A Curse Dark as Gold

ELIZABETH C. BUNCE

Arthur A. Levine Books

An Imprint of Scholastic Inc.

Library of Congress Cataloging-in-Publication Data

Bunce, Elizabeth C.

A curse dark as gold / by Elizabeth Bunce. — 1st ed.

p. cm.

Summary: Upon the death of her father, seventeen-year-old Charlotte struggles to keep the family's woolen mill running in the face of an overwhelming mortgage and what the local villagers believe is a curse, but when a man capable of spinning straw into gold appears on the scene she must decide if his help is worth the price.

ISBN-13: 978-0-439-89576-7

ISBN-10: 0-439-89576-6

[1. Mills and mill-work — Fiction. 2. Blessing and cursing — Fiction. 3. Uncles — Fiction. 4. Orphans — Fiction. 5. Sisters — Fiction. 6. Ghosts — Fiction.] I. Rumpelstiltskin (Folk tale) English. II. Title.

PZ7.B91505Cur 2008

[Fic] — dc22   2007019759

Acknowledgments

Weaving this tale was by no means a solitary endeavor. For their help and support along the way, I must thank my own Friendly Society: Barb Stuber, Christine Taylor-Butler, Diane Bailey, Judith Hyde, C. R. Cook, and the other amazing women of Juvenile Writers of Kansas City. Thanks to my parents, for never once uttering the phrase "fallback career," and to my first critique partner, my brother, Scott. Special thanks to Cheryl Klein and the team at Scholastic (especially for bearing with my affected period spelling). Extra-special thanks to Erin Murphy. And lastly, to my husband, Christopher, for always being there. If I wrote you into a story, no one would believe you were real.

Chapter One

When my father died, I thought the world would come to an end. Standing in the churchyard in my borrowed mourning black, I was dimly aware of my sister Rosie beside me, the other mourners huddled round the grave. Great dark clouds gathered over the river, and I knew them for what they were: The End, poised to unleash some terrible wrath and sweep us all right out of the Valley. I let go my hold on Rosie's arm, for I was ready to be swept away.

Yet, somehow, I found myself still standing at the end of the service. I stooped and cast a handful of earth atop the casket, accepted a lily from the vicar, and joined the train of black-clad figures trailing back to the Millhouse — all the while wondering what had gone wrong. Surely at least the mill would mourn his passing, and I would find the old wheel splintered and cracked, riven from its axle, ground to a standstill in the wheelpit.

In the millyard, the old building stood as ever, casting its vast shadow over the house and grounds. Far above where the stones met the roofline, an old sign, so faded and weather-beaten as to be near illegible, spelled out STIRWATERS WOOLLEN MILL: MILLER & SONS, SHEARING. There was no

Miller now, and there had never been any sons — just two half-grown orphaned daughters, a crumbling ruin of a water-mill, and the mountain of debt it was built upon.

"Charlotte." The voice at my shoulder was gentle but insistent, and I turned to see Abby Weaver, big with child, standing beside me. The black gown I wore, twenty years out of fashion and so tight I could scarcely breathe in it, had been her mother's. Abby squeezed my arm and steered me into the Millhouse.

The entire village had crowded into our parlor — Father's workers and all our neighbors — toasting the dead with ale from Drover's and feasting him with food brought by the Friendly Society. Plump, stolid Janet Lamb was carving a ham by the fireplace, while Jack Townley poured out ale from a vast oaken cask balanced on a bench I didn't recognize. I stood in the doorway and removed my bonnet with great dignity. Once it was free from my head, however, I lingered there, crushing its black beribboned brim with trembling fingers, utterly uncertain what to do next.

"Charlotte?" I turned toward the voice; it was Rachel Baker. Her normally unflappably cheerful face was lined with concern.

"Have you seen Rosie?" I said in a faint voice that did not sound like my own. "I've lost her —"

"You haven't lost her," Rachel said firmly. "She's in the kitchen with the Lamb boys and Tansy. Eating. Like you should be."

I almost managed a smile. "You Bakers think food is the answer to everything."

"Well," she said reasonably, "it's a start."

I made to head for the kitchen, but as I moved through

my home, I was surrounded from all sides — swept into a dozen sympathetic embraces, a plate of ham and biscuit pressed into my hands, tea fairly lifted to my lips.

"Thank you," I murmured — or I meant to; I am not at all certain anything came out. "Thank you all. My father . . ." I faltered, staring at their faces, a mixture of concern and ale-flush, and spoke the plain truth. "My father would have loved this."

"Ah, miss, he were a good man, and will be rightly missed." Eben Fuller clasped my hands in his. I swallowed hard and tried to answer back, but my words were lost in a wave of condolences I did not wish to receive and remembrances I could not bear to hear. I was propped up between Rachel on one side, Mrs. Hopewell on the other, as the villagers exchanged touching stories of Father's kindness, or amusing ones of his misadventures in the wool trade.

"'Twas a queer sort, but a good man for all that," old Tory Weaver was saying. "I remember when he came here, full o' grand plans for the old place, and not a notion in his head how to run a woollen mill."

Janet Lamb eased through the crowd with a mug of ale, to sit beside the old jackspinner. "Tory, do you remember teaching the master to shear sheep?" She laughed. "Thought he'd never get the hang of it! Must have lost half a crown's worth of wool from that first ewe alone, then, eh?"

"Aye — that weren't nowt compared with the time he rigged up some fool machine to mechanize the shearing," Jack Townley put in. "Near scared the poor sheep to death, he did!"

"Ah, he did all right in the end," Mercy Fuller said gently. "Haven't we survived this long, then?"

A heavy hush fell over the crowd as all eyes none too subtly turned my way. I bit my lip and tried to think what to say, what words to utter to keep the conversation flowing — but I was tapped out, empty. Suddenly it was all too much. This house, always so quiet with Father here, was filled with too much noise, too many people, too much black . . . and too many unspoken questions I did not know how to answer.

I stood up abruptly, and something clattered to the floor as my knee knocked against a little table someone had dragged into the center of the room.

"Please excuse me." I think I said it, but it didn't matter. Somehow grief gives you license to be rude. Without another word to anyone, I shoved through the crowd of mourners toward the back door and fresh air.

"Those poor girls." I heard the voice behind me as I passed, the cluck of sympathy, the sighed replies: "Aye, and after the debts are paid off, they'll be left with nothing. It's a sorry business, all round. You know what the master was like — a goodly soul, but no head at all for money."

"When word gets out that Stirwaters has no miller, folk'll be swarming around like flies to a carcass, waiting to see 'em fall. Mark my words — we'll be lookin' for new work by month's end."

I wrapped my arms around myself, as if I could somehow hold my world together, and fled up into the mill.

Inside, my steps sounded big and hollow banging up the stairs. I came out into the spinning room on the second floor, all its long, still machines waiting for someone to come and direct them. I knelt there in the shadows under the rough brown rafters, listening to the gears shudder overhead. From a distance I heard the water rush over the wheel, swift and cold and fueled by snowmelt upstream — the vast, steady heartbeat of the mill. I traced my finger over the split floorboards, the rivets driven into patches where the wood had grown too thin. I knew the path of every uneven board in these floors, the very spiderweb of cracks in the walls; the leather belts and iron gears and moss-covered wheel said *home* in every sigh and rustle.

Stirwaters had witnessed the birth of this town, had watched generations of Shearing-folk pass through its doors, pace these floors under their rhythmic labor, pass into memory again. Our little mill was not merely the center of our world, it was also the heart of Shearing. We had grown up knowing that the village was built up around the mill, and ran still to the rhythm of the waterwheel. Every other business in the village — the inn, the bakehouse, the blacksmith and joiner — was here to serve Stirwaters and its workers. If the mill went, there would be no reason for anyone to stay, and the sweet sympathetic cluster of townspeople banded together in my home would be cast to the four winds like dust.

My father's voice seemed to echo in the room: *We don't own this mill, girls; we are merely stewards here.*

Rosie found me, minutes or hours later. She floated into the spinning room with nothing at all like her usual pell-mell gait, settled herself beside me, and put her chin on my shoulder. After a long moment, she said, "Do we close the mill?"

I turned and looked at my sister for the first time in days. She looked miserable and pale, bright hair pulled tight under her veil, blue eyes ringed with red. Black did not become her, and suddenly I knew I could not stand to see her in it another day. I gathered my sister into my arms and held fast to her, under the gentle murmur of the gears.

"Is it Sunday?" I asked, and when she shook her head, I gave my answer: "Then we do not close."

By God's grace or sheer chance, the world did *not* stop turning, and Stirwaters's millwheel kept right on turning with it. I spent the next days tucked away in Father's office, answering letters and counting out pay slips, and not looking up to see his empty chair, or the cloak rack by the door that held no ragged gray topcoat. Rosie took over the mill-works, a jumbled affair of ancient machines and spare parts cobbled together until Stirwaters resembled nothing in the known milling world. She had been Father's shadow these last few years; she knew the mill as well as anyone.

The millhands, for their part, had seen too many mill-ers come and go to pay much mind to James Miller's pass-ing. The loss of the miller was a minor upset, at worst, a hiccough in production, to be smoothed over by experienced hands until some long-lost cousin or nephew arrived to take up the reins. But Rosie and I were the last of the line; no one was coming to pick up what Father had let drop. Stirwaters was *our* responsibility; it was our duty to ensure that the old mill did not slip out of Miller hands after five generations.

Thus I began my career as the miller of Shearing village. And if there is any reason the world did not stop in its procession and toss us all into the void, it can only be because I was too stubborn to let go. Though we were whittled down to nothing, scoured and battered and stripped clean, we rallied together through the end of winter and the first uncertain days of spring, and before we knew it — long before we were ready for it — the turning of the days brought us round to woolmarket, and the official start of my first season as Stirwaters's miller.

It was a cool, damp morning in early March, and I stood in the kitchen at the Millhouse, watching the first flocks of sheep toddle toward Stirwaters's woolshed. Like a shifting grey-white sea, they bumped and nudged one another as they flowed into the yard, while a mist drifted up from the river and cloaked everything in a silver shroud.

"I can't go out there," I said, still gripping my mug of long-cold coffee.

"What?" Rosie turned to stare at me. She was half into her cloak already, and half out the door. "What are you talking about?"

"I'm not ready —" I said. "It's too soon —"

"You'd better *get* ready, missie, because the wool is here. The men are here. And they're waiting for you, Mistress Miller. Unless you expect Jack Townley to buy our wool for us."

That *would* have been a disaster, and any other time the very thought of it would have made me smile. I had to get hold of myself. There were dealers from all over the Gold Valley waiting in the woolshed, ready to supply Stirwaters with the wool we needed for the year's run. And unless I was there to buy it, there would be no run, and the determination I had professed these last weeks would be no more than empty bravado. But to step forward, to face the world and say, "I am the miller now" — to be the *final* word on whether we turned left or right, went ahead or held fast — no, no. I wasn't ready.

Rosie prized the mug from my hand, dumped my cloak over my shoulders, and thrust my bonnet into my hands.

"I can't do this," I protested again, as my sister shoved me out the door.

"Don't be an idiot," she said. "You were born to do this."

Rosie herded me toward the woolshed like a recalcitrant ewe, but once in the shadow of the old building, I felt a strange sense of calm. Our woolshed is beautiful in the morning, with sunlight pouring in the high windows, the wood floors polished to gleaming by generations of oily fleeces. With the barn doors swung wide, it was as bright inside as out, and the crisp spring air smelled of wool and the lavender tucked in among the fleeces to chase away moths. I breathed in the odd but lovely fragrance, and prepared to step across the threshold.

"Aye, mistress, make way!"

I jumped aside to let George Harte, a young upcountry shepherd, pass by with a donkey train, their broad backs heaped high with burlap-wrapped fleeces. One of the donkeys dropped a donkey-mess right where I'd been standing. Rosie choked back a laugh and gave my shoulder a friendly push. The Stirwaters workday had begun.

"Right." I smoothed my skirts, straightened my bonnet, and marched inside. "Mr. Woolsey," I called to the squat, sturdy farmer baling fleeces a few yards away. "Have you brought me any of those hogget ewes you promised last fall? I'll give you sixteen for the lot, if they're as fine as you said they'd be."

This had been my game, every year, and I was good at it. Not as good as Mam had been — but Father was a disaster, and we were under strict orders not to let him near the woolshed on Market Days. I liked the rhythm of the bargaining, the give and take of offer and counteroffer, the nudge and tap and gentle tug to see how far I could get.

Other wool towns have a bustling marketplace, an official Wool Hall overseen by the Wool Guild, even a weekly cloth market. But not Shearing. Although the town had grown up when Stirwaters turned a disorganized country sheep market into a proper village, Shearing had never quite fulfilled the dreams of our founding ancestor. But we were still the Gold Valley's wool market, and so, for a few short weeks each year, everyone piled into the only building in town big enough for such an event: Stirwaters's woolshed. Wool, sheep, traders, and all stumbled over one another, and the normally spacious and peaceful shed became a scene of pandaemonium.

Over the next several hours, I passed among the woolmen and their fleeces, dodging sheep and sheep-messes and the representatives of other mills along the Stowe, who smiled at me approvingly, giving me nods of encouragement as I sailed by. It was a fine season for wool, but I should have to be careful how I spent my meager budget. I combed through packs of snowy pale fleeces, dug my fingers deep into the backs of plump, placid ewes, and twisted prices down shilling by shilling, penny by penny.

"Eighteen shillings for these Stowewold ewes, and thirty even on the Merino. Mr. Colly," I added, seeing the stocky woolman hesitate, "you've already shorn them. What a waste it would be to have to pack up all these fleeces and haul them back upvalley, and it not at all certain you could find another buyer before the moths get to them."

Mr. Colly burst out laughing, by which I knew I'd won. "Ah, I know why my nephew thinks so highly of you lasses," he said. He sobered for a moment, and looked me up and down with the keen eye of a stockman. "Ye've grown, lass — and it looks good on you. You keep this up and you'll be rivalin' your mam soon enough."

I had to take a very deep breath to keep my voice from shaking. "Thank you, sir. And can you send Harte down to the mill later? Rosie's dying for him to take a look at that tangle of gears by the fulling stocks."

Mr. Colly nodded. "How is that sister of yours? All sass and vinegar like her mam, I'll wager."

"I sometimes think it's a good thing the millworks are in such disrepair. She'd probably run wild if she didn't have something useful to do."

"Ah, never Miss Rosie," he said. "She's more sense than that. The pair of you — worth more than many a man's son."

"Well," I said, "it's a good thing, because we're all this old place has." I gave Mr. Colly a wave and went down the line.

The clamor and bustle of sheep and men filled the shed, mingling with the other, more curious stirrings that always seemed to characterize Shearing's wool market — shears that went inexplicably dull; unheard noises that spooked the sheep; possessions that were at hand one moment, vanished the next, then turned up hours later in the most improbable locations. Generally folk shrugged and laughed it off; a few murmured, "Stirwaters," with a roll of the eyes and a shake of the head; still more adorned their flocks with red and blue ribbons, or marked their bales with chalk symbols — just in case.

Adding an edge to the frenzy this year was the presence of a man from Pinchfields, a big new mill in Harrowgate.

He had slipped into the crowd and might have remained anonymous if a buyer from Burlingham hadn't pointed him out to me. We'd never had a wool buyer from Pinchfields in Shearing before, and there was something strange about him. He haunted our woolshed — like a ferret in a dovecote, Rosie said — looking down his nose and scratching notes in a little book he carried everywhere. Moreover, he had no eye at all for quality, buying without a second glance stock the rest of us had rejected — discolored lots, older fleeces, wool with too much cotting and canary stain.

"I don't understand it," I said to Rosie. "What's he up to? He can't use that any more than we can. It'll ruin his run."

"Maybe he doesn't care. His factory's so big he can put out anything he wants."

"But won't his customers care?" I persisted.

She just looked at me. "I suppose we'll find out."

The wool he was buying came so cheaply it would cost Pinchfields almost nothing to produce their cloth from it. In turn, they could sell that cloth for much less than anything Stirwaters could make. They'd bury us in no time if they could keep up that sort of business. And they knew it.

Late that afternoon I was haggling over a fleece with the fat ewe still wearing it, deep in negotiation at shear-point. Not the craftiest of creatures, sheep nonetheless have instincts that tell them who they must and needn't mind. Old Bossie had taken my measure straightaway and, judging me a novice, was little inclined to cooperate. She struggled in my grip — I swear she would have bitten me if I'd let go her jaw even for a moment. Smeared with lanolin from knees to bosom, I at last managed to pin her beneath one leg and was just starting to drive the shears through the clotted wool on her belly when the Pinchfields man sauntered up to me and gave a big look around the room.

"Such a quaint place you have here, Miss Miller," he said. "It's all just so charmingly old-fashioned."

Blood flooding my cheeks, I bent my head low over the sheep to hide my flushed face. "We're very proud of Stirwaters's long history," I mumbled.

At that moment, the great stupid ewe heaved free of my grip, yanking the shears from my hand. They clattered against the floor as Bossie sprung away to the safety of the feed pen, dragging her half-shorn fleece behind her on the ground.

The man from Pinchfields laughed, a small, ugly sound like the grating of rusty metal. "Oh, very proud, I'm sure. Well, if you're ever in Harrowgate, I do hope you'll return the honor and come to Pinchfields. I've no doubt you'll be impressed. Everything's new. But, well —" here he paused and drew something from his waistcoat pocket. "We just don't have the prestige of an old, distinguished label like Stirwaters on our cloth." He held out a scrap of muslin wrapping, revealing the stamped Stirwaters coat of arms on the fabric.

For a moment I didn't understand. Then something echoed in my mind: *like flies to a carcass.* I rose to my feet, heedless of my tangled skirts. "And you won't," I said. "Stirwaters is not for sale."

"Are you sure about that? In my experience there's a price on everything. What would you say to, oh, two hundred pounds?" He fished in his waistcoat for his book, which was fairly bursting with banknotes. "You'd keep your home, of course; we wouldn't have any interest in keeping the mill running."

I stood straighter, but my cheeks were red from outrage now, not from shame. "Sir, I'm afraid you misunderstood me. Stirwaters isn't for sale, at any price."

"Oh, come now — five hundred. That's more money than you'd see out of this place in your lifetime. You're a fool not to take it."

"This is a wool market, sir, not a *mill* market. I suggest you take your offer somewhere else."

The man from Pinchfields leaned his narrow frame over me. "Look here, you stupid girl, this is the last time you'll see an offer this good. Eight hundred. Take it."

His thin face was close enough for me to see the tobacco stains on his teeth, cringe from his sour breath. I shook my head.

"Curse you Millers for stubborn fools! I guarantee you — six months from now, a year — you'll be wishing you'd sold."

I hadn't noticed that a crowd had gathered, watching us, until Jack Townley stepped forward. A sizeable man, he stood quiet and calm beside me. "I believe the lady said no, sir," he said in an easy voice. The man from Pinchfields looked around. Besides the wool-buying crowd, we were surrounded now by the bulk of my Stirwaters family, who make a formidable presence when they put their minds to it. George Harte and Eben Fuller ambled up behind Jack, followed shortly by Janet Lamb, casually brandishing a baling hook.

The Pinchfields wool buyer eased back and smoothed his jacket with his wiry hands. "Is that how it is, then?" He tucked his book and the money back into his coat and gave another glance round the woolshed. "That's a shame, Miss Miller. I know I'd hate to see that infamous Stirwaters curse get the better of you."

I drew in my breath. "I'm sure I don't know what you mean."

He smiled thinly. "I mean, Miss Miller, that if I were you I'd reconsider our offer — before your name and label are all you have left to sell."

Chapter Two

TWO weeks later, Tom and Abby Weaver left us. The millhands had been loyal and supportive immediately following my father's death, but as the strain of uncertainty began to wear on everyone, workers deserted us like rats fleeing a burning hayrick. We lost good people in those days — a skilled carder, weavers, a finisher, a man-of-all-work. I watched them go with a mixture of grief and resignation. Who could blame them? They were Harrowgate-bound, or Burlingham, or Stowemouth . . . to seek their fortunes somewhere fortunes may be made.

But it was not all losses. George Harte, having had his arm twisted by Rosie to look at the millworks, stepped one foot inside Stirwaters and could not seem to pull himself away again. With the blessings of his uncle and his black collie, Pilot, he traded his shepherd's crook for a spanner and installed himself in the spare rooms at the woolshed. I was more grateful than I could say — an act of faith like that was precisely what I needed just then. The presence of Pilot, patrolling the millyard by night with her sharp eyes and even sharper bark, was likewise a comfort. We had never been scared at Stirwaters, but we had never been alone, either.

One afternoon I sat in the office, frowning over our ledger books. Somewhere between my dismay over our oil bill and the amount still owed to the undertaker, Rosie came flinging into the office, bearing the post. With a sigh, I sorted through the letters she cast onto the desk. Past-due notice, bill, another bill — probably a notice that we were *about* to become past due . . . Maybe we could get by without eating this spring.

"Charlotte, look at this! Who do you think it's from?"

"Not another one from Pinchfields, I hope," I said, distracted by the incomprehensible handwriting of our teasel supplier. Since Market Days, we had received two more offers from the Harrowgate factory, each more elaborately generous than the last.

"Not unless they've started putting perfume in their offers."

I looked up sharply. "What did you say?"

Rosie broke the seal on her letter, and now I could smell a faint flowery scent from the paper. "It's written in purple ink," she said.

I peered in closer. "Are you sure that's for us? It sounds like somebody's love letter."

Rosie turned it over to look at the address. "It has both our names on it. And I don't see why it couldn't be a love letter," she added indignantly. "I can't tell who it's from — the ink is all smeared here." She unfolded the note. Her eyes grew wide, and she held the letter up for me to read.

"Does that say 'Wheeler'?" I asked.

She was starting to smile. "It does indeed."

Mam's brother? I took the letter from her hand.

My dearest girls,

Please forgive the tardiness of my condolences; I have been travelling abroad and only just heard of your father's death. What a dreadful shock; how tragic that you two are all alone now. It brings back the sadness of your dear mother's death all those years ago, and I wept when I heard the news.

I hope this note finds you both well, but I shudder to think what you have been going through. Be assured that you will not be alone for long now; I am making haste to come to Shearing immediately.

Yours affectionately,
your uncle,
Ellison H. Wheeler, Esquire

We had never met our mother's brother, but I could almost remember her speaking of him fondly, if I tried. Some years her junior, he would have been a child when she left home. I read the letter over and over, trying to bring up a picture of the man, as if doing so could conjure my mother, too — and Father with her. I forced back a sudden sadness and squeezed Rosie's hand. She smiled at me, but her eyes were very bright.

We spent the next several days preparing for our uncle's visit, waiting and watching anxiously for his arrival. I pictured a masculine version of Mam, with her same round face and reddish hair, a sturdy man in workaday clothes who would embrace us roughly, tousle our hair, and speak in low, thoughtful tones. Rosie had him shorter, with a paunch and a pipe and a big jolly grin beneath a receding hairline.

We could not have shot farther from the mark.

One sunny morning late in the week, I stood outside Stirwaters, watching the churning wheel send mist into the glittering air. The pretty scene concealed a grim truth. Built of limestone and slate, the building should have withstood the elements for centuries, but time and neglect had taken their toll, and the mill looked much older than its scarce hundred years. I studied the old building, the moss and lichen spreading up the stones, the crumbling mortar, the broken windows that let wind and rain spray through the workrooms. Inside, things were just as bad — cracks in the floors so wide you could drop a hammer through them; plaster falling off in chunks. Here and there a half-hearted attempt at patching or repair had been made over the years, but it always seemed as if ruin had the upper hand.

"What are you looking at?" Rosie asked, coming round my shoulder and peering up at the mill.

"Why haven't those missing slates on the roof been replaced? And this decking —" I kicked at the rotted boards. "It's falling apart; someone is bound to put a foot through that and break an ankle."

"Someone?" Rosie said, eyebrow cocked.

"Very well. I don't want the first impression Mam's brother has of us to be that we're an utter ruin. She'd be ashamed of what's become of Stirwaters."

Rosie was smiling. "I think it's a fine idea. Let's round up the troops."

As the millhands drifted in, we tried to recruit help patching holes, sealing cracks, scrubbing moss and lichen, whitewashing, limewashing, and painting. My suggestions met a mixture of sullen, earthward gazes and the odd snicker.

"What is it?" I demanded. "If it's about the extra work, I'll pay overtime."

Amid the feet-shuffling and muttering, Jack Townley spoke up. "Mistress, do you really think you're the first one to try to fix the old place up?" He shook his head. "It's always the same, then, ain't it? New miller comes in and puts a few patches on, tidies up the workrooms, buys a new machine. But it don't take. Why do you think your da' turned into such a tinker? Because this mill don't *want* to be fixed up."

"The mill doesn't want to be fixed? You can't be serious." But the faces of my workers, grim and set, told a different story.

"Nay, Mistress. We all know you don't want to hear it, and aye, we'll do our best by you and put paint or nails where you like 'em, but you wait — in the end, it won't make a spit of difference."

"What nonsense. Harte —" I turned to him.

"Ma'am, all I know is I can't get that number three jack to work. If it's not rust, and it's not mechanical . . ." He shrugged. "Ask Rosie what she thinks."

Rosie shook her kerchiefed head. "I've seen repairs take as often as not in this old place. You just have to appreciate its . . . spirit."

I nodded, satisfied, and glanced over my assembled workers again, but missed a face in my count. "Where's Bill Penny?"

Somebody snickered. "Mayhap he's been taken by fairies."

"You mean spirits? Dead drunk at Mrs. Drover's, I'll wager." I shook my head. Why hadn't I listened to my father? He never would hire a Penny, called the lot of them lazy drunk and unreliable. "If anyone sees Mr. Penny, be certain to mention that I will dock him a day's pay for every hour he misses this week." Not that I would — but just then I was sore tempted.

"Nay, Mistress —" I looked over. Young Paddy Eagan, a serious lad who'd quietly worked his way up from runner boy to apprentice spinner, was shaking his head, dark eyes wide and urgent. "Annie Penny — they're our neighbors, the Pennys — says she hasn't seen her da' in three days. Took off into the hills one day and just disappeared."

"Well, he wasn't taken by fairies," I said. "That's absurd."

"It's spring, though, ma'am — April first, it was, and a Friday at that — that's when they're like to snatch you."

"April first? All Fools' Day? God help us." More likely Bill Penny had "took off" into the hills to escape the wool-washing, or the roof-thatching — or Mrs. Penny. But it did little good to say as much. For all our practicality, Gold Valley folk are stubbornly superstitious, happy to blame the least little oddity on the Fair Folk or the Old Ones. Everyone has their corn dollies, their kitchen imps, their blue door-steps and windowsills. Any outsider driving through the village would think it quaint country fashion — all that blue at the front of houses — but in truth it's a warding: meant to keep fairies and spirits where they belong, up in the hills and away from decent folk. I had never paid any of it much mind.

I tipped my hat back and regarded everyone. "Is there anything else we need to blame on spooks and goblins? Good. If we're quite finished, I believe we all have work to do. And if you put so much as a *speck* of blue paint on those doors, Jack Townley, I swear to God I will sack you so fast you'll be in Trawney before you realize you're out of a job!"

I went to bed that night weary but satisfied from a hard day spent scraping moss from limestone. Repairs progressed slowly — Stirwaters folk might drag their feet and grumble, but their work was loyal and true. I felt sure we would at least *look* a little more sound when our uncle arrived.

We had shuffled our bedrooms in anticipation of his visit, and I was now in Father's room (neither Rosie nor I had been ready to have a stranger — even an uncle — sleeping in his bed). Half undressed, I sank onto the edge of the old iron bedstead and looked round me. This room, with its worn counterpane and faded red paper on the walls, had always seemed warm and comforting when Father was alive. Without him, it was merely dark and shabby. Low bookshelves sat into the walls by the fireplace, their books untouched, unread, coated with a layer of soot and shadows.

I bent low and retrieved one, blowing the dust from its spine as I heaved it up onto the bed. In the flickering candle-light, the drawings inside seemed to come alive. Before he inherited Stirwaters, my father had trained to become a mapmaker, and over the years he'd compiled an atlas of maps and drawings he'd made of the Gold Valley. How I had loved this book as a child! I had spent hours folding out the long pages across my lap, tracing the lines of rivers or the curving ornamental script. Here was a map of Shearing, showing Stirwaters at center, with the bakehouse next door and the smithy across the road, our names marked out in tiny precise letters that bore little resemblance to my father's usual untidy hand. Here a view of Stirwaters, the building cut open to reveal the movement of gears inside. One of my favorites was a map of the land surrounding Haymarket, where Mam and our uncle had grown up. The land, heavily wooded according to the dark swirls etched onto the page, spread out into the hills before smoothing out to green farmland. Lakes like blots of ink dotted the hillside, each with a haunting, beautiful name. I had wondered over each strange site in turn, trying to picture the occasions that had given rise to Gallowstock, Simple Cross, or Bone Weir.

I looked at it now, following the twisting roadway from Haymarket west toward Shearing, imagining the path that had brought Mam and Father together, and the road that now led our uncle here. Back again to Shearing, where Rosie and I were held fast — tonight the cutaway Stirwaters seemed oddly foretelling: block after block chipped out of the mill, leaving only a windblown ruin clinging to its foundation.

A scratch at my door pulled me from my musings. The door creaked open, and there was Rosie in her nightdress, candle stub held aloft. "I'm too tired to sleep," she said, cupping her hand to puff out the flame. "I'm sure I won't be able to walk tomorrow, after being up and down that ladder all day. Is that Father's old atlas?"

Her hand reached out to touch the inky crosshatch of Stirwaters's millwheel. We climbed into bed together, as we had more and more often these last weeks, and Rosie took the album, turning to a pen-and-ink rendering of a spinning jack, each belt, gear, and spindle given the same meticulous detail, all the way down the long carriage.

As she turned the pages, something fluttered to the counterpane. I picked it up — a dried sprig of some herb or tree; hemlock, perhaps. I twisted it before my lips, breathing in its dusty perfume. On one page, Father had done a study of all the old local superstitions: sketches of the charms and symbols used to bring luck or ward off evil, notes on various customs still observed. There was a list of things one mustn't do on Friday — frightfully comprehensive, from getting haircuts to getting married; a hex symbol like a mystical compass rose, rubbed in with a smear of purple; one of the twisted straw effigies known as corn dollies. That was just like Father. He had spent one entire summer trying to learn the knack to tying the straw, only to abandon it when another passion seized him in the fall.

One entire summer during which he'd let the millworks fall into disrepair, the weavers fend for themselves, and the bills all go unpaid.

Not native to Shearing, Father had been fascinated with the traditions of the Gold Valley. When Mam was alive, she had scorned them, but gently, with humor; after her death, it was almost a mania with him. He became convinced that all the mill's troubles — from sheep that gave poor fleeces to workers who showed up late — were to blame on the legendary Stirwaters Curse.

The Stirwaters Curse. I had grown up hearing those words every time something went the least bit awry. True, we Millers did tend to more than our share of bad luck — from the very first Miller of Shearing, old Harlan, who had built Stirwaters and this house. But down through the years of market collapses and roof collapses — which could happen to anybody — one dark thread bound the Millers apart from ordinary ill luck: No Miller had ever raised a son who lived to inherit Stirwaters. The mill had been handed down along a crazy zigzag path from brother to cousin to nephew . . . to daughter. Stirwaters could only be inherited by Millers, and Rosie and I were the only ones left.

It was all foolishness, so far as I could tell. There wasn't anything to be done and no blame to lay for bad wool; and a little more diligent management would clear up the rest of our problems. And as for the sons . . . tragic coincidence, nothing more.

But Father would have none of that; it was easier to believe in some nefarious supernatural force that meant us ill, than it was to buckle down and do the work. He had even spent a hundred pounds one year for a so-called cunning man to "lay" the curse — one hundred pounds that could have bought a newer spinning machine or paid our Cloth Exchange license for twenty years. Or made sure Rosie and I had shoes that fit and dinner on the table every night.

With Rosie lost in Father's atlas, I leaned my head against the bedframe and closed my eyes, telling myself it was not disloyal to hope that my uncle — even now hastening down those winding paths — might bring good things to this family.

Sunday afternoon we heard the crunch of wheels on the shale drive and ran upstairs to peer out the garret window in the landing.

"Is that him? Oh, that can't be him!"

"No," I said finally, staring at the man in the carriage and thinking of the violet ink and perfumed paper of his letter. "I think it must be."

The carriage pulled right up below us, so close we could see the gleam of gold thread in the passenger's coat as he gestured to the coachman. Now, don't believe that Shearing — for all our country ways — is a village devoid of any sense of propriety or fashion; we are not. But our mode has certainly never tended toward embroidered waistcoats at midday or such elaborately powdered hair. This — *this* was our Uncle Wheeler?

The gentleman sprang down from the carriage, and I caught a flash of violet stockings and large, terribly shiny shoe buckles. He brushed something invisible from his tapestry sleeves and picked his way across the shale to our doorstep.

Rosie pulled herself away from me and hurried down the stairs.

"Wait," I called. "I think we should change our clothes." We had worn nothing special for this first meeting with our kinsman, just our everyday dress from life at the mill — plain, serviceable, and old.

Rosie gave me a look. "Good," she said. "I'll just put on the blue silk I wore to meet the king, and what will you wear?"

In the end we went as we were, though I was tucking strands of my hair into place as Rosie opened the front door. Our caller drew back, one slender hand at his cravat, and regarded us with . . . what? What did that look say? I squeezed tight against Rosie and twisted another strand of hair back behind my ear.

"Uncle . . . Mr. . . . Wheeler?" I said at last, and the gentleman in my threshold swept the ostrich-feather hat from his head and bowed low.

"Ellison Wheeler at your service, my dears." He stepped inside, and Rosie and I took a quick step backward, out of the range of that hat. "Dear Charlotte," Uncle Wheeler said, holding his arms wide. "You are the very picture of your father. I'd have known you for James's child anywhere."

I smiled, surprised. No one ever said so; was it true?

"And Rosellen, such a beauty! Have you broken many a young man's heart?"

"Not lately, sir." Rosie's voice sounded flat, but she did have the grace to curtsey.

"Here now, have your girl bring in my trunks, and we'll just get to know one another." He removed his gloves — kidskin white as snow, with hands beneath nearly as pure — and strode into the parlor.

Dismayed, I twined my fingers in my apron strings behind my back. "I'm afraid there isn't anyone," I finally said. "Won't the coachman bring them?"

He spun to face me. "No servants? Oh, my poor dears. No wonder everything looks the way it does. We must take care of that, first thing. But certainly, Rosellen, fetch the coachman. I have some little trinkets in there for you both, so don't let him drop them."

I took a deep awkward breath. "Rosie and I are both so glad you've come to visit. Won't you please sit down? I'll fetch us some tea." That was Gold Valley strategy: When all else fails, bring in the food.

I got Uncle Wheeler seated on the faded sofa with the warmed-over coffee and dry cakes and, my courage failing me, went to help Rosie with the trunks. After dragging two big portmanteaux and a hat case up to my bedroom, we divided forces. Rosie retreated to the kitchen to fix the supper she'd been planning for days, and I returned to our uncle.

I paused outside the parlor doorway to smooth the wrinkles in my dress and adjust my cap. "I do hope you find your room comfortable, Uncle Wheeler," I said, swinging open the door. "It's not the biggest, but it's our warmest, and it has a lovely view of the mill."

Uncle Wheeler had risen, circling through the parlor and finding all its flaws and inadequacies. He closed the drop-front of Mam's cherry secretary, which stuck and had to be wiggled into place; stroked a finger down the windowpane; cast his gaze over the tarnished candlesticks, the chipped china lamp, the faded rag rug. When he saw me, his smooth face crumpled with sympathy. "Oh, my dear girl," he said, holding his arms wide. "My poor, dear niece."

I hung back, not certain I welcomed an embrace from this sparkling stranger; but it seemed rude, so in the end I leaned in, and he briefly draped his arms about me and brushed my cheek with a whisper of a kiss. His hands were very soft, as if he rarely doffed those gloves, and I was very conscious of my own callused and ink-stained fingers. The powder on his wig smelled of lilacs, sweet and peculiar.

"I should have come sooner," he said. "But my business in Harrowgate detained me, and — no matter. I'm here now. You girls have grown into such lovely young women. I'm sure your father must have been bursting with pride."

I flushed, willing it to be true. "Thank you, Uncle. And I'm so sorry that you —" I'd been about to say, *that you've missed him,* but realized with a stabbing pain how foolish it should sound. "I wish Father could have been here; I know he would have loved to see you. He'd have wanted — things just weren't the same after Mam died."

Uncle Wheeler gave a cluck of sympathy. "Such sadness you girls have known. And such responsibility *you* have had to assume, as the eldest. How like your mother." He smiled sadly and brushed a strand of hair from my cheek. It was suddenly too intimate; the last man to stand beside me at these windows had smelled of engine grease and lanolin, and I could not bear to think of that, not with my uncle looking at me with such kindness I might weep. I pulled away.

"I'm sorry, Uncle, I —"

A sudden rattle of china broke the stillness of the moment. I seized on the sound with relief. "That's Rosie. I'd better help. You must be wanting to freshen up, sir, after your long journey," I added rather belatedly.

He gave me a thoughtful look. "Yes, thank you, my dear, I think I shall."

With that I fled into the familiar warmth and clatter of my kitchen.

"Look at this!" Rosie cried, waving a wooden spoon at the pots hung over the fire. "Egg and barley stew? Turnips?" She jabbed brutally with the spoon at the mixing bowl cradled in her arm. "There was a roast at the butcher's, a beautiful six-pound standing rib roast. And a rack of lamb you would have wept over!"

I looked at the meat turning on the spit. "Well, what did you buy?"

"Rabbit!"

"Oh."

"I have a trout," she said a little wildly. "I could make a cream sauce and stuff it with raisins —"

"No —" I said, maybe a bit too hastily. "That trout's showing its age. We'll do better with the rabbit." I saw the pie she'd been rolling out. "What's that, then?"

"Currant."

"Well, there you go. We have lovely currants."

"We have lovely currants in June, when they're ripe! Those are dried currants!"

"Rosie, it will do." I put a hand on her shoulder and made her look at me. "Mam's brother?" I said gently.

She looked unconvinced, but finally nodded. "Mam's brother."

I watched her shake off the bad humor in the way only Rosie can manage. With a savage thrust, she gave the spit a turn that almost shook those poor rabbits into the flames, but we finished the cooking in a state of relative calm.

While we waited on the pies and whipped the dining room into a splendor seldom witnessed in Shearing village (Rosie unearthed three crystal goblets that almost matched, and even found a tablecloth that hadn't been attacked by moths since its last public appearance), our uncle retired upstairs to dress for dinner. Rosie and I had barely managed to take off our bonnets and pat back our hair, but Uncle Wheeler was elegant in black velvet and silver, a lace cravat foaming at his throat. Our uncle's conversation was lively and intimate; he shared stories of his childhood with Mam in Haymarket, though I confess it was difficult to imagine this fancy gentleman as a boy.

Our uncle's polished manners put Rosie's and my country graces to shame, and nothing we could do seemed right. In her anxiety, Rosie had burnt the rabbits, and the stew had a skin that no amount of stirring would dissolve. The turnips were turnips, and I don't know what happened to the pies after I got hold of them, but they certainly didn't turn out like currant pie is meant to. Finally, long after Rosie and I had given up on the food, Uncle Wheeler took one last sip of wine, wiped his knife on his napkin, and pushed his chair back from the table.

"Splendid, girls," he pronounced. "One gets so tired of the rich food abroad and in the city. It's so novel to have good simple country fare every now and again."

Rosie sprang up from the table as if she'd been cut free from a trap. "I'd better do the washing up," she said, but Uncle Wheeler caught her by the hand.

"Nonsense, Rosie, that can wait. Let me show you both what I've brought you."

We adjourned into the parlor, where Uncle Wheeler opened up one of the portmanteaux. It was like something from a fairy story — treasures we could scarcely imagine: a painted silk fan for me, depicting a gentleman dressed quite like our uncle, reclining on a settee with a matching young lady and a frolicking dog. A pink *peau de soie* gown in a flurry of lace and ribbon, sized for a girl half Rosie's age. Delicate kid slippers. A pot of rose-petal jam that Rosie seized upon with appalling relish. I beheld the trove with some bewilderment; what on Earth would we *do* with these precious things? But I recovered myself, I hope in time: "Thank you, Uncle. Everything is truly lovely. I'm sure we've never seen their like before."

He smiled and shrugged briefly. "Ah, mere trifles. Just a few things I picked up here and there, as I saw them. I know how young ladies like pretty things." He gave a small cough. "Although it seems I may have miscalculated Rosellen's age by a bit. . . . No matter, no matter. But look here — I have something special for each of you." He dipped into the bag once more, and brought out two very different items.

Rosie's was a porcelain miniature of Mam, delicately done and barely recognizable as the mother I had known — a young woman with cascading curls and lace at her bodice, hands crossed genteelly in her lap. She gave a cry and pressed it to her breast, as if the painted Mam could feel her heart beating through the glass. We had no other picture of her, and I'm sure Rosie could barely remember her face. This was a treasure indeed.

"And Charlotte." Uncle Wheeler produced a small leather album and passed it over to me. I undid the ribbon and let the case fall open in my lap.

Inside was a letter from my father. I knew his hand immediately, the slant of the lines down the page, the blots of ink at the end of words, the threadlike scrawl of the script. I could almost reach out and hold that hand, the long fingers — just like mine — spotted with ink from gripping too close to the nib. But his hand hadn't held pen to this paper for more than ten years; it was an old letter, written just after our mother died.

Dear Wheeler,

I cannot believe she has gone — and the boy as well. Even with the girls here the silence in this house is unbearable. I seem to hear her voice in every room, only to enter and find nothing but emptiness. I don't know what we'll do without her, and but for the children I should not care. She has left two small angels behind her, motherless babes now. I don't know how much they understand. Charlotte is silent and somber, but Rosie cries constantly and asks where her Mam has gone. Gods! This is no place for children, not without a mother. But my girls are all I have left now. I fear for them, Wheeler; how can I raise them alone? And if something should happen to me . . .

You are the only family they have left now. Errie would want you to care for them should they be left alone. Promise me you won't forsake them — promise me you'll look after my girls.

Yours in sorrow,

James

I held the album with tight fingers and bit my lip. I would not cry now, before a virtual stranger. But Father's grief — still fresh, as if the leather case had preserved it all these years — struck me with such force it was hard not to weep for his pain. What sort of gift was this, I wondered. What was my uncle trying to do, by sharing this letter with me now?

Uncle Wheeler wore a strange smile as I looked up at last to meet his gaze. Did my mother have those green, green eyes? I thought she did.

"So you see, my dears, why I *had* to come. I swore to your father that I would look after you. It was the only thing he ever asked of me." He slid closer to me on the sofa.

I nodded, a heaviness welling up in my breast. There were a dozen questions I wanted to ask him — we knew *nothing* about him, after all — but they all seemed rude and ignorant, and I could not think how to pose them. I closed the little album and turned the fan over in my hand, spreading then collapsing its gilded ribs. "Is this what girls in the city are used to? These dresses and — and fine things?"

"Oh, and more," he said. "The balls, the young men, mixing with the finest society. Why, they —"

"I don't suppose there are many who —" I swallowed hard. "Who run businesses, are there? Or who . . ." I trailed off. I knew there were girls who worked, of course, but I did not think their prospects ran quite to silk and kidskin. I was suddenly not certain where in the order of the world Rosie and I fit in.

"Run businesses?" Uncle Wheeler looked confused. "My dear, what an odd notion."

Rosie broke in. "What she means is —"

"Never mind, Uncle. It was a foolish thing to say. "

Uncle Wheeler nodded with understanding and squeezed my hand. "My dear girls, you must have no fear that what became of my sister and I will befall you — that you'll be left to fend for yourselves in the wide world. I have put my own interests aside while I come to tend to you girls."

"What does that mean?" Rosie said. I stared fiercely at her, as if the strength of my gaze alone could make her behave.

"Oh, Rosellen, we shan't worry about that now. We'll just concern ourselves with the immediate crisis, and get on from there."

"Well, the immediate crisis is we haven't any money."

"Rosie!" I could have smacked her, but Uncle Wheeler took it in stride.

"No, no, Charlotte — it's quite all right. Rosellen's ingenuousness is one of her many charming assets." He withdrew a beaded purse from his jacket and popped it open. "Now, I haven't brought much cash, of course, but what I do have is yours. What do you think you'll need, by way of pin money, housekeeping, that sort of thing?"

I stared at the purse, glittering amethyst and silver in the lamplight, and tried to reason how much money such a man might carry. The fan, the slippers . . . his ostrich-plumed hat alone would have been more than two weeks' wages for my best-paid workers. His very pocket change might well see me through the month — or more.

Still . . . he was my uncle, and he had just lavished us with gifts. I bit my tongue and asked for half of what I wanted. "I think, perhaps, sir, five pounds?" It was a small fortune, and awfully brazen to expect anything near that much —

"Done." Uncle Wheeler counted out the coins and pressed them into my hand. "And don't hesitate to ask, my dear. You shan't worry about money any longer."

Chapter Three

The next day, one last icy winter blast escaped the hills and swept down the Valley, shuddering through town and ripping up thatch and shingles and spring bonnets brought out too early. Up in Stirwaters, the glass rattled in the sash and lamps would not stay lit. Though the calendar read April, winter still had us in her grip and was slow to let go.

It was bad luck all around — nothing more — that Harte was working a fitting on the other side of the wall, just as the tail end of that cold wind flung round the corner of the mill and caught the edge of the old, faded STIRWATERS sign. At the same moment, Paddy Eagan was trotting past from the dyeshed, tucked into the lee of the building for protection from the wind. With a tug from the wind and a bang from Harte, the old plank — twelve feet of hard, weathered elm — swung down off the stones and struck young Paddy in the head, knocking him to the hard, cold earth.

I heard the screech and creak as the wood pulled free, Pilot's frantic barking, and the shouts as the millhands ran for Paddy. I ran out into the yard as they were lifting him from the ground. He was pale as wool, a trickle of blood from his hair, but awake.

"Good Lord!" I cried. "Bring him inside. Janet, fetch

something to cover him with." I yanked off my apron and pressed a corner of it to Paddy's scalp. He winced, but gave me a weak smile.

"Time to fix that sign, eh, Mistress?"

"Shh, Paddy, don't talk. They've gone for help — Mr. Hale will be here any moment."

I should have known better. On a day like that one, with an obvious omen like our sign crashing off the building and nearly killing our apprentice spinner, they'd never send for the apothecary. It should have been no surprise when young Ian Lamb returned fifteen minutes later with the Widow Sarah Goodeye — known around the village as Biddy Tom.

I knew Mrs. Tom only slightly, and when she swept across my threshold, something in me drew tight and still. A tall woman dressed in red homespun, she wore a white cap over her steel-colored hair and a woollen shawl round her square shoulders. She gave me a cursory nod as she knelt beside Paddy and began to sew him up with brusque, competent stitches.

"He's cold," she pronounced. "Someone fetch some spirits." Several flasks appeared in an instant. She shook her head at the crowd as she took one and poured out a measure for Paddy. "The rest of you have a drink as well."

Truth to tell, Biddy Tom was probably at least as able as Mr. Hale — maybe more so in a real emergency. Not just the town midwife, she also did most of the horse-doctoring, and dog-doctoring, and hen-doctoring in the village. The fact was, Shearing had an apothecary because it was fashionable to have one, but no one took him seriously. For "real" medicine, most everybody appealed to Biddy Tom.

I stood in a corner up against the empty wool press while Mrs. Tom took over my finishing room. Low light from the waning day set the room deep in shadow, despite the oil lamps burning overhead. The fulling stocks kept up their steady slosh and thump as the hammers fell against the sodden cloth, beating the fibers tight together. The pounding was like a heartbeat in the mill, low and hypnotic. I felt myself pulled into their rhythm as the dusky room seemed to shift around me.

Soon Biddy Tom had Paddy sitting up, flushed with liquor, telling his tale for the crowd. He made it sound exciting, and his audience, likewise warmed, drank up every detail. But I hugged myself tight and swayed a little with every fall of the stocks, seeing the old sign come swinging down, over and again.

Bad luck. Nothing more.

"You too, Charlotte Miller."

I jumped. Biddy Tom was right beside me, holding out a flask. I shook my head, but she pressed it on me. Her pale eyes seemed to look right down inside me, and before I knew it, I was choking down a much-too-large gulp of some truly dreadful home-brewed gin.

"That's better."

I didn't see what was better about it, but I held my tongue, which was more than everyone else was doing. They had already turned the event to legend, expanding the tale as they passed it among themselves.

"'Bout time, too," Jack Townley was saying. "Hardly seems right to start the season without the old curse popping up to bite us in the tail."

"Things go in threes," Janet Lamb added. "Best be on watch, now."

"Aye," someone added, counting it out, "There's young Paddy and the sign, and then —"

"*Stirwaters is not cursed!*" I said it much louder than I'd meant to — or maybe I didn't. "I won't have such talk in the mill, do you hear me?"

Jack, Janet, and the others looked at me, cheeks red, emboldened by gin and excitement. Mistress or not, right then I was still the little girl they'd teased with tales of haunts and curses.

"Nay? What about Lonnie, then?"

"Aye, Lonnie!" Everyone nodded and I felt my own cheeks redden.

"Lonnie Clayborn is a clumsy fool! He had no business on that carding engine — and you, Jack Townley, should have known better. He's lucky he only lost a finger!"

There was silence for a moment, until Paddy piped up. "What about your da', miss?"

"What about my father?" I found myself stared down by my entire staff. I stood straighter. "Mr. Hale said his heart gave out."

"Died in the mill, he did."

"Of course he died in the mill! Where else would he die?"

"And your mam?"

I stared at them, growing cold and hot by degrees. I could have used another belt of Biddy Tom's gin, just then. "My mother?"

"Aye," Janet Lamb said. "Your poor mam, dyin' without a son like that."

"Hasn't been a son born to Millers these last five generations," someone added.

"Not and lived."

This was really too much. "Indeed? And what of your own family, Jack Townley? There hasn't been a Townley girl as long as anyone can remember. Is that a curse, too?"

"Well, the way my wife tells it, 'tis." Townley grinned amid a burst of laughter. I was about to sputter back some response, when Biddy Tom's thin reedy voice broke through.

"Ah, there's no curse on this place," she said, and everyone fell silent, all eyes turned toward her. "Bad luck in spades, maybe, but there's a difference." She tucked the flask inside her kirtle and gathered up her shawl. "Paddy Eagan, stay away from falling signs for a bit and you'll be right as rain come the weekend. And you, George Harte, mind your hammering on windy days. Charlotte, show me out."

I followed Mrs. Tom back out into the dusky afternoon, hugging my arms against the chill. Mrs. Tom fixed her cap more snugly on her head and looked up into the wind.

"Pay them no mind," she said, bundling into the grey shawl. "Curse won't breed where water runs past. Anyway, land here's too strong for it. That's your problem, Charlotte Miller — not a curse, just a powerful lot of magic, and none of it knowin' which way to work itself."

I stared at her, patience failing me. Hadn't we bad luck enough without talk of curses and magic calling the devil down on our heads?

Mrs. Tom took my arm. Her hand was unexpectedly warm and fleshy, and I flinched. She gave me an odd soft smile that cracked the lines around her eyes. "Ah, missie." She shook her head. "Your mam never believed, either. Just remember: There's practical, and there's practical. Don't let your pride get in the way of your seeing."

She squeezed my arm a final time, whipped the shawl round her shoulders, and stepped out into the wind, which fell to a breeze and then stilled altogether as she carried on up the lane.

Something about Biddy Tom had always made me uneasy, ever since I was a little girl and she treated Rosie for fever. I remembered it too clearly for comfort — I was only six or seven, and Rosie was near death, burning red and dry as paper to the touch. She'd been sick for days, and none of the remedies from Hale's had helped. Finally, when Rosie turned cold and quiet one night past midnight, Father sent for Biddy Tom. I was scared of her — scared of her red cloak and scared of her low voice and scared of her too-clear gaze. I stood in the corner, holding tight to Mam's skirts as the simples woman lifted my baby sister from her cradle and turned her this way and that, holding her too close to the fire as a packet of herbs smoldered in the embers, filling the room with heady, acrid smoke. Eventually Mrs. Tom went home, Rosie got well, and life went back to normal.

But barely a year later, Mam and our baby brother died together, and Biddy Tom couldn't do anything to help them. I knew what Father thought — everyone knew it or thought it, though no one said it aloud: Biddy Tom had done *something* to steal Rosie from death, and either God or the devil had claimed Mam and Thomas for payment.

All that was long past, and Rosie could barely remember it. And though Mrs. Tom hadn't done anything for Paddy but what any competent physician would do, I couldn't help wondering what other, stranger remedies she carried in that bag of hers. It was something that did not bear thinking of.

I was heartily glad to be home for dinner that night, grateful for the distraction and novelty of my uncle's presence. We had left him all the day to fend for himself; he had still been abed when we rose, no doubt weary from his long journey, and we had not had the chance to return home for lunch. I had assumed he would wander over to the mill when he wanted us, but he had apparently found enough at the Millhouse to occupy himself.

"Now, girls." Uncle Wheeler drained his wineglass and set it down with a delicate tap. He was dressed for the evening in a costume of robin's egg blue and butter yellow, and I wondered if he had any plain clothes stashed away in those portmanteaux. "It's time we discuss getting you settled."

"Settled how, sir?"

"Why, find a buyer for the mill and get you married off, of course."

Rosie choked on her wine, and it took a clap between the shoulders to revive her.

"A buyer?" I said, scarcely loud enough to be heard.

"Married?" Rosie had turned scarlet.

Uncle Wheeler smiled. "Of course," he said. "You can't mean to keep on in this fashion. The very idea of you girls working in that dangerous old mill . . . goodness, a boy was nearly killed there today! I'm sure this can't be the life your parents would have wished for you. You'll take my advice and forget this nonsense. Start looking toward a proper future for yourselves."

A bite of sausage burned in my throat. I took a sip of water to force it back down again. "But, sir, Stirwaters is our home. We couldn't think of selling it."

That smile widened as Uncle Wheeler dabbed at his fingers with his napkin. "Charlotte, please. Look at yourself! You're working yourself ragged. In fact, I think our first order of business should be to find you some help around the house."

"We really can't afford to pay a serving-maid —"

"My dear, I think you'll find there's always money for the truly important expenses. I do understand that this is a change for you, from the way you've been raised. But you come from quality — at least on one side — and I will not have you wasting your lives in this rustic little backwater. So tomorrow morning I'll have a look over your books and see what can be done about arranging the sale. Rosie could probably marry on her looks alone, but for you, Charlotte, we'll need some sort of settlement."

I lowered my fork to the table and tried to order my thoughts.

"Uncle," I said, "you must understand. It's not just a matter of Rosie and me. There are other families depending on us as well."

"Those families are not my concern. Your father entrusted me to look after you two girls, and I must do what's in your best interest."

"And Father trusted *us* to look after Stirwaters!" Rosie said.

"Rosellen, truly. You must learn to control those little outbursts."

Rosie glared at him, her cheeks flaming. "We have had *some* offers," I said hastily.

His head whipped toward me, the little tail on his periwig flipping around his neck. "That's my girl! Now —"

"But please, you must let me handle it," I said. "Stirwaters has been in our family such a long time — I do feel that *we* must be responsible for its future." I tried to smile, hard as it was with Rosie staring at me as if I'd plunged the bread knife into her heart. "Please."

He was silent a long moment, watching me out of those green eyes until it seemed he could see right inside me. I dropped my own eyes to my plate.

"All right, then," Uncle Wheeler said finally. "Perhaps it's too soon to discuss this. But I'm all you have left in the world now. I should keep *that* in mind, if I were you, Charlotte." He blotted his lips one final time and rose from the table. As Rosie and I sat there in dismay, his expression softened. "I'm sorry. You must understand, I am only trying to do what's best for you both. We'll leave this issue for the time being, but do think about what I've said. You could both marry well, you know; there really is no need for all this."

The week did not improve from there. I spent the next morning in the dyeshed, dodging gossip about Biddy Tom and going over the inventory with Stirwaters's dyemaster. Father had always stressed that Mr. Mordant was the finest dyer in our part of the country and we could not afford to lose him. He kept no apprentice, and worse, no dyebooks. He made everything up according to memory, behind closed doors, with an air of secrecy that had made a younger Rosie suspect him of witchcraft. Given the strange smells that emanated all hours from the dyeshed, it was no wonder she'd thought him brewing potions in there.

Mr. Mordant's secrets made Stirwaters famous for a glorious array of color. Buyers at the woollen halls knew to look for "Stirwaters Blues," a waterfall of mazareen, Prussian, and a rare, deep logwood only he could make. Keeping Mr. Mordant employed (not to mention happy) cost an arm and a leg, but he was worth it.

"Fustic!" Mr. Mordant rummaged among rows of dusty jars and battered packets. He knocked one of the jars off the shelf with his elbow, catching it a heartbeat before it shattered.

"Sir?" I stepped out of his way as he pushed past, and bumped up against one of the great steaming vats. I put my hand on the rim to steady myself, and yanked it back with a hiss. The wool within roiled and turned in the bubbling violet stew. Blowing on my scalded palm, I did my best not to breathe the fumes, hot and foul as a chamber pot.

"Fustic! I must have it here somewhere. Can't make a decent gold without fustic. That straw-colored cassimere your mam likes so much won't come out right without it."

"But —"

"Ha! Here we go, lass." He pulled a ragged paper pouch from beneath a stack of empty jars and peered inside it. "Won't last the season out, this. Have to get more."

"All right," I said again. "How much, and from where?"

He swiped the list from my hands. "I'll do the ordering, *mistress*. You won't get my secrets this year!" He broke into wild, crowlike laughter.

I stood there, stunned into silence. How had my father done this? The man was clearly crazy. And then I had my great inspiration.

"You know," I said, "I've heard some interesting things about the reds coming out of Springmill this year."

He raised his head slowly, a look of cunning in his dark eyes. "Never. Not Springmill?"

"Oh, yes. Nearly as good as the imports. Or so I've heard."

He was quiet a good long moment. I watched him draw a circle with his foot on the stained earth floor. Finally, he sidled up to me and, in practically normal tones, said, "I'll just make up a list of the things that I need, lassie, and bring it up to the office later this afternoon. Don't worry about a thing. Springmill reds, my foot!"

I let out a measured sigh. "Mr. Mordant, I do wish you'd consider taking an apprentice."

"I'm not dead yet, missie!" he said, a little too cheerily.

"No, that's the point, sir. At the very least, write down some of your recipes. You could keep them in the strongbox in the office, if you like. Safe and sound."

His narrow lips pursed tight. "Can't write them down. That's how the other ones trick you."

"The other ones?"

"Other Ones, missie, Other Ones!" he said impatiently. This time I clearly heard the emphasis — the Naming. "You Millers," he said, "always writing, writing, writing." He ripped the list right down the middle. "Put everything down where it can be seen by anybody. And what good's that ever done you? Nay, They'll not trap *me* that way, They won't!"

He kicked the fragments of my inventory into the

embers beneath the dyevat. "Never you mind about Them. We're safe from 'em here," he said, patting me on the arm. "But I'll tell you what, lass. You send that pretty sister of yourn down here once-a-while, and I'll show her one thing or another."

I looked round the little dyeshed, at the pots and bottles and little packets, and thought about the real magic Mr. Mordant pulled off in here. "I could learn it," I said.

Mr. Mordant eyed me for a long moment, then shook his grizzled head. "Nay, lassie."

"Why not?"

"Because you don't want to know how things are made round here — not really."

"That's not true! I'm every bit as interested —"

Mr. Mordant's hand fell on my arm and stopped my mouth. He pointed to the wool boiling in the vat. "Lass, if I put this here wool to rinse in water drawn upstream from the mill, it won't come out as dark or pure as if I rinsed it in water drawn downstream."

"But that doesn't make any sense —"

"No, it don't. And there ain't no reason to explain it, neither, but that something gets in the water at Stirwaters and makes it take color better. Something . . . not natural. This mill, it has *moods*, lass, queer humors. Like a person — fair one day and foul the next, and you've got to know how to listen to it." He nodded and turned away again. "And that's what you don't want me to tell you. So you send that sister of yourn. She don't mind what I'll have to teach her."

He took up his heavy stone roller and began to grind up a bundle of bark, clearly finished with me for the day.

*   *   *

Rosie grabbed me on my way back into the mill. "It's about time you showed up! Tansy Eagan's in your office!"

"Tansy Eagan! What can she want?"

"Oh, I'm sure she'll tell you." She lifted a corner of my stained apron. "Where have you been all this time?"

I said nothing — yet — about Mr. Mordant's offer (let alone his moods and humors). No need to push my luck this morning.

Tansy, a tall, gangly girl about Rosie's age, was pacing furrows in my office floor. "Ah," she said as I cracked the door. "I've come for me brother's wages."

I looked her over as I came inside, doffed my hat, and sat down. She had the look of the queen hen about her — proud, puffed, and strutting.

"Pay day's Wednesday — bearing-home day, you know that." Stirwaters always paid out wages on the day each week when our weavers brought back their finished cloth and fetched home the yarn for new work.

"Heh," said Tansy, with a smile that showed her cracked teeth. "Won't be no more bearing-home for Paddy. Our mum's decided this place is too chancy. She'll be keepin' him home where it's safer now."

Paddy's wages were nearing those of a man grown. Mrs. Eagan must be mad to make him quit. "What's he going to do?" I asked. "Is she taking him to the loom?"

Tansy sniffed. "Can't think so. I'm her 'prentice. Be workin' me own loom soon enough." She held out her wide, angular hand. "The wages?"

Tansy tapped her foot impatiently as I counted out the coins (with a few extra we could not spare, for I was fond of Paddy and shuddered to imagine him home all day with

Tansy and her mother. Spun from the same wool, those two were). "Have you got me mum's yarn, then?" she asked when I was done.

"No, I have not. Come back on Wednesday."

She shrugged. "Mum wanted me to tell you that she'll be askin' more for each piece."

"What?"

"Your piece rate's too low. Her sister in Burlingham makes three pound a week, and you best keep pace or you'll lose your best weavers."

I leaned back slowly into my chair, torn between disbelief and anger. The piece rate for weavers was set by established tradition and overseen by the Wool Guild, and Peg Eagan had no call to try and raise it for herself. Three pounds! That raised the price of the cloth she wove to nearly its market value. Even if I could afford such a rate, I'd be a fool to pay it. I'd never get it back — not on plains and packing cloths.

Tansy watched me smugly, letting her words sink in. It was a hard matter — Paddy had taken a goodly share of their family income, and if I cut off mother and daughter as well . . . It was no small thing to send a family into ruin. But if Mrs. Eagan wouldn't see reason, what could I do?

"Well, Miss Eagan, I'll be sure to let your mother know if something comes up for that rate."

Tansy's smile faded as she took my meaning. She tucked Paddy's wages into her bodice and glared. "You'll be sorry. Just you wait. Me mum'll have words to say about this!"

"Give my regards to your brother," I said. "There will always be a place for him at Stirwaters."

Tansy slammed the door so hard a bit of plaster fell off the lintel.

For the next several days, Stirwaters attentions were divided among carding and spinning and the fixing of broken steps . . . and gossip about my uncle. It was just as well; I'd grown heartily sick of hearing about falling signs and our visit from Biddy Tom. Who was this strange gentleman, folk wanted to know. Was he to be the new master? Despite my own misgivings, I did my best to assure them that he wasn't. There had been no further mention of selling the mill, but each morning at breakfast our uncle made polite inquiry about the state of our affairs, and every night at dinner, gentle commentary on the state of our health and dress. True to his word, he even engaged a serving maid for the Millhouse: Rachel Baker, who donned a white cap and apron and took to calling Rosie and me "Miss," as if she hadn't known us all her life.

I was determined to look on this development as a sign that Uncle Wheeler intended life to continue in this vein. He knew how Mam and Father had loved it here; surely he could see that staying was the best thing for Rosie and me, as well. Indeed, I often saw him standing in the millyard, gazing at the mill buildings and the river as if drinking in the view, and I believed that he felt Stirwaters working its way into his bones, as well.

Reassured, I turned my full attentions to Stirwaters. If Rachel and Uncle Wheeler could polish up the Millhouse, surely I could do the same for the mill. The repairs I had asked for continued apace; we had managed to unstick the yardside doors and rebuild the back steps, and if the windows were still broken, at least now they all had solid casements. We had not yet replaced the fallen sign, however, and repeated efforts to rehang it ended in failure.

"I can't explain it, Mistress," Harte said, scratching his head with his hammer. "There's no earthly reason the bolts won't take, but every time I get up there, the stone just crumbles away."

"It's dry rot," I said. "The place is riddled with it."

Harte gave me a long, even look, but finally nodded. "I'll get some paint, then, Mistress."

At the end of the week, I found Mr. Mordant in the yard, mixing up a big batch of whitewash under a fine sky.

"Bad day for dyeing," he said when I stopped by, indicating the weather with a nod of his head.

"How's that, then?" I asked. "Is it too cold?"

Mr. Mordant broke into wild, braying laughter. "Nay, missie! Friday!"

I closed my eyes. *Friday.* Of course. Still, since he had the whitewash, there was one particular project I was eager to take on myself. I hauled bucket and brushes up to the spinning room, which was badly in need of attention. Most of the walls were exterior and stone, but a few were plaster, and I doubted they'd had fresh paint in generations — certainly not the back wall, where someone, long ago, had put a hex sign. The wall was worn and sun-faded, the image dim with age. Its original colors and swirling designs were hard to make out, especially where the plaster had chipped away. It dated back farther than anyone at Stirwaters could remember, and I doubted anyone took much notice of the thing, or could remember why it had been painted there in the first place.

Picturing the wall fresh and gleaming white, I applied brush to plaster with relish. As I painted, I imagined replacing the superstitious symbol with a painting of Stirwaters's coat of arms, the gold millwheel on a green shield, crowned by a ram. Harte could do a splendid job emblazoning our arms there. I stepped back to appraise my work — and promptly kicked over the pail of whitewash.

Cursing, I scrambled to catch the spill, mopping up my sodden boot and utterly ruining my skirt in the process. I ran for rags and water, leaving white footprints everywhere, and was on my knees scrubbing frantically when I heard a sound like crows behind me.

Mr. Mordant was bent over the righted pail, laughing coarsely. "Told you, missie. What did I say, then?"

"Friday," I snapped. "Fine, Friday. Here, help me get this up."

When we had the floor as clean as possible, only faint white streaks seeped into the grain of the floorboards to betray my clumsiness, Mr. Mordant helped me gather up the rags and bucket. As he eased himself off the floor, supplies in hand, he stopped cold, staring at the wall.

"Ah, lassie," he said quietly. "Ill done, I think. 'Twere ill done, indeed."

I gripped my bundle tighter. "What are you talking about?"

Mr. Mordant gave a long sigh. "That mark's been up there all these years, and ain't nobody painted over it before. Never wonder why? Did you not think, then, that whatever that thing were warding against, it's still out there?"

I could not get the dire look in Mr. Mordant's eyes out of my mind. I kept telling myself he was nothing but a queer old man having a jest, but it was no good. The workmen's insistence that Stirwaters did not want to be repaired did little to ease my mind. New blocks set into place worked loose by the following morning, a crack patched here sprang up again a few inches away. And every time I passed the newly white wall, I thought I saw the old colors of the hex sign — a shadowy, faint impression, but certainly more than imagination. *It's the whitewash*, I told myself. It always took several coats.

But it didn't. No sooner than a second — and then a third and fourth — coat of paint had gone up over the hex sign, the colors seeped through again.

Rosie watched me, altogether too silent for my taste.

"What?" I finally said at the end of the fourth coat, sweaty and exasperated.

"I just think maybe you ought to leave it alone," she said. "You heard what Mr. Mordant said."

"That's ridiculous. There's no —" I stopped, hearing Harte's voice echo in my mind.

Rosie must have heard it, too. "No earthly reason you can't paint that wall?"

I was too hot to feel the chill. I mopped my forehead with my paint-speckled apron.

"Fine!" I said at last, addressing the wall directly. "I give up! You win. I'll even send Harte up to repaint the fool thing."

Bold against the fresh white background, the newly painted hex sign looked like a great watchful eye gazing over the mill.

Finally, we reached a state where we could call the repairs more or less complete. The mill was cleaner, certainly, enjoying a fresher, brighter aspect and fewer cracks and crumbles. Patches were put on thin spots in the floor, and if their corners popped up occasionally, we just tapped them down firm again.

Harte never did manage to rehang the sign, but STIRWATERS WOOLLEN MILL was now spelled out in glorious barn red on grey, lichen-free limestone.

"Shall I stop now, then?" Harte called down from the ladder. "Or do you want the rest?"

Rosie and I watched from below. "What do you think?" Rosie asked, her hand on the black collie's head. "It looks a bit bare, just that — but the rest of it's not really true, then, is it?"

"'Miller and Sons, Shearing,' just as it's always been," I said. "We did not go to all this work not to see the name Miller on this mill."

Chapter Four

Somehow life slipped into its usual spring rhythm. We spun and carded and dyed our new wool, and sent it out into the village to be woven, and we brought it back again, ready to be finished and bound up for sale. And then we did it all again. We were spared falling signs and over-turned dyevats for a few weeks, and if anyone whispered of curses or spirits, they did not do so in my hearing. Rosie and I, too, became accustomed to Uncle Wheeler's presence in our home. Meals were more lavish, certainly; if we weren't careful, we should outgrow all our clothes. And even if we were made all too aware of our rustic manners and coarse country ways, surely it was worth it, to have a full larder to come home to every day.

One bright day in May, despite having awakened to one of Rachel's luxurious breakfasts, I had descended into a perfectly foul mood by afternoon. Mr. Weaver was training me to take over for Paddy Eagan at the spinning jack, and I'd spent hours winding and rewinding the spindles for the long machine — all two hundred sixty of them — until I had the knack of the quick light twist that sent the thread reeling up the bobbins. And the headache and sore wrists to prove it. Running the jack was skilled labor that took years to master, and there was no way I was going to pick it up, not in one springtime of lessons squeezed between my other labors.

"Now, lass — are you with me? You've got to go slower on the backward pass, or you'll break the — aye, as I was saying. Here, now, stop the whole thing." Without so much as a sigh, steady old Tory shifted the gear into neutral and sent me down inside the assembly to fetch the ends of the broken threads.

"Ah, Mistress," Tory said when I emerged, "why don't ye take a break? You've done better than anyone could expect."

And you'll be glad to be rid of me, no doubt, I thought. "Very well," I said, "but I'll be back."

"Ah know ye will," Tory said softly, turning back to his spindles. "You wouldn't be a Miller if you weren't."

I scowled my way down the narrow steps and into the airless finishing room, where I was met by Lonnie Clayborn, who came swinging round the corner, breathless.

"Mistress — there's a gen'leman skulking about like, out in the yard." He gestured clumsily with a hand still thickly swaddled in a filthy bandage.

"Do you mean my uncle?"

Lonnie shook his head. "Nay — some city feller. Like them what was at Market Days."

The Pinchfields man? I stormed out of the mill and into the yard, where a young gentleman in a cassimere suit had hyp-notized Pilot into a belly-up puddle of lolling tongue, drooping feet, and swishing feathered tail.

"I thought I had made myself perfectly clear," I announced to his black felt hat. "We are not some flystruck carcass for the picking!"

The man slowly raised himself up from the shale drive and brushed at the dust on his trousers. "I — I'm a little confused," he said. "I'm looking for Stirwaters, and I seem to have found *that*, but —"

"Aye, and we're still not for sale!"

He doffed his hat, shoved a hand through his long sandy hair, and replaced the hat once more. "No, still confused," he said cheerfully. "I was hoping to speak to whoever had taken charge of the estate. I've come from Uplands Mercantile, in Harrowgate."

I felt my face turn absolutely scarlet. "Oh, Lord — you're Mr. Woodstone! I have your letter —" I scrabbled through my apron pockets and found it. It had come some days before, and I'd been meaning to answer it, but work kept getting in the way . . . some nonsense about a bank, and — "Here, I'm so sorry. I thought you were — well, never mind. I'm Miss Miller," I added, somewhat belatedly.

"You? But I was expecting children — you know, little girls in pinafores and pudding caps?" He laughed. "Here, let's start over, shall we? Randall Woodstone, at your service. Miss Miller, if you could tell me where I might find whoever's responsible for the mill's affairs now."

I peered up at him through the visor of my hand. He was a sizeable fellow — not that tall — but he wore his clothes well, particularly that black jacket. I judged him to be a few years older than myself. "You seem to have found her."

The banker looked taken aback. I was getting used to that expression. "But how old are you? That is — surely you have some sort of guardian, or an agent, at least?"

I gave the little smile I'd been practicing for such occasions. I hoped it made me look serene and competent. Rosie said it made me look half ill. "No, indeed, sir. Now if we've quite established that, shall we get on with whatever business has brought you to my mill?"

"Right. Miss Miller, I'm afraid it's about your loan. With the unfortunate passing of Mr. Miller — your father — and the mill's subsequent lack of stable leadership . . . I'm afraid that the bank has decided to call in Stirwaters's mortgage."

"Our what?" I squeaked. That was too large a matter for even Father to forget to mention. The millwheel sounded, suddenly, very loud. "Mr. Woodstone, there must be some mistake. I am not aware of any such debt on the mill. Please, may I see the papers?"

Mr. Woodstone handed them over. I glanced through the sheets of neatly lettered vellum, but could not seem to make sense of them. The only thing that was clear — altogether too clear — was the name James Miller, in great implacable script right at the top of the first page. And on the last page, the scrawling illegible streak of ink that was my father's signature.

"Oh, mercy."

"Miss Miller — here, why don't you sit down?" Mr. Woodstone steered me over to the millrace and plopped me down gently on the stone wall. "I understand this must be quite a shock —"

"But I don't understand. When did he take this out? It says — but this was only a year ago. Where did the money go?" A sudden sickening thought struck me. "How *much* did he borrow?" I scrabbled through the pages.

A great warm hand reached in and gently pried my fingers from the mortgage papers. "Two thousand pounds," Mr. Woodstone said quietly. "Around nineteen hundred now. Not that I'm sure that's much comfort."

I choked out a blunt laugh. "Not a lot, no. What does that mean, call it in?"

Mr. Woodstone's expression was very serious. He had a kind face, even beneath all this bad news. "Miss Miller, I was sent here to collect the full amount."

"Two thousand pounds?" He may well have asked for two million — or two hundred. I didn't have it. Mr. Woodstone nodded. "Or?"

"Or we foreclose. I'm dreadfully sorry —"

I sat there on the mossy stone of the millrace, dimly aware that somewhere Mr. Woodstone was still speaking. I fanned the mortgage papers and beat them before my face. I had never fainted, but this would be the moment for it. It was here, then: the End I had felt looming at the funeral — here in the form of a kind-faced young banker from Harrowgate. The water trickled by below us, a faint whisper and splash in the afternoon sun; but I heard it as the blood of Stirwaters draining away.

"But you can't," I said suddenly, before I was aware that I was planning to say anything. "Don't you understand — Stirwaters is the heart of this village. Twenty-two people work at this mill, and we supply income to dozens of farmers in the Valley and beyond. How can you foreclose?"

Mr. Woodstone regarded me with eyes the color of the Stowe. "Miss Miller, I know it sounds heartless — but that isn't the bank's concern."

"Then make it your concern," I said desperately. "Please — come inside. Meet Eben Fuller, and Mr. Mordant, and Harte — and my sister. See some of the people who will be affected if you force Stirwaters to close. Does your bank find it profitable to send an entire village into ruin?"

"Miss Miller —" I do not know what Mr. Woodstone might have said next, for at that moment the church bell rang the evening hour, and the old mill doors creaked open, spilling the millhands into the yard. I rose hastily, suddenly fearful that I might be seen with this banker and — and what? Be thought party to some illicit assignation?

Mr. Woodstone, all etiquette, rose with me. He watched the millhands pass us by, frowning slightly.

I saw my advantage and went for it. "Mr. Woodstone, please. Isn't there any way to convince the bank to — to let us have more time? My father only passed away a month ago; there must be some provision for such an event. It's the height of the wool season, and Stirwaters's stock goes to market soon. Surely we can make *some* kind of arrangement."

As we stood there by the water, my Stirwaters family strayed past: plump red-faced Janet Lamb, cheerfully berating her son Ian; old Tory Weaver, who had evidently given up waiting for me, shuffling his stooped way across the shale yard; Jack Townley — always met at the gates by pretty Mrs. Townley and a handful of small, perpetually dusty boys. Ruth saw me, and gave a wave.

"Very well, Miss Miller," he finally said. "I could at least spare the time to let you make your case. I was instructed to take an inventory of your assets; but I see that we're losing the daylight, and perhaps tomorrow would be a better time to have a look at the mill?"

"Thank you, Mr. Woodstone," I said, and did not quite let out all my breath until that sleek cassimere coat was halfway to Drover's inn.

*   *   *

Back inside Stirwaters, I found Rosie midway up a ladder, fitting a gear with Harte. I caught her eye and beckoned angrily. She slid down and met me in the office. "What happened to you? Mr. Weaver said you disappeared an hour ago —"

"Did you know Father took out a mortgage on the mill?"

"He what? But —" Her eyes widened. "No, of course I didn't know. Why would I?"

I slammed the papers down on the desk. "You two were always so close; he talked to you about everything."

Rosie's expression softened. "What happened?"

Wearily, I sank down on the desk and related all the banker had told me. When Rosie was suitably pale from the news, she shook her head sadly. "Father never said anything — never *would* have said anything about it to me. You were the one he talked to about money."

I made a sound that was meant to be a laugh, but came out somewhere between a cough and a sob. "He never talked to me about money," I said. "I spoke to him about it, but it was always a wave of his hand and, 'Don't fret so. Things will take care of themselves.' Oh, aye, and look where that's brought us, then."

I tapped my fingers on the binding of the ledger, wherein the debt was *not* recorded, and sighed. "He's coming here tomorrow, to take an inventory for the bank. We've got to show him we're worth saving."

Rosie gave a mirthless laugh. "Oh, I'll show him a thing or two."

"I wish you wouldn't," I said. "He did seem awfully sorry about it."

She raised an eyebrow, but squeezed my shoulder. "Things *will* be all right."

"How?"

"Because you'll think of something. You always do."

I followed Rosie home with none of her misplaced confidence. It was all very well to tell Mr. Woodstone that our stock went to market at the end of summer, but the fact was, we'd never bring in two thousand pounds — or anything close to it. I'd been hoping to scrape together a few *hundred* pounds — enough to pay all my workers, hire a new jackspinner, and replace the broken glass in the spinning room windows.

It seemed all my grand plans would have to wait.

Dinner that night was a stiff and awkward affair, made perhaps even more strained by Rachel's presence, leaning over my shoulder to ladle soup into my dish or refill my glass. Uncle Wheeler kept pausing to give instruction on any number of details she hadn't managed to his satisfaction. The joint was overdone, the aspic was too cold, the wine not what he'd ordered. For Rachel's part, she kept up the serene and patient expression she wore for difficult customers at the bakehouse and said nothing but "aye, sir" and "thank you, sir."

I watched the sumptuous dishes come and go: leek-and-cream soup, braised sweetbreads, stuffed duck; and all I could think of was the mortgage. What had Father done with that kind of money? It hadn't gone into the mill, that much was plain.

"My dear Charlotte, you seem distant tonight. Are you unwell?"

I started and splashed soup onto the tablecloth. "No,

Uncle, surely not. Just a long day." My uncle reached out and stroked my arm with his thin hand. Lace that must have cost twenty shillings a yard frothed round his wrist.

"My poor girl. You've had such a strain lately. All this work, on top of your recent tragedy. A delicate constitution like yours needs *rest* after such a shock."

"She hasn't got a delicate constitution! She's healthy as an ox."

I heard a clatter from the kitchen, I think to cover up a muffled laugh.

"Thank you, Rosie. Uncle, truly, I believe work is just what I need right now, and —"

Uncle Wheeler clucked his tongue. "This is exactly what we were discussing the other night. It's all very well for a lady of consequence to *own* an enterprise such as your little mill, for an income, of course, or a dowry. But somewhere else, naturally, managed by some competent laboring class fellow, with an agent — or a relative — to oversee the finances. But actually running a — factory — herself?" He gave a distasteful sniff. "Well, that's hardly done."

"Mam did it," I said a little sullenly.

Uncle Wheeler's green eyes narrowed slightly. "Well. And look where that brought her. I'm very serious, Charlotte. Reconsider your position. I know your father took pride in that Miller stubbornness, but it's hardly a virtue in a young lady."

And whatever thoughts I had of confessing my latest financial difficulties to my uncle went straight out of my head at that.

*   *   *

I slept poorly that night and was at Stirwaters early, taking advantage of a few moments' peace to check the cloth drying on the tenterhooks. Like two parallel farm fences, the tenters cross a wide field behind the millpond for thirty-five yards. We could have used a third, but it was one of those vexing mysteries of Stirwaters: The third tenter always fell down, or sagged in the middle, or tore the cloth, or was got at by goats; so we coped with two. That day we had two of Mrs. Hopewell's pieces stretched out, dove grey satinette and a blue flannel, running along the river like its reflection. I walked the rows, checking the cloth for flaws. The cloth had come loose from a couple of the hooks, so I knelt down to refasten it, tugging the selvage taut and even.

"Ahoy, there! Miss Miller?"

I spotted an unfamiliar pair of creased riding boots beneath the cloth, briskly making their way my direction. The cloth was seized with a fit of perversity and would not reach to the hook, just as the boots stopped right on the other side of the tenter.

"I say, do you need a hand there?"

And I, with my great backside thrust gracelessly into the air, looked up to see my father's banker grinning down at me. Flushing hotly, I abandoned my selvage and burst to my feet.

"Mr. Woodstone! Is it your custom to go skulking about in tenter fields?"

I could see he was trying not to laugh. "I resent skulking," he said amiably. "I did call out. Good morning, Miss Miller."

He had exchanged his black suit for a coat of brown baize — heavy for the morning — and the scuffed and creased boots. His hair was tied back loosely with a ribbon, and he wore no hat, no waistcoat. If I hadn't known better, I could easily have mistaken him for one of my country neighbors. Before I could answer, he stooped low beside me and pulled firmly on the cloth, slipping it easily onto the great iron hook.

"You can't think much of me after yesterday," he said. "Let's start fresh, why don't we?" He rose and held his arm for me to take. "Miss Miller, would you do me the honor of showing me your mill?"

I spent the better part of that morning leading Mr. Randall Woodstone on a tour of Stirwaters, from the spinning room to the tenterhooks, the felting room, the finishing room, the wheelhouse. All the while, he trailed at my heels, taking everything in and asking perceptive questions about the millworks: How efficient was the power train? What was our average return on a length of cloth? Did we buy our wool locally or was it imported? He noted my answers in a rather battered record book, no doubt taking our measure for the bank fellows. *Is Stirwaters worth saving? If only their stock could bring in another two hundred pounds. Such a shame. . . .*

Rosie, contrary to my concerns, was at her charming best, not even one gold curl out of place. If the banker thought it strange to find a young girl installed in the wheelhouse, walking him through the workings of the great waterwheel and its many smaller replicas, he gave no sign of it. Still, the farther along we went, the faster his pencil scurried across the pages of his inventory book, the more pointed his questions became. I read the look in Rosie's gaze: Was he sizing us up to save us — or skewer us?

Mr. Woodstone and I followed the gears from the wheelhouse upstairs, along the path the wool took in the mill. As we passed through the spinning room, he paused before Jack Townley's carding engine. "And what does this do?"

"Mr. Woodstone, please don't touch that!" I scuttled closer and yanked his hand away from the razor-sharp carding cloth. "We've already lost one finger this spring, and I should hate to impede your ability to — to draft up mortgage papers and such."

Mr. Woodstone let out a great laugh that echoed off the stones. "Duly noted." As I explained how the machine combed the matted wool into smooth fibers ready to be spun, Mr. Woodstone took notes: *Carding engines (three),* I fancied he wrote, *fifty pounds apiece.* "Very good. What's next?"

Undeterred, I led him straight past my spinning jack to Tory Weaver's, where the old jackspinner eased the long carriage forward into the mill room, drawing the threads out like a fine white web. Mr. Woodstone stepped in close and watched the hypnotic rhythm of Tory's motion with the jack, which was like a slow, peculiar dance, as he alternately drew out the frame, and then pushed it back again.

"Spinning is at the heart of our operation here, and Stirwaters was built to accommodate these machines," I said. "It's a skill that takes years to master. Mr. Weaver, how long have you been at Stirwaters?"

Tory leaned back and regarded Mr. Woodstone from wizened eyes. "Ah, I'd say I been here through the last three masters. Not countin' Miss Charlotte, of course." He gave me a crinkled smile.

"Very impressive, sir. Would you mind if I gave it a try?" He eyed me sidelong. "I trust there's nothing dangerous about *this* machine?"

I felt my mouth hanging open, like some country simpleton, and closed it with what was surely an audible clack of my teeth, as Mr. Woodstone shucked off his baize coat and let Mr. Weaver guide his hands into place on the spinning frame.

"So that would be Charlotte's father, then, and what, your grandfather?" Mr. Woodstone asked, watching the carriage frame advance under his touch. Mr. Weaver gave me a sharp look.

"No, sir. My father's cousin. Stirwaters has a — strange history in that regard."

"But it's always been in the Miller family?"

"Oh, yes, sir. We're a family operation."

Mr. Woodstone looked up from the spinning jack and regarded me levelly. "And after you, Miss Miller?" The mill floor shuddered with the rumble of water beneath us.

I swallowed hard. "There's no one."

"No cousin, no uncle, no long-lost brothers?"

I shook my head.

"I see," Mr. Woodstone said quietly, as the gears thumped steadily overhead.

A few more passes with the carriage later (during which, I grudgingly noted, Mr. Woodstone broke *no* threads), the banker relinquished his claim on Tory's jack, with what seemed genuine thanks. He passed me his little book to hold as he shrugged back into his jacket, and I was very well-behaved and did not peek once.

"So how does all this thread become cloth?" Mr. Woodstone asked, flipping back through the pages of his notes. "I don't see any looms here."

I shook my head. "No, sir. Weaving is sent out. There wouldn't be any room for the looms here, first of all. And besides, they belong to the weavers — they aren't the property of Stirwaters." I may have said that a tiny bit more forcefully than necessary, but Mr. Woodstone did little more than twitch his eyebrows before scribbling yet another notation.

He snapped the book closed. "Well, if you don't mind, I think I'd like to see some of this famous cloth of yours. I believe I heard something about blue dye?"

I nodded. "Oh, yes, sir. Come this way, I have a new piece in the office."

I set off across the spinning room, my skirts swinging in a wide arc as I walked. I was halfway to the stairs when Mr. Woodstone called my name. I turned back, and saw with dismay that he had stopped before the wall painted with the hex symbol. *Don't ask, don't ask*, I silently pleaded, but Miller luck struck again.

"I say, this is . . . unusual. Not the sort of thing I usually encounter in the businesses I survey."

My heart sank, but I plastered that serene, half-sick smile on my face. "Just our little . . . emblem. A sort of symbol for Stirwaters." Well, why not? It was as fitting as anything else.

He traced a finger along one gold-edged swirl. "Ah, yes." He dipped into his jacket pocket and pulled out a figure of plaited straw. "I found this on the floor by one of the machines. Corn dollies? Very, ah, thorough of you, I'd say."

I stared at it, all the force of my will resisting the urge to snatch it back from him. Blast Father and his charms and curses! "Mr. Woodstone, I can assure you, we are not *all* superstitious rustics in Shearing."

"Miss Miller," he said. "I would never suggest it."

And after that, I was relieved to fairly slam shut the door to the office, cutting off Mr. Woodstone's view of the hex sign.

He slid easily into a chair and leaned back, crossing his legs, while I fetched a length of logwood blue plush, fresh from Janet Lamb and the finishing room, and unfolded a yard or two over my arm, so Mr. Woodstone could watch the light disappear into the depths of its velvet-soft raised nap.

"No one else makes this color," I said. "It's exclusive to Stirwaters."

"How much will something like that go for?"

I refolded the cloth. "I'm going to ask twenty pounds for this. And there are two more bolts just like it."

Mr. Woodstone let out a long whistle, and I suppressed my smile.

"Well, you've managed to impress me," he said. He spread his book open on the desk, chewing on his lip and nodding as he read. I found the habit terribly distracting, and had to look away.

"Is that good?"

He sighed and sat straighter. "I don't know, Miss Miller. When your father came to us, he was very determined. His mill and his daughters, that was all he cared about. I can honestly tell you I understand his affection — for everything. But it isn't up to me, not completely. I'd like to see you make a go of it, truly I would. But you'll have to show the bank that you're worth a two-thousand-pound risk. Can you do that?"

I met his eyes. He had trusted my father with an absurd amount of money — his poor judgement, but I would not allow Stirwaters to suffer for that. "What must I do?"

Mr. Woodstone outlined the terms. I would have to make an "earnest payment" of six hundred fifty pounds by the end of summer — he could extend the deadline to after Market, but no later. After that, regular payments could be made over

68

the course of eighteen months. It was not as good as I'd dared hope — not as good as if I'd been a man, certainly. Father's loan had been for ten years; the bank, apparently, was not willing to take such a chance on me.

"If you miss a payment, Miss Miller —"

He didn't finish the sentence. He didn't have to. We both knew what would happen.

At long last, I led Mr. Woodstone out into the yard, where the afternoon sun bathed Stirwaters in golden light. He stopped and shielded his eyes with one hand, gazing out over the mill building, the dappled green pond beyond it, and the silver wheel, turning lazily in the slow water. Taking advantage of the moment, I brought him closer to the building, on the pretense of offering him a drink from the water-butt. A plume of mist rose from the water, making the very air glitter.

"I say, that's really beautiful, isn't it?" he said softly. I did not let him see my smile.

"Shearing folk say this mill has a mind of its own. That Stirwaters knows what it needs, and calls its caretakers to it. That's how it's managed to stay in the family so long."

"Do you believe that?" Mr. Woodstone's voice was quiet, but I sensed no mockery in it.

"My father did. He used to remind us that we were only keeping Stirwaters in trust for future generations. And, Mr. Woodstone, you must believe that I will do *anything* to ensure that that trust is not broken."

Mr. Woodstone stepped closer to me. "Miss Miller, I —" But at that moment, I heard the telltale creak of the Millhouse door, and I jumped, pulling away from the banker.

My uncle was just emerging from the house. In a coat of salmon pink velvet, he crossed the shale toward us, pulling on his white gloves.

Mr. Woodstone watched him with surprise. "I say — isn't that Ellison Wheeler?"

"Yes — he's my uncle. He's been staying with us since Father — while we get settled."

Mr. Woodstone rocked back on his heels. "Really? He's quite a well-known . . . figure at some of the old clubs in Harrowgate, you know."

I frowned, wondering about my banker's acquaintance with my uncle. That was all I should need.

Uncle Wheeler paused about ten paces from us. "Good day, niece. I'd not have thought to find you loitering about the yard in the middle of the day. And who is your . . . companion?"

"Randall Woodstone at your service, Mr. Wheeler. We've not formally met, although our paths have crossed. I believe we belong to the same club." He held out his hand.

Uncle Wheeler drew back and pursed his lips. "I hardly think that likely, my boy."

"The Westmoreland? You must be missing the amusements there, I daresay. How are you finding the country, then? A little dull for your taste, no doubt."

My uncle smiled thinly. "You'd be surprised."

I did not want him to learn the nature of Mr. Woodstone's business with Stirwaters — not when he had a banker so convenient to discuss the matter of selling — so I broke into their exchange. "Uncle, Mr. Woodstone was an acquaintance of my father. He's been in Shearing on business, and has just dropped by to offer his condolences."

"What a very small world, indeed," my uncle said softly. "What sort of business?"

"Banking business," Mr. Woodstone said with an easy smile. "And what sort of trade are you engaged in, Mr. Wheeler? I never did quite know."

"Ah well — a little of this and that, you know, my dear boy. Of course, my chief occupation right now is the welfare of my nieces." He took a measured step closer to me, until I was within the circle of his lilac perfume.

"What a generous gesture," Mr. Woodstone said. "The Mistresses Miller certainly are fortunate to have such attentive relations."

"I'm sure. Now, my dear, you mustn't keep Mr. Woodstone any longer. I'm sure he has important matters to attend to. Come along now; your luncheon is waiting for you." One salmon arm round my shoulders, my uncle made to steer me toward the Millhouse.

Mr. Woodstone took a quick step forward and bowed low, catching my hand on the way. "Miss Miller," he said, meeting my eyes with great solemn grey ones. "Please do not hesitate to call on me if I can be of *any* assistance. Good day." He gave my hand the faintest of squeezes before letting it drop, bowed again to my uncle, and disappeared, whistling, down the dusty road.

Chapter Five

"*And* that's how it stands," I concluded, looking over the grim and set faces gathered for bearing-home day. I had been very frank about the nature of Mr. Woodstone's visit earlier in the week. "I won't hold it against anyone who wants to leave now. Mercy, didn't you say your sister could find you a place at Woolcroft?"

Mrs. Fuller looked at me with stricken eyes. "Oh, Mistress, I never could! Not with Market coming up — you'll need those cassimeres."

"Nay, Mistress," Jack Townley spoke up. "You'll not be rid of us so easily, then. We're not going to jump ship and leave you empty-handed just when you need us most."

Those were kind words, and they warmed me — I only hoped they wouldn't regret them.

"We've got to get that money," I said to Rosie later. We were up in the office, making up the inventory books for the Cloth Exchange, but I couldn't focus on the task. "They'll stay here and starve, or they'll drift off to other towns, and either way it'll be the end of Shearing. I can't let that happen."

Rosie sighed. "Well, there's one quick answer."

Eyebrows raised, I waited.

"Uncle Wheeler."

I scribbled furiously in my inventory book. "No."

"For goodness sake, why not?"

"If I tell him we need six hundred pounds, it will mean another lecture about selling the mill."

Rosie lifted up my inkwell and turned it over in her fingers, watching the ink roll round the crystal. "So, this is about pride, then?"

I snatched it back from her. "No, it is not. I'm telling you, there's no *reason* to tell Uncle Wheeler, because it won't do any good. A debt like this is precisely the leverage he's looking for to make us sell."

"Maybe he doesn't really want us to sell. Maybe it's just the only way he thinks he can help us. But if he knew he could give us some money —"

I shook my head. "He has no interest in Stirwaters. If we needed money to buy ballgowns or finance a début season in the city — I'm sure he'd be more than generous. But he wouldn't see any value in putting money into a dying mill." I looked at my sister. "We've just got to do well at Market, is all."

So spring burned into a roaring hot summer, and Stirwaters bustled along. We felt the loss of the Eagans, but the others picked up the slack where they could, and slowly, piece by piece, the finished cloth built up in the woolshed. As I began to tag and label the bundles for Market, I fancied some Stirwaters ancestor smiled down on me. Mercy Fuller's cassimeres were as fine as I'd ever seen them; Mr.

Mordant outdid himself in the colors pouring out of the dye-shed. The pressure of the looming debt was bringing out our best work.

Those were good days, then; the first in ages. We had our tasks laid out for us, and as we worked to the rhythm of the turning wheel, our thoughts followed the Stowe, downriver, to Harrowgate. To Market.

It was considered bad luck to talk openly about Market too early; too many things had been known to go wrong, in the past. But it didn't stop the occasional whisper or broad, proud smile as I walked past someone's workstation. "When our Charlotte goes to Market" became a thread of hope, a blessing breathed over the cloth: "We'll get a good price for this'n, when our Charlotte goes to Market."

We had the same problems we always had, of course. There was something wrong with one of the gears in the spinning room, and no amount of tinkering by Harte and Rosie could repair it. One morning Jack Townley's carding engine just *stopped*, and though Rosie examined it frame by frame and gear by gear and pronounced it perfectly sound, it wouldn't start up again. He stood by the stilled machine and stared at it, dumbfounded.

"Go home and play with your boys," I said. "We'll hold your wages." He nodded and went off, but I thought I heard him mutter something as he left — and when he returned the next morning, he fixed a plaited straw figure firmly to the engine's frame, and after that it ran just as smoothly as anything.

"But —" Rosie began.

"Don't say a word." My voice was thin with warning.

Still, despite the little headaches, I found the rhythm of

work at the mill soothing. I loved to stand in the spinning room, or under the shadow of the millwheel, and let the heartbeat of Stirwaters thrum through me. I could look at those old stone walls and speak the plain truth: I was doing my honest duty as the miller, and Stirwaters was doing the work it was built for. As May gave way to June, we received a packet from Uplands Mercantile Bank repeating the terms of our arrangement, with a brief but cordial letter from Mr. Woodstone, wishing us well. As I weighed the crisp stationery in my hands, I actually believed he meant that.

Of course, our world at Stirwaters now included Uncle Wheeler as well. His interest in the mill was casual, at best; he still had not set foot inside the building, and seemed disinclined to do so. I supposed I couldn't *make* someone love Stirwaters; perhaps you had to be born to it.

How he occupied his days was still of some mystery to me. He occasionally hired a horse at Drover's and rode out for the day — sometimes to Haymarket, sometimes on errands unreported. "Gentlemanly pursuits," old Tory Weaver suggested when I posed such musings aloud. I did not know what those might be; all the men I had ever known spent their days *working* — or shirking work, which is a dedicated pursuit of its own.

I suppose every enterprise has such a fellow, and at Stirwaters, ours was Bill Penny. Often as not he'd fail to show up, and when he did appear, he was not always entirely sober. Still, he did his work in his slow, haphazard way — simple tasks that nonetheless had to be done: tidying up in the woolshed, keeping the sluice gates clear of debris, minding the fire for Mr. Mordant. Though he got dark looks from some of the millhands, I wouldn't entertain suggestions that I fire him.

Letting the Eagans go was one thing — sly they might be, but they also looked out for themselves. I had no such confidence that Bill Penny's family would survive without the meager income Stirwaters provided.

One bright, warm afternoon I came upon Ian Lamb drawing water for the dyemaster, and something tugged at my memory.

"Hold there," I said, stepping up beside him. He paused and straightened, squinting at me under the sun. "I'd like you to draw that water upstream, if you would, Ian."

"But Mr. Mordant said —"

"Humor me. Tell him I want two batches of whatever color he's brewing up. Half upstream, half down." I wanted to see for myself whether Mr. Mordant's strange ideas were more than just fancy.

"Mr. Mordant won't be pleased, then," Ian said. I just looked at him, until he shrugged. "Yes, ma'am." He dumped the vat straight back into the Stowe and, whistling, ambled up past the mill. I must have heard those words a dozen times that afternoon, as news of what I'd done scurried through the mill. But the dyemaster kept his complaints to himself.

A few days later, Ian poked his head into the office with the news that the cloth was ready. I followed him down to the yard, where Mr. Mordant and Rosie were rinsing out the great lengths of dyed wool. It was Lincoln green, a color Mr. Mordant could probably dye in his sleep. He hauled an armful of it from the water, rich and deep as the hills at dusk. He nodded to Rosie, who heaved at another bundle of cloth, unfurling the sodden fabric like a sheet fresh from the washbasin.

I looked at it solemnly. "Upstream?" I asked, and she nodded. Even soaking wet, there was no comparison. Mr. Mordant's was the wild rich color we were known for; the other was . . . ordinary.

"But that doesn't make any sense. Why didn't the color take?"

Mr. Mordant just eyed me levelly. "I told ye, missie. That's Stirwaters."

"One of its 'humors'?" I gazed down at the mill, tucked in dusky shadows despite the glaring sun. "Dye it again." Leaving my sister and the dyer to their work, I strode to the edge of the river, as if the rippled grey water could tell me Stirwaters's secrets.

There was scarcely even a breeze off the water on a day as hot and still as this one. Downriver, at the small village landing near Hale's and Mrs. Post's, a barge had docked, one of the boats that paused there once every week or so. That afternoon, in among the rivermen unloading the cargo onto the landing, I saw my uncle, jauntily propped on a black walking-stick, in casual conversation with one of the bargemen.

Curious, and glad to leave behind the capriciousness of Stirwaters for a moment, I strolled to join them. I bade my uncle good day, and the bargeman's head jerked up in surprise.

"She's never your niece, then!" he exclaimed, wiping his hands on his linen breeches. "Why, I've been watching this lass since she were no taller'n a teacup!" He laughed heartily.

"To be sure, it isn't Captain Worthy! I hardly recognized you without your beard!" It had been years since I'd seen the old riverman, and I allowed him to kiss my hand. "Uncle, forgive me — surely you and Captain Worthy aren't acquainted!"

Uncle Wheeler smiled wanly. "Ah, no. No, my acquaintance is with the *owner* of this vessel." He gestured toward the barge, a gaily painted affair of red and blue, with a flock of black birds in full flight swirling all across one side. The legend of the shipping company, Porter & Byrd, was emblazoned in gold across the birds.

"Oh, aye? And ain't that something," Captain Worthy said. "Them Byrds or them Porters, then?"

Uncle Wheeler glared down his nose at the man. "Quite. Charlotte, the, ah, captain here was just telling me that Porter and Byrd is expanding their routes into the Gold Valley."

"How splendid," I said. "We could use more traffic on this river, I think. What will your cargo be?"

"Ah, bit of everything, I'd say. We've some sugar and coffee today, and were hoping to leave with some wool, but it looks like we left it too late in the season."

"I'm afraid you'll have me to blame for that, sir. We tend to buy early at Stirwaters."

Captain Worthy gazed up toward the mill, toward the tenterfields, where the Lambs were taking down a bolt of blanket cloth to make room for the green flannel. "I say, I wouldn't mind getting my hands on some of that cloth you folk make," he said. "A pack of that Stirwaters Blue would go a long way to makin' up for the wool, I think."

I smiled. "I think that could be arranged. We've got most of it earmarked for Market, of course, but there's always some to spare, for old friends."

"Charlotte, truly —"

I glanced at my uncle. "Sir?"

Uncle Wheeler was smiling, I think, but the look was slightly sour. "My dear, let's not waste this gentleman's time. Surely you understand that Mr. Worthy was simply making conversation."

"Nay, I were —"

My uncle cut him off with a slicing flick of his cane. He drew me aside. "Now, my dear," my uncle said, *sotto voce*, "Have a care for what you're doing. It's all very well and good to be generous, when it's called for. But if you hope to succeed in your father's business, you'll need to keep your head about you."

"But Porter and Byrd —"

"Is a very prestigious shipping firm. Tightly run. I know the family well. They certainly wouldn't allow their common staff to go about making bargains on their own. That fellow has an official manifest stating the cargo he is authorized to carry, and you can be sure there would be consequences if even one pound of coffee was unaccounted for." His look at Captain Worthy said volumes. "Believe me, Richard Byrd keeps a close accounting on his assets."

"What are you saying? That Captain Worthy would make a bargain with me —"

"Belowdecks? Yes, my dear, I'm afraid so."

I frowned, my gaze travelling between my uncle's face and Captain Worthy's barge. I supposed it was possible; it wasn't as if I knew the man well, after all, and Uncle Wheeler was certainly more worldly than I. The cloth trade is heavily regulated, and it wouldn't be the first time someone tried to skirt the Exchange fees and tariffs to make a few shillings on the side. Still, the penalties for smuggling are high, all round, and one thing Stirwaters did not need just now was more risk. I allowed my uncle to make our farewells, and returned to the hot steamy work of the mill.

I put thoughts of Captain Worthy from my head, and spent a long, hot afternoon at the mill, which ended in fine Stirwaters fashion when I collided with Mr. Penny as he lumbered round a corner, hauling a barrel of lant. The stale urine splashed all over me, and it took some doing to disentangle myself from the barrel, Bill, and his mumbled apologies. I hastened home to strip down to my stays and petticoat before the foul stuff could soak through.

I clattered down the steps from my room, the stained dress rolled up in my arms. As I rounded the corner on my way to the kitchen, I caught sight of something in the parlor. My uncle stood with his back to me, looking out the tall windows, an empty wineglass in one hand, the bottle in the other. He had doffed his tapestry coat and thrown it carelessly across the back of the sofa. I stepped closer, thinking to bid him greeting. But as I put my hand to the doorframe, my uncle very deliberately set his glass on the windowsill, pressing down on the rim with white knuckles, until the stem snapped.

He turned his head, and I ducked out of sight.

That evening our uncle was quieter than usual, staring into his wineglass as Rachel filled it, over and again. There were no comments about our dress, no criticism of Rachel's cooking. Indeed, he ate very little, and rose and quit the table just as Rachel brought in the final course.

"What's got into him tonight?" Rosie said.

I shook my head. I had no idea, but I could not shake the feeling his queer mood had begun that afternoon, with the barge from Porter & Byrd. I was still mulling it over as I followed Rachel into the evening air to retrieve my gown from the wash line. She stopped to help me take it down, and drew in her breath sharply.

"Charlotte — look there! What is that?"

I glanced to where she was pointing — at a ragged dark mist floating in the breeze across the river — and dropped my clean dress onto the shale. "No!" I hiked up my skirts and ran for the tenters, where that afternoon we had hung Mr. Mordant's green flannel to dry. I skidded in the damp grass and had to catch myself on the corner of the fence, but I had already seen enough. The beautiful green cloth was in tatters — great gaping cuts in the fabric, every few yards, slashed with a knife.

"Who would do such a thing?" Rachel gasped, right at my heels.

I shook my head, staring around me into the trees, straining to see — what? Who? The grass was trampled all along the row, but that could have been the culprit's feet — or my own.

Chapter Six

*T*he next morning we pulled the damaged cloth down from the tenters, and though Rosie had scoured the field and the margins of the wood, there was no more evidence of who had damaged the cloth than there'd been by moonlight. And if anyone in the village had witnessed the vandalism, they were not forthcoming.

"I can't even imagine who might hate Stirwaters enough to do something like this," I said, twisting free a shred of green flannel caught on the hooks.

"I can," Rosie said. "The Eagans, for one — not Paddy, obviously. But his mam and sister? I have no trouble thinking they did it."

I pondered this. The Eagan women, angry at being let go, were just lowdown enough to take out their revenge on our cloth. And Tansy *had* threatened me — after a fashion. Furthermore, Harte was certain Pilot hadn't barked, which meant the vandal was someone the collie recognized. "I never should have sacked them."

Rosie made a strangled sound. "Of course you should have — and Mam would have done it ages sooner. They're out for nobody but themselves. Trouble is, there isn't anything we can do about it, not without proof."

She was right, of course. And the loss of the cloth was a bigger blow than I was willing to admit. Market was drawing ever nearer, and without enough cloth we might come up short of Mr. Woodstone's bill. I couldn't afford to lose even one bolt. Though Rosie grumbled, I hired Bill Penny on full-time to patrol the tenterfields.

"You're crazy," she said. "He'll just drink away his wages and sleep away his shifts — and anyone could tiptoe right over him to get at the cloth. We're better off with Pilot —"

"Yes, and Pilot's record is hardly shining, is it? Rosie, I had to. No one else has time to watch the tenters; and besides — I feel bad for them. Maire's pregnant again."

Rosie snorted. "Everyone in this town is not your responsibility, you know."

"Of course they are." But I said it so softly she never could have heard me.

Still, with Bill on the job, no more cloth was damaged. Neither Rosie's sleuthing nor the millhands' gossip could produce the guilty party, and in time we put the incident out of our heads. We had to — with Market approaching, there wasn't much time for any other thoughts.

I had never before been to Market, and truly, the prospect was more than a little daunting. Buying wool at our local spring wool fair was one matter; the Harrowgate Cloth Exchange was another world entirely: a massive, labyrinthine empire housed in a riverside warehouse whose name of Worm Hill did little to inspire confidence. Any clothiers that produced more than a certain amount of cloth each year sold their wares through the Exchange, from large-scale factories like Pinchfields, down to smaller mills like ours. The buyers ranged from shipping magnates to drapers, but if you wanted more cloth than it took to make a new bedgown or frock coat, you came to Worm Hill. Stirwaters was an insignificant presence there — we could only afford a fortnight's rent on a stall each summer, and the taxes were crippling — but the bulk of our fortunes were made, or broken, at Worm Hill.

It wasn't altogether customary for a clothier to accompany the stock personally. Father had gone every year, but he'd also relied on a Harrowgate agent to keep him in line. No agent was willing to take me on, of course; my letters of inquiry had all returned with brusque but polite apologies. Although demand for Stirwaters's cloth was never in doubt, my father's reputation was questionable enough that no one would ally himself with his underage daughter.

Still, I would not be entirely alone. Uncle Wheeler had embraced the prospect of accompanying his niece to her metropolitan début, insisting that I let him make our travel arrangements and that I acquire some new clothes for the affair. Rosie and I salvaged what was left of the ruined green flannel, and worked late into the evenings cobbling together a new travelling frock.

I spent hours pasting swatches into our sample books and making and remaking our price lists. Had I not helped Father prepare for this every summer of my life? I opened up Father's atlas to his depiction of the Exchange. The spidery letters scrawling out WORM HILL had given me a delicious chill when I was a child . . . the carefully marked-out rooms and stalls, a somber reassurance during the weeks each year when Father left us. Now the thrill they gave me was something even more tangible. This year it would be *my* cloth in that little stall on the third floor; this year it would be Charlotte Miller's chance to show the world what Stirwaters was made of.

Finally, near the middle of August, everything was ready. I was ready.

And then the letter came.

It was one of those brutally hot afternoons we see in late summer, where the very air glitters and it is difficult to breathe. I retreated to the woolshed, where the limestone walls kept out some of the heat. Sunlight filtered down through the windows and cast the colored bales into jewelled hues: from pale creamy buff to deepest Saxon red; moss green to Lincoln green; robin's egg blue to mazareen; dove grey, pearl grey, oyster, and charcoal. I looked them over with satisfaction, picturing how I'd like to display them at Worm Hill. The satinettes in one pile, perhaps, or all the blues together. It was good work; we could be proud of ourselves this summer.

I moved from bale to bale, binding and labelling each bundle, making notes, and didn't hear Harte until he was right up on top of me.

"Mistress, you'll hurt yourself doing that alone. Let me get that end for you."

"Harte, I've been doing this since I was ten years old," I said, but slid aside and allowed him to lift the bulk of the weight. "You learn a thing or two in a house without brothers."

"Aye, and with a young lass like Miss Rosie to run after, too, no doubt." Harte laughed and moved to the next bale. "You're looking ready to leave, then. Won't be the same around here without you, you know."

"Where goes the wool, follows the miller," I said.

Harte leaned in to retrieve the twine. "Rosie's fit to burst with envy."

I had to grin. "I don't think Harrowgate is ready for Rosellen Miller, do you?"

Harte shrugged. "Never been. Give me the hills and the sky and the river."

"The sheep and the dirt and the —" I mopped my face with my apron. "The perspiration."

"Amen, Mistress." Harte grinned and pulled a calico handkerchief from his trouser pocket. Something crunched as he patted his hand against his hip. "Ah — and there I forgot. Don't tell Rosie. I was supposed to give you this —" He held out a rather crumpled envelope.

"Oh, Harte. She didn't bully you into fetching the post again, did she?" I unfolded the envelope, and my heart gave a little skip when I beheld the postmark: Harrowgate. Another letter from Mr. Woodstone?

I should have been so lucky. This came instead from Worm Hill. No preamble, no pleasantries:

It having come to the Attention of the Trustees of this Exchange that your firm has been operating without benefit of President, Foreman, or known Agency and therefore in Violation of the Bylaws of the Wool Guild, it is necessary to Inform you that the stock stall formerly held by Stirwaters Woollen Mill of Shearing has not met the requirements for Renewal. Thereto you will Quit all plans to display your stock, cloth, or other Wares within the grounds at Worm Hill, or in the general Vicinity of Harrowgate. Petitions for Reinstatement will be entertained at

*the next meeting of this Board and though seldom do Open stalls
become available, finding that your Firm meets with Approval,
Entry will be made on your behalf in the Queue.*

Yours respectfully,

Arthur M. Darling, Trustee

Worm Hill Cloth Exchange

*N.B. Copy of notice filed with Guild of Uplands Wool
Merchants*

"Not bad news, then?" said Harte — but he addressed
my departing back. I had balled up my skirts and marched
off across the millyard. I slammed into the Millhouse kitchen,
where Rosie and Rachel were bent over a pan of rolls.

"We've been *blacklisted!*" I flung the letter to the table and
wrenched my bonnet from my head. Rachel abandoned her
mixing bowl and came to read over Rosie's shoulder.

Rosie stared at the letter as if it were some sort of foul
insect she'd discovered crawling out of the millpond. "Those
greedy blackguards!"

"*Rosellen Miller!*" My uncle stepped into the kitchen.
"Here, let me see — what's all this fuss about?" He read the
letter swiftly, then folded it again, sharpening the creases with
his fingertips. "Well. This is terribly distressing. But perhaps
it's for the best. I have said you were working too hard, and
now you've gotten yourself all upset. Baker, please bring my
nieces some tea." Uncle Wheeler gave a flip to the skirts on
his jacket and slid into a chair. "Charlotte, dear, do sit down
before you fall down."

I was too angry to move. "How can you say it's for the
best? I have a hundred bolts of cloth in the woolshed, and

nowhere to sell them! And unless I sell that cloth, I'll never be able to pay back —"

Nearly too late I felt Rosie's eyes boring into me. I stumbled to a halt. "All my workers," I finished lamely.

Uncle Wheeler sighed. "I'm sure your workers will find other jobs. Charlotte, *do* sit down so we can talk about this rationally. Baker! Where is that tea?"

"I don't want any tea," I mumbled sullenly, but was too tired, suddenly, not to sit. I slumped into a chair across from my uncle and sank my head into my hands.

"It would seem, now, that we have two options. Their chief complaint seems to be that Stirwaters has no leadership —"

"What rot! What's Charlotte, then?"

I put a hand on my sister's arm. "You know Father left no will. If I'd been a boy, they wouldn't even question my claim. But as it is . . ."

"But can't we do something?"

I shook my head sadly. "If we fight this, the Wool Guild could take Stirwaters from us."

"Well, that's easily rectified," my uncle said.

"Go on," I said carefully.

"I would be happy to step into the role, of course; take the reins, as it were."

"You!"

"Of course," he said again, smiling confidently. "I am here to help in whatever capacity necessary."

I nodded slowly, unable to address this idea, yet. Losing Stirwaters would be a catastrophe — but having someone like Uncle Wheeler, however well-meaning he was, at the helm was nearly as unthinkable. Stirwaters was a *Miller* property; it had never been otherwise. And Uncle Wheeler had no interest in the wool business; how could we be sure he'd make decisions that were in Stirwaters's best interest?

And, to speak plainly, I wasn't ready to give it all up just yet. "You said two options," I said tentatively.

"Ah, yes," Uncle Wheeler leaned back in the chair. "This, of course, would be an excellent opportunity for you to sell."

Rosie burst to her feet. "Never!"

"Rosellen, calm yourself."

"No, I *won't*," she cried. "It's past time someone around here got angry! You sit there and smile at us over your wine —" She turned to me. "And *you* — you're just going to let them pick and scheme and chip away at us?"

"What are you talking about?"

"What else? Pinchfields! Oh, you *must* see this is one of their schemes! They're obviously in league with these trustees, or the Wool Guild. . . ."

I watched her with dawning horror. Was it *possible?* Oh, mercy — it would make so much sense: If they could keep us from selling our stock, they could ruin us. *You'd best reconsider, before your name and your label are all you have left to sell. . . .*

"Now, girls," Uncle Wheeler said, "let's not be irrational. Scheming against you? Oh, surely not. To what purpose? You told me yourselves that this business is fraught with risk. It would hardly take a robber baron to judge that Stirwaters hangs on by mere threads. Rosie, I won't have you spouting nonsense and upsetting your sister.

"Now." He lifted the teapot and poured us each a fresh measure. "I must impress upon you the importance of viewing these events in the proper perspective. Perhaps this is a sign that it's time for you to give up your foolish attachment to your father's little operation."

"But I don't understand. I thought you wanted to help us."

"Rosie, dear, of course I do. That's why you must listen to reason now. I was willing to play along with your little fancies, for your mother's sake. I know how fond she was of the mill, after all. But it's time you saw sense."

Rosie shook her head and pulled her hand out of Uncle Wheeler's soft grip. My uncle had opened his mouth to speak, but I rose to my feet. "Uncle, please," I said. "We appreciate everything you're trying to do, but as I said when you arrived, we simply *can't* sell the mill. It's impossible." I added, much more confidently than I felt, "We'll just have to find somewhere else to send the cloth."

Up in the bedroom, I peeled my damp stays from my body, splashed some lukewarm water on myself, and slipped into a clean shift. The air was stifling; no breeze at all lifted the curtains on the open window. I collapsed onto the bed and watched the late sun burn the afternoon into dusk as I turned futile thoughts over and over in my mind.

Rosie arrived with a tray from Rachel, dumping it unceremoniously beside me. Grabbing a roll but not eating it, she paced between the window and the bed, a frown creasing her forehead. She had a fire building in her, and there was nothing for it but to let it burn out. Finally she said, very quietly, "Maybe it's true, what they say."

I pulled myself up on one elbow. "What?"

Rosie looked at me. "You know. The curse. No — listen. We've had more than even our share of bad luck this year. Father, and then the mortgage, and the cloth — and now this?"

I sighed. "Rosie, honestly. Everything that's happened has a rational explanation. I think your first theory made more sense."

She sat down beside me. "Pinchfields?"

I nodded grimly.

The news was all over the village by morning. Shearing gossip is a force of nature; besides, what was the point in keeping it a secret? I passed through a crowd of pale, questioning faces as I went to unlock the mill doors. I lay a hand against the rugged wood, but made no move to open up.

I turned to them. "It's all true," I said. "Everything you've heard."

"What'll you do, then, Mistress?" Eben Fuller asked. His voice was gentle, but I was bone weary and thin on patience.

"I don't know. Look, go home, all of you. There's nothing to do here today."

"But, Mistress," Mrs. Hopewell said, "it's bearing-home today."

"Go home," I repeated. "Call it a holiday, call it — call it whatever you like. But there's no reason for any of you to be here. Not today. Not . . ." I meant to say, "Not anymore," but I just couldn't get the words out.

A strong arm took me by the shoulders, and I was grateful

for it. It was Harte, of course, and with a few calm words, he got everyone to disperse.

I had told the millhands to leave, but I could not take my own advice. Despite the baking oppression of the mill, I climbed up to the office. My father's atlas lay open to the map of Worm Hill. I lifted it to put my finger on our stall, my lost, forfeit stall, and nearly dropped the book.

It read *Pinchfields* in curvy, spidery script. I closed my eyes tight, sure I was imagining things. A count of ten passed before I looked again, and surely as the turning wheel, the word remained. My hands shook, and I slammed the book shut and clutched it to my chest.

A person needs rest after a shock. Maybe my uncle was right. Maybe I was finally breaking under the strain.

"Charlotte?"

I started. Rosie had followed me up, and with cold hands I opened the book for her. Her eyes grew wide and then looked straight at me. "Is this some sort of prank?"

I let out all my breath in one great rush. Of course, that's all it was. Just nasty commentary from a disgruntled millhand. But no one had been up here —

Rosie studied the page, rubbed at it with a finger, scowled. "You can't change *Stirwaters* to *Pinchfields* this tidily, not without leaving some mark. This is clean; nothing's even been rubbed out. How?" She looked at me, wonder in her eyes.

I grabbed it back from her. She was right — for all I could tell, this page had read *Pinchfields* for ten years. All traces of our own name had disappeared. It was impossible. Involuntarily, I felt my gaze rise from the atlas to the far wall, where the violet-and-gold hex sign watched over us like a great angry eye.

Chapter Seven

That dark mood prevailed for the next few days, that unshakable sense of some threat looming toward me from the distance. And no wonder, I suppose: If I didn't come up with Mr. Woodstone's money, we were doomed. Desperately, I pulled the packs apart in the woolshed, separating the plain cloths from the fancier sorts. I could sell the kerseys at market fairs in the Valley, I thought, and perhaps Mrs. Post's customers would be interested in the plaid blanket cloth. But such sales were crumbs and scrapings, at best. There was nowhere I could divest myself of one hundred lengths of cloth. Not in time. If only I hadn't dismissed Captain Worthy's offer so hastily. . . .

I kept thinking I must *do* something — fight it somehow, file a protest with the Wool Guild, or write to someone: to the bank — to Mr. Woodstone. But I didn't dare. As I had told Rosie, the Wool Guild could challenge my claim on Stirwaters too easily; and while Mr. Woodstone had seemed nice enough, his loyalties were with the very people who wanted to take my mill from me.

For her part, Rosie was uncharacteristically silent those days, carrying Father's atlas with her and ducking my gaze when we passed in the mill. I put her down as stewing, and deservedly so, but when I did chance to meet her eyes, she looked merely thoughtful, and not angry. I ought to have suspected she was up to something; she is never that meek unless there is trouble afoot.

The millhands kept coming back to work, of course, however futile that work was seeming by the day. As was custom, the Friday we spun the last of the spring wool, we all took a half-holiday, although it was difficult to summon up the proper festive mood. Instead of the traditional afternoon toasting the season (and the miller) with Drover's ale in the yard, that year everyone just trickled off home. I lingered in the shadow of the millwheel, listening to the water dribble sadly into the pit.

"I don't know," I whispered back, the rough cool stones digging into my shoulders.

I watched the grey planks of the millwheel cut through the low water, steady as an executioner's blade falling, over and over. Green lichen stained the weathered boards, and the sound of the water was a mere dip and murmur in the hot afternoon air. I could stand there for hours, gazing into the depths of the pit, looking for answers that would not come. Better to just collect Rosie and head home.

I found her in the spinning room, in the widest clear space between two aisles of machines. She was silhouetted against the glare of the windows, and I could not immediately make out what she was doing. She crouched on the floor, a circle drawn round her in white chalk. A stub of a candle, ground into wax on the floor, sat beside her, the smell of tallow sour and rank in the room. The room was uncharacteristically silent, the turning gears a mere whisper in the still air, no sound at all from the slow-turning wheel.

I stopped in my tracks and stared at her. Her back was to me, and I watched her pause to glance at the floor, where Father's atlas lay open at her feet.

"Blood to bone, I summon thee," she read aloud, casting something to the heart of the circle with a fling of her right hand. "Hearth and home, I summon thee —"

"What in God's name are you doing?" I cried. I took three long strides and arrived at Rosie's side. Grabbing her by the elbow, I yanked her to her feet. "Have you lost your senses? What is this — is that *mandrake*? Did you take that from the dyeshed? If you got one speck of red on my spinning room floor —"

"*Your* floor? I have wept and sweat and bled for this mill every *bit* as much as you have." She turned away. "Blood to bone, I summon thee —"

I glanced down at Father's book, to the passage she'd been reading from: *To Summon Faerie Aid.* "Oh, for mercy's sake! Why not stand by the pulpit at church and ask angels to intervene?"

"I've done that," she said.

I couldn't bear it. She looked so lost, and so young. It was easy to forget she was barely more than a girl, when I felt so old. I wrapped her in my arms and pressed her head to my shoulder. "I know you want to believe all those old stories. But this is nothing but superstition. Stirwaters needs help, *real* help. Not some fairy story you found in a book."

"Ha," she said, pulling away from me. "What we need is a miracle."

"I don't think this family is eligible for miracles. Rosie, I'm tired. Let's get this stuff cleaned up before someone comes in and sees it." I bent to collect the scattered remnants of her "spell" — a bowl of salt, the black candle, a packet of herbs wrapped in muslin. "Where did this all come from, anyway? Did you raid the dyeshed? Or —" I looked sharply at her as I recognized a dried flower I knew hadn't come from Mr. Mordant's supplies. "Don't tell me you've been to see Biddy Tom."

She looked sullen. "So what if I have?"

"I can't believe you'd waste what little money you have on this rubbish. If Mam were alive —"

I never had a chance to finish, for at that moment Rosie looked past me and turned absolutely pale. She grabbed me by the arm and pulled me standing. Someone was in the room with us, casually leaning against the hex sign.

"Beggin' yer pardon, misses." The figure stepped into the light, not some eldritch savior from Fairyland, but a perfectly ordinary, somewhat shabby man of about my father's age. A bit stoop-shouldered, in a coat much too large for him, he lifted brown fingers to his hat brim and nodded genially.

Rosie still clutched my arm. "Welcome to Stirwaters!" Her voice was pitched somewhere between gaiety and hysteria.

"Was there something we could help you with, sir?" I said.

He took another step toward us. He had a queer sort of shambling walk, as if troubled by rheumatism. "Well, I was thinking there might be something I could help *you* with," he said. "That is, you might have some work for someone like me."

I looked him over — just an itinerant tradesman in workaday clothes and a battered hat, with unfashionable red side-whiskers and small eyes, as if he squinted over his work. My father had sometimes worked with such people — men with a knack for some odd trade or talent.

He'd put them up for a few days or weeks while they did their work, until the urge to travel struck them once again. *Wanderers*, my father called them, often with a hint of longing in his voice.

"I'm afraid not." I shook my head. "We're nearing the end of the season, and —"

"Give the man a chance," Rosie muttered from behind that bright smile.

"We can't pay the workers we have, you know that."

Rosie ignored me. "What kind of work do you do?" She was flushed with excitement, her hair tumbling down into her face, bonnet hung against her back.

"Oh, you'd say I'm a man of all trades, with a few special skills." He stepped closer still, a gold watch-chain glinting across his plaid waistcoat. "If you'll allow me to demonstrate, I do think I could be of some help to you here."

I smiled tightly. "You'd have to be able to make gold appear from thin air to be much help to us now, I'm afraid."

"Gold, you say?" he said, scratching his head through his hat. "Well, not out of the air, maybe, but —" He reached toward Rosie, who stood strangely still under his advance, and drew a length of straw free from her hat. I started to protest the liberty he was taking, but something stopped me. From out of a pocket in his jacket appeared an old-fashioned hand-held drop-spindle, the kind no one uses anymore, and he sent it spinning with a turn of his hand.

Slowly, as we watched, he drew out the straw and spun it — *spun it!* As if it were a roving of wool! As the spindle bobbed and twirled, something — I could not quite see what — pulled out from the brown straw and through his knobby fingers, and where it should have gone onto the spindle, the finest strands of gleaming golden threads appeared. Around and around the spindle went, and the glitter of gold turned with it. I could not take my eyes away.

"What alchemy is this?" I heard my voice say, quiet and far away. "What sleight-of-hand?" Abruptly the spindle stopped, and the spinner held it up for me to examine. It was full, spun tight with thread that indeed looked more like gold than straw.

I pulled out the last twelve or eighteen inches and could not credit what I saw. It seemed to be truly gold thread — purely gold and nothing else, no carrier thread to tame the metal to the shape; if I held it tightly for a moment, the heat of my hand would soften it, and it took merely a pinch of my fingers to break the strand. Yet something told me that this thread would weave well and embroider even better: the sort of thread that could make a clothier weep for the perfection of it. I tugged at the bit of straw still dangling from the end, hoping to see where and how it fastened to the thread. It pulled free with only a bit of resistance.

I could not work out how he had done it. Perhaps he had fed the spindle with thread concealed in his coat-sleeve. Perhaps — *perhaps it was real.*

"Charlotte!" Rosie was babbling on excitedly; I hadn't heard a word she'd said. I looked up and blinked at her, seeing only the glitter of gold before my dazed eyes.

"What do you think?" she demanded.

"I —" I faltered and worked my face to find coherent thoughts. "We're not set up for metallic thread. It takes a machine like a winch, not a spinning jack. . . ." But my words were senseless: There before me — in my own hands — was the proof. I forced myself to stand straight and hand the spindle back to its owner. "Sir," I said, "I don't know who you are or where you've come from, but I don't believe this is anything we're interested in."

"Charlotte!" Rosie squealed. "Have you lost your mind? Isn't that just what you asked him for?"

"This is madness. And furthermore, you know we can't afford it."

"My rates are reasonable," the spinner said. "I'm sure we can work out some bargain that's agreeable to all of us."

"Fine," I said a little wildly. "What are you offering?"

He turned and eyed the office appraisingly. "If you fill a room that size with straw, I will spin you equal measure in gold thread."

"In exchange for what?" The very room seemed to be spinning around me.

His bright gaze fell on my hand. "I rather like your ring," he said.

I stared at my hand. The only ring I wore had been Mam's — a cheap paste pearl in a silver plate setting. "Why?" I said. "It has no value."

A slow smile spread beneath the ruddy moustache. "It has to you," he said.

I looked at my penny-ring and then the full spindle of gold thread he still held before my eyes. Rosie grabbed my arm and pulled me into the far corner. "What's the matter?"

"We can't do this."

"Why?"

"Rosie, it doesn't make any sense! He's obviously a

charlatan or — or something else I don't even want to contemplate. Why on Earth would he come to Stirwaters to give us a room full of gold in exchange for a pearl ring that's not even real?"

Rosie held my arm tightly. "Charlotte," she said, and there was not the faintest trace of desperation in her voice. I should have known then not to listen to her — she's always at her most persuasive when her plans are at their wildest. "I agree, it's all a bit . . . curious. But what are we risking, *really*?"

"What are we going to do with gold thread?"

She didn't even falter. "Sell it, of course; or give it to the bank, or take it to the smithy to have it melted down. What does it matter? It's *gold*."

"But —" I looked past her at the little man in his shabby coat. He had gone back to twisting his hat; the gold spindle lay harmlessly on the corner of a spinning jack. Behind him, in my office, were the mortgage from Uplands Mercantile Bank and the letter from the Cloth Exchange.

"No more mortgage, no more Pinchfields," Rosie said, reading my mind. I pressed my fist to my forehead for a count of ten, then turned back to the spinner.

"Very well," I said finally. "Come back this evening. We should have your straw by then." I edged past him into my office. "Let me just get some paperwork drawn up for you to sign."

The man was shaking his head. "I'll not sign my name to anything in this mill again," he said. "If that's all the same to you."

I paused. "Have you worked at Stirwaters before?"

"Oh, aye," he said. "All the Millers have known my work."

"Really? What's your name, then? I've probably seen you in the records."

He looked out my office door at the work floor beyond. "Oh," he said, as if considering the idea, "let's say Jack Spinner."

Something cold spread through my breast. "That's no kind of a name."

"It's all the name I need, here." He gave a slight smile and tipped his hat. "Tonight, then. I'll be back at sundown."

After he'd gone, I paced the office. "Straw!" I muttered. "Why not sand? Why not sows' ears?"

"That's silk purses, not gold thread," Rosie said with a grin.

"Oh, it's all the same. Rosie — aren't you the faintest bit disturbed by this?"

"Why? From what I can tell, he's the answer to our prayers." She shrugged. "Or something."

"But *jackspinner?*"

"Perhaps his mother had a sense of humor."

"He's lying," I said.

"Or he's lying. Who cares?"

I glanced through the office door, to where the hex sign was cast in the fading light. My father's atlas still lay open on the floor, in a circle of cinders. I strained to hear the water-wheel, but only silence pressed in around me. No, this just *wasn't* possible.

I picked up the spindle from where it lay and fingered the thread. For all my misgivings, I knew no mechanism that could create such luxuriously fine strands of gold. If this Spinner could do it — however he did it —

Oh, Miller pride! I *wanted* Stirwaters to produce things of such quality and beauty. If no one would ever see the cloth we'd made that year, I at least wanted *something* to show for our efforts. I wanted to pay down our debts.

And I had nothing to lose.

Chapter Eight

Finding the straw was another matter entirely. Shearing, for all its small size, is too much town and not nearly enough country to have bales of straw lying about for the taking; certainly the amount *we* needed would raise more than a few eyebrows. Rosie advocated substituting river rushes for the straw, on the grounds that powerful magic ought to overcome any such small obstacle. I argued a stricter interpretation, even if she could gather enough from the edge of our pond (of which I was by no means convinced).

As usual, Harte came to our rescue. Rosie spun him some outrageous story about baskets or bonnets and rich city folks, and he amiably agreed to borrow a wain from some upcountry kin and collect the straw from the farms of his neighbors. "Anything for Stirwaters," he'd said with a grin. "You folks are family now."

"He thinks he's helping save Stirwaters," I said to Rosie late that afternoon as Harte and Pilot set off. "Won't he expect to see these bonnets?"

Rosie glanced back at him. "Don't be silly — you know Harte takes no notice of such things. Besides, he *is* helping save Stirwaters."

I stared at her, but couldn't figure out what to say.

We spent the rest of the afternoon clearing out a store-room in the garret above my office, making a space for Mr. Spinner to perform his . . . labors in. It was hard going; most of the jumble was odd bits of machinery parts, gears and old handles and spare belts gathering dust and mold in our attic. I swept out a colony of moths that had made a lovely home in an old cast-off length of baize (now hopelessly ruined), and Rosie dusted an ancient hand spinning wheel to gleaming perfection. The wheel spun freely; our machinery, at least, would cause no problems for this enterprise.

We adjourned at teatime. Rosie decamped back to the Millhouse to assess the situation at home and fetch us some nourishment. I brushed down my clothes, fixed my hair, and took a dip from the water-butt. Fixing my hat more snugly on my head, I ventured out of the millyard onto the solid, sure footing of the roadway, and followed the path downstream to where Nathan Smith kept his forge.

We had no jeweller in the village, nor any bank. Uncle Wheeler would be able to tell me in a heartbeat, I was sure; but I could hardly consult him on such a matter. No, our village blacksmith seemed the only person I could turn to for what I needed to know. The traditional reputation smiths had for being tight-lipped wouldn't go amiss, either.

When I came upon him in the smithy yard, the last slanting rays of daylight made his oddly slight frame seem strange and ethereal. I clutched the small skein of thread in my apron pocket. He saw me lingering there, holding fast with one hand to his gatepost, and called out to me.

"Mistress Miller, what can I do for you?"

I found my voice, telling myself it had been too long a day with too much work in too much heat, with too little air and not nearly enough food. "Mr. Smith," I replied, forcing my feet to carry me closer to him. I pulled the skein out and held it toward him. "I was wondering if you could tell me what this is."

He stared at it for a long moment before laying aside his tools and wiping his sooty fingers on his apron. He took the thread from my hand. "You mean, can I tell you that it's what you think it is?" He handed the skein back as though he wished to be rid of it quickly. "It's gold." He said it simply, with a little shrug of his thin shoulders.

"Are — are you sure?"

Mr. Smith gave a curt nod. "Gold's not something you mistake easy. You can be sure of it, Mistress. Good or ill, however you came by it, that's gold you've got there."

I blinked at him. He seemed to be disappearing into the shadows more than ever now, and it was nearly impossible to make him out, all soot-covered, in the darkness.

"Mistress Miller." He held out his hand, something dark and heavy in his grip. "Here. You take this." He took my hand and pressed a heavy iron ingot into my palm. "That's cold iron. You don't mistake that one, either."

With a swallow, I nodded, not sure at all what was going on. "Yes," I said anyway. "Thank you, Mr. Smith."

"Right," he said. "Hold on to that, Mistress. You don't know when you might need it."

He turned back to the forge and walked away, leaving me standing in the yard, the ingot in my hand.

True darkness hadn't fallen after all, and I walked home in a sun-dazzled haze, keeping firmly to the center of the road and well clear of any shadows. With the weight of iron in one pocket and the skein of gold in the other, I felt a bit silly over the odd spell that had befallen me in the smith-yard, and for the moment, at least, I convinced myself that all was well.

Harte finally pulled in at dusk, driving a hay wain, look-ing harried but just as cheerful as ever. Behind him, the wain was loaded high with a tumbling yellow heap of straw, enough and more to fill the garret room. Rosie beamed at me trium-phantly, and Harte dismounted, passing me the little purse — still fairly weighty.

"Got the lot for two shillings, Mistress — quite a bargain, if I do say so. My old uncle was more than willing to help you Millers out, when I explained things."

I stared desperately at Rosie. "You got Farmer Colly involved?"

He grinned. "Aye, and my mam wants to know, are you starting a cottage industry making corn dollies, then?"

I snatched the purse back. "Yes, that's exactly what we're doing. Thank you, Harte. And tell your mother and uncle how grateful we are when you see them next."

I regarded the straw in the cart. We should have to carry it all, armload by armload, up three flights of stairs through the mill. At least the mill was empty; we could work in relative secrecy, without the eyes of Shearing gossip watch-ing us. Finally, after dozens of trips up and down that left my legs rubbery, and another half hour of sweeping up the straw we'd dropped along the way, the garret room was full. Harte showed remarkably good spirits, never asking us once why we were carrying it so far from anywhere sensible, and out of gratitude I invited him for supper. He cast a brief glance toward Rosie, who was washing up in the water-butt.

"Ah, I think not, Miss Charlotte. I mean to go down to

the river and wash up myself, then I'd like to hie to my own bed, I should think. That farm labor? Hard work for a city feller like me." He laughed and flexed a strong arm that had been doing heavy labor all his life. "Good night, ma'ams. Miss Charlotte . . . Rosie."

Sundown came all too soon that evening, and despite all our preparations, before we were quite ready, our tradesman, our new "Jack Spinner," returned. He was waiting in the office as Rosie and I trudged our way back upstairs, sitting on the edge of my desk and flipping through the pages of my father's atlas.

"Mr. Spinner," I said wearily. "You've returned."

He eyed me levelly. "We had an arrangement," he said, and the clipped edge to his voice grated like the scrape of iron when it sparks. "A bargain is a bargain, in my book. Don't you agree, Mistress Miller?"

I swallowed, my throat dry. "Indeed," I said. I twisted my mother's pearl ring from my finger and held it tightly in one hot fist. Rosie fidgeted beside me. Whatever my doubts, this was the only solution that had yet presented itself, and the thought of Uplands Mercantile foreclosing — or of the man from Pinchfields sniffing his pointy-nosed way through my mill, his stroking fingers on my machines . . .

I breathed deeply, walked to my desk, and withdrew my keys. I pulled off the one to the garret room and handed it to Mr. Spinner. He looked at the key in his open palm a moment, then looked at me expectantly. I passed him the ring, which he slipped onto his rough, stained little finger.

"Your straw is waiting for you. Rosie will show you where." I lowered myself steadily into my chair and opened my ledger book. "Oh, and Mr. Spinner," I called as they were leaving, and I was proud of how steady my voice sounded, "when can we expect the work to be completed?"

He stopped in the threshold and looked at me. There was something appraising and thoughtful in that gaze, and it made my skin crawl, but I forced myself to meet his eyes. "I should think I'll be done by morning," he said easily.

"By morning?" Surprise squeaked the words out of me, and I was sorry I'd asked, for all at once the nature of the work we'd ordered sprang right back to my fullest attention. Rosie must have seen something in my face, for she shut the door behind them quickly and carried him away to the garret room, just a few feet and ancient floorboards above my head.

Rosie finally left as well, after considerable argument. We had already missed both tea and dinner; someone would have to deflect Uncle Wheeler's questions, and both Miller girls' absence from the Millhouse overnight was utterly untenable.

"But why does anyone have to stay at all?" she asked. "And why should it be you?"

"I'm not leaving a stranger alone in the mill all night. This is my responsibility. Besides — you're a better liar than I am. You'll think of something to tell Uncle Wheeler."

I settled down to a long night of waiting, alone in the mill with . . . with whatever he was. I closed myself in the office, thinking somehow to protect myself behind doors, but the creaks and thumps of the old building, as familiar as my own skin during the day, struck loud and startling come nightfall. I could tell myself over and again I didn't really believe it, didn't *truly* think a man in the attic could spin gold from straw, but for now we were at his mercy, and I am not ashamed to admit I was frightened.

Rosie had left me well stocked with lamp oil and a good tinderbox, but it was cold comfort against the darkness, the eldritch power, and the sheer ancient age of the mill. What I found comforting by daylight seemed strange and haunting now. I fancied some force in the mill objected to the presence I had brought into it — objected to the magic worked upstairs by the curious little man who called himself after one of my machines. I huddled into my chair and told myself not to be foolish, but every sound of settlement, every sigh of the wind, each snap or rustle down through the floors, seemed a voice of disapproval. I wanted to bang my fist against the rough stone walls and cry out that whatever I did, it was all for Stirwaters.

I tried to work, to determine what use I might make of gold thread, but I could not concentrate. At last I pulled volumes of old ledgers and rosters from the shelves and sought references to a Jack Spinner — but of course there were dozens of such entries, and none of them germane. I went through Father's papers, but his wanderers weren't well recorded. Nowhere could I find mention of any tradesman quite like the man in my attic.

I could not stop my eyes from lifting to the hex sign on the wall outside my door. I could not explain what I had seen that afternoon, what was even now taking place on the floor above me . . . but neither could I discount it. I had *watched* him spin straw into gold; Mr. Smith had verified its authenticity. It might be a parlor trick, but if so, it was an elaborate one — and for what purpose? No, try as I might to convince myself otherwise, for once it was simply easier to believe it was real.

Eventually I must have dozed, there at my desk, my cheek against the leather of an old ledger book, my hand still on my pen. How long I slept there I could not say, but my heart nearly gave out when, somewhere past midnight, my door burst open with a sound like musket fire. I jumped straight up in my chair and grabbed for the nearest weapon — the iron ingot from Nathan Smith's forge — my heart beating frantically against my ribcage.

"Miss Charlotte?" Against the darkness of the doorframe, Harte stood out like a ghost in his white nightshirt, which apparently had been hastily accompanied by his trousers and boots only moments before.

"Harte!" My voice came out far shriller than I meant it. I tried it again. "Harte," I said, in what I hoped were calmer tones.

He stepped in a few paces, still staring at me in bewilderment. "What are you doing here, ma'am? It's well past midnight. I saw the light and thought I'd better check on things."

How could we have been so careless — to forget that our Harte's window looked directly into the office, making any light we burned there clearer than a full moon on a cloudless night! Hastily I wracked my brain, trying to remember where the garret window looked; would Harte have seen it, coming from the woolshed?

"Miss Charlotte?" Harte repeated, coming fully into the room now. "Are you all right?"

I forced a smile to my frozen lips. "Yes. Yes, thank you, Harte. Just — finishing up some work for the morning. I'll be going soon. No need to worry — I shan't forget to douse the lamp."

He grunted. "I should think not — you'll need it to get home by on a night like this. Dark as the devil out there, if you don't mind, Mistress."

"No, not at all. Thank you." Still a bit breathless, I stared at him, willing him silently to leave, that ridiculous smile still plastered on my face. Harte gave one last glance around the office and, still frowning, left me. I knew we had aroused his suspicions, and doubted very much that he intended to slip meekly back to the woolshed and sleep the rest of the night away.

Somewhat comforted, in fact, by his watchful presence, my fear gradually gave way to curiosity and then impatience. *Morning*, he had said. I did not know by what rules such magic was bound; I could not risk disrupting the spell too early. Finally, when I could make out the color of tree branches outside, I rose and patted smooth my skirts and hair. Taking a deep breath to steady myself against the slightly sickish feeling of staying awake all night, I went upstairs.

I did not knock; the door was mine, after all. I put a somewhat shaky hand to the worn wood and pushed it open.

He was gone. Somewhere in the night, after finishing his work, Jack Spinner had disappeared. I was in no state to work that out — he could not have come downstairs without passing my office. Using whatever powers had brought him to us to begin with, he seemed to have vanished back into that fey realm without sound or sign.

But it didn't matter. In that moment I thought wildly that *nothing* would ever matter again: Everything we would ever need was laid out before me. Gleaming reels of thread were stacked chest-high all along one wall, like rows of corncobs. They glittered with the sheen of gold, casting their own beautiful light all through the room. I took a few steps into the room, but my feet failed me and I sank to the floor. It couldn't be real. I put out a hand to touch the nearest spool, but my fingers paused a few inches from the gold. I couldn't bear to break the spell just yet. I merely sat there, speechless and stunned, staring at the hill of riches before me.

After a moment I felt my heart begin to beat again, quick and steady and very loud. Still hesitant to touch the spools, I began to count them. Not believing my first result, I went back and started again. Three more times I made their measure, each with the same number at the end.

Oh, mercy — what had we stumbled into? Frantically, I unwound one bobbin . . . then another, tearing at the thread to uncover the deception. Five or six more, deep into the stacks, sure there must be ordinary thread beneath the gold. I pulled the entire length from one spool, counting the times it made the span of my arms. At last I sat in the heap, my head spinning with exhaustion and disbelief and the sheer impossibility of the numbers, and for the first time in more months than I could remember, I did nothing.

Rosie found me, not much later, before anyone else could chance upon me. Her little shriek aroused me, and in her excitement she grabbed my arm and yanked me standing. She squealed and whirled about the little empty space in the garret, laughing with a mad delight. I resisted being drawn into her dance of ecstasy, until at last she wound down and, breathless, gave me her crooked grin.

"Oh, you are no fun at all, Charlotte! You do see the gold here, right? I'm not imagining it?"

"I see it," I said, keeping calm from shock alone. I leaned back against the doorframe, pulling closed the door.

"Well?" Rosie demanded. "How much is there?"

I felt the laugh bubble across my lips, even as I tried to suppress it. "Nine hundred and eighty-one spools."

Rosie's mouth fell open, but no sound came out. I threw my arms around her. "It's enough to pay Mr. Woodstone."

For a glorious, shining moment, I thought I heard music — great, swelling hymns soaring to Stirwaters's rafters. But it must have been the water crashing off the wheel.

Chapter Nine

That glorious, soaring feeling lasted a few hours, but reality finally did me in. The truth was, the utterly fantastic situation we'd found ourselves in left me with a new problem: how to divest ourselves of these riches, and convert them into the cold cash we needed for the bank. I could hardly deliver a barrel of gold thread to Mr. Woodstone's doorstep and call our debt paid. In the night I'd had the ghost of an idea, no more, and now set myself the task of putting flesh on its slight bones.

"What are you looking for?" Rosie inquired, as I rifled furiously through a stack of old copies of *The Merchant Draper* journal. Father hadn't kept up the subscription in years, but these old almanacks had been my childhood storybooks. At last, triumphant, I found the page I was looking for. It was twelve years old and faded nearly invisible, but I flashed it open to Rosie.

"This."

Rosie peered in, curious. "A recipe for lace starch?"

"No, you ninny. *This.*" I spread the pages open on the desk. A half-page advert, decorated with a curious little illustration of a cherub, announced:

The House of Parmenter
PASSEMENTIER
Dealers in fine Goods, Lacework, and Trims

Gold & silver Threads
for
Needlework or Decoration

For sale to the Trade or Publick
Spring Street, Harrowgate

Rosie studied it a long time. "That's good," she said finally. "That's very good." She flipped the journal to the cover and pointed out the date. "How do you know they're still operating?"

"Because," I said, "Mrs. Parmenter sent those lovely lilies for Father's funeral."

Rosie was grinning broadly. She smacked her hand down on the desk. "See? See, I told you you'd think of something!" She sobered. "Look, you'd better get home. I don't know what time Uncle Wheeler came in last night, but —"

I nodded and pulled myself up from the desk. With a weary sigh, I remembered something. "Harte was here."

"What? You mean last night?"

I nodded. "I don't think he saw anything, but he was certainly suspicious. We'll have to be more careful in future."

Rosie barked out a little laugh. "In the future? Are you planning on making a habit of this, Mistress Miller?"

"You know what I mean," I snapped; but in honesty, even

I wasn't entirely sure. What had I meant? My thoughts ran to the strange scene yesterday at the forge, and I suppressed a shiver.

I set off for the Millhouse and breakfast, but Rosie lingered, determined to protect the cache of thread from prying eyes ("and Eagans," she added darkly) by covering the garret window with canvas and fetching a hefty padlock from Mr. Smith's.

"What'll you tell Uncle Wheeler?" she asked as I slipped down the stairs.

"What? Oh, I shouldn't worry. I'll just mention that we had a fairy man in overnight who spun us several hundred pounds worth of gold thread, and all our problems are over."

True to Rosie's prediction, my uncle was in the parlor when I finally got home, basking in the glow from the long windows, serene and polished in robin's egg blue. There was no way to get past him without comment. It took a great effort not to touch a hand to my hair or flutter my fingers down my skirts. What must I look like — did I have any stray golden strands clinging to me anywhere? It was too late to check.

Uncle Wheeler lowered his newspaper and beckoned me in with one long finger. I hesitated, but thinking of no good excuse, found myself drawn into the room. I sat beside him on the faded sofa and tried to arrange my skirts to hide their wrinkled hems.

"Now my dear," my uncle began, "I'm afraid I have been quite lax in my duties toward you girls these last weeks, and for that I must express my regrets."

"Oh, no, Uncle —"

He silenced me with a lift of one manicured hand (where *was* he getting those manicures?). "This is my fault, of course, for not being firm enough with you. Running about at all hours, unchaperoned . . . do you realize that you'd be cut from every circle of society if word got out?" He paused. "But we are not here to discuss that at the moment."

I lifted a hand to my mouth to suppress an unladylike yawn. "Do please continue, Uncle."

"Now, I'm sure it's disappointing to have your little pastime come to an end, of course, and I know how attached you were to the mill —"

"I beg your pardon — what?"

My uncle looked mildly taken aback. "I was speaking of this matter of the Wool Guild, of course. You can't mean to simply go on as if nothing has happened. Please don't think I'm doing this to be cruel — of course I'm not. But you *must* see reason. Let me propose something to you — don't be hasty, now; just listen for a moment before you say anything."

"And what is that, sir?"

"Well, I believe you'd told me that you'd received an offer of sale on the mill. From — who was it again? A Perch — Pinchfields, was it?"

I nodded, suddenly wary.

"Now, I've made a few inquiries, and —"

I had been sinking into a fog of weariness, but at this I snapped back. "You've *what?* How could you? I told you I would handle it!"

Uncle Wheeler's tongue flicked over his lips. "Yes, well. Evidently that was an error in judgement on my part. Charlotte, as your guardian, I feel obligated to do what is in your best interest, and as I believed initially, that is selling the mill."

I could not believe it. After all we'd gone through! I was so tired I could do little more than sputter angrily, but Uncle Wheeler ignored me, forging ahead.

". . . to speak with them. I believe that I've settled on the most advantageous arrangement, as I'm sure you'll agree when you've had the opportunity to compose yourself and look at this with reason." At this, Uncle Wheeler rose and smoothed down his jacket. "And now, I do believe Baker has been holding our breakfast."

I was escorted, then, to a meal I was in no state to consume. I wished to tell him that it was no longer necessary to consider selling, that I had the means for saving Stirwaters at hand — but nothing on Earth would compel me to mention Jack Spinner. Uncle Wheeler ate steadily and fastidiously, one finger crooked away from the corners of teacups and toast points. He frowned when Rosie bounced in, flushed and breathless. She took a moment to compose herself, smiled sweetly to Uncle Wheeler, and slid into place beside me. I stared at the food on my plate but could see only the face of the Pinchfields wool buyer, sneering at me.

A sudden sharp pain in my ankle turned my focus to Rosie, who had kicked me beneath the table. She was chatting away cheerfully with Uncle Wheeler. I took a deep gulp of scalding tea and sat straighter, forcing myself to attend to them.

"I think that sounds like quite a sensible plan, Uncle. Certainly you must take advantage of the felicitous timing, as you say."

"What are you talking about?" I asked carefully.

Rosie grinned at me. "Your meeting with Pinchfields in Harrowgate, of course. Uncle Wheeler has everything arranged. Wasn't that thoughtful of him?" She jabbed at a slice of nectarine with a tiny fork. "Uncle, did you try these? They're divine."

I stared at her in horror, but the pieces slowly began to fall into place. As my sluggish thoughts finally caught up with my sister's, I nodded.

After breakfast I cornered Rosie in the kitchen. "Are you witless? What am I going to say to Pinchfields?"

"I think you ought to concentrate on what you plan to say to Mr. Parmenter."

A smile crept about her lips, and I couldn't help myself. I hugged her.

I spent the next days satisfying myself that I could leave the mill in safe hands for seventy-two hours, checking and rechecking the wool in the shed and the strongbox in the office, and cautioning Rosie beyond her endurance.

"Enough!" she cried at last as I was quizzing her about the key to the great lock on the garret room. "I won't let anyone up there; I won't burn down the dyeshed; I won't let Bill Penny run the carding engine. Mercy, Charlotte — anyone would think you didn't trust me!" And with that she stormed off.

I gave the locked mill doors one last tug and stepped out into the yard to see Biddy Tom across the road, stooped over the verge, gathering greens from the edge of the fence. All at once, she stood up straight and looked right at me.

"Charlotte Miller," she said with a nod; and though her voice was no louder than common, it carried like a shout across the road. I found myself crossing the lane to meet her.

"Good day, Mrs. Tom."

She nodded again and bent for a handful of yellow blossoms. "Keyflower," she said. "Good for headache and insomnia. Wood sorrel" — here she indicated spindly weeds trailing through the fence — "for fever. By the way, your place smells a bit funny, like. Come by and I'll get you some sage to burn, clear your air a little."

"It always smells funny," I said. "It's the dyeworks."

She smiled then, reedy and wiry as her herbs. "That weren't what I meant, and you know as much. Odd air hereabouts."

The gall of it! If we had "odd air," *she* was half to blame for it! All at once, the events of the last days became too much, and everything spilled over. "Did you sell Rosie those — things? Potions, and — and mandrake root?"

Biddy Tom eased herself upright and eyed me levelly. "Sell them? You know better than that, Charlotte Miller. I never sell anything to anyone. Did your sister come to me for aid? That's her business."

"You leave her alone! She's just a girl — she doesn't know any better —"

"Are ye her mam, then, or her sister?" She reached for my shoulder, and I wasn't quite quick enough to flinch away. "Miss Rosie's plenty old enough to know what she's about. It's hard to watch your sister in pain —"

"Rosie's not in pain!"

Mrs. Tom's lips twisted slightly. "I meant *ye*, lassie. You think it's easy for Rosie, all you've been through? She only wants to help, and you haven't left her many ways of doing that, with your managin' this and takin' care of that."

"Rosie helps," I protested. "We couldn't manage without her."

" 'Tain't what I mean." She tucked the herbs into pockets in her apron and lowered herself back to the grass. "You've a lot of weight on those young shoulders, Charlotte Miller. Let Rosie hoist her fair share."

"By painting symbols on the floor and chanting nursery rhymes?"

She looked sidelong at me. "Oh? And what happened?"

I clapped my mouth shut. After a moment I said, "Nothing happened, of course."

"Oh? I'd not be too sure of that, lass. That big city trip you were planning is back on again, I see. And I don't believe the rumors that it's because you mean to sell at last." The old woman actually winked at me!

"Yes, it's back on," I snapped. "And it has nothing to do with any chalk drawings or mandrake root or — or wood sorrel or sage! So stay away from my sister and good day to you!" I spun on my heel and launched myself back home again.

"Charlotte Miller."

Against my will I turned back.

"You mind what I said about clearing the air hereabouts. Don't you presume everything is as it seems by broad daylight."

"What is that supposed to mean?"

But Mrs. Tom had slipped away into the golden afternoon.

Chapter Ten

*W*e arrived in Harrowgate after a day and a half on the road, bouncing over dry ruts in an airless stage compartment filled to choking sweetness by Uncle Wheeler's lilac wig powder. As I had my head half out the coach window for most of the journey, I beheld quite the prospect driving into town. The narrow valley and green hills of home gave way to a flat broad plain, through which snaked the wide grey river and miles of endless golden pasture. We could see the city long before we arrived there, its staggered rooftops and church spires rising up from the landscape like a queer, manufactured mountain range. An arched iron gateway marked the transition from Country to City, and the packed-earth roadway instantly became cobblestones. Everything seemed both huge and curiously close, as if you could stretch an arm out the carriage window and touch buildings on both sides. Of course, you were more likely to have your fingers bitten off by the neighboring carriage horses, clattering past with an astonishing, inexplicable speed.

Uncle Wheeler had spent the journey instructing me in all manner of city matters: distinguished personages whose paths we may happen to cross, the history and inhabitants of the great houses we passed, the best corner coffee-houses and streets for marketing. It was like someone had breathed life into a penny tour book, and I had only to turn an eye this way or that, and receive the full accounting. I supposed it was understandable; to my uncle, we were home at last.

But as we drove into the city, he did not relax, as I should have done, coming home after months away; by contrast, he became more excitable by the minute, animated and flushed beneath his powdered cheeks.

"Why, Uncle," I remarked as we passed the bustling Stowebridge Market, my uncle's hands on the grip of his walking stick white with exertion. "Anyone would think you were nervous!"

At once he withdrew, easing back into the carriage seat and crossing one stockinged leg over the other. "Nonsense, child," he said languidly. "It's merely the heat of the compartment."

And since I was beating my bone fan rapidly at my own face, I could hardly argue with that.

Uncle Wheeler had scheduled our appointment at Pinchfields for later that afternoon, which gave me scarcely enough time for my most significant errand. Fortunately, he did not object to my paying a call on "an old acquaintance of my father's," and after settling ourselves into the well-appointed inn, my uncle hired a cab to take us across town to the passementerie shop. Round through the foreign streets of Harrowgate we drove, through bricked lanes and grand wide roads crowded with traffic. It flashed by me in a blur; I was too preoccupied to marvel at the unfamiliar landscape. Rehearsing my lines in my head, I clutched my reticule and resisted the urge to reassure myself that the little spool of gold thread was still within. For his part, my uncle was at last mercifully silent, as well.

The House of Parmenter was literally an old green townhouse nestled in a row of residences in a modest neighborhood. The carriage pulled to a stop by a curtained bay window where a young woman sat sewing. Uncle Wheeler looked up long enough to sniff, before pulling open the heavy door for me.

A grandmotherly woman in a feathered hat waved us in. Her crewelwork dress, with its silk piping and foot-long bullion fringe, made her look like a walking advertisement for Parmenter goods — or a walking sofa. "Good day, good day!" she warbled.

The girl in the window, a much, much younger copy of the woman, looked up from her needlework with a coy smile. She stared openly at Uncle Wheeler, who lingered in the foyer behind me as the older woman shuffled out from her heaps of paperwork and samples.

"My good man, what can I do for you? The House of Parmenter is at your service. Custom embroidery? Lace cravats? The finest imported silk thread?" Mrs. Parmenter looked me up and down through tiny spectacles. "Or perhaps a wedding costume for your young lady, hmmm . . . Mother-of-pearl buttons, linen mantua-lace light as air . . ." She swept a tape from the desk and advanced on me like a matador.

"I think not," Uncle Wheeler said in clipped tones that let all the air out of poor Mrs. Parmenter. "Charlotte, do get on with whatever your — business here is. I will await you in the carriage. Do not tarry." He turned toward the door and paused, his hand lifted toward a length of silver braid. He examined it for a moment with some evident scorn, and then said, "Have ten yards of this sent to Burke's and Taylor. I fancy a travelling coat."

"Heh," Mrs. Parmenter said, as the landing door closed with a snap. "And I'll be sure to hurry that along, won't I?" She gave me a great wink. "Who are you then, dearie?"

I started, quite unable to be nervous in the face of this reception. "Charlotte Miller, ma'am. I've come —"

Her blue eyes grew wide. "You're never James Miller's girl!" She bundled me to her bosom in a flutter of gold lace. "Oh, my dear. Go right up, go right up. Mr. Parmenter will be so pleased to see you. Such friends, your father and my Irwin, you know."

Mr. Parmenter's office was no tidier than Mrs. Parmenter's desk. A bright workroom under a flood of cracked skylights, it was crowded with desks and tables piled high with sample books. Tacked up on every wall were scraps of gold lace, silk fringe, and braids and trims of every conceivable design.

"Hello?" I stepped tentatively over a box of spools. "Mr. Parmenter?"

Mr. Parmenter emerged from the muddle, a slight older fellow with thinning hair well-waxed and curled, his neck draped about with yards of trim like a tailor's measuring tape. "What did you say your name was?" he said, peering at me in some confusion.

"Charlotte Miller, sir. I've come from Shearing. Your wife — that is, the lady belowstairs, seems to think you knew my father, James?"

Mr. Parmenter was scribbling notes on a scrap of parcel-wrapping. "Hmm? What's that? Oh — clothier, I believe.

Some odd bits about that business, though — you'll want to stay away from them."

"No, Mr. Parmenter — I *am* Miss Miller." Clearly, talk would get me nowhere. I opened my reticule and withdrew the spool of gold thread and set it on the worktable. It shone like sunlight itself in the brightly lit workroom, a radiant coil of pure gold that made Mr. Parmenter's other luxurious wares seem tawdry by comparison.

Mr. Parmenter stared at the spool for the longest moment, his mouth half open, a blot of ink blooming at the end of his pen. At last he composed himself and gave the thread the same suspicious examination it had endured at my own hands.

"Where did you get this?" he said, almost reverently.

"Tradesman. Can you use it?"

He eyed the thread as if afraid to give away his eagerness. Oh, that was a look I understood very well! "How much can you supply?"

"Oh, nearly a thousand of the like. Can —"

"My dear, you are the answer to my prayers! Wait — did you say one *thousand*? Of this? Are you pulling my leg, then, miss?"

"No, indeed, sir. I am quite serious."

He turned to me, and a flood of words poured out of him. "You can't imagine what a trial it's been this season! There are outrageous taxes on local gold, and tariffs on imported gold are so bad the lacemakers can't afford it, and if you could get me one *hundred* spools of this by the end of the month you will absolutely save my life. A thousand!" He broke into a little giggle, rummaging through a heap of tambours and ledgers and uncovering a receipt book. "I can offer you ten shillings sixpence per spool. I know, it's low —"

"I need fifteen."

He pursed his lips. "My dear, I can't even sell it for that — and that's retail. I can maybe go up to twelve shillings — maybe twelve and six . . ." He shook his head sadly.

"Mr. Parmenter, what are the wyre-drawers charging these days? It must be close to four or five pence *a yard*. I'm offering you a bargain at fourteen and six." I stepped in closer and rolled the spool toward him, the gold thread pouring onto the desk like a ribbon of light.

"Will you take thirteen?" he asked in a small soft voice. I forced myself to breathe easily. That would bring us some twelve pounds short of Mr. Woodstone's bill — but I had managed to squirrel away a little money during the summer, and Mr. Woodstone did not seem the type to quibble over farthings.

"Very well, Mr. Parmenter, I think we have a bargain."

"Splendid!" He scrawled something in the register, and ripped the cheque from the booklet. "Now, miss, I'll give you forty percent now, and the balance when we fetch the stock."

"Mr. Parmenter, I'm afraid I'm going to have to ask for ready money."

"But, miss — I couldn't possibly. Oh, there's no way —"

Feeling wickeder than sin, I reached for the spool and slowly drew it away. Six hundred pounds was an absolute fortune, and I had no reason to assume the Parmenters had that sort of money lying about for the taking. Still, it couldn't be helped — if this was the only way . . . but I had to be careful. I had more to lose here than Mr. Parmenter.

He watched me with quavering breath, then scowled and tore up the first cheque. "Fine, although I shudder to think what Bessie'll do to me when she finds out."

I allowed myself one deep breath. "Thank you, sir. The stock is available immediately."

"Oh? Good, good. I'll send a man for it at the end of the week." He eyed me over his spectacle rims as he passed me the money. "Are you sure you don't have a source for silver as well?"

I smiled and shook my head, and Mr. Parmenter led me to the doorway. "Mr. Parmenter, what did you mean about staying away from the Miller business? What was odd about it?"

He scowled, the little eyes bleary. "Odd? Whatever gave you that idea? Nonsense. Now, if we can ever do business together again —" and he hurried me right down the stairwell before I could so much as blink back at him.

As I made my way downstairs, I could not suppress my smile. It wasn't exactly Worm Hill Cloth Exchange, but I think I did not do too badly in the end.

Uncle Wheeler had not quite made it past the foyer, having been detained in conversation by the girl in the window, a sharp-featured beauty who had turned her arched eyebrows like a weapon on my uncle. He was leaning casually in the doorframe, bending over her slightly as she laughed and swept her curls from one shoulder to the other. I clattered down the last few steps as gracefully as a dairy maid. At my entrance, she gave me one scornful look and stabbed her stitching brutally with her needle.

"All done, Charlotte?" Uncle Wheeler murmured absently. He drew the young woman's hand to his lips with an alarming smile, and blew a kiss through the air across her wrist.

She blushed very prettily as Uncle Wheeler took my arm and steered me outside.

"Pretty thing," my uncle said.

"She's no older than I am," I said.

"Well, we've talked about that before, Charlotte — you're quite of a marriageable age. As am I, when it comes to that."

"She's just a seamstress," I said cruelly — just to see what should happen. Uncle Wheeler dropped my arm abruptly and turned his smile on me.

"Yes, but she'll have a lovely afternoon now, won't she?" He stepped toward the waiting cab and held out a hand. "Come along now, we don't want to leave the gentlemen at Pinchfields waiting."

My stomach turned, and I was more than happy to climb into the carriage, where the noise of traffic inhibited any further conversation.

Pinchfields was a misery: an ugly, dark, filthy, stinking nightmare of industry, crouched on the banks of the Stowe like a great hulking beast, covetously gripping its sere acre of land and spewing black smoke into the heavy air. Two vast buildings, their red brick faces barely broken by windows, wound round themselves in a tangled labyrinth until it was impossible to make heads or tails of anything. The river slinked beside, so slow and rank I could barely believe it was the same Stowe I had lived beside all my life.

Uncle Wheeler was enchanted. "The factory is only five years old, Charlotte," he said as we alit from our hired cab. I could not credit it. Its dark walls and grimy windows spoke of ages and ages on this spot, and surely they had dogged our footsteps at Stirwaters longer than that! Yet as we approached I saw the cornerstone, stamped with the date, implacable as the walls themselves.

We were shuttled through an iron gate, where a Mr. Edgewater, a stout man in middle age, sweating and mopping his wilted wig with a silk handkerchief, was waiting for us. He shook Uncle Wheeler's hand heartily, but barely noticed me.

"Welcome, welcome," he huffed, striking out for a barred door in the brick wall. "I am instructed to give you the grand tour. I'm sure you'll be very impressed. We've made some recent improvements in the weaving rooms —" He halted, apparently out of breath, and cast his glance back toward us. "That is, rather — well, come along, then." He shoved us forward into a dim, clanging workroom.

"What is that noise?" I cried before I could stop myself. It truly seemed as though we'd stepped into the belly of a dragon — dark and hot, with a roar and a hiss so loud I barely heard my own voice.

Mr. Edgewater laughed, and it was not a friendly sound. "Steam!" he cried, loud above the dragon's breath. "That's steam, my dear girl. No clumsy waterwheels here — we use only the very latest equipment." He pointed to the ceiling, at the snaking network of painted pipes shuddering slightly in their bindings. I followed them with my eyes, up through a hole in the ceiling. Wool works best in heat and damp; if Pinchfields had found a way to create those ideal conditions, it didn't matter how poor their raw materials were. They could make it up in the processing.

We followed Mr. Edgewater through five floors in two buildings with hundreds of workers in thrall: children barely old enough to dress themselves and hollow-eyed girls hunched, flushed and coughing, over their machines, where the stench of sweat and sickness overpowered even the smells of wool and grease. It had none of the light and room of Stirwaters, nothing of the view and air; no space even to step back and take a breath. The workers might have been chained to their machines for all the freedom they had to move about; they stood and worked in a slow, dispirited trance.

By happenstance I chanced upon Abby Weaver there, working a massive plying frame, her nimble fingers red and blistered, cheekbones standing out too clearly in her face. She started when she saw me (as surely I did as well).

"Mistress!" she cried, looking up briefly before turning back to her work. The threads she was winding into yarn had skips and slubs in them, an uneven batch of workmanship that would never have passed at Stirwaters. She pinched at odd bits of the yarn, as if trying to mend the errors before it became *her* sloppy workmanship, but to no avail.

"Where's Tom?" I said, pitching my voice above the din.

"Home," she said, slipping aside the rings and spools. "He broke his leg and lost his post. He's watching the baby, at least."

What kind of "home" must they have here, this lost branch of my Stirwaters family? A windowless room on a back alley somewhere, their children never to run in the willow groves or splash in the streambed? I clutched my purse with stiff fingers and realized that Abby was shouting at me.

". . . a machine here that weaves by itself," Abby was saying. "You should go look; they say it's a wonder!"

"I'm sure!" I called back. With great effort I managed to leave Abby there. Thoroughly sickened by the whole place, I made myself follow my uncle and our guide.

Soon enough, we entered a vast room of almost unfathomable depth, stocked with row upon row of looms — twenty, fifty — I lost count. One girl worked two or three, and she was not weaving: She was watching. The machines *themselves* were weaving — the shuttles flying back and forth through the sheds, the battens banging up and down in a deafening, oppressive rhythm. I stepped forward, drawn into that clattering nightmare as if it had hypnotized me.

This was it, then, the end of the world I had felt upon us when Father died. It wasn't fire or famine or debt that would destroy us. This was Progress. Stirwaters wasn't venerable, we were just *old*. How could we survive in the face of this massive, inevitable newness? I wanted to escape those stifling rooms and the beasts that lived there, devouring my future with every steaming breath.

"Shall we step into the office?" Mr. Edgewater's voice broke into my thoughts.

"Indeed," Uncle Wheeler said with a sniff. "It is a bit close in here."

Mr. Edgewater brought us to a closed door on the highest level, glassed over and ill-fitting in its frame. I could see shadows moving behind the frosted panes. Our guide tapped obsequiously on the glass, and a liveried clerk stepped out and bowed.

"Miss Miller," he said, the first person in this entire factory to call me by name. "Mr. Darling will see you now."

I adjusted my hat and took a step forward, then stopped, frowning. "I'm sorry — Mr. Darling, did you say?"

The clerk nodded, ushering us over the threshold. The little office was stuffy, windowless; the smell of fresh paint hung in the air, but the dark walls were sweating from the steam.

From behind a delicate turned-leg desk rose a gentleman in a black velvet suit, far, far too warm for the room. He was thick round the waistcoat, heavily jowled, his mouth turned down in a perpetual frown. Upon seeing me, he gave those bent lips an upward twist, trying to affect a smile.

"Miss Miller, do come in, come in! Such a delight to have you here at our little" — he coughed — "establishment. What did you think?"

"Mr. Darling?" I said. "You're Mr. Arthur Darling?"

"Primary shareholder of Pinchfields, I am."

"And trustee of the cloth market?" I was trembling, unable to believe my stupidity.

He nodded. "I'm glad to see that your uncle has been able to talk some sense into you, Miss Miller. Trust me, you will not regret an alliance with Pinchfields." He drew a sheaf of papers from the desk, tidied their corners, and smiled at me — a great wolfish smile, complete with shining teeth. By God, he had sale papers all drawn up already! This wasn't just a friendly tour . . . I had been lured into a snare!

I glanced at Uncle Wheeler. He was leaning easily against the doorframe, studying his fingernails. I took a deep breath of the stifling air.

"Mr. Darling," I said, and I am proud of how my voice carried. "I and all the Millers will be cold and dead before you get your filthy hands on Stirwaters."

I swiped the papers off that ridiculous desk and tore them in two, scattering the pieces on the brand-new rose-print carpeting.

That mad fire sustained me all the way through the mazelike corridors to the open air and the waiting carriage. I clambered up and took several deep breaths to steady myself. I was almost calm again when Uncle Wheeler sprang in after me.

"You stupid girl!" He grabbed my wrist and twisted it up toward my face. I gasped with pain and surprise, and could not breathe with his face so close to mine. "Do you have any idea what that little display cost us?"

I wrenched my hand from his. "Cost *us?* What did you think — I would meekly sign over my home? I'm afraid you've been quite deceived, Uncle. Rosie was right. They must be plotting something. Your Mr. Darling? He sent the letter from Worm Hill. It can't be coincidence." I rubbed my sore wrist and matched him glare for glare.

He licked his thin lips and frowned delicately. "Well," he said at last, "I suppose that does look rather suspicious. But, my dear, I beg you to reconsider. If this factory has that sort of influence, what chance do you have? Surely you recognize the hopelessness of your situation now."

I sank into my seat, gripping my reticule with both hands, where my "chance" was safely tucked away — my precious cheque from Mr. Parmenter. "Never."

Uncle Wheeler leaned in over me. Beads of perspiration stood out beneath the white of his wig, and the lilac scent had gone faintly sour. "Charlotte, please — listen to me. You can still go back in there, and —"

I pulled away and gave a rap to the back of the driver's box. "Take us back to the hotel," I said, with such finality even Uncle Wheeler could not protest.

That night, I found it impossible to sleep. The day's excitements — the confrontation at Pinchfields; the too-heavy hotel supper, shared in stony silence between my uncle and myself; and — most of all — the fat cheque from Mr. Parmenter haunted my efforts. Something was nagging at me — some unease I could not name. I lay still as a board in the too-soft bed and stared at the wardrobe door where I'd hung my reticule. Surely it was only the burden of carrying so much cash on my person; the sooner I ferried it to Mr. Woodstone's possession, the better. I imagined scheming innkeepers slipping into those cupboards in the dead of night, by means of secret doors cut through the walls behind them. I'd been living far too long with Rosie, to conceive of such a thing. But I climbed out of bed nevertheless and retrieved it, checking for the thousandth time that Mr. Parmenter's cheque was still inside. I tucked the little purse beneath my pillow, my arm through its strap. But I was only somewhat comforted.

Chapter Eleven

In the morning Uncle Wheeler rapped on my door as I finished dressing. He looked me over with that strange appraising glance before sweeping it across my chambers. I forced myself to smile my good-mornings, wrenching my thoughts from the purse at my side.

"Oh, good," he said. "You're up. I have some business to attend to this morning, so I will be leaving right after breakfast. You —"

Relief made me careless. "Well, that works out nicely, then. I wanted to go out myself —"

His gaze darkened momentarily, and I saw my mistake. But rather than delivering a lecture on propriety, Uncle Wheeler dipped into his waistcoat pocket and consulted his watch. Snapping it shut impatiently, he said, "Oh, very well. Just do try to be back by noon, and don't make a spectacle of yourself." He slammed out of my room without a backward glance, and I blinked at the doorway in surprise.

The offices for Uplands Mercantile Bank anchored a city square near the river, just up the street from Pinchfields. The bank stood, solemn and white and heavy, at the crown of the square. Stone steps stretched all along the front, rising slowly to white columns and a line of bronze doors, black with age and city smoke. I tried to imagine Mr. Woodstone climbing these steps each morning, and the picture in my mind of the young man in his scuffed boots and brown hunting coat did not mix at all with this austere backdrop.

I made my solitary way up those steps, nodding to the liveried footman who held the door for me as I entered.

Everything inside the bank was shiny: marble tiles, deeply polished wood counters, a domed ceiling with a map of the world in colored glass. I wondered how my father had ever thought to come inside such a place, let alone found courage to ask for money. I was here with money in my purse, and *I* wished to flee back down that gleaming hallway, down those white steps, and all the way back to the dusty road and mossy stone walls of home.

Somehow I took myself up to the counter and placed myself at the foot of the line forming at one of the booths. I was the only woman there, and I felt curious eyes upon me. I stared resolutely at the back of the gentleman in front of me, until a little cough sounded at my elbow.

I turned to see a small man, smartly dressed and bespectacled. "Is — is there something I can help madam with?"

"Yes," I said. "Thank you. I'm here to see Mr. Randall Woodstone." I said it too loudly, and the curious glances turned to outright stares. I suddenly realized how I must look — a girl alone, in a shabby printed dress and no cloak, asking after a young gentleman banker. Thankful for my hat to hide my flush, I added clearly, "My name is Charlotte Miller. I'm here on business for Stirwaters Woollen Mill, in the Gold Valley."

My bespectacled clerk relaxed. "Of course, Miss Miller. Right this way, please. Mr. Woodstone's offices are on the second floor." He led me off into a maze of glassed doors, cold walls, and further marble stairs. The clerk finally stopped before one door that looked the same as all the others, opened it, and ushered me within.

"A Miss Miller here to see you, sir." The clerk bowed and disappeared.

"Charlotte!" Mr. Woodstone sprang up from his desk. He was in his shirt sleeves, his jacket tossed casually on the chair behind him. "That is — Miss Miller. This is a surprise. Come in, come in!" He fumbled for his coat and shrugged into it awkwardly. There was a great crease down the front, and he looked as though he'd spent the morning shoving his hand through his hair. He leaned across the desk to shake my hand. I withdrew Mrs. Parmenter's cheque from my reticule and held it before him in both hands. His eyes grew wide.

"I say, you did it!" He took the check and stared at it a moment, then hit it on the edge of his desk, like a punctuation mark. "Well done — extraordinary. I knew you had it in you. Everything fare well at the market, then?"

I gave my too-short skirt a tug I hoped he couldn't see. "Yes, well. We had a stroke of luck."

"Well, you were due one. Here, Miss Miller — sit down, won't you?"

"Look, Mr. Woodstone —"

"Call me Randall," he said with a wave of his hand, fumbling through some papers on his desk.

"Mr. Woodstone, I'm afraid that isn't quite the amount we'd agreed upon. But if you'll allow me to send you the rest when I return to Shearing —"

He shrugged. "No matter. You're good for it." He gave me

a smile that went right to my bones. As I was sorting myself out, he put a stack of papers before me on the desk. "All right, then. Here are the papers for your loan. I've taken the liberty of redrawing them to reflect the new payment schedule."

As we filled out the new paperwork, ominously now in *my* name, not my father's, Mr. Woodstone chattered on like an excitable little boy. "You're not in the city alone, then, surely? No — let me guess. Your esteemed uncle. Where is the gentleman, then?"

I must have looked a bit guilty, for Mr. Woodstone laughed. "Flown your fetters, have you? I can't blame you — but why all the secrecy? Haven't you told him about me? The loan, that is?"

I shook my head, uncertain how much to tell him. I wanted to like him; he was *terribly* likeable, like an earnest dog — but he was my banker. Still, I was grateful to have someone to confide in, if only slightly. And I rather felt I'd paid for the privilege, frankly. "I don't know. He thinks I ought to sell out. I'm sure he means well, but —"

Mr. Woodstone shook his head. "But you're holding out?"

"Well, of course," I said. "I can't just give up. There have been Millers at Stirwaters —"

"Since the beginning of time." He smiled. "Your father said something much the same. Look, I have to say — I'm awfully sorry about all of this." He waved a careless hand over the papers spread on the desk. "I can't help feeling somewhat responsible —"

"But that's ridiculous," I said. "Why should you? Did you force my father to incur a debt he had no hope of repaying?"

"Charlotte," he said gently, and I realized I must sound more bitter than I thought. "We never would have loaned him anything he couldn't afford to pay back. He must have believed he had the means."

"He always believed he had the means. That was the problem." An uncomfortable silence fell over the stuffy office. Mr. Woodstone studied the papers in front of him, drumming his fingers against the desk. They were as ink-spattered as my own, but strong — as if he did something in his off-hours besides scribble in record books. "Look, Mr. Woodstone, you don't know *why* my father took out this loan, do you?"

"I assumed it was for capital improvements to the mill," he replied. "That's the reason he gave us, and — oh. Given what you showed me at Stirwaters, I'm guessing he never made them?"

I shook my head grimly, but a thread of a whisper flitted across my thoughts: *This mill don't want to be fixed up. . . .* I shoved it aside. "No. He spent a lot of time tinkering with new ideas for machines, but he certainly can't have spent two thousand pounds on that."

Mr. Woodstone eyed me thoughtfully, until the intensity of those greyish eyes made me look away. "I'm afraid you have a mystery on your hands, then. We don't require that our clients show us evidence of how they've used the money — only that they pay it back. I'm sorry, Miss Miller. I wish I could tell you more."

Somewhere I heard a clock chime the quarter hour, and I started. "Dear me, what time is it?"

"It's gone half past eleven," he said. "Why?"

I rose from my seat and bundled together my hat and reticule. "I promised my uncle I'd be back by noon. I'm sorry, Mr. Woodstone, and thank you — but I must go."

He rose with me. "Here, surely you'll allow me to walk you to the cab stand. It's the least I can do."

As we descended the stone steps into the square, Mr. Woodstone rambled on blithely, inquiring after the wonders of the city I'd witnessed: Had I seen the portrait exhibition at the Royal Gallery? The Botanic Gardens? Taken tea at the Mayfair Hotel? I shook my head and replied that I had been here only on business and hadn't had the opportunity for anything else.

"Well, that's a great pity," he said. "You and your uncle must accompany me to the opera tomorrow night — as my guests, of course. My father keeps a box, but we never use it. . . ."

A horrifying image of myself sandwiched between Mr. Woodstone and Uncle Wheeler, in my faded yellow dress and threadbare shawl, nearly brought me up in my tracks. "Oh, but I'm afraid that's impossible," I said with admirable smoothness. "We're leaving this afternoon."

"But —" Mr. Woodstone paused — "so soon? I thought you were here for a fortnight. When will I see you again, then?"

I shook my head, wondering how it could possibly matter to him.

We had reached the cab stand, where rows of carriages waited for passengers. Mr. Woodstone selected one for me, gleaming black and open to the air. After he gave the driver my address and paid the fare (ignoring my objections), I turned to him.

"Mr. Woodstone," I said. "You put your faith in me when others would not have done. Why?"

He looked only slightly taken aback. He combed his hand through his hair, which had never quite recovered itself, and shrugged. "Let's say I have a lot of respect for girls — young women — who have to step up and take care of their entire families." One hand on the coach above my head, he looked down at me. His eyes had gone blue in the bright day. "My mother died when I was born, and I was raised by my sister. My four sisters, really — but mostly Rebecca, the eldest. I see what you're trying to do, and, well, she'd never forgive me if I let you fail."

Something in his words, or those alarming eyes, or the sudden warmth of the waning morning, caused a piercing tightness in my breast. I could not answer that, and so I said, "Four sisters? And I thought Rosie was a handful."

Mr. Woodstone laughed aloud. "Trust me, your Rosie can't have *anything* on my Marianne." He rapped on the carriage frame and offered me his hand as I stepped up inside. He may have held it just a moment or two longer than necessary — or that could have been my imagination. "Good day, Miss Miller."

As the carriage flew along the cobbled streets, giddiness and relief overwhelmed me. I had succeeded in my business at Parmenter's, survived my trip to Pinchfields, and relieved myself of a third of my debt. It seemed my Harrowgate début had been quite the triumph after all! I eased back in my seat, determined to enjoy the ride. When I alit at the Colonnade Hotel, I hesitated. I should still have to smooth over the awkwardness with my uncle that had arisen from the scene at Pinchfields, and I did not relish the prospect. Instead, I crossed the street during a gap in traffic, to a little public house with a white-striped awning and a view of the park across the way.

I had a few moments and coins to spare; I could treat myself to a cordial.

I stepped inside and was just about to remove my hat and sink into a booth by the window, when I heard a familiar voice pitched slightly above the other conversation in the room. I looked up and froze. Well in the back, tucked away nearly out of sight near the kitchen, was my uncle. His back was to me, but I would know that robin's-egg blue coat and lilac-powdered wig anywhere. He was deep in animated conversation with another man I knew — the Pinchfields wool-buyer. It had to be him — he had the same dark angular face and narrow features, the same derisive sneer that had made Rosie say he looked like a ferret.

My breath caught in my throat. What on Earth had brought those two together — and with such urgency — this morning? I could tell from my uncle's demeanor that this was no friendly renewal of acquaintance, no casual breakfast between old city friends. I studied them from behind the cloaks a moment longer, straining to hear clear words among the murmur of their voices, watching for shifts in the Pinchfields man's ugly face. I wanted to march up to their table and confront them, but I didn't dare. Before they could see me, before the barmaid could cross the creaking floor to ask me in, I fled the pub and clattered breathlessly across the street and up to my hotel room.

I longed to question Uncle Wheeler, all the long drive home. But there were other passengers on the stage — and what would I say? *"I've been spying on you, and I demand you tell me what you and Pinchfields are scheming!"* There should be fewer people on the drive tomorrow; perhaps by then I'd have time to form the perfect question, the one that would force my uncle to give up all his secrets. But as the miles rolled past, it began to seem all the more innocent. What had I truly seen? That their meeting had something to do with Stirwaters, I had no doubt. But my uncle *had* arranged for me to discuss a sale with them; surely the man from Pinchfields had merely been urging my uncle to talk sense into me. Nothing more sinister than that.

I turned to my uncle, willing him to give something away, but he merely smiled at me absently and patted my hand with his gloved fingers. I heard nothing more about Pinchfields, and though I was still curious, I was grateful for that.

We arrived late at the inn due to delays on the road caused by the movements of sheep and the vagaries of wealthy passengers who chose, at the last moment, not to travel. Uncle Wheeler was by then in a foul and imperious mood, made no more amenable to discover that they had given away our rooms, and the only accommodations available were a single room on the top floor (for Uncle Wheeler, naturally), and a cramped but tidy cupboard overlooking the stable yard. There was scarcely enough room to turn around in, but it had a bed and thereby satisfied all my requirements. We had missed dinner, but Uncle Wheeler's persuasion garnered us trays of cold meat and bread. I barely tasted mine, and was asleep in minutes.

But I did not sleep well. In the dark of the night I awoke to strange noises — laughter, I thought groggily, and something like a henhouse being ravaged by foxes. I mumbled something rude and rolled over, folding my inadequate pillow over my head. A moment later, the raucous concert hit fever pitch. I knew further sleep was hopeless, so I pulled myself out of bed to peer out the window.

There was a cockfight going on. A full moon shone down on a ring scratched out in the dirt, glinting on scattered feathers and the gloss of blood. The noise was incredible — the cheers of the spectators outmatched only by the shrieking of the cockerels as they charged and struck at each other with the cruel spurs bound to their claws. I'm a country girl — I know what eventually becomes of most livestock. But goading two dumb animals into mortal combat, merely for sport? This was barbaric. Nauseated, I turned away.

But not fast enough. The moon shone bright on something else that night — a puff of white, bent over the rim of the ring — and I had to take another glance. Uncle Wheeler knelt at the edge of the pit, his glittering coat flung behind him in the dirt. He was shouting and crowing along with everyone else, banging his fist against the ground. I stared at him a long, long while, unable to credit the transformation — that my genteel uncle had somehow become this bloodthirsty, wild-eyed creature.

When the match finally ended, the losing cockerel a shredded and broken heap in the center of the ring, Uncle Wheeler rose up from the earth and patted a strand of his wig back into place. A splash of something dark marred his shirtfront. A stout, squat country fellow leaned in menacingly, gesturing with a meaty hand. Uncle Wheeler slapped his hand away and flung something at his feet. I thought I saw the glint of silver, the flutter of a banknote. He stooped and grabbed his jacket from the ground, and stalked off into the night, the tapestry coat balled up in his hand.

*   *   *

The next morning I rose and dressed slowly, turning the scene in the yard over and over in my head. I knew that men of society gambled: tasteful games of cards played over glasses of port, wagers on carriage races, rolls of the dice. But blood-sports by moonlight at country inn yards, while their nieces slept upstairs? I did not know what to make of any of it.

When I finally arrived downstairs, it was to find Uncle Wheeler — somehow powder fresh as always — involved in a heated argument with the innkeeper. Stares from the staff and other guests followed me as I joined him.

"What's the matter?" I said, and it took one sniff from Uncle Wheeler and the set jaw of the innkeeper for me to understand. *Oh, mercy.*

"How much is it?" I asked, opening up my reticule. The innkeeper looked sympathetic, and I realized he thought I must be well accustomed to this. Flushing hotly, I counted out the money, and the innkeeper actually patted me on the arm. I could hardly get out of there fast enough.

Uncle Wheeler was quick on my heels. "Charlotte, wait — it was a temporary misunderstanding. A mere miscalculation! I must have underestimated the expenses of the trip, and didn't carry enough cash. I assure you, I would have worked it out."

"Of course," I said, very quietly. I pulled a few more notes from my purse and pressed them into his hand. He looked at them, the oddest expression on his face, before closing his fingers around them. Thankfully, the stage pulled up at just that moment, and I climbed in, grateful for the presence of a dour old woman in mourning black and the scowling pug dog on her lap.

Chapter Twelve

I was welcomed back to Stirwaters a hero. Rosie had encouraged premature speculation about my success, and when I swept in off the stage late that afternoon, a cheer went up in the mill rooms.

"That's our Charlotte!" Janet Lamb fairly beamed as I passed by her workstation in the finishing rooms.

"Ah, lass," Jack Townley said, "heard you gave Pinchfields the boot. Well done."

I smiled back. "Yes, I don't think we'll be hearing from them again." But I seized Rosie by the elbow and dragged her into the office. "What did you tell them?"

Rosie grinned and gave me a fierce hug. "How did it go?" she demanded upon releasing me.

"I sold the gold thread."

She nodded. "Good. And?"

"And they'll be sending a man for it this week."

"And?"

"And I got a good price for it."

Rosie made a moue of impatience. "But what happened at Pinchfields? And did you see that banker again?"

I untied my bonnet strings and related the details of my journey, from the awfulness of the Pinchfields workrooms, to the grandeur of Uplands Mercantile. Rosie listened raptly, all the way to my conclusion that the trip had been a grand success.

"Well, then, what's the matter?"

I sighed. You cannot hide things from Rosie. Reluctantly, I told her what I had witnessed of Uncle Wheeler's odd behavior, fearing she'd take it badly.

To my surprise, she merely nodded grimly. "We should have known Pinchfields would try a trick like that. They probably contacted Uncle Wheeler and arranged the whole thing, and when it didn't work out, they sent the wool buyer to pressure him. That's all."

I bit my lip, seeing the sense in her words. "And the gambling?"

Rosie shrugged. "Men gamble. It isn't pretty, but I don't see what it has to do with us."

"I don't know. You didn't see him — he was . . . changed."

"Well, you're a sight to behold yourself, before you've had a cup of tea in the morning, but there's nothing sinister about it." She squeezed my shoulder. "Come on, they want to celebrate. Jack Townley brought a bottle of port. It's hideous stuff, but what can you do? By the way, they think you've found a buyer for the cloth, so you might get to work on that."

I went to smack her on the back of the head, but she was too quick for me.

Despite Rosie's reassurances, I was still uneasy. I had seen something in my uncle that troubled me, and I did not know what to think. In the days after our return, Uncle

Wheeler's absences grew more frequent. At least we knew the reason for those now: If he rode out north on a Friday morning, a peek at the latest broadside revealed a horse race in Trawney; an absence of an evening was likely to be a game of cards at Mrs. Laidlaw's. Since he was as serene and gracious as ever at home, however, I had to agree with Rosie. What our uncle did with his leisure time was his own business. When he returned one evening and presented me with an enamel snuffbox in the shape of a swan, he was in such high spirits that I began to think all was forgotten from the incidents in Harrowgate.

Indeed, why should I let my uncle's behavior cast a pall over the trip? Bolstered by my success with Parmenter's and by Mr. Woodstone's faith in me, I began to research in earnest a plan for the cloth. I thought I had not had such a bad idea, to consider contacting Captain Worthy and the shipping firm of Porter & Byrd; and though I knew my uncle was opposed to the idea, I wrote and sent them swatches of our fabric. I was barred by Guild regulations from selling the cloth wholesale anywhere in the country, but Porter & Byrd would have the export licenses to ship it overseas. And if that did not work out, there were other shipping agents, other small operations scattered about the countryside that I would contact. And if *that* did not work out, I would strap the cloth to my back and hawk it door-to-door like a peddler.

The morning the couriers arrived from Parmenter's to fetch the gold thread, Stirwaters was in fine form, causing a scene that was almost comical — had it happened to someone else. I suppose we were due an incident; we had had nothing truly peculiar happen all summer (the obvious event with Mr. Spinner notwithstanding). Rosie and I had spent an afternoon boxing up the gold thread, exchanging it with the spools of wool thread that we'd had packed for market. Once the crates were stacked and sealed, no one would ever suspect they held anything but ordinary thread.

The courier came by boat, pulling alongside the mill in the low water. A tall man in a linen waistcoat and straw boating hat climbed ashore, followed by a sturdy lad of thirteen or fourteen. "Jim Threadgood, for the House of Parmenter," he said, with a tip of his hat. "I'm here to pick up a shipment."

Rosie was waiting in the attic with the key to Mr. Smith's great lock, but when she fitted it into the keyhole, it would not turn. Her subsequent attempts likewise made no further headway.

"Are you sure that's the right key?" I asked, though there could hardly be any doubt.

But no amount of coaxing (or swearing) could release the lock. After the four of us made good effort, with that key and every other on my ring, Rosie stared at me in desperation, and I sent her after a rasp to file the lock away. Once the lock was freed, the door would *still* not budge, and Mr. Threadgood was starting to look distinctly put-upon.

"I say, what's going on here?" he demanded.

"Oh, that's just the spirit of the mill," Rosie said, gritting her teeth as she pulled on the door, "playing a little joke on us."

"She's not serious," the courier said.

"Of course not," I said soothingly. "Mr. Threadgood, why don't you and your boy head over to the bakehouse next door, on us. They're bound to be serving lunch soon. We'll get this straightened out in no time, I'm sure."

When they had gone, I gave the door a mighty tug. "Open *up*, you great fool thing!"

Rosie squeaked in dismay. "Oh, don't make it angry! We'll never get it open."

"This is absurd," I said. "We've got six hundred pounds worth of gold thread behind there. Fetch Harte and have him bring up an axe. We'll chop down that door if we have to." I gave the latch one last frustrated yank, and to my surprise it sprang open under my hand.

"Ha," Rosie said, staring at the open doorway. "I guess you just need to know how to talk to it."

"Oh, shut up," I said. "Get Mr. Threadgood back up here before it decides to close on us again." And for good measure, I shoved a crate of thread hard against the door and planted myself in the threshold until the courier returned.

The little successes of those days were soon overshadowed by sadness in the village. One hot day in September, little Annie Penny fell into the river behind her father's croft and drowned. It should have been impossible, in that heat with the Stowe so low, but she caught her foot in a tangle of reeds, and was lost by the time anyone missed her.

No great friends of anyone in the village, the Pennys were still "ours," and no one would begrudge their respects to a child. We gathered in the churchyard under a lying sky — bright and cloudless as any May Day — and I thought how unfair it was that Annie's death could go unnoticed by the heavens, which had mourned so over my father's grave. I am certain I shall rot all eternity for it, but for once I was relieved that not all disasters came with Stirwaters looming behind them.

And then I saw Maire Penny staring at me. No one had stepped forward to loan Mrs. Penny any mourning clothes; she was dressed in the same stained frock she wore every day, her two youngest children hanging from her hands. She had wrapped her head and shoulders in a black shawl, but her eyes burned out accusingly. Mr. Penny stood beside her, clutching a bundle of rags I took for handkerchiefs. It was not until I had torn my gaze away from his red and swollen face that I realized the bundle was a limp, faceless doll.

The service was scarcely over, the handsful of earth barely tossed down upon the tiny coffin, before Maire snatched her hands from her children and clutched her gravid belly with a free hand. "You!" she cried at me, her voice hoarse and ragged. "No good has come to this family since my Bill took up with you Stirwaters folk! I begged him to stay away — everyone knows what goes on down there — but two shillings a week were more important than his family. Not that we saw the money — spent it all on drink, he did —"

Mrs. Hopewell slipped her arm around Mrs. Penny's shoulders. "Hush, Maire," she said, "not on Annie's day. . . ."

But Mrs. Penny would not be consoled. "No! I'll say my piece. That mill is a *blight* on this village! It steals children, it breaks up families, and I'm gettin' out of this accursed place afore I got no family left! I don't need your Miller luck touching my lot!"

I stood rooted to my spot, my mouth fairly open with shock. Surely it is a bitter thing to lose one so young, and a little madness is understandable, but her words cut deeply. I could not find the will to quit the churchyard, and at last only I and Bill Penny still lingered.

Bill fell to his knees beside the grave. One hand was balled up at his mouth, as if he hoped to hold in his grief, the other clutched the ragged doll. With a great sobbing breath he dropped the doll into the grave. He mumbled something inaudible, and I finally pulled myself together to depart. This was a private grief, and none of my right to share. But as I started to leave, Bill rose to his feet.

"You stay there, Annie-girl, you hear me?" The words were slurred and anguished, but too impossible to mishear. "Don't you pay us any visits. You bide with Hester and little Billy and don't leave your rest, now. By cloth and bone, so mote it be."

And as I watched, Bill Penny spit into the freshly dug grave of his daughter.

I spun on my heel and fled, a cold sweat down my back, and stumbled headlong into Jon Graves, the undertaker. He had been waiting at a discreet distance for the family to leave, that they should not witness his labors.

"Easy there," he said, catching me gently as I turned my ankle in the dry road.

I mumbled something like "How clumsy of me" as I righted myself.

"It's a sad business," Mr. Graves said.

"It's dreadful." I could not quite pull myself back to the world — that image of Mr. Penny spitting. . . . "People's children oughtn't die." Even I was surprised at the bitterness in my voice.

"Ah, miss," the undertaker said with a sigh, "we all of us die, and only the Reaper knows the appointed hour. 'Tis odd, though — Shearing hasn't had a drowning since Stirwaters were built."

"What?" As unpredictable as the Stowe was, that seemed impossible. "Why not?"

Mr. Graves shrugged and leaned on his spade. "Can't say. Some folks'll tell you it's the tribute the Friendlies pay every year at Shrovetide."

Every village or tradesman's group has a Friendly Society organized for just such a purpose — to pay funeral expenses or carry a hungry family through a lean season. I couldn't see the Pennys among their numbers, though, and I could not stop my next thought: *If they had paid the Friendlies, maybe the river would have spared Annie.*

Mr. Graves continued. "Others'll tell you it's because of what happened the last time — you know, at Stirwaters."

I glanced at him sharply. "I *don't* know. What happened?"

"Ah, miss, it's probably no more than just old village gossip — you know how tales spread. I don't rightly know the details, meself — there weren't a funeral, after all. But there were some kind of trouble during the building, somebody fell into the river, and were drowned. No more than that, miss — so you can stop looking at me like that."

I pulled myself together. "I'm sorry — it's just, I've never heard of this."

"Ah, and you can pay it no mind, then. T'only reason it's remembered at all is for being the last drowning in this village. Till now." Mr. Graves glanced at the churchyard. Mr. Penny had finally left. "I'm sorry, miss. Sad duty calls. But if you're wondering more about it, 'twouldn't surprise me if the mill had some record of it, somewhere. You look there."

I didn't look. I had had enough of drownings, and death, and grief. I wanted to turn to problems I knew and could solve, and let the long dead rest in peace.

We saw little of Bill after that; Stirwaters was all but idle until we could sell the cloth, and there was not much work for him, nor did he show up seeking any. Annie's death had cast a shadow over the last days of summer, and those were grim and quiet days for us all.

When I did not hear back from Porter & Byrd, I wrote half a dozen other shipping agencies, drapers' shops, and haberdashers, but (excepting one dressmaker who ordered two lengths of black cassimere in anticipation of a heavy season for funerals), one by one word came back: *No, thank you.* Or variations on the same: *We bought our cloth at Worm Hill; was there some reason Stirwaters could not sell by normal channels?* &c. It began to look hopeless, and though our next mortgage payment was not due until the turning of the year, I should soon have to consider whether to buy any fall wool; and if I did not buy fall wool, my workers should all go hungry.

I was thus occupied in a miserable circuit of my thoughts one afternoon, and did not look up when Rosie slipped into the office, bearing the post. With a wave of my hand I let her sort through it, and she gave me the catalogue.

"The teasel people seem to think they'd like to be paid," she said, casting one note onto the desk. "Dexter's sent a new price list for dyestuffs, and Mr. Woodstone wants to know if we've lost any more fingers . . . ?"

"What?" My head snapped up and I snatched the letter from Rosie.

"Oh, *now* you care."

Mr. Woodstone's note was brief but merry, asking after our progress and health and reminding us that he was at our service, should we need anything. There was no mention of our debt, but he did note that his father was particularly impressed by Stirwaters's accomplishment, just above the words *Yours faithfully*, and a schoolboy-tidy signature I was becoming familiar with. I found myself flattening out the creases with my fingers, tracing the ink on the page as Rosie prattled on about the remaining post.

"Who do we know in Stowemouth?"

All at once Mr. Woodstone's letter was forgotten. "That's Porter and Byrd," I said quietly, hardly daring to hope. It would surely be another excruciatingly polite refusal.

It was not, although neither was it such a stroke of fortune to turn our fates around in one breath. Mr. Byrd sent his regrets that he was unable to respond sooner, but if our cloth was still available, he was very much interested in pursuing an alliance of our firms.

> *Unfortunately, we did not receive your correspondence in time to arrange a place for your stock among our current shipments, but if you were prepared to wait until after 1 January of the coming year, we anticipate the overseas market then to be more amenable. Further, we are prepared to offer you the prices stated in the accompanying document, as well as a one per cent commission on sales, less a twenty per cent share of all tariffs and customs fees.*

Please respond with all due haste if these terms are agreeable.

"January is a long time off," I said.

"Only three months. And a bit."

"A lot can happen in three months." I glanced over the proposed price list. "And we'd be losing money on some of the stock. We could have done better at Market."

Rosie nodded. "But think of your cloth — *your cloth* — shipped to the far corners of the earth. Laborers in tropical plantations wearing Stirwaters kersey, governors' wives dressed in Stirwaters shalloon."

I bit my lip, and with a heavy hand wrote back my brief reply:

The proposed terms are agreeable. We will hold the stock until the new year.

Yours sincerely,

C. Miller

Chapter Thirteen

That long, strange summer finally drew to a close, and then, as smoothly as if someone had pushed a lever for it, autumn was upon us. The Gold Valley shone in all her amber glory, the trees along the river making a dazzling yellow parade from Blue Corners to Delight. At the end of October, when warm days are fewer than the chill ones, and golden sunshine gives way to grey mist, the Gold Valley celebrated harvest season with a travelling festival that rotated through the villages. Every three or four years, it made its way to Shearing.

Even with a woolshed full of unsold cloth, the merry-making was contagious, and I was determined to put aside my concerns for a few hours. The fair amounted to a market day in Shearing; we might even make a few sales. Get enough cider and music in people — even Gold Valley folk — and they'll do all sorts of unexpected things.

The morning of the fair was brisk, but sunlight promised to burn the cold from the air by noontide. We opened Stirwaters for tours and sales and hosted a cidering in the yard as we'd done in Mam's day. Harte painted a glorious banner on a bad run of white broadcloth and hung striped bunting from the upstairs windows. I took my place by Stirwaters's doors, while Rosie showed off the millworks to visitors. Pilot sat at my knee, scrutinizing the folk who entered her demesne, and I trailed my fingers in the feathers of her sharp ears. She was curiously silent that morning, almost smug, so I was not expecting to hear a low, cheerful voice say right in my ear, "Shall I take the penny tour?"

I looked up to see Randall Woodstone, of all people, standing at my elbow. I noticed that he had cut his hair; the soft fall of bronze had been trimmed away to the clean style we favored in the country. It made his eyes stand out very brightly in his tanned face.

"Mr. Woodstone!" I said cleverly, but if my cheeks were red it was only because of the cool morning air. "Come to check on us?"

"I hear this is the place to be this weekend." He dipped a hand into his pocket. "Charging for tours, I see? That seems a very sound business practice. Your uncle's idea?"

I grinned. "Rosie's, actually; the girl is a mercenary. Put your money away, sir. You know perfectly well you're welcome at Stirwaters any time."

"As your banker, I must advise against that. You should take any income available." He was still smiling, and I let him lay the coin in my palm.

"Well," I countered, "it seems rather foolish to take your money when I'll just turn around and pay it right back to you. So, here." And I put the penny right back in his hand, a cheeky grin on my own face. I was behaving with appalling forwardness, but somehow I couldn't check myself. Fair weather.

He looked at the coin for a moment before turning his grin on me again. "Well," he said. "Since I have just come into some money, won't you let me buy you some cider? I hear it's the best in the village."

I glanced back to see Rosie watching us, leaning against the wall in her dress of apple red, a matching specimen of that fruit at her mouth. She gave me a significant look and then turned away. Oh, why not? Rosie could greet for a while; anyone who worked for us could give tours. I was going to let a young man buy me cider.

Later, facing each other across a makeshift table of planks and barrels, we toasted the day with ancient wooden mugs.

"Careful." I laughed as he took a deep draught from his mug. "That's the good stuff. Trawney's best, straight from the orchards. It'll go right to your head, Mr. Woodstone."

He set the mug down heavily, but the look in his eyes was very clear. "Charlotte Miller," he said gravely, "I have asked you *repeatedly* to call me Randall. Now I'm afraid I'll have to insist upon it."

I widened my eyes. "Well," I said, "if you *insist* upon it, very well." I was laughing a little, but he was serious.

"Let me hear you say it."

"All right," I said quietly. "Randall. *Randall*. Is that better?"

The smile had returned, brighter than ever. He reached across the table and took my hand. "It's perfect."

I stared at my hand in his, aware that my heart was beating awfully fast, and I stood up abruptly. "Come," I said, forcing the merriment back into my voice. "I believe I owe you a tour."

"Where are we going?" he asked, and Rosie would be proud: I laughed at him.

"I thought you came to see the fair." And, of all the cheekiness, I lifted his half-empty mug to my lips and drained the contents before spinning off into the festival crowd, my banker at my heels.

I don't think I'd ever seen the harvest fair in quite the same light as that day with Randall. All the familiar sights seemed new to me, from the sheep-judging to Mrs. Carter's pickle stand, the children's games and the church raffle. Randall threw himself into the spirit, signing up to guess the bullock's weight and compete in target practice at the shooting stall. I must confess he showed up rather nicely; Edward Handy is generally considered Shearing's best shooter, but Randall beat him twice out of three.

"By the gods, man!" Edward bellowed after the third round, clapping Randall on the back with his meaty fist. "You must come for the pheasants in November!" He looked at me appraisingly. "Your family wouldn't go hungry with a gun in those hands. Cider here! Cider all round for the man who beat me — and his lady." Here he winked at me — a man I've known all my life!

"But we're not —" I started to protest. Randall caught my hand and laughed.

"Best to just go with it," he said under his breath. "You know how these country crowds can get out of hand." So we had another around of cider, this time with our neighbors, and just for good measure, I threw in one of Mrs. Carter's famous pickles for Randall.

Afterward, breathless and still laughing, we left the crowds and walked along the ridge of the river. I stopped to lean against a tall poplar. The world was spinning just slightly, and I had to catch my breath.

"I say, are people around here always so friendly?" Randall said.

"Village life," I said. "You're indelibly linked to Stirwaters now."

"Ah. Shall I check my coat for black marks?" He grinned, but I shook my head.

"No, indeed. I shall not be held accountable for any misfortunes you suffer as a result of your association with Stirwaters. Let it be said now."

He frowned, a furrow appearing between the sandy brows. "Come again, then?"

"Oh, haven't you heard? Well, let me give you the full accounting. The winter after Stirwaters was built, the river upstream changed course. A landslide diverted the water through flatter land, dispersing much of the water's power." I clapped my hands together sharply. "Just like that. Overnight, this little bend in the Stowe became an impractical site for a mill, and Harlan Miller became first in a long line of hard-luck Millers."

"Oh, come now! That sort of thing could happen to anyone."

I smiled grimly. "That sort of thing happens to the Millers with regularity. Once there was an epidemic that killed almost all the sheep in the Valley, and another year there were floods all summer so the wheel couldn't turn. Believe me, your mortgage is no more unsettling than any other catastrophe Stirwaters has weathered."

He turned his gaze to me from the river, and something flashed in those changing-color eyes. "But you've got something those other Millers never had."

"Oh? And what's that?"

"You've got me."

My mouth fell open, but I had to laugh. "Are you going to change my luck, then, Mr. Woodstone?"

He looked me straight in the eye. "Miss Miller, you may count on it." Before I realized it, he had slipped his hand behind my waist. Nothing more — he held it there, barely touching me. I held my breath for two or three heartbeats before speaking.

"What is that for?" I said, my voice surprisingly steady.

He smiled slightly. "I wanted to see if I'd like it."

"And?"

He leaned in. "I like it." And that smiling mouth was suddenly upon my own, kissing me, one of those ink-stained fingers tipping my chin up to meet him. I've no idea what I did; surprise overwhelmed me, and I only remember the feel of his lips against my mouth and the sweet cidery taste of him.

He turned away after the briefest moment and stared out over the river. I said nothing, listening to the blood roar in my ears.

"Charlotte," he said after a long, long moment.

"Randall," I whispered.

The golden sunlight bounced off the water, and the crisp breeze carried the sounds and scents of the festival to us. Very aware that his hand was still on my waist, I couldn't move. I wasn't sure I wanted to.

"There's a lot about this village to like," he said softly. "I think there might be enough to make me stay here." And I could think of nothing at all to say to that.

"Did we see everything?" he asked suddenly, his voice returning to normal.

"What?" The word flew out of me, louder and sharper than I'd intended.

"Is there more to the fair? Did we see everything?"

I let my breath out in a long rush. "No," I answered slowly, grappling for self-control. "No, there's much more. The food stalls, and a church blessing — but that's tomorrow — oh, and the round dances."

Slowly he slipped his hand away from my back. "Then shall we continue?"

I threw up my hands. "Oh, why stop now?" I said, and if I'd known what was coming later that night, I *might* have said that with considerably less tartness. I might have.

The rest of that mad afternoon passed in a confusion of revelry and absolute stone-faced ordinariness from Randall. He said nothing at all about the scene on the river bank — no word about his bold touch, certainly nothing about the kiss. Perhaps he routinely kissed young ladies by the riverbank, and I was to think nothing of it. By the time we'd collected his winnings from the bullock's stall (a bag of apples and a voucher from the butcher's), I had resolved to do just that.

We sat together at dinner, with no less than a friendly distance between us. His mood at least served to steady my own nerves, and I managed not to spill stew on myself and kept up my end of the conversation with dignity.

"How do you suppose Rosie's getting along at the mill?" he asked, mopping up broth with a hunk of brown bread.

"Good heavens, I'd forgotten all about her!" I said.

Randall's eyes widened. "That must be a first."

"Are you deliberately distracting me?"

"Is it working?"

I glared at him. I wanted him to know I was not some silly country maid, to be seduced with one stolen kiss. "Hardly," I said, in what I hoped passed for dignified tones. "In fact, I must be getting back now. Thank you for an . . . entertaining afternoon, Mr. Woodstone." I pulled my feet free of the bench and turned away. He caught my hand.

"Charlotte, don't —" he said. "It's been a lovely day. Let's not spoil it. I'm sorry."

"Just what are you sorry for?" I said, pulling free from his grip.

He rubbed his hand with the other and looked at me. "I — I'm not sure, exactly." He sounded so helpless and forlorn that I burst out laughing.

"Oh, come on. The round dances are starting, and you don't want to miss those."

Randall was a fine dancer, certainly better than I, but that wasn't surprising, with his rich city upbringing. Moreover, he was fun. He passed between partners with cheerful ease, handing each girl off to the next man with a laugh and a smile. I must admit to paying him rather more attention than I ought; I wound up treading on Edward Handy's foot, missing a turn, and nearly colliding with Josie Hale and Robbie Lawson. Finally, I gave up and excused myself, retreating to the edge of the stage to watch. But Randall saw me and bowed out, too, handing off his partner to mine as the music started up again. He was flushed and breathless, and for some reason that made my heart falter in its rhythm.

Night had fallen, the chill returned. I wrapped my arms

round my chest and noted that Randall made no overtures to assist me. I told myself I was glad of it, and concentrated on watching the dancers.

"I heard a rumor on the dance floor," he said.

I looked at him sharply. "Oh?"

"Oh, yes." He sounded very serious, but there was a playful gleam in his eye. "Nora Butcher told me that Robbie Lawson is going to marry the apothecary's daughter."

"That's Josie." I pointed her out. "She's the village beauty. Every lad in Shearing has wooed Josie Hale at one time or another." Miss Hale was at that moment dancing with our Harte, her dimpled cheeks pink with exertion, her dark hair falling loose from its pinnings. Mine was as well, for that matter, but Josie made it look like an asset.

"And," Randall continued, "Mrs. Butcher also says that Prudence Sharp only won the mince pie ribbon because she adds laudanum to her sauce."

"My goodness, you're learning everything tonight."

He leaned back and examined his fingernails. "I also heard that a certain foreign-bred banker has designs on one of the miller's daughters."

"Oh, well," I said lightly, "you can't believe everything you hear."

And then I looked at him, and all levity fell away. Randall watched me, finally serious for the first time in that long, long day together. I took a step back. He grabbed my hands. "Charlotte, let's do it. Let's get married."

Had I heard him right? I pulled my hands away and gripped the railing behind me. Married? Could he mean it?

But as I looked at him in his fine brown country suit, his city hair trimmed away, the relaxed way he leaned against the fence — even *now*, of all moments! — suddenly, it didn't seem like such a strange idea. He was a good man: kind, reliable. He came from a well-set family and had secure employment. I wasn't likely to find a better prospect among the men in Shearing; in fact, I'd never dreamed of making so good a match. Marrying Randall Woodstone could solve so many problems. This was the opportunity of a lifetime. I was not so foolish as to pass it up.

I met his eyes at last, to see him watching me, gently, with his clear, easy gaze. It was a nice face, one I could be happy looking into every day.

"All right."

He swept his arms around me and lifted me bodily off the ground, my heart beating frantically against his chest. How long he held me like that, I cannot say, but I think one song ended and the next began, and before long, the dancing brought Rosie round to us. With the barest glance at the expression on my face, she abandoned her partner and joined us at the gate.

"You look like you've swallowed a live fish," she said. "Where on Earth have you two been today?"

"Your sister is going to marry me," Randall said, his voice thick with emotion behind the grin. Rosie let out an absolutely unrestrained whoop of delight.

"Never!" she said, and fairly jumped into his arms. I had to drag her off him; she was beating him on the back with her fists. She fell back and, hands on her hips, she looked him over appraisingly, as if she'd never seen him before.

"When?" she demanded. "When did all this happen? Oh, I don't care!" Whereupon she smacked poor Randall once again, hard on the shoulder. "I've always wanted a brother.

I can't imagine one I'd like more than you. Oh!" she cried. "I must tell *everyone!* Can I tell everyone?"

Randall and I stood there, grinning like fools. "I suppose so," I said, and before I could say another word, Rosie had kissed him on the cheek and dashed off across the dance floor. I thought for a moment she would interrupt the dancing and make a very public announcement, but we were spared that. She stopped and whispered something to Rachel Baker, who turned to stare at us, grinned, and ran off the stage.

"Rosie," I said, smiling and shaking my head. I looked at Randall. Smiling still, I crept in closer to him, and he put his arm around my shoulders. His arm tightened around me. It was nice; I found I liked it very much.

"Are you quite sure you don't have a brother at home for Rosie?" I sighed, laying my head back against his shoulder.

"Rosie's well taken care of already, Charlotte." He pulled his arm free and pointed across the stage, to where Rosie was deep in conversation with Harte. Their matching golden heads were pulled close together, a slow smile spreading across his broad face, her cheeks flaming red. Of course . . . Rosie and Harte. How could I have missed it? My heart felt altogether too full, as if it would burst should anything else wonderful happen that night.

"Oh!" I said, a little helplessly. "Oh! Oh!"

Randall pulled me in tighter, and kissed me again.

Chapter Fourteen

I *didn't* sleep at all that night, and no wonder, I suppose. The festival mood had evaporated, leaving the old cautious Charlotte in its wake. How could I marry Randall Woodstone? I barely knew the man; he certainly did not know me, and I was sure he would not want to. And furthermore, he lived in Harrowgate! I hadn't been thinking clearly — somehow I had overlooked the fact that the moment we were married, Randall Woodstone would sweep me away from Shearing and Stirwaters and everything that meant anything to me.

Whatever the morning brought, I would have to seek out Mr. Woodstone . . . and go back on my word. A new pain stabbed through my breast, and I told myself it was only the inconceivable thought of a Miller breaking a bargain.

Morning finally dawned, exactly as yesterday had not been: damp and drear, a heavy fog down across the valley floor. Rosie woke at last, and the smile she gave me almost undid me. Well, if I were going to tell Mr. Woodstone I couldn't marry him, it certainly couldn't go any worse than telling my sister.

I broke the news as she did up my stays, and in her shock she gave the laces a yank that almost cut off the blood supply to my head.

"Have you lost your mind?" She gave the laces another mighty heave and tied them off. "You must have. Are you running a fever?"

I sat on the edge of the bed. "No, but I think I must have been yesterday."

"No. No. I will not have this! For once in your life you made a quick decision — and it was the right one, for pity's sake. I will *not* let you talk yourself out of this!" But she looked more sad than angry — a red, wilted version of herself as she fought to hold back tears. I drew her down beside me and put my arm around her.

"Hush, love," I said. "It's for the best. It wouldn't work."

She hugged me back, but whispered, "It *would* have worked. That's what scares you."

Dressed at last, I came downstairs and bypassed even the thought of tea, certain that any small delay might just finish me off. Say thanks for small blessings — Uncle Wheeler was nowhere to be seen. I practiced my lines in my head, kept my composure as best I could, and stepped out into the cold foggy morning.

And nearly ran headlong into Randall.

He was coming up the walk, in an ash-grey suit, and of course I didn't see him in the fog. But he saw me, in my bright flash of russet against the Millhouse, and bounded toward me. Before I could react, he caught me up in his arms and kissed me. I was breathless when he finally let me go.

"Good morning," he said. "Did you sleep well? I haven't slept at all. You wouldn't believe — well, never mind. Here." And he held out a small parcel, crudely wrapped in tissue and twine.

"What's this?"

That little lopsided grin made its return, turning my insides to jelly. Curse that Randall Woodstone.

"Well, apparently, word got out that I had dared ask for the hand of the prized Charlotte Miller — without a ring! Oh, let me tell you, Charlotte, your neighbors are *fearsome* when they put their minds to it! I hardly escaped with my skin."

I couldn't smile back. I was trying to, but I just couldn't make my face obey me.

"Anyway, they'd have driven me straight out of town if I hadn't promised to beg your forgiveness with at least some token of my affection. Unfortunately, my mother's engagement ring is on my sister Rebecca's finger, and, well, Shearing has no jeweller."

"You noticed that?" Wherever did I find my voice — and for such a comment?

He gave a little laugh. "Well, yes. However! It was my great good fortune that there is a fair going on at the moment, and I was able to find you something among the goods both exotic and mundane." He pushed the little parcel toward me, and somehow I found myself reaching out and accepting it — just when I had sworn to myself I would break it off.

It was nothing more than a dish of plainware pottery, a simple decoration round the rim. In its center was a crude transfer of a watermill, and around the edge was a motto: GREAT COURAGE BREAKS ILL LUCK, it read, and I know right then my heart just stopped beating altogether.

Very quietly, Randall said, "Will that do?"

Great courage breaks ill luck. What else could I do? I nodded.

He tried to find that ever-present smile of his, but seemed to have some trouble with it. I wanted to reach out my hand and touch my fingers to his lips — wanted to in the most painful way — but I kept tight hold of the little dish. And then Randall's arms were around me again, squeezing all the air from my lungs. I held him back, still clutching tight to the tissue and my dish, and it was a long, long moment before I realized that his face pressed tight against my shoulder was just a little damp.

The weather that day remained dismal, as if to remind us that joy is transitory, and the lot for folk in Shearing is ever one of misery and gloom. Those suffering the aftereffects of too much autumn revelry found it particularly lamentable, and spared no effort sharing this revelation with their neighbors. The visiting merchants packed up early and quit town, as did the upcountry fair-goers, and the festival market collapsed with a damp sigh.

It seemed Randall's proposal was not the only excitement witnessed in Shearing overnight. A brawl had broken out over a game of darts at Drover's and turned into a riot that spread into the street, causing the literal collapse of one rented market stall and several pounds' damage to the stock (crockery or fruit; it was not agreed upon). Three people were held in expectation of the magistrate's arrival, and I was not surprised to hear Bill Penny and Peg Eagan named in the account.

At midday, we gathered in the churchyard for the village blessing, a soggy and cheerless lot — all excepting my betrothed, who held me in a grip as if he were afraid to let me go, and chattered on endlessly, his eyes bright and animated.

He held fast to me all through Mr. Hopewell's rather lackluster benediction, and afterward insisted on joining the crowd in stacking wood for the bonfire.

"This is an old village tradition," I explained to Randall, to stave off any questions. "We always burn a bonfire from All Hallows' Eve through All Souls' Day."

"A light, to guide the year's departed to their rest."

I looked up sharply, a damp stick poking into my palm. "I never heard that."

Randall nodded, his gaze somewhere up in the hills. "This weather isn't looking good, though. They'll never get the fire going in this rain."

I looked across the churchyard, to where the heavy sky glowered over the still-white headstone of my father, and the new green grass of Annie Penny's grave. I broke my sticks and cast them onto the heap. "It's all foolishness, anyway," I said.

Back at the Millhouse, I shook the rain from my cloak and hung it to dry before the kitchen fire. As I arranged its folds, I noticed that the shoulder, where I had spent the day pressed against Randall's side, was still dry. I touched it gently, lifted it to my face and breathed in deeply, but nothing lingered there except the scent of damp wool. I sighed and let the cloth drop.

I found tea brewing over the fire and the post laid out on the table; I carried both into the parlor. Uncle Wheeler sat at my mother's desk, the very picture of silvered elegance: one lean leg tucked artfully behind the other, arm raised in the act of dipping a quill into an inkwell.

"Well," he said. "And where have we been this fine day, miss?" There was a quality in his voice I did not quite recognize.

"It was the vicar's blessing, sir. The whole village was there."

"Ah, yes. And was Mr. Woodstone there?"

I set my tea down unsteadily. Rumor runs on quick little feet in Shearing, but I had not expected it to reach those particular ears so soon. "Why do you ask?"

"You know perfectly well why. Coyness may be a virtue during courtship, but I do expect frankness at home."

Well, I should have to tell him eventually; it was not as if I could suddenly appear with husband in tow and expect it to go unnoticed. "Very well," I said. "Yes, Mr. Woodstone was there. I've decided to marry him."

He turned his cold gaze on me. His face had gone positively scarlet, even beneath all that powder. "You've decided?" he said, so faintly I could scarcely hear him. "*You've* decided? And who do you think you are?"

I fumbled for words. "It's a good match —"

"It is preposterous. You? Marry a *banker*? Look at yourself! Your shabby little shopgirl look may serve you well in Shearing, but out in the world everyone will see you for what you are: a fortune-hunting orphan! You'll ruin your reputation. I won't allow it." He shoved himself away from the desk.

Suddenly, I understood. "All your grand talk of high society and ambition for me and Rosie — it was all lies? You mustn't aim too high, Charlotte — a husband called Smith or Butcher is plenty good enough for *you*." I was trembling, anger closing my throat.

He made no reply, just skirted the room in a stream of

spring green damask, his gilded heels soundless on the rug. As he paced, I watched him will away the flash of fury that had betrayed his feelings, don his usual calm like slipping into a new coat.

He came to me and took my ink-stained fingers in his fine soft ones, holding my hands gently. "My dear, I am only thinking of your happiness. Of course I want you to marry well. But the most successful matches — like your parents' — are equal ones. I've no doubt your Mr. Woodstone thinks he is doing you a grand favor. But think of it — how will you feel among his family, his friends? No, my dear, it's been my experience that such unbalanced matches seldom end up happy."

He gave my hands a squeeze, and I swallowed hard. I knew how right he was. About all of it.

But I had also glimpsed behind his mask. No amount of powder or perfume could hide it from me now. Speak what he would about my happiness, something else about Randall's proposal bothered him.

Still, my uncle's comments, like burning nettles, were not easily brushed off. Who was I to aspire to such a match as Randall Woodstone? I was still brooding the next morning when Randall called for me at the Millhouse. Somehow he had learned we never use the front door, and gave the kitchen door a hearty rap that had Rachel springing to open it long before I could pull myself up from the table.

"Mr. Woodstone!" Rachel turned to me and winked. "Come in out of the damp and get yourself some coffee."

I looked round the kitchen in dismay. Our mismatched dishes lay scattered on the butcher block, and the chimney had taken upon itself to smoke that morning. I couldn't bear Randall to see me here. I scurried to the door and dragged my cloak off the hook.

"That's a tempting offer," Randall was saying, "but I've come to take Charlotte walking." Whereupon he offered me his arm, and I slipped out beside him.

Randall led me through the village, past Drover's, and up the long road leading out of town. It was an awful morning for a walk, chill and damp and windy, and I huddled in my cloak, while Randall tried to keep his arm around me.

"You're awfully quiet this morning," he said as we passed the remnants of the festival market and started up the long hill. "What's on that mind of yours?"

I sighed and looked at his fingers, twined in mine. "What are we doing, here?"

He regarded me with some surprise. "I thought we were walking. But that isn't what you mean, is it?"

"How is this going to work?" I cast my hand in a vague circle, meant to encompass Randall, me, the village . . . and I know not what else. "This — marriage, I mean."

He looked at me gravely. "Well, first we'll stand before the vicar, and you will say, 'I do,' and then I will say, 'I do,' and then we'll live happily ever after."

"Be serious. *Where* will we live? What about Stirwaters, and Rosie?"

"Charlotte." He pulled me toward him until my face was in the hollow of his throat and I had to tip my head back to see him. "I expect Rosie will sort herself out just fine. And as for the rest of it? I don't have any intention of changing anything.

You have your work, I have mine, and it's a very great pity that they are not conveniently located to one another, but we will work around that. And as for where we'll live, well, I *do* have a suggestion about that." And he turned me bodily, until I stared up the hill to the ivy-bedecked walls of Woolhampton Grange, Shearing's only grand house, which had stood empty for years.

"I've taken it to let, but I thought it had better get your approval first. It's all a bit dusty and grim, but there's a view of the mill you will not believe."

I looked from the mansion to Randall and was momentarily speechless. "You mean I won't have to leave Stirwaters?" I finally managed.

"Never. I want that house filled to bursting with fat, noisy Miller-Woodstone children."

And at that moment, even with the icy wind whipping us to the bone, I could almost believe it was possible.

"What about the mortgage?"

He looked at me quizzically. "What about it? My records indicate that Stirwaters still owes more than twelve hundred pounds."

I nodded, wary. Randall burst out laughing and kissed me on the forehead. "Truly, Miss Fretsome, if I'd thought for a moment you'd let me pay it off, I'd have done it already. But I'm no idiot. Besides, I'm going to need every farthing to maintain you in the fashion to which you've become accustomed."

I had to laugh. "Oh? Do you think your salary will cover patching my shoes and darning my stockings?"

"If we budget carefully, just." He pulled me closer and whispered into my hair. "I want you to wife, Charlotte. On whatever terms you're comfortable with." Grinning, he squeezed my hand and set off up the hill, with me in tow. "Come on, let's see what this grand old lady has in store for us."

Randall stayed in town the rest of that week, putting our new affairs in order and setting the long-empty Grange to rights. Some days I would join him, wandering through the cavernous halls and trying to imagine myself living there. Even magic-spun gold seemed easier to believe sometimes. But then I would stand in the dining room and look down upon the village, to where Stirwaters sat in the misty distance like something out of a picture, and it was hard to decide which was the more eldritch realm.

Randall often joined us for dinner at the Millhouse that week, and my uncle's opinion of him seemed only to improve, though it was still difficult to tell if he had changed his mind about the match. I found myself watching them both during those meals, trying to catch another glimpse behind my uncle's powdered mask, but the candlelight, conversation, and rich food disguised him well.

One afternoon I was coming downstairs from changing when I heard a snatch of conversation coming from the parlor.

"My dear boy, I do hope you plan to talk some sense into your wife. Perhaps once you're married she'll give up this ridiculous attachment to the mill."

I froze, my hand halfway to the parlor door.

"Oh, I doubt that, sir." That was Randall's voice, and then a pause — I imagined him lifting a glass of brandy to his lips. "I think you underestimate her."

"I'm sure you'll find a way to manage her. Come now, you can't mean to burden yourself with that old pile of stones! It's a money pit, my good man — she'll bankrupt you with it. But you could make a tidy sum if you sold it."

"You think so?" Randall said. "I'd like to hear more about this plan of yours."

I drew back, my breath quickening. At that moment, a voice said, directly at my shoulder: "Those who listen at doorways never hear anything good."

Rachel gave my shoulder a friendly push and winked at me. "Get in there, then. I shouldn't keep that one waiting, if I were you." And, to leave me no choice in the matter, she reached over my head and pushed the parlor door open.

"Miss Charlotte, sir," she said, in her very best dutiful-servant voice.

Randall and Uncle Wheeler stood together by the fireplace, the flickering flames casting them into devilish red shadows. I could not read the expression in Randall's eyes; my uncle had his gentleman's mask firmly set. I looked from one to the other, wanting them to finish their conversation, baldly discuss my future there with me present.

My uncle set his glass down with a clink. "Charlotte, honestly. Do you mean to stand there gawp-mouthed and staring all evening? Mr. Woodstone will think you were raised by rustics." He turned to Randall. "I do hope you find her easier to manage than I have. I've found her quite uncontrollable."

Randall only smiled.

We passed the rest of our wait for dinner in an awkward silence. Randall kept trying to get close to me, but, still nervous and uncertain about what I had overheard, I pulled away from him, until at last we were off in the corner by the secretary. My uncle gave us a pointed glance, so Randall squeezed my hand and slipped away to a more seemly distance. I did not squeeze back.

I thought how different this meeting ought to be — how friendly it would have been if my father had been here, instead of my uncle. More scattered and haphazard, perhaps — Father seated on the floor amid a flurry of papers, detailing some scheme for Randall; Rosie and I tripping over one another in an effort to scrape together something edible; the sound of laughter and cheer throughout the Millhouse. If I closed my eyes, could I bring those visions to life?

I did not. My gaze fell instead on my mother's desk — free now of dust and finger-smudges. Only a corner of paper peeking out from behind the drop-front showed anything amiss. I automatically reached for the door to straighten the paper. It was a letter, scribed in Uncle Wheeler's violet ink. But the hand was different — strained, somehow, not his habitual florid sweep of ink across the page.

Glancing cautiously toward my uncle — whose face was turned resolutely to the fire — I reached back into the desk and drew the paper toward me. I heard a cough, and started. Randall, his eyes firmly on mine for a moment, leaned in toward my uncle.

"I say, Wheeler, you must have some opinion on the new filly at Crossbridge."

Uncle Wheeler was examining his brandy in the firelight. I held tight to the door of the desk as he launched into a detailed analysis of the horse's faults and virtues. Randall shifted casually, until to face him Uncle Wheeler must have his back to me.

I stared at Randall — that must have been deliberate, hadn't it? Hastily, I read:

Sparrow — by God, where are you? I have been up and down the countryside looking for you — to the Flats, to Stowemouth — even Yellowly! If you think this fox-and-hound game amusing, I assure you I take no such pleasure in it! I told you I would come back for you — your brother couldn't keep me away from you forever. But perhaps you've forgotten me. Perhaps you've foresworn our love. Perhaps I was only a springtime amusement after all. ~~When I left Ward —~~

It stopped, as if the writer had been interrupted. My heart lurched guiltily — I was trespassing on something private here — but I could not draw my gaze away. Was it possible that this note had been written by my own Uncle Wheeler? That last was smudged out, in a great angry blot like a bruise, but eventually I made out the word: Wardensgate.

"I don't know, sir, I think she'll surprise us all," Randall said — a bit too loudly. My eyes flew toward him, and I saw that my uncle was turning. I had only time to slide the page back into the desk and lift the lid closed once more.

As we adjourned for dinner, Randall drew me aside. "I say, what was all that business in there?" He sounded merely curious, amused. I managed to smile.

"What would you say if I told you I was reading my uncle's love letters?"

His eyes flew wide and he suppressed a laugh. "I'd say you're starved for romantic correspondence of your own, Miss

Miller, and I must remedy that." He swept his arm round my waist and kissed me briefly.

"Have you ever heard of a town called Wardensgate?" I said when he let me go. "I think my uncle may have lived there for a while, before he came here."

He frowned. "I've heard of it — but, Charlotte, it's not a town. It's the debtors' prison."

Chapter Fifteen

My wedding day dawned bright and chill, a fairy-frost dusting the hills and woods and turning the village road to silver. In my suit of cornflower blue plush, and clutching my nosegay of orange blossom, I was escorted through the village by a gay procession of my neighbors, determined to subject me to the full battery of Gold Valley superstitions: a sprig of ivy in my hair, sixpence in my shoe, a layer of linen gauze veiling my face, ushered round the church three times sunwise before being allowed at last to enter (left foot first). I was breathless and half-frozen by the time I wrestled the veil from my bonnet and collapsed into the pew beside Randall.

The ceremony was brief and tender. We rose between the benediction and the sermon to declare ourselves. I had a moment's panic when I uttered the words, "and all my worldly goods I thee endow," but Randall, while promising to love and cherish me, encircled my waist with his arms, and I felt a strange sort of easy peace, as if the Valley had given a great restful sigh. I sank back down into the pew, Randall's hand warm in my gloved one, and marvelled that my life could be so altered in no more than ten minutes' time.

Afterward we adjourned to the Millhouse for as lavish a wedding breakfast as Uncle Wheeler could arrange.

Randall's eldest sister, Rebecca, a cheerful, matronly woman who trailed her daughters behind her like ducklings, directed the affair with a brisk and competent air that even my uncle was forced to respect. Randall's nieces were sweet, stair-step girls who smiled shyly and called me "Aunt Charlotte" from the start.

I was torn away from my new family by the tidal force of my neighbors, laughing, kissing, and offering me their congratulations. I embraced Mercy Fuller and three young Fullers, all bedecked in their Sunday finery, and was seized in a massive bear hug by Jack Townley, who lifted me bodily from the floor.

As I shifted my hat back into position, I turned and came face to face with my uncle, who was dressed to fit the morning in ivory damask and an abundance of lace. "Well, Charlotte," he said in his lazy voice, "I trust you'll forget all about us here, now that you've caught yourself your banker husband."

I blinked, unable to tell if he was joking. But I just smiled and said, "Oh, trust me, Uncle, I shall *never* forget you." Impulsively, I embraced him. "Thank you, for all of this. It's lovely, truly."

I drew back and he smoothed out his coat and sleeves. "It's nothing," he said. "It's only my duty, after all."

As he slipped away into the crowd I wondered again about the letter I had read. Had Uncle Wheeler been in debtors' prison? The image I had — of drafty dungeons populated by beggars in rags and ill-fed vermin — did not reconcile with this powdered gentleman of refined manners and scornful disdain for modest living. Randall had me half-convinced I must have read it wrong. Surely it had said Warfield, or Woolston, or any of half a dozen things. And if it had said Wardensgate, that did not mean Uncle Wheeler had been an inmate there. Rosie, suspicions aroused, had gone back to check one night when our uncle was absent from the Millhouse, but had found nothing at all in Mam's desk but an empty ink pot.

As I was pondering these matters, Randall crept up behind me and caught me round the waist. I gave a squeak of surprise as he spun me in his arms and kissed me, in a fashion not at all seemly for a married couple in public. I felt my head swim, and pulled back, breathless. He was looking very much the country gentleman this morning, in a coat of dove grey, the selfsame ivy-and-orange pinned to his collar. I reached up to straighten the posy, and he regarded me solemnly.

"Charlotte," he said, his eyes searching my face for something. "Are you happy?"

I caught a glimpse of my uncle in the corner of the parlor, holding a glass of wine before him like a shield, and felt my face crack with the strain of smiling all morning. I clasped my new husband round his neck. "Yes," I said. "Oh, yes."

After much disentangling of ourselves from embraces and congratulations, we finally managed to quit town near sunset. Randall's father had sent an extravagant wedding gift: a glossy black carriage and two equally glossy black carriage horses, christened Blithe and Bonny by one of Randall's nieces. The thing had Uncle Wheeler positively in raptures. He examined every inch of the trap, extolling the virtues of the perfectly matched horses, the finely balanced axle.

"I say, you do know your way about a carriage," Randall

said, giving Blithe's (or perhaps Bonny's) neck a friendly thump.

Uncle Wheeler slipped out from beneath the trap's polished undercarriage. His coat sleeves were shoved back, his wig askew, and he was almost smiling. "Yes, well." He took a moment to brush down his cuffs and melt back into his statuesque self. "Harness racing. The sport of kings."

Whatever Randall said in response to that was obscured by Rosie grabbing me and hugging fiercely, as if afraid to let go. She pulled back at last, beaming. Suddenly, urgently, I wanted the world to share what I was feeling.

"I'm going to make Harte foreman," I said, although it fell well short of all I really wished at that moment. But Rosie's smile grew even wider, so it was enough.

At last, our luggage loaded aboard the trap and our well-wishers growing weary, Uncle Wheeler took my hand and helped me alight beside Randall. "My dear." He nodded slightly. "Woodstone, I wish you well of her. Good day."

We took our honeymoon in Delight, a spa town in a part of the Valley known for its mineral waters. Alternatives were suggested — Harrowgate, the coast, even overseas — but Randall would have none of it.

"What?" he cried, scandalized. "Be the only man in Shearing who didn't take his bride for a honeymoon in Delight? No, madam. I have my pride."

So it was Delight or nowhere, and I must admit that I was not sorry to share the little pleasures of that lovely village with my worldly husband. Although I did point out that even the innumerable charms of Delight would be long exhausted by the end of our fortnight, he merely laughed and said I didn't understand the purpose of a honeymoon.

And, indeed, he was quite convincing about that; and all I shall record here is that we missed both breakfast and the luncheon buffet at the hotel our first day, and that I came to understand why so many young wives produce children three-quarters of a year after their weddings.

There are three things to do in Delight in winter: take the waters, sit in the Gallery at the Baths after having taken the waters, and shop. Even despite my looming mortgage payment, I let Randall convince me to release my tight grasp on a few pennies, here and there: the mantua-maker's shop, where I was measured for what seemed a whole new wardrobe; the staymaker's, where I was laced into my first new corset in years. I told myself I was spending household money now, and that I had a right to a share of it, but even so, it was a strain. Still, there is something to be said for shoes whose soles are still unpatched, skirts whose hems have not yet been stepped on or splashed with wool wash.

One afternoon we stopped in a fancy-goods shop to buy needlework supplies for Randall's sisters, and as Randall bent over a case of pretty little sewing tools, I drifted away to the display of threads on the far wall of the shop. Fine-spun crewel wool hung in a rainbow of hanks beside a row of silk floss in every hue. I put my fingers up to brush a skein of mazareen blue, but my hand stilled in midair.

There near the window, in obvious pride of place, wound about with their yellow monogrammed House of Parmenter labels, were a dozen or more glittering skeins of golden thread. I didn't need to look to appreciate their depth of color, their perfect sheen. I did not need to touch to know the weight and feel of that gleaming thread. I remembered Nathan Smith's reluctance last summer to touch the charmed gold. I understood it, now.

"My, that's pretty," Randall said, coming up behind me. "Emily will love this, Charlotte; don't you think?"

And what could I possibly do then but smile as my husband bought a dozen skeins?

Later that evening, Randall drew me aside before dinner and slipped an arm round my waist.

"What's this?" I said.

Randall stroked the blue plush collar of my wedding ensemble, which I had been wearing almost every night to dinner, it being my finest gown by unquantifiable yardage.

"Close your eyes." I felt him fasten something to my bodice, and when he lifted my fingers to his lips and bade me open my eyes — I gasped. Pinned to my collar, just above my heart, was a lovely brooch of shining red enamel, hanging from a bar of gold like a jewelled cherry. My fingers trembled as I touched the gold scrollwork border, the engraved forget-me-nots, the glitter of a garnet at each floral heart. "But why?"

He cocked his head at me, changing-color eyes gone blue in the dusky light. "Why not? The man in the shop told me garnets are good luck. Besides, I'm still trying to make up for the engagement ring." Randall took my hand and kissed it again, and then my lips. "But look — it's not just a brooch."

He turned the pendant over in his fingers, revealing an elegant timepiece, each numeral marked out in gold, with tiny filigree hands pointing to the hour.

"See, it's a perfect Charlotte gift. It *looks* lovely and delicate, but inside, it's completely practical."

Something fluttered in me at that, a little thrill through all my bones. "I don't need you to buy me jewelry." My voice was scarce a whisper.

"And I promise never to do it again." He drew me close to him, brushed his lips against the hair at my temple. "Truly, Charlotte, it's only money."

Only money. I laid my head against his shoulder and held my hand to the watch until the metal was as warm as blood.

One chill grey morning at the end of our first week in Delight, I was taking a turn about the Gallery at the Spring Rooms. The long, colonnaded porch overlooked the baths and fountains, its tall arched windows pulled tight against the winter. A few hopeful snowflakes struggled through the clouds and died on the warm glass. Wives did not mix with their husbands in the Gallery, so I was squeezed together with a twittering family from Harrowgate, as we sipped our silver-bound cups of spring water and tried to pretend it was not quite so vile. Truly, what made anyone think we should like to drink the same hot water we'd all been *sitting* in?

The steam from the springs kept the Gallery toasty, even in snowfall, and my neighbor at the window fanned herself as if it were the height of summer. Thinking I should die of boredom before the afternoon was out, I took a peek at the pendant-watch to check the hour.

"My, my," the woman said, swiftly exchanging her fan for a lorgnette. The glass pressed to her face, she greatly resembled a bird of prey — perhaps an owl. "A little wedding gift?"

"You're Mrs. Woodstone, aren't you?" said one of her daughters, a pretty girl younger even than Rosie. Before I could respond, her mother swept her scrutinizing gaze over me and my unfashionable flannel dress.

"Woodstones. Hmph. A good old Harrowgate family," she said, as if I was to be reassured in my selection by her approval. "They don't mix much in society, of course — but that just means they're not getting themselves involved in scandals. But I don't know *you*," she added pointedly.

"No, ma'am. I'm from Shearing."

"Hmmm," she said, settling back into her silk plumage. But she added charitably, "Well, everyone must come from somewhere, I suppose." She looked suddenly thoughtful and tapped her daughter with the fan. "That reminds, me, Jane, you'll never guess who I saw leaving the Empress Dining Room this morning. Virginia Byrd!"

Jane gasped daintily. "But I thought she was out of the country. I haven't seen her since Kitty Darling's house party that spring."

"Nursing a broken heart, I heard," her mother agreed, with less sympathy than one might have hoped. "Whatever became of that beau of hers, anyway? Such a dreadful scandal! You won't remember this, of course, Mrs. Woodstone, but they were *the* couple, about two seasons ago. Everyone was sure he was going to offer for her, and then all of a sudden —" She lifted her hands in a helpless gesture.

"But wasn't it too mysterious," piped her daughter, "how he just disappeared? Broke the hearts of half the girls in town." She sank back into her chair with a sigh that was half-swoon.

"You *know* it had to have been that brother of hers," argued the other girl. "The man Virginia loved would never have played her false! And the way Richard just whisked her off afterward —"

"Well, *I* heard he ran afoul of some of his friends and took a holiday —" The mother dropped her lorgnette dramatically. "— in Wardensgate!"

I sat up abruptly. "Wardensgate! Debtors' prison?"

The owl nodded solemnly.

"Well, I can believe it," her daughter said. "The way he went through wig powder alone — half the perukiers in Harrowgate must have had a claim on him!"

Oh, had she really said that? I gazed into my glass of foul water with dismay, beginning to wish I hadn't drunk any. But, oh, they went on.

"Well," the sister stressed, "if he ever shows his face in Society again, I'd like to give him a piece of my mind for how he treated poor Miss Byrd!"

"You may have to queue up," the mother said. "Arthur may be wondering what's happened to that fifteen hundred Mr. Wheeler owes him! My dear Mrs. Woodstone, whatever is the matter? Here, Cora, give her a clap on the back. That spring water is enough to make anyone choke!"

I was grateful when the time came for Randall to fetch me away from there.

"Darling, you look a little flushed. What say we get some fresh air?"

I couldn't have agreed more. It had suddenly become far too close in the Spring Rooms. I took his arm and we walked out into the night. "What have you been doing all this time?" I asked him.

He stifled a yawn. "Looking at the snow, out the downstairs window, with a man called Treacher."

"I see. And was he very interesting?"

"I shouldn't think so — he hadn't any teeth and was deaf as a post. Charlotte —" he turned to me suddenly, a certain desperate urgency in his now-grey eyes. "Are you as bored as I am?"

I met his gaze solemnly. "Worse."

He grabbed my elbows. "Wonderful! Let's get out of here, shall we? Let's go home."

Chapter Sixteen

*W*e set off deep in the heart of morning, after one last sumptuous Delight breakfast, the shining black trap from Mr. Woodstone fitted out with runners now instead of wheels. The flurries of the previous afternoon had turned into one of the Gold Valley's rare snowfalls, blanketing the roadway in white. Beneath my new travelling cloak I wore my garnet timepiece, pinned close to my breast.

Randall's eyes shone in the glittering sunlight, his collar pulled up firm against that broad jaw, his bronze hair lightly frosted from a brief fall of snow when we first stepped out of the hotel. Smiling at the thought that I *could*, I reached a hand out of my muff and brushed the snow away. He looked at me and caught my hand, giving it a quick, warm squeeze before lifting it to his lips.

"Mrs. Woodstone," he said formally, and though I'd been hearing it all week, off Randall's lips the name sounded bold and lyrical . . . and permanent. It sent an odd, quick flutter to my belly, as though we'd hit a dip with the carriage.

"Mr. Miller," I answered impishly.

"Oh, Charlotte," he sighed, and before I knew what happened, he bent low, brought up a handful of snow from the roadway, and dumped it over my head.

"That silenced you, didn't it?" he gloated as I sputtered and gasped. I gave him a little shove that caused the horses to wander a bit in their path, but we rode the rest of the way in companionable silence, bundled together beneath the sheepskin wraps. The warmth from his body next to mine chased away the strange feeling in my stomach, and I tried to forget the odd moments that had marred the perfection of our first days together.

We came into Shearing at last, chilled and red-cheeked, and it was as though we had driven the carriage out of one world and into another entirely. Here, upon the banks of the river, the winter had wrought not snow, but ice — half an inch at least, coating every rooftop and bending trees to the earth. Branches shuddered in the wind, sending icy shrapnel down upon the roadway. The road was a bed of glass-sharp chops and furrows, treacherous footing for the horses and rough going for the trap.

"My God!" Randall pulled back on the reins to steer round a fallen limb. As we skirted the Stowe, we saw a sight that had me half out of my seat: ice on the river. Ice on the river, above my millwheel. The Stowe was frozen solid. It was all I could do not to tear the reins away from Randall and hie the horses through the village at breakneck speed.

Randall led us straight to Stirwaters. I should have understood what it meant that he did that, then, but at the time it seemed only natural. Of course we should want to stop at the mill first; where else? The moment we pulled into the shale drive, I alit from the carriage without a look back. I broke into a run but slipped hard on the icy ground, barely noticing that Randall was there to lift me up again. With a bit more care, I made my way around the Millhouse to the mill, past the frozen pond, and stopped dead when I came within sight of the wheelhouse.

A crowd had gathered, all frantic gestures and bewilderment — Rosie, Harte, Uncle Wheeler, a handful of villagers. I saw Robbie Lawson and the Hales with Janet Lamb, stout and billowing in her winter wear. They parted some when I came among them, but no one spoke to me. To a man, they all stared at the massive oak millwheel, the frozen water that held it fast, and the deadly, splintering crack through the beams that held the wheel in place. The great old wheel, locked into the ice below, had wrenched free from its axle and now hung bent and crooked, one side treacherously lower than the other.

Rosie stood deep in low, frantic conversation with Harte, up near the base of the wheelhouse. They fell silent as I reached them, and Harte shook his head.

"The drive shaft snapped," he said. "It's a hard freeze. I wouldn't have believed it, but there you have it." He waved a helpless arm toward the tangle of wood and stone. Dear old Harte — how exactly like him to take it personally.

Rosie said, "I suppose we're just lucky it hasn't happened before, but Shearing hasn't seen a freeze like this . . ."

"Ever," I finished.

"But that's impossible," Randall said. "It's only been snowing for a day or two — how could the river have frozen solid in that time?"

A shiver overtook me that was more than just the icy morning. *The river changed course, a plague that killed half the sheep, floods* . . . a broken millwheel. Hard-luck Millers, indeed. I reached up to touch the crack in the wood, and was somehow surprised that the mill did not flinch under my hand as I probed its wound. I certainly felt the pain from that ghastly break — coarse and raw and searing, so fierce it blinded me.

"Can we recover?"

"From this? Oh, aye," Harte said, but his voice was grimmer than usual. He was studying the wheel, his hand up, fingers spread, taking quick measurement. "In spring, when this thaws and we can drain the pit to make repairs. Until then . . ."

"We have no power."

"That's about the size of it, Mistress."

It was the worst possible note on which to start the new year. Although we had our cloth promised to Porter & Byrd, which would cover our next mortgage payment, after that — what? Without the millwheel, we could power none of the machines — not the carding engines, not the spinning jacks, the plying frames, the fulling stocks. We were crippled.

And it was a curious thing, to stand in Stirwaters with the mill silent and still, no gears rattling overhead, no water rushing by underfoot. The mill felt strange and empty. Dead. I wondered if it felt itself gone still, its great heart torn from its chest, its limbs sundered from their brain. The thought gave me an eerie sort of chill, and I shoved it aside, but firmly. Rosie took it badly, as if her own heart were wrenched from her. She haunted the silent wheelhouse, heedless of the icy wind whipping through the ruined walls, and looked at me, stricken, when I'd call her name. It was going to be a long winter.

My homecoming as a married woman was thus a subdued one. As I lingered at Stirwaters that first awful afternoon, conferring with Harte and Rosie, Randall slipped off to the Grange to unpack us, and when at last I dragged myself out of the mill and into the evening, Rosie had to stop me climbing the stoop into the Millhouse.

"Go home," she said, a trace of weary irritation in her voice. "Your husband is waiting."

Confused for a moment, I hesitated, and then forced a laugh. Helplessly, I held out my arms, and my sister almost fell into them. "What are we going to do?"

She hugged me fiercely, pulling back at last. "We'll be all right," she said, a furrow creasing her brow, and though I nodded, I wasn't sure either of us believed her.

I trudged up the long hill to the Grange to find that Randall had been busy in my absence, turning the stiff, formal dining room into a space nearly as warm and intimate as the Millhouse kitchen. A fire blazed in the hearth, and we ate hand to hand across a corner of the vast oak table, borrowed silverware clinking cheerfully on the hand-me-down plates. We had forgotten to buy our own, and the Bakers had come to our rescue, loaning three or four of everything from the bakeshop, from the chipped coffee mugs to the mismatched bowls, plus their daughter Colly and a roast-hen dinner.

"It's a sad state of affairs when the miller and the banker can't feed themselves without help from a nursemaid." I laughed.

Randall smiled and squeezed my hand. "We'll send for a catalogue from the shops in Harrowgate tomorrow." He traced a pattern on my palm with his fingers. "Do you want to talk about the wheel?"

I winced. "Yes," I said automatically, and then shook my head. "No. I don't know. How do you talk about something you can't even bear to think of? But Rosie says she'll get the wall patched up, temporarily, and if anyone can build a mill-wheel, it's Harte. . . ."

Randall sat there, a look of concern on his straightforward face, stroking my hand. He might have been an ostler sooth-ing a nervous horse, and the firelight and the warmth and the great heavy drapes behind me seemed a palpable barrier between me and the troubles at Stirwaters. Absently, I reached up to touch the timepiece at my breast. This was what Randall did for me — this moment of tranquility, this stalwart defense against the volleys hurled at me daily. But I sensed a fragility in that barrier, and I vowed then that I would let nothing dis-turb it. Whatever else happened, *this* was sacred. I think that was the moment when I truly drew Randall close in to me, alongside Rosie and Shearing and Stirwaters. These things were mine, and I would let no harm come to them.

The ice gave up its grip on Shearing within a day or two, thawing the village into mud and debris. There was not much damage, overall — a few fallen limbs, some loose shingles. Only Stirwaters had received a mortal blow. After the initial cleanup, Harte took advantage of the break in his duties to head home for a spell, and Randall delayed his return to Harrowgate, as though I had gone fragile with the injury to my mill.

"For heaven's sake, I shan't go mad if I sit idle for one min-ute," I exclaimed in exasperation once, as Randall expressed concern over my well-being yet again. "Besides, it's not as if there isn't work still to be done — cloth doesn't finish and catalogue itself, you know."

Rosie had been to the joiner's; she knew the cost of the new wheel and shaft, and I had told her to order them, but she dragged her feet. Oh, she had excuses: The joiner had to order the right-sized bolts; the log for the shaft was too green. I took her at her word, until she descended on me one chill morning and beckoned me into the office.

Rosie spread an armload of papers across the desk: schematic drawings of Stirwaters and its workings, sketched-out maps of our land and the river, pages and pages of calculations. I thought they must be Father's; the hand was his, and we were forever finding scraps and scribbles he had left behind.

"Where did you find these?" I asked, sliding one long drawing from beneath its fellows. It depicted a new millwheel — a much larger one — driving the Stirwaters power train.

"I didn't find them," Rosie said. "I've been working on them for days. Well, with Harte's help. He's not much with pen and ink, but he's something of a genius when it comes to machines."

"You! But what is it all?"

"Look —" she indicated the schematic before me. "These are plans for the new millwheel. I think we could increase the horsepower half again if we went with this design. It will take some tinkering, since it reverses the direction of flow —"

Oh, it was a grand idea, and she had such hopes for it! She talked on for a few more minutes, pointing out the elements she'd put so much time and care into — how Rosellen Miller would put her mark on Stirwaters for still and all. Her eyes were bright, her face flushed.

"If we just replace the old wheel, how much will that cost?"

"About fifty pounds."

I cringed, though we *should* manage to save back nearly that much from our dealings with Captain Worthy. "And this larger one? And everything to fit it into place?"

"Perhaps three times that."

"You know we don't have that kind of money!" I hadn't meant to burst out like that.

Rosie sat stiffly in her chair. "I thought maybe Randall might advance us some funding."

"You can't be serious! How can you suggest such a thing, after what we've gone through to get *out* of debt to him!"

"Yes, well — things are different now, aren't they?" She was glaring at me, her jaw thrust out stubbornly.

"And that is precisely the reason we will not even entertain the notion. I'll not take advantage of Randall's wealth!"

"Well," Rosie said slowly, "that's why you married him, isn't it?"

I slapped her. I don't recall *meaning* to do it — somehow my hand shot out and struck her across the face, leaving a bright pale mark on her red cheek.

Her own hand flew up to the spot, her eyes wide as gear-wheels. I stared back in horror, but an apology would not form itself on my lips. After the briefest moment, Rosie shoved back her chair and swept all her papers carelessly together. I saw she was fighting back tears.

"You're just like Mam, you know that?"

"It's too big a risk," I said, but my voice was very small.

"It's always too big a risk," she said. "Father would have understood!"

It was my turn to feel the sting of a blow. Blinking against the burn in my eyes, I mumbled, "Dreams, Rosie — that's all Father's ideas ever were. That's all this is."

But she was already gone.

With the unbearable silence of Stirwaters pressing against me like the air of a tomb, I wandered back up to the Grange. The wind was like a whip of ice in my face, and I was numb and breathless by the time I crested the wooded hill. One curiosity of living at the Grange was that our nearest neighbor was Biddy Tom. She occupied the old gatehouse on the property, a sturdy lime-washed cottage nestled in a tangle of spruce and heather. It was not actually all that near — a few minutes' struggle through the wood, or a longer walk by the roadway — and since her plot of land was not part of our lease, I seldom saw her. Perhaps when Spring opened up the world we would turn neighborly, but the very thought of it gave me a chill not part of the winter afternoon.

I found Randall hard at work outside, wrapped in his frock coat and hat, hacking viciously at a black thicket with a rather large set of hedge shears. An axe lay buried in the remains of a tree struck down by the ice storm. His pale cheeks — chapped red with cold — broke into a wide smile, and he lifted a gloved hand in a big wave.

"What are you doing?" I said, coming closer. We stood in the shadow of the dining room window, the stone eaves arched gloomily overhead, traced with the skeletons of last year's ivy.

"Well, once I got the last of the storm debris cleared, I thought I'd get a head start on spring."

"You cleared away all those damaged trees?"

"Of course," he said. "Who did you think had done it? Little Colly? Well, she helped some." He bent over the hedge and brushed his frozen lips against mine. "Mercy! We'd best be careful — we'll stick together in weather like this. Why don't you head inside and get warm? There's water boiling in the hearth. I'll be in as soon as I get this demon hawthorn beaten into submission."

"I think it's winning," I said, just as he yanked his hand back from the hedge with a hiss. "Those thorns will stick through anything."

Holding the shears at a rakish angle, Randall surveyed the property. "It's a grand old park, or it will be, once I convince the woods to give it back." As he moved around the hedge, he elaborated on his plans for the garden and the yard. He showed me the strip of verge where he planned a bulb garden, the run-down carriage house ("Imagine having the horses and trap right here at home!"), the brick terraces overlooking a "vista" of the Valley floor. Every corner of the property would have Randall's touch — fresh stonework, new plantings, a glass-paned summerhouse to enjoy the mature roses.

I listened with growing unease. How could he make such plans? This was not our house, not our land to dig up and repot as we chose. And to look ahead — five, ten years for some of these ideas. It was dizzying.

"My father made plans like that." I said it without thinking, and Randall took it for response to some comment I had not even heard.

He squeezed my hand. "Then that's what I'll do first."

Inadvertently, I shivered.

"Darling, you're freezing. Let's get you inside and start

on that tea." He put his arm round my shoulders and steered me back to the front of the house. We paused briefly to peek at our bedroom oriel, its paned window sparkling in the waning light. A twisted, black-trunked tree reached its stunted branches toward the glass.

"What's this?" I asked, fingering the gnarled wood.

"Lilacs. There's this one, and a whole copse of them by the morning room terrace."

I recoiled, snatching my hand back. "Cut it down," I said. "Cut them all down."

A few nights later, Randall and I called at the Millhouse for dinner. I had seen little of my uncle since my wedding, and though I confess I did not experience quite the proper regret, I supposed it a duty I should not dismiss so lightly. Thus my new husband and I, gaily bedecked, arrived at the Millhouse like company, and were ushered in across the parlor threshold by Rachel as if we were strangers. Truly, I almost felt like one, under the brief gaze Rosie rewarded me with.

I stood in the parlor and looked at the home that was no longer my own. My new shoes felt odd and awkward on the Millhouse floor; I could not feel the smooth uneven boards, and found myself seeking, with my toe, for the loose one near the fireplace. I saw my unfamiliar reflection in the old smoked mirror, and remembered looking at the room this way, all those months ago when Uncle Wheeler had first come. I put a hand up to touch the china lamp, turned now so the crack was at the back, and stilled my fingers in the air.

"Rosie," I murmured, half from curiosity, and half to fill the silence that had risen up between us, "what's happened to the prize cup?" The silver plate trophy, won generations ago by some unnamed Miller in some Wool Guild competition, had stood so long on the Millhouse mantel that it had made a permanent ring for itself on the painted wood.

"I've no idea," she said curiously. "Uncle Wheeler must have decided it was too low, and had Rachel move it. He's been doing that for weeks now." She drew me closer to the fireplace, and in a hushed voice said, "Charlotte, he's been acting strangely ever since you left. The trophy, then Mam's candlesticks . . . and then last week he came home in the middle of the night, half undressed — in his shirtsleeves; no jacket, no waistcoat. In the *snow*."

A picture I had never quite been able to banish rose in my mind: of my uncle, bent over a ring drawn out in the sand, blood marring his blouse. I shook my head and tried to think what to tell her, when Randall strode up and gave her a companionable punch to the shoulder.

"Rosie, you're looking well. Won't you come see us at the Grange?" She brightened like a candle flame and gave him a very sisterly hug. Randall, smiling, squeezed her back. Uncle Wheeler finally joined us, and I must say he did not look so different after a few weeks' distance. I felt a curious sensation of distaste when I beheld the embroidery on his waistcoat, but bit my lip and quelled it. I should never be able to look at gold thread, it seemed, without thoughts of Jack Spinner. He drew me forward for a fluttering embrace, still scented very strongly of lilacs.

After dinner, Randall eased himself into the armchair facing the fireplace. "What are your plans these days, Wheeler?"

"My plans, my dear boy? What can you mean?"

Randall crossed one long leg over the other. "Well, you must feel as though your duties here are coming to an end, with Charlotte married and everything getting settled so nicely. You must be anxious to get back to your life in the city."

"Why, Woodstone, I wouldn't dream of it! With Charlotte gone, looking after Rosie has become my *full* occupation."

Rosie made a muffled sort of sound, and then coughed politely into her sleeve.

"Well, that must be tiresome for a man like you. No doubt you've had plans set awry by this . . . arrangement? Schemes, plots, irons in the fire?" Randall spoke easily, almost carelessly, the way men of society must be accustomed to conversing. "Your niece can't need that much looking after; why, she's in the mill half the time anyway! You don't want to be saddled with a ward, not when there's a perfectly felicitous alternative."

Uncle Wheeler had a singularly peculiar expression on his face. "I'm afraid I don't know what you mean."

"I mean, my good sir, that I — with Charlotte's blessing, of course — would be more than happy to, as it were, take Rosie off your hands."

Rosie's eyes leaped with delight, and she caught my hand.

"What a splendid idea," I said. "Rosie, why didn't we think of it? Oh, Uncle, do say yes — we wouldn't think of detaining you in Shearing one moment longer than necessary."

Uncle Wheeler coughed. "Why, Charlotte, anyone would think you *eager* to be rid of me!"

I felt myself color. "Oh, no, Uncle — it's only that we know how tedious it's been for you here these last months — and we're so grateful to you —"

"I think what my wife is trying to say," Randall broke in, "is that while she is deeply appreciative of all you've done for her, there really is no reason for you to prolong your stay here."

He was smiling still, that easy, casual expression he wears so well — but his voice had a firmness to it I did not recognize. It seemed almost like a challenge.

But Uncle Wheeler did not rise to it. He gave a gentle, mild laugh, and settled back into the faded sofa, his cup at his lips. "My dear boy," he began, but at that very moment there was a crash, like the sound of all the plates in the house breaking at once, followed by a scream.

"Rachel!" Rosie and I were on our feet at once, sprinting for the kitchen.

It was a shambles. Rachel stood in the hub of a ring of broken glass and crockery, splattered broth and vegetables on the floor. She was spewing a stream of unintelligible obscenities — and she was bathed in red.

"Rachel, my God, you're bleeding!" I rushed to her, lifted her apron to her face, but she waved me off.

"No, no — it's cherries. Spoilt now." Still trembling slightly, she pointed to the utter ruin of a tart. "Daft vandals!"

"What?" Randall was right on Rosie's heels. The cause of the destruction, a brickbat, dripping with syrup, lay amid the rubble. Randall stooped for it, brushing off a speck of broken glass. "Here, there's a message." He untied the scrap of cloth, now sticky and stained with red, from around the bat.

" 'You've been warned.' What the devil is that supposed to mean?"

I shook my head, just as dumbfounded. "But who threw it?"

Randall turned and flung open the kitchen door, stepping out into the night. "There's no one — *oh*. Charlotte, you'd better come out here."

Chapter Seventeen

Randall reached a hand out to me, and I gingerly stepped across the shattered glass and strewn food to the doorway. "Oh, mercy!" The words stuck in my throat and came out a strangled squeak.

It looked as though a great storm had struck the woolshed and the yard, scattering our stock to the four winds. There was cloth everywhere — pieces of it. Scraps, snips, slices. Whole packs, bound for transport, had been torn apart and shredded to rags. The woolshed doors were wrenched clean off their hinges and banged crazily against the stone walls. Someone had broken into the dyeshed and overturned the vats and scattered dyestuffs into the liquid streaming over the yard. What looked like a great grey blanket floating across the yard — or a ghost in a smoky shroud — revealed itself to be several yards of silver cassimere, slashed to ribbons. I stooped for it, wrapped some round my hands, lifted it to my face and waited for it to whisper its secrets to me. It was sticky and damp and reeked of ammonia; I cast about and found that the barrels of lant outside the mill had been tipped on their sides, to let their foul contents leech onto the ground and the remnants of my cloth.

The entire stock — every bale, every bolt, every yard of cloth. Every kersey, every baize, every satinette — destroyed. Willfully. Gleefully. Maliciously. This was not just one or two lengths, vandalized on the tenterhooks. This was a massive act of unfettered aggression. An attack on Stirwaters. On me.

"Who did this?" Randall said. He was still clutching the brick, and I thought he looked as if he'd like to throw it at someone.

"Does it matter?" I asked, futilely trying to piece together a tear in the silver cassimere.

"I'll say it does," Randall said. "When I get my hands on whoever's responsible —"

Rosie flung herself into the yard, straining into the darkness as though she could see the culprits lingering in the fringe of wood, pointing and sniggering at us.

"Rosie, it's no use," I said. "They'd be long gone by now. We'd never find them."

Randall looked from Rosie to me. "Well, you must have some idea!"

"An idea, maybe. But no proof. Someone who knew that Harte would be gone, and that's the entire village."

"The entire village wouldn't do this. Now, think! While we have time to fetch the magistrate and round them up!"

I shook my head. "The magistrate won't be here until Sunday month, and by then all the evidence will be gone."

Randall grabbed for his hair and remembered too late that he had cut it off. His hand hung, helpless, before his face. "Blast — I forgot. Small towns."

*   *   *

The mess — both inside and out — took hours to clean up, while my uncle fretted and tut-tutted and lifted not a single white manicured finger to help us. We swept up as much of the damaged cloth as we could, bundling it into old wool bags (the vandals had even destroyed the wrapping-cloth), but I knew we'd be finding bits of flannel and satinette in tree branches and under shrubs for a long time to come. Randall rolled up his shirtsleeves and held the woolshed doors as Rosie fixed the hinges; afterward she pronounced her brother-in-law "a proper hand with a ladder and block."

But among all the mess, there was no sign of the culprits' identity.

"I don't think one person could have done all this," Randall said. "Look." He gave the righted lant barrel a push. "Even empty, this is heavy."

"But the locks weren't broken," Rosie said. "Whoever did this *unlocked* the woolshed. Only Harte and Charlotte have keys, and Charlotte's never left a door unlocked in her life."

"You have Harte's keys," I reminded her gently. "He left them with you when he went home, remember."

She looked horrified, and took off for the Millhouse. A moment later she returned, breathless and brandishing the ring with a look of such relief I thought she'd cry. "They were right there, under my pillow. Right where I left them. Unless —" she gave a stricken sob. "Unless *I* left it unlocked."

"Hush, love. It wouldn't have mattered if you did. Look what they did to the doors — do you think a thing like a lock would have stopped them? Besides, after what happened with the attic room —" I stopped myself, unwilling to draw that thought to its conclusion.

Rosie had no such qualms. "What? It won't open a door so we can get our thread out, but it *will* open a door to vandals who want to destroy the woolshed?"

"That's how things work around here, isn't it?" I said bitterly. "It's capricious."

"Who's capricious?" Randall said, causing us both to start. He had wandered off, looking for evidence, and we had forgotten him.

Rosie and I exchanged a sharp glance. "Peg Eagan," I said, half at random, and added pointedly to Rosie, "Look, *whatever* happened, there was clearly some human agency involved. Go see if you can find out where the Eagans were tonight."

The news was all round the village by morning. The millhands, who had not quite stopped coming to work even with the millwheel broken, trailed in after sunrise, shocked and furious. Jack Townley was ready to form a lynch mob, and Mercy Fuller dug her hands through the scraps we'd collected, mewing over each in turn. "Ah, this one's the kersey Mrs. Hopewell were so proud of!" or "Not my black baize!"

And I? I floated around the millyard, like a ghost in true, unable to summon up the resolve to do — whatever I must do to see Stirwaters past this. Randall found me, wandering helplessly through the shale, turning up bits of rock with my toe and collecting stray scraps we had missed.

"Charlotte, we must talk about this! You know the stock's a total loss."

I nodded, neatly stacking the scraps I had gathered. They were still damp and reeked of stale urine.

"But surely you were insured?"

I stared at him, wanting suddenly to laugh, hysterically. "Insured? Who can afford insurance?"

We had no stock. We had no wool to make more, no mill-wheel to drive the machines to make more, no time at all in which to consider the matter. Captain Worthy was coming at the turning of the month, and our payment was due to the bank a few weeks later. And now I had the banker suddenly too close for comfort, reminding me at every turn of the dire strait we were in. "I'll think of something," was all I could say, until my voice colored from despair to impatience.

The vandals were still unidentified. If the millhands had their suspects, no one spoke of them in my hearing, and our own efforts had come to naught.

"Mrs. Drover swore up and down that both Tansy and Peg were in the public room all night." Rosie kicked at the ground in frustration. "I still say they were involved — somehow. I saw Tansy at Hale's yesterday, and she just grinned and did this —" Rosie made a gesture with her fingers, pantomiming scissors.

I drew back my lips in distaste. "That's just Tansy, being Eaganish."

"What about this Pinchfields?" Randall suggested. "You said they've threatened you — maybe they sent a henchman down to rough you up a little. Has there been a stranger in the village recently?"

I gave a mirthless laugh. "If there was, he hides his business better than any person in the history of Shearing. No, maybe —" I faltered, frowning.

"What?" Rosie and Randall echoed one another, but I shook my head. I'd been about to say perhaps it was one of our own, but when I weighed them in my mind — Jack Townley, the Lambs, Mr. Mordant . . . I couldn't bear the thought. For once, it was almost easier to believe in a curse.

Thus the days ticked away toward our deadlines, and I just sat in my office and stared out over the pond, as the rustles and sighs of the mill twined their way inside my head. If I had paid them any mind, I might have thought I was going mad. But the truth was, I was out of options. I could perhaps sell the scraps to be ground up for processing, though I would never get the value the whole cloth would have brought from Porter & Byrd. Randall tried to offer his help, but I would hear none of it.

"Look, I do wish you'd reconsider," he said, a week after the destruction of the cloth. We were eating lunch at the Grange, a hearty Bakehouse-prepared meal of bean soup and steaming brown bread. "You're running out of time, and we have the money, or we can get it. It just doesn't make sense for you to be so resistant."

I scowled over my bowl. "No. I'll not have you risking your fortune on Stirwaters, too."

"It's hardly a fortune," he said with a laugh. "Besides, it's our money now."

"Six hundred pounds *is* a fortune. And it's *your* money, and Stirwaters is my mill. It's my responsibility, and I'll not have it said that you're married to a —" Uncle Wheeler's words on my lips, I faltered, my quarrel with Rosie still too fresh in my mind.

"Married to a what?" he asked. "Charlotte, who said anything of the sort?" He reached across the table, but I pulled my hands back.

"I did not marry you for your money, and you did not

marry me for my mill," I snapped. "Stop fussing — I'll figure it out." I rose and began clearing the table with a vast clattering of dishes and silverware, until Randall threw up his hands and marched out into the yard, to pick up his hedge shears and hoe.

I bit my lip and watched him leave. Our honeymoon was drawing to a close. Soon he would be heading back to Harrowgate — with or without our mortgage payment — and I would be here, in Shearing, with the same problems I always had. The looming certainty of that was more than I could bear, suddenly, so I bundled myself up in my cloak and hat and wandered down the hill to Stirwaters.

To my surprise, my sister was in the finishing room. She had an odd air about her, distracted, faint — as if she were waiting for something. She started when she saw me, and I couldn't tell if she was suddenly frightened, or relieved. She reached for me, but dropped her hands. "Charlotte, don't be angry."

I stared at her a moment. "What did you do?" But as I looked at her, her jaw set but a measure of fear in her wide blue eyes, I knew. Suddenly, I *knew*.

I turned and pounded upstairs as fast as I could.

"Charlotte, wait —"

I turned back. Rosie was a few paces behind me. "I didn't —" She made a helpless gesture with her hands. "Truly, Charlotte, he just showed up."

He was there, in my office, sitting on the corner of my desk and leafing through Father's atlas. I stopped short in the doorway, struck with such relief that for a moment I could not breathe. Rosie caught me up and took my hand, and I managed to recover myself.

"Mr. Spinner," I said, straightening my bonnet, which I had not bothered to straighten these many days. "How pleasant to have you call again." I was aware how shrill and ridiculous my voice sounded — but I could not care.

"Aye." Mr. Spinner nodded, his ruddy whiskers bobbing slightly. "I see you've come to some distress with your property since I was here last."

I nodded, foolish, eager.

"Bad luck, that. Need a hand, then, ladies?"

The wind howled round the mill and rattled all the glass in the casements. I felt a moment of clarity and reason, and seized upon it.

"Yes, Mr. Spinner, but —" I pitched my voice as calm as I could make it. "I'm afraid that we haven't any need for gold thread at present. Have you any other skills?"

Jack Spinner lowered my father's atlas to the desk. "Oh, and what are you wanting for, these days?"

"Cloth."

Spinner nodded approvingly. I forged on. "We have some damaged yardage. Is there anything you can do —"

"Something happen to some of that famous Stirwaters Blue? Well, I was a passable hand at the loom, in my day. I may be able to piece it back together for you." He paused and eyed me pointedly, his gaze travelling between my face and my bodice. "I hear you pay fair wages to your weavers, Mistress Miller."

I put a hand up — and felt my fingers brush the enamel timepiece. Randall's gift. I hesitated.

Spinner saw. "Ah, well, if I can't help you, I can't help you. I'll just be on my way, then, I suppose."

"No, wait."

"Charlotte, no!" Rosie clutched my arm, but I was unpinning the watch. *It's only money.* I told myself I did not feel the prick of tears as I dropped the crimson bauble into Jack Spinner's outstretched hand, where it glittered with the gloss of blood.

"The loom is in the attic. Follow me. Rosie — start fetching in what's left of the stock."

The ancient loom stood deep in shadow beneath the sloping eaves. Spinner brushed past me and made his shambling way toward the machine. The low sunlight seemed to follow him, until he stood with one hand raised toward the loom, all shadows swept from the corner. He eased himself onto the bench and gave a few passes with the shuttle, still in place after all these years.

"Ah," he said, in that queer, rusty voice, "Helen's loom. Good old machine, this one."

"I beg your pardon?" I drew forward, curious.

"But what's this, then? Someone's been tinkering, I see." He stooped low, giving a push to some lever beneath the body of the loom. A pulley carried the motion through the machine, and it shuddered. "Heh," Spinner laughed. "Look at that. I'll hardly have to do *any* work."

He beckoned for me to hand him something; I spied some old brown canvas under the window, and pressed a corner of it into his hand. At his touch, it began to unravel — slowly, inevitably, as if it lost all memory of having ever been cloth. Spinner began to whistle, a lively tune that clashed with the howling wind outside.

"Now, Helen. Currer's wife, and mistress of Stirwaters in her day." He whistled a few more bars of his song; the threads of the canvas wound themselves onto the quill, until the shuttle was full and ready to weave. Spinner gave the shuttle a tap with one hand. "Fine lady, she was. Mother of Simon, mother of Aaron. Good lads."

Helen — Currer — I shook my head. Mercy, what was he talking about? Currer Miller was the second keeper of Stirwaters, more than eighty years ago.

"Oh, and we mustn't forget Hap, now . . . such a shame what happened to him —"

"I'm sorry?" I said.

"Oh, no, you're not," Spinner said, a thread of darkness suddenly in his voice. "Not really. Those boys mean nothing to you."

My mouth was open to ask him to explain himself, but Rosie returned at that moment, dragging the pack bag of scraps behind her.

I spent the next half hour helping Rosie load the cloth into the attic. We quarrelled briefly — we seemed to be quarrelling, briefly, more and more these days — over who should stay in the mill overnight; I felt it my duty, but she pressed me to return to the Grange, and not leave Randall to wonder over an absence that should be impossible to explain.

"It's Uncle Wheeler's Friday card game," she said. "He won't be home before dawn, and by then he'll be in no state to wonder where *I* am."

Spinner promised us that the work would be completed

by morning, and that no one would mark the strangeness of its origin. And perhaps he was right. Why should they? Who on Earth would guess that the cloth appeared by magic?

In the dark of that night I woke, shivering, for my husband had rolled over in the bed, taking the blankets with him. I lay there a long while, listening to Randall's breathing. Its rhythm could not soothe me, and I found myself fumbling for the little timepiece, and a candle to read it by — but of course there was nothing, and I fell back onto my pillow, stricken. Eventually I rose and crept through the dark, unfamiliar hallways of my new home, to the great dining hall and its view of Stirwaters's millpond.

How different it seemed in the dead of night, from the cosy, candle-lit room where Randall and I had eaten hours earlier. Now the room was deep in shadow, the ancient furniture looming eerily in the darkness. The carvings on the fireplace, lit up by a shaft of moonlight through those enormous windows, seemed to leer at me, their twisted faun-faces reminding me sharply of Mr. Spinner. I drew back the curtains enough to look down on the pond, but the wheelhouse was not visible, and I could not see if any light still burned in the office. The Millhouse was dark as a grave.

Even my new dressing gown could not warm me against the chill seeping through the glass, and I found myself longing to slip back beside Randall, under the crewelwork hangings, and warm myself against him as he slept. The peace of that sleep was what I wanted more than anything, the ease with which he threw off the worries of the day with his boots and his waistcoat and, snoring softly, banished the troubles of the night.

"Charlotte." Randall's voice was a warm thread of air across the room, and his arms were around me before I could turn round. Softly, I let him drape the blanket around my shoulders, and laid my head against his chest.

"I looked everywhere for you," Randall said gently.

"Liar," I breathed. "You did not."

He brushed his lips against my neck. "No," he agreed. "I knew you'd be here." Here where the windows looked down on my mill, my sister, my home . . . what had been my life up to now.

"Randall," I said, wrenching up the subject from where I knew — even then — it should lie buried. Especially then.

"Hmmm?" His voice came slowly; I think perhaps he had already begun to fall asleep again, there against me, wrapped together in the blanket I had made for him — my Miller wedding gift.

"I gave the watch to — to be pawned."

I felt him stiffen. The soft liquid flow of his body had gone; his arms around me tightened. "I wondered," he said quietly.

I blinked back tears. He had noticed, after all, and I had waited too long, probably, to mention it. I turned, and the blanket fell away from my shoulders.

He looked so vulnerable, my strong Randall, barefoot in his nightshirt, his hair all tousled, wrapped tightly in the green plaid blanket. But his eyes were dark and alert, and I did not know what to make of him.

"To buy more cloth from other mills," I added quickly. "If there's still time, before —"

He shook his head, cutting me off. "No," he said. "I understand."

I had never heard his voice so curt. I took a step toward him, reaching out, trying to explain the inexplicable. "My uncle knows a pawnbroker, and —"

"Your *uncle?*" His voice rang out, sharp and disbelieving. "Oh. I see."

"I had to, there was —"

Randall put up a hand, silencing me. In the darkness I couldn't see the look on his face. I did not want to. After a dreadful pause, he turned on his heel and pulled the blanket tight about his shoulders as he strode out of the dining room. "Come to bed now, Charlotte; it's freezing."

I didn't follow him. I sat, still and frozen, staring down at Stirwaters until dawn.

Chapter Eighteen

By the time I got back to Stirwaters, the mill was full of cloth. Like the gold thread before it, it was fine work — preternaturally fine. From tissue-thin fabrics light as air, to thick warm blanket cloth, it was all here, and ready; it required no fulling, no finishing, no sentence on the tenterhooks. It was simply *done*. Yet somehow, within Spinner's handiwork, I could still see *our* cloth. I could flip back a corner of black yardage, and see the flash of mazareen blue satinette it had been, in another lifetime.

"No one is going to believe this," I said. "I don't believe it."

Rosie had concocted an alibi for all this cloth: It had come to us downriver, from mills in Burlingham and Springmill (I'd apparently spent the past several days writing frantic pleas for assistance), arriving late in the night on a much-delayed barge.

"Don't worry," she insisted. "No one will question it."

"But that's crazy. And where did we supposedly get the money to pay for this? You know the watch wasn't worth anywhere near this much." I put my fingers to my collar, where the timepiece had hung so briefly.

Rosie looked at me, all innocence. "I don't know that. Do you know that?"

I gave it up.

We packed up the cloth, waited for Porter & Byrd to collect it, and said no more about it. Captain Worthy arrived on schedule, in his sunset-painted barge, and I stood on the dock and prayed nothing would give me away.

He greeted me warmly, picking through the packs with undisguised pleasure. "I say, your cloth's even finer than I remember it. Well done, lass. Mr. Byrd will be well pleased, indeed."

I felt myself color under my hat brim; hopefully he took it for feminine modesty. Selling the gold thread to Parmenter's was one thing, but this — this felt counterfeit. I was almost more relieved to see Porter & Byrd's barge depart with the cloth than I was to hand their cheque over to my banker.

Although Randall never mentioned the watch again, I could tell it was not forgotten. Indeed, I could scarcely look at him these days without a pang of guilt that overshadowed any relief I might feel over securing Stirwaters's safety. As he prepared to return to Harrowgate, I sat on the edge of the grand bed and watched him stuff his suit coats and breeches into a battered portmanteau.

"Look, I'll be back as soon as I can — two weeks, maybe three. Are you *sure* you'll be all right here by yourself?"

I nodded, suddenly not sure at all, and my fingers tightened on the bedpost.

Randall leaned over me and brushed my hair with his lips. "That's my girl. Now, don't fret about things. You've made your payment, and you've got me and the bank off your back for a few months, right? Try not to dwell on what happened — it's just a little bad luck, is all."

I scowled. "I warned you."

"Well, we'll take out an insurance policy straightaway — and don't argue: I'm going to make it a condition of your loan, in fact. And then you won't have to fear a little bad luck anymore." He turned back to his packing. "I wish you'd get Rosie up to stay with you. I'd feel a lot better about going."

I shook my head. "She won't. She doesn't want to leave Uncle Wheeler alone in the Millhouse."

Randall gave the straps on the portmanteau a sharp tug. "Uncle Wheeler. Of course not." He turned to me, his lips drawn tight. "Charlotte —"

"What?"

He shrugged and shouldered his bag. "Never mind." He stepped closer and held out his arms. I slipped off the bed into his embrace, but there was a stiffness there that may well have been more than the weight of the portmanteau on his back. Watching him drive out of the village, flicking the reins against Blithe and Bonny's rumps, I could not decide if the feeling in the pit of my stomach was loneliness or relief.

Though we had weathered the immediate crisis with the cloth, the matter of the millwheel remained unresolved. Weeks after the accident, the old wheel rested, still as a gravestone, against the race-side wall of the mill. Harte and four of the strongest hands had taken it down and left it there, and I could hardly bear to look at it. The wounded paddles looked like a mouthful of broken teeth, and I found myself running my tongue behind my lips whenever I passed by.

It stood between Rosie and me like a wall we could not reach across. Stubborn as we both were, we had rarely quarrelled up till now. I could always count on her fire dying down as fast as it had flared up, and within minutes or hours she would be wiling me out of my own anger. But that was before my marriage, before I moved out of our home. I could not count on her to have cooled off by dinner, if I was not there to share that dinner with her.

I tried to talk to her, but she would only shrug and say it didn't matter. She had something like her old Rosie cheer when she said it — but now I had begun to doubt my ability to judge her moods. It troubled me, and I drew away, so I would not have to notice.

Finally, when it became futile to wait for a thaw between the Miller sisters, Harte decided for all of us that it was time to rebuild the wheel. He had returned to Shearing, ready to work, and found Stirwaters idle still. So he'd grabbed his tools and marched off toward the race. I felt a sigh go through me, as though the mill itself had been holding its breath for weeks. Following him out into the yard, I nursed some concern for his plans. He had worked so closely with Rosie on her scheme for the new wheel; should I have to talk him down to Earth as well? I needn't have worried: I found him crouched down beside the old wheel, carefully taking its measure on a scrap of old wood.

It became a spectacle. Millhands flowed out and took up their cheery, ale-warmed positions as Harte gauged and scribbled. Bent across the gudgeon, his head down at his knees, he let out a long whistle.

"Mistress, come and have a look. What do you make of that?"

I swept over, bundled tight in my cloak, and peered in closer. Upside-down now, under the grime of age, was the maker's mark for Stirwaters's first millwheel. I could barely make out the letters, until a rare shaft of sunlight broke through the clouds and shone right on the nameplate:

WHEELER & SONS, LTD. HAYMARKET

I reached out to touch it, expecting to feel a spark, a jolt. . . . I knew I was seeing something important, but its meaning would not reach back out to me. I pressed my hand against the brass, willing it to give up its secrets, but all I got for my trouble were dirty fingers.

"How very odd," I murmured, at a loss for what I wanted to say.

"Ah, not so much, Mistress," Harte said. "In those days there probably weren't but one or two places to get such a big wheel built."

"Aye," Ian Lamb added. "Old Man Miller didn't have the services of Harte and Miss Rosie, did he?"

"You ought to show that to Squire Wheeler." Townley grinned. "See how he'd like all that tarnish on his name!"

Everyone laughed, but I felt the chill go through me then. I looked Rosie's way, and her eyes met mine at last. She sidled closer for a better look at the nameplate, and as she touched the brass, I reached down and touched it with her. No jolt, no sudden fire of understanding . . . but I bit my lip, and Rosie looked at me with wide, wide eyes.

I knew then I wasn't imagining things. There was some meaning here, an old secret long hidden beneath our very feet, some significance deeper than the mere purchase of a millwheel. Wheelers involved in the building of Stirwaters? What could that mean?

Building the new wheel took Rosie away from Stirwaters for whole weeks of workdays. She and Harte would be gone most mornings by the time I'd made my own way down the hill. I did pass the joiner's on that route, where I often saw Rosie and Harte bent over their work together. Mindful of Randall's suspicions of their budding romance, I did not intrude. I was relieved to see them side by side again, and relieved, too, that the wheel was at last underway; but I could not help but feel Rosie's absence still more keenly.

I felt more alone than ever.

Cloistered in my office for long, idle hours, I made a project of documenting Stirwaters's history. Mr. Mordant had accused Millers, once, of writing everything down, and it was true. There were records going back to the days of Harlan Miller — memorandum books, schemata, old dye recipes and weaving patterns. There were shelves of the stuff in the office, and boxes more stashed in the attic and cellar. It was all a terrible jumble; it would take weeks to sort out. Long dull weeks I must fill anyway.

In the cellar, at the bottom of a bin of mouse-shredded receipt books, I discovered bound volumes of personal journals — one for nearly every miller to hold my post. There was no volume for my father, of course; the record of his tenure was sketched out in the atlas he had drawn. What should such a book from my hand document, I wondered. The very last Miller, recording the end of days at Stirwaters?

I sat back on my heels on the damp floor and stared at the stone foundation walls. A crack big enough to fit my hand in stretched from the ground to the ceiling, with bits of mortar pushed out of place by time or burrowing rodents. All at once Jack Townley's words sprang back to me: *This mill don't want to be fixed up.* Was that it, then? We could patch cracks until Judgement Day, hang new millwheels and put up fresh paint, but all of it could never disguise one cold fact: Rosie and I were the last of the Millers. Stirwaters should only last as long as the Miller line — and when the last Miller passed into history, so would the mill?

I carried that thought with the journals up into my office. It *fit*, somehow — like a bolt sliding home, like a key releasing a lock . . . and one by one all Stirwaters's secrets should tumble out at my feet. But *why?* The world did not conform to so neat a pattern; families died out, true, businesses too . . . but things were not interlinked so securely outside of fairy stories and nursery rhymes.

And curses.

I recoiled from the thought. Then, like a farmer poking at a snake to see if it is quite dead, gingerly approached it once again. I laid the word, letter by letter, out in my mind. Curse. A curse on Stirwaters. A curse on the Millers. Which? *Both?*

Using the back of one of Rosie's sketches for the new wheel, I charted a family tree for Stirwaters. Once I had the patriarchs sketched in, I had to dig deeper into the records for their families. I began with Father's predecessor, Joseph, a distant sort of cousin who had died peacefully at home (so said the obituary from the Haymarket *Crier*) at the age of eighty-six. His only child had been a son, died in infancy. Among

Brandon's gaggle of nine children, three boys dead of scarlet fever. To Currer's Hap and Simon — a cart overturned. From our own wee Thomas, back to Harlan's pride and joy, Josiah, who made it into adolescence, but no further, my chart showed eleven Miller sons who had failed to inherit the mill from their fathers. A black mark drawn over each name painted the grim picture. Not only had these boys died before they could take Stirwaters — they died before they reached adulthood.

Every single one.

"Oh, mercy," I breathed, and a breeze shuddered through the mill.

I wanted to weep for them all, all those lost boys of Stirwaters. How many, like Thomas, were poor babes whose names never even made the record? Thomas was only there because I was here to remember him. Each name on that chart — and how many more? — represented sisters who'd lost brothers.

Mothers who'd lost sons.

I shoved the records across the desk and kicked back my chair, leaving my pen to pool ink on the family tree. I did not care. I had to get out of there, away from the mill and whatever darkness was even now reaching its tainted hands into my family.

I had told no one. I'd been ill for a few days in February, dizzy and weary, with a poor appetite; and Randall, home from Harrowgate for a bank holiday, insisted I stay abed for two entire days before he would release me. As my symptoms lingered I began to suspect that something besides a touch of winter illness caused them.

When I was certain, and I had made up my mind against my will, I took the longer path by the roadway and called on my neighbor, Biddy Tom. Standing on her shadowed doorstep, I wished I had brought Rosie with me, but until my own suspicions were confirmed I didn't want to get her hopes up.

Mrs. Tom's cottage sat in a shady grove overgrown with oak and mountain ash, and an angry-looking vine, winter-naked, sprawled crazily up the wall and across a window shuttered tight behind it. I could barely make out specks of once-blue paint through gaps in the vine. The same blue decked the frames of the other windows, the lintel, and glowed like a great blue eye on the arched door. A "friendship door," we called it — split top and bottom, each half swinging independently. Today both halves were tightly closed. A painted hex circle in reds and yellow — not quite flowers, not really birds — hung where a window should have been, and a faded garland of fall leaves, battered some by the rough winter, curved above my head.

I dropped the hammer of the knocker against the door, my heart jolting once in echo. A moment passed, in which I contemplated my escape, before the upper door creaked inward, and Mrs. Tom's calm face peered out at me.

"Charlotte Miller. I wondered when you'd be coming down to see me. An August babe, if I'm not mistaken. Well, don't stand there gawping in the cold — come inside, child."

The upper door swung back, and I heard a snap as Mrs. Tom refastened the bolts that held the door together, and then the whole blue arrangement receded inward once more. Pursing my lips, I stepped inside Biddy Tom's house.

And was immediately surprised. What had I expected? Something queer and dark, haunted by shadows and nameless things? The cottage was bright and airy, sunlight streaming in through lace curtains and casting the tidy parlor in cheery light. A whitewashed floor and faded rag rug, polished furniture, the sparkle of pewter and glass on the mantelpiece — there was nothing eldritch here. Nothing stranger than a massive spinning wheel by the fireplace — as long as the hearth and probably as high as my shoulder — and a large panel painting of five serious-looking men above the settle.

"My boys," Mrs. Tom said, "my Tom, and Small Tom, Henry, Peter, and Stephen."

"What — what happened to them?" I asked, wondering faintly which one of the strapping fellows in the picture was "Small" Tom.

Mrs. Tom burst out laughing, a hearty sound, and warm, like the lowing of cattle. "Nothing happened to them, girl. Small Tom and Henry took to sea and took wives on the coast. Peter is a joiner, and Stephen runs a public house in Trawney. Of course, my Tom died years ago." She gave a wave of her hand, as if the loss of a husband were something to shrug away as casually as a gnat or a fly. "Now, let's get a look at you."

After she had declared me in perfect health, and given me what must be a standard litany of new-mother reassurances, Mrs. Tom asked me to tea. I could scarcely refuse; Gold Valley neighbors do not decline one another's hospitality. And though I confess a strong urge to depart as soon as possible, it was quelled by a mixture of curiosity and absolute dead ordinariness. The midwife's cottage was like every other home in Shearing; what had I to fear?

Besides, I had too many questions.

Mrs. Tom brought the tray, a sturdy, workaday display of

plain china and warm biscuits. I offered to pour out, but she waved my hand away. I nibbled my biscuit in silence, a silence that grew as the afternoon light waned, and Mrs. Tom made no move to light lamps. Finally, she arranged her hands in her apron and looked at me across the tea table.

"Well," she said. "Say your piece."

I meant to protest, but those clear pale eyes were too intense. I set my cup down and met her gaze. "What causes a curse?"

She frowned slightly, as if to bat my question aside as gently as she had my hand. But a moment passed and she seemed to change her mind. "Anger," she said, and the word rolled over me like low thunder. "Dark, fearful anger — jealousy, resentment, pain. And, usually," here she shifted in her chair, like a cat tucking and settling in, "violent death."

"And bad luck?"

"Ah," she said. "Now, that's different. A curse you can't do much about, but find way to break it. Luck, though — lass, you make your own luck. Bad things happen in life, misfortunes fall to everyone in turn. Just a part of the changing years, and nowt to worrit over. You just decide how to face it, is all."

I frowned. Easily said. But an image rose up in my mind: a picture of a mill on a small brown dish. "Great courage breaks ill luck," I whispered.

Mrs. Tom smiled. "Aye, lass. That it does."

I bit my lip. "What breaks a curse, then?"

She didn't answer for a long moment. The sunny parlor was deep in slanted shadows now, golden light chasing the tracery of lace against the faded floor. Finally, Mrs. Tom began a slow, rhythmic nodding, as if to herself. "Well, now," she said quietly. "That's another thing entirely." She rose from her straight-backed chair and crossed the room to a cabinet set into the wall. Opening it, she drew her hand along a row of books, her fingers hanging scant inches from a selection. "First," she said. "You must know who set the curse. That story's been trailing around Stirwaters a long, long time. Any notion why? What dark dealings in Miller past are hidden in those stones?"

"None!" I said, but too quick, too sharply. What did I truly know? Miller or not, my father had been a stranger here, and the miller before him. Stirwaters had changed hands too many times to keep all her memories alive. But what had I told Randall? *Stirwaters calls its keepers. . . .*

The name *Wheeler* had been on the millwheel, on the very heart of Stirwaters, all these years. My uncle's name. Was that simple coincidence? Was Uncle Wheeler's presence here part of some old, old design? And if the turning of the great wheel had brought us all back together again, Miller and Wheeler, then for what purpose?

Anger, pain. Violent death.

Scarcely aware I did so, I clutched a hand to my belly. Mrs. Tom noticed, and came back to sit beside me, the book she sought forgotten.

"Lass," she said gently, "put talk of curses out of your head. If there's one thing bad for wee babes, it's worry. Forget an old woman's nonsense, forget the gossip and the foolish stories. Go home to that husband of yourn and raise up a big brood of Woodstone babies. Forget you ever heard the word *curse*."

"I can't," I said. "I can't afford to."

I rose to my feet and thanked her for the tea. She shook her head but followed me to the door. "You come back in a

232

month or two, hear me? Or any time. My door's open to you, Charlotte. If you need a friend."

I felt those strange pale eyes on my back all the way to my own doorstep, but I was halfway home before I realized something: My mother had been a Wheeler, which made me one, too.

And so was my baby.

Chapter Nineteen

Finally, in the middle of March, the millwheel was ready. It arrived by cart from the joiner's, led by Rosie and Harte, the rest of the village trailing behind like a parade. It was the work of two days to set it into place — and the event of the season. Like a barn-raising among country neighbors, everyone pitched in to help, millhand or not. Even Uncle Wheeler strutted about like a squire, overseeing the proceedings with an air of administrative authority.

Taking advantage of a day that was almost pleasant, we closed the sluice and emptied the spillway, draining the water from the wheelpit. It was a job we should have done every year, to clear debris and silt from the pit, but like everything else it had been neglected. I hadn't seen the wheelpit empty since I was a little girl. It was a great half-barrel carved out of the earth, lined with grey stone caked with mud. As the water drained away, the pit was overrun by scampering, bare-legged boys eager to burrow through the silt in search of treasures washed into the headrace.

"You lads be careful now," Harte yelled as Jamie Handy shoved little Dan Fuller facedown into the muck. Danny howled with rage and grappled for Jamie's feet with clay-caked fists. Eventually he made contact, and spilled Jamie's legs right out from under him. Everyone laughed, even those of us who knew better.

"Sixpence!" one of the boys shouted. "A real silver sixpence!"

"Ain't that Tansy's shoe, what she lost last summer?"

And so the account rang up, all the detritus of the years, collected in the bowels of Stirwaters. Coins were the property of their finders, but anything whose ownership might be determined was strewn in a filthy strip along the bank. I fell into the column filing past to study the items, amazed at their variety. For a frugal people, we certainly managed to lose our share of things.

Among the battered shoes, broken crockery, and odd bit of harness, there was another sort of booty entirely. I collected no fewer than five straw figures, crudely formed and rather the worse for wear for their dunking in the pond. Stuck with pins or dressed in rags, they had the appearance of sad little victims of sacrifice. One of the wet figures in my hand, I glanced round at my neighbors. Who had flung these manikins into the water, and for what purpose? Was this the "tribute" paid by the Friendly Society? Toss a corn dolly into the Stowe every spring, and the capricious river will spare you and yourn?

I shook off a shiver and gathered up the corn dollies from the bank. I found Mr. Mordant across the pond, watching the to-do from a respectable distance. He was leaning against the fence, whittling a chunk of wood with a blade no longer than his thumb.

"Mornin,' missie." He nodded to me. "What you got there?"

I showed him. "I found these," I said. "I — I'm not sure what we should do with them."

Mr. Mordant gave me a long, appraising look, his pipe dangling from his lip. "Good girl," he said finally. "Tha' done right. Seems to me we can go two ways: cast 'em back into the wash, for there they were meant to stay — or toss 'em onto the fire, for they done their job already."

"Have they?" I found myself asking. Didn't Annie Penny attest to their failing?

The old dye master glared at me. "You know better'n ask a question like that."

Biting my lip, I shoved the figures toward him. "Here, you decide how they should be . . . dealt with." I was happier not knowing. I did hear from Rosie, though, several months later, that she had seen them in the dyeshed, all lined up along the windowsill.

As Mr. Mordant collected the dollies from me, I heard the squish-slap of wet boy's feet against the shale and looked up to see the youngest Lamb running toward us.

"Mistress, Mistress!" he cried, catching me up. His soaked knee breeches dripped onto my skirts. "Ain't this your mam's ring?" To my astonishment, he held out a tiny circle of tarnished tin, all the silver gone, topped by a begrimed paste pearl. "Mam says it were yours." Before I could speak, he scampered away again.

Mr. Mordant grinned at me, dark gaps in his smile. "Now, how 'bout that?"

I showed the ring to Rosie later that afternoon as we were washing up in the butt.

"What do you think it means?"

Rosie held the ring over the water for a long moment, as if watching waves and eddies through the circle. "That it's probably too much to hope your watch will turn up?"

Helplessly, hysterically, I began to laugh.

The following day we hoisted the new wheel into place. Less a spectacle than the empty wheelpit, today's work drew a smaller audience, and a more idle one. Anxious to begin work anew, the Stirwaters folk hung round the wheelhouse, getting underfoot, in case some task might present itself promptly once the new wheel was turning freely.

I stood in the lee of the wheelhouse, watching Rosie and Harte work side by side. Like two parts of one machine, they were well matched, moving easily in one another's rhythm. Rosie would reach out a hand blindly, and Harte would fill it with whatever tool she needed. I wondered what it might be like to have that connection with Randall.

"Fine piece of work, ain't it, Mistress?" I turned to see young Ian Lamb beside me, his mother, Janet, with him. "Still, wouldn't it have been grand to see a great new wheel runnin' the old place?"

Janet gave him a look to curdle cream. "Tweren't nowt wrong with the old design," she said stoutly. "No need to go meddlin' with what's been fine enough all these years. And ain't no call to go diggin' up parts what's been sealed off for good and all. Buried is buried, if you ask me."

"Buried!" I said. "What's buried?"

"Nowt's buried," Janet said, shoving her hands into her apron pockets. "Just talkin' about the past, is all."

"Yes, but you said *buried*," I insisted. "Is there something buried under Stirwaters?"

"'Course not. Where did you hear that fool notion! You're gettin' as queer as your pa, then, I daresay, Mistress. Buried under Stirwaters!" She laughed — a bit too heartily.

Something *I'd* tried to bury sprang up vividly in my memory. "Do you know anything about a drowning at Stirwaters?"

"A drowning!" Ian's attention snapped back quickly enough.

Janet cuffed him hard on the shoulder. "No, I do not," she said, her voice firm. "I have never heard such a thing, and I've been here thirty-four years this spring. Ah, Mistress." She gave me a firm smile, as if to close the matter. "Don't pay no mind to the spoutin' of a fool woman plenty old enough to learn when to keep her fat mouth shut."

I frowned at her in silence a moment longer, meeting her stubborn gaze. She turned away before I did, giving her son a shove.

I had little time to reflect on that conversation, for Randall drove into town just in time to see the new wheel hauled into place. I watched him park the buggy in the yard and toss a coin to one of the lads, who led the horses away.

"Haul away, lads, easy there!" bellowed Harte, and I looked away for a moment, to watch the men heave hard on great levers and lift the wheel enough to slide the blocks beneath. When I looked back, Randall was jogging over the slick wet grass.

Suddenly, I saw him fall.

I saw his boots hit a slippery patch, watched him lose his footing, gasped as he pitched headlong into the pit. I heard the great painful crack of the rotted sluice gates giving way, sending the pent-up water racing down the channel like a burst of storm tide.

I stifled a scream and grappled against the wall for a handhold. I squeezed my eyes closed for a count of five and then looked up again, and all was as it should be. The work continued — Randall had paused to chat with one of the hands — and up the race, the sluice gates still held fast. No one else had seen it — yet it had seemed so *real*! I pressed a hand to my waist and took several ragged breaths. Ten feet below me, the cold damp stones of the wheelpit lay smooth and worn beneath the curve of the wheel.

Fighting vertigo, I stared back at them, waiting. *What is it?* I asked them silently. *What are you trying to show me?* Was it a message — or a threat? I was still staring at the pit when Randall slipped in beside me, circling my waist with his arms.

"It's freezing out here. Here." He draped his frock coat round my shoulders, and I stood stiff and still, smiling and pretending I was glad to see him there.

I could not stand to watch them all crawling around the empty pit much longer. Pleading a chill, I retreated inside the mill, with Randall's overwhelming approval. At first I just sat, listening to the clamor of the work outside. Harte's voice hollering, the creak of the ropes . . . but as I listened, the sounds seemed to shift, subtly — a shout, in a strange voice, thickly accented — a sound of hammer on stone. I could not hear the river, not even a gentle ripple as it flowed past the mill.

I started, as out of a dream. *Oh, mercy.*

I yanked book after book from the shelves, flipped through pages, tossed them aside again. May Day celebrations, funeral bills, awkward transitions of handwriting as the mill changed hands, over and again through the years. But nothing I sought, nothing near old enough. We had records going back to the days of Stirwaters's founder, but none at all from the building of the mill. And I could not credit that.

Rosie came in at length and found me pacing the office, the ledger from Edmund Miller's day in my arms. "We're getting ready to open up the sluice," she said. "Start the water flowing again. We thought you'd want to see."

I barely heard her. "They dammed the river, didn't they?"

Rosie paused. "Who?"

"When they built Stirwaters — they had to dam the river. When the water wasn't running past — *that's* the only time a curse could be laid down. Biddy Tom told us, remember? And that's when someone drowned here — it must be the same person."

She came in a few steps and pried the volume from my hands. "That's some trick," she said, "cursing somebody with your lungs full of the Stowe."

"I thought you believed all this!"

"Well, when *you* say it, I've got to admit it starts to sound a little cockeyed."

I sighed and leaned against the desk, one hand pressed to my skirts. Rosie came to me and put an arm round my waist.

"What's wrong?" she asked. "You're not yourself lately."

And wasn't that the truth.

Harte and Rosie's work proved true: In place at last, the new wheel functioned beautifully. As it turned easily in the water, so turned the seasons, and before we knew it wool market days were upon us again. After a year, I should have felt more confident, strolling into the woolshed to face the woolmen, but I didn't. I bought less wool than last year and paid more for it. I wasn't pushing my luck.

"Wouldn't it make more sense to buy *more* wool, and have a cushion?" Rosie protested; but I disagreed: Better to prepare for the worst by having less to risk.

I wanted to check this theory against my husband's expertise, but Randall was absent more often these days. I knew he was working hard at the bank, in anticipation of our baby's birth, so he could be here with me more afterward — but I was torn. I wanted him here with me, and yet I didn't. I couldn't look at him without seeing him flail and struggle under the rushing water of the millstream. And so I helped him pack, and loaded him onto the carriage or the stage, and said nothing.

With the new wheel up, and the spring wool tucked away in the woolshed, the season got off to a robust start. Porter & Byrd had renewed their confidence in us, sending us a modest commission cheque and placing another hefty order. Halfheartedly, I submitted an application for reinstatement at Worm Hill, but it no longer seemed necessary to pin our fortunes on the Harrowgate market. Mrs. Parmenter sent a cordial letter offering to buy more gold thread, should we find ourselves in possession of more of the same. Hastily, I shoved that note to the back of a desk drawer.

The millhands seemed happy to be back at work, as well. Now that hands were no longer idle, tongues were likewise busy once again. And the chief subject of examination that cold bright spring? The Miller progeny.

I hadn't expected to keep it a secret long; Shearing

gossip is like another tributary of the Stowe, after all. But I was unprepared for how swiftly I became the subject of rapt attention and unbidden advice. I smiled thinly and bore it, feeling like the prize heifer at a stock show.

"She's carrying high, like her mam," said Mrs. Drover, weeks before anything of the sort was remotely perceptible. "That means a girl."

"Aye," concurred Mrs. Hale. "Make sure you drink a lot of milk, now, lassie; and stay clear from too many flowers. You don't want the wee lass to grow up wandersome."

"Why is everyone so convinced it's a girl?" Randall asked, amused, one bright afternoon as we rode home together from fetching the post and restocking the larder. Mrs. Post had just, with utter seriousness, advised a preparation of mole's feet and spearmint, hung round the neck. I hunched down inside my cloak, not wanting to answer him. Spoken aloud, the notion would sound preposterous, but I knew the truth of it. Millers had no luck with boys; better to hope from the start the baby would be female.

"They're probably right," Randall continued. "After all, in seven tries, our mothers only managed to produce one boy. One in seven odds — fairly good in favor of our little foal being a filly!" He reached over to pat me on the belly.

"Two in eight," I whispered, flinching away.

"What?"

I said it a little louder. "I had a brother once: Thomas. He lived a week. That's when my mother died."

Randall slowed the carriage and turned to me. "My God, Charlotte, why didn't you ever tell me?" He put one strong arm round my shoulders and squeezed tight. "Did Mrs. Tom say there was any cause for concern?"

Hadn't she? But I shook my head.

He tipped my chin toward his face and kissed my fore-head. "There. You're young and strong; there's nothing to be afraid of."

I laid my cheek against his chest, straining to hear his heartbeat through his coat, but all I heard was the groan and creak of the old millwheel, spilling Millers down into the raging river one by one.

Things were little better at the mill. As if Stirwaters were determined that I should get no work at all done this year, the millhands would not let me near my spinning jack, citing old Gold Valley superstitions that the babe would grow up to be hanged! Woolwashing, dyeing, and fulling were like-wise out. So was standing for too long, climbing too many stairs, or working too near a window. I lost track of which of these precautions were for my protection — and which for theirs. Never mind that pregnant workers had made their way through Stirwaters for generations; this was a Miller baby, and no one would take any chances.

I must admit, I was less scornful of such beliefs than I had once been.

One afternoon as spring hinted toward summer, I worked late in the office, tidying up some figures in the account books. At last, satisfied but weary, I rose from the desk and bent all over to work the stiffness out of my spine. As I stepped out into the empty spinning room, I glanced toward the wall with the hex sign and started, my heart in my throat.

A figure stood in the shadows there, shoulders hunched. It took me a moment to realize it was Bill Penny, who I'd not seen in months. He had changed over the winter, shrunken and aged; he seemed half the size he'd been at his daughter's funeral. His clothes hung on him like sacking, and there was a huge, unmended tear in the sleeve of his coat. It looked as though he'd been sleeping in it, but the eyes he turned to me were sober ones.

"You pulled all the water out," he said, twisting his hat in trembling fingers. "I saw you."

"What? Oh, the wheelpit. Of course — we had to. For the new wheel."

"Did you see him? He comes here, sometimes, you know."

"Who's that?" It had been a long afternoon and my feet hurt. I was looking forward to propping them up on the petit-point footstool in the parlor at the Grange while Colly rubbed my swollen ankles with peppermint oil. I was not attending him as closely as I ought.

"Did you know my Annie?"

I shook my head. "No, Mr. Penny, I didn't." I had seen her, of course — it was hard to mistake the Penny children — but they kept to themselves, and I had no occasion to meet the girl.

"She were such a pretty 'un," he said — which was patently untrue, but hardly a thought you'd begrudge a mourning father. "She had such pretty brown eyes, like two ripe chestnuts. An' she carried her dolly wi' her everywhere."

I nodded. "I saw it — at the funeral." I had hardly meant to make that admission, but I could not retract it now.

Bill's eyes burst open and he broke into a laugh that made me reconsider his sobriety. "Ye saw that, did ye, miss?

I tricked her, I did! She'll stay down if she got her dolly, won't she?"

The bleary eyes were beseeching. "Of course she will," I said, not at all certain what I was promising.

"But you'll tell me, won't you? If you see her? You'll tell Bill Penny if his Annie-girl comes round here."

"Comes here! Why should she come here?"

Bill nodded solemnly, conspiratorially. "Because this is where all the ghosts come."

I went cold.

"You know, miss — they're all around ye. The young lad, and th' angry one, and the master that was —"

I held my hands tight at my sides. "My father?"

A creak on the staircase nearly undid me. I looked up to see Harte framed there, his expression uncharacteristically dark.

"Is there some trouble here, Mistress?" he asked, glaring at poor befuddled Bill.

"Of course not, Harte. Please find Mr. Penny some task where he can be useful." I uncoiled my fingers and gave them a stretch. Harte gave me a long, appraising look before nodding.

"As you wish. Come along, then, Penny." He caught him by the arm and was none too gentle steering him from the room. The last words I heard were "come back when you've cleaned yourself up."

Harte returned a few minutes later, during which time I'd moved to the office, but had not managed to rouse myself from the fog I'd caught from Mr. Penny. What had he meant? Was I now to believe we were not only cursed, but haunted as well?

Harte let himself into the office. "They've all gone home now, Mistress," he said. "And if you don't mind, I'll be locking the place up and heading back to my rooms."

"Of course," I said. "Thank you, Harte."

He lingered in the doorway a moment longer, and then came all the way in and sat down on the corner of my desk. He lifted the iron ingot, hefted it, and then set it down again. "Look, Mistress," he said. "Don't think I'm forgetting who's master here, but I don't like this."

I frowned. "I'm not sure what you mean."

"I know you're trying to be charitable, and that's well and good, but that Penny's a bad sort. Your Mrs. Baker and my own mam were sisters, as y'know, and Maire Stokes — Mrs. Penny that was — grew up right nearby them. They'd tell tales about those folk as would make your hair curl, ma'am. Peas in a pod, that Maire and her husband. I think they'd make the Eagans look like the saints themselves." He grinned, but I could tell it was only to pacify me. He saw nothing amusing in his words. "Can you tell me what he said that had you so shook up?"

I frowned. "What?"

"Ah, Mistress — I saw that look on your face from clear 'cross the spinning room. Like you'd seen a ghost. Now, I don't know what you and Miss Rosie have been up to here at all hours lately, and it's none of my business, at that — but when a man in your employ frightens you, I think I'm fair within my rights to speak out against it. Is he threatening you with something?"

"Threatening me?" Something made me want to tell Harte the truth. About everything — come clean there and then. I didn't dare, of course, but I did own what Bill Penny had said. "He says he sees ghosts here."

Harte's face was grim. "I'm sure he does. With his taste for drink, he probably has all kind of dread visions. And having buried three children? It can't be easy to stand in his shoes, Mistress, I'll give him that much. But it don't change what I've said. I'll stand by whatever you decide, of course. I'm just askin' you to think twice how badly we really need another hand round here."

Chapter Twenty

I could not bring myself to discharge Bill, sound as Harte's advice was. Part of it was charity: How could I pour salt in that poor man's wounds? But the measure was my own selfish curiosity. If Bill Penny truly saw ghosts — and I told myself I did not believe it; Harte was right and they were naught but drink-phantoms — but if he *did* see them, I half wished to be close by when they appeared. I could scarcely explain this even to myself. My world was like a glass tipped on its side, reason flowing out and . . . something else flowing in. Could Bill's ghosts somehow make sense of all the strangeness that I had witnessed these last months?

And there was another reason. *The master that was . . .* Was my father in that congregation? Did he still linger, guiding my hand? I voiced the thought to Rosie, and she crowed with laughter.

"Aye! And we want him guiding your hand, so fine a job he did of things when he was alive." She shook her head. "You're wasting your money and your sympathy on that Bill, Charlotte. He's a shiftless old sack, drunk or sober, and you'll never get the work out of him you're paying for."

Not that it was costing any sort of fortune. I only paid Bill for days he worked, and in the months that followed, those were fewer and fewer. Neither did I pay much mind to gossip that placed Bill Penny with the Eagans almost as often as he could be found at Drover's. And it was all for naught — for in all the long hot months that followed, I never saw so much as a queer shadow near him.

The cold bright spring dissolved into a damp, oppressive summer, of a heavy overhanging sky that would neither rain nor clear, but life at Stirwaters settled into an unusually smooth rhythm. Our next shipment to Porter & Byrd was building up in the woolshed; they had this season put in special requests for particular cuts and weaves of cloth. Stirwaters Blues were making their name, it seemed, farther afield than any Miller had previously dreamed. It even seemed possible that we might make our last payment to Uplands Mercantile with a bit of a cushion to spare.

One afternoon I was surprised to find Bill shambling about my office, mumbling to himself, his trembling fingers shifting over the bookshelves, the desk.

"What are you doing in here?" I said, sharper than I intended. "Go home. Have something to eat."

"I haven't seen her," he said mournfully. "She never comes home, and I thought she might come here, where the boy is."

"Annie's not here," I said gently. "She died last summer, remember? Bill — maybe you oughtn't be here. This place isn't good for you. . . ."

"I thought she could see me, now that I'm here all the time. But I got confused — and then I took my knife and did it just like he said —"

"You what?"

He shook his head, urgent for me to understand. "I cut up them bales, right, what were all in bad colors? He said it frightened them, that they couldn't come anymore if it were there. And I said maybe we could just *move* it, but he said it weren't good enough."

I stared at him in dawning horror. "*Mr. Penny, did you cut all that cloth?*"

"Oh, aye — he told me to."

"Who?" My voice was stricken, shrill.

Penny pulled back like I'd slapped him. "The master. He gave me a present if I did it."

I barely heard that last part; all I saw was the millyard in moonlight, swirling thick with scraps of cloth like dust motes. I grabbed for Bill, shaking him by the shoulders. "What did you do? What did you do?"

"Mistress!" That was Harte, crossing the room in long strides to pull us apart. "What in the world's going on here?"

"He — he slashed the cloth," I said breathlessly. I had no idea why I was so upset — was it that Bill had done it, that *ghosts* had told him to . . . or that I'd erred so in my judgement of him? Harte gripped my shoulder tightly until I was calm again. Bill had broken down sobbing, like a frightened child. "Mr. Penny," I said loudly. "You must go home, and you must never come back here. Do you understand me? Do you understand?"

Harte shook him until he met my eyes. "You're sacking me?" Bill said, and he suddenly sounded completely lucid.

"Yes, Bill," I said, as the millwheel crashed and roared.

*   *   *

I woke in the night when a pain stabbed through my breast. I shot up in bed with a gasp, fearing for the baby. But it was no more than a moment before I realized I felt no *physical* pain. Panting as if from a nightmare, I clutched at the sheets and stared into the darkness. A second pang gripped my heart, and I knew something was wrong. I shook Randall awake.

"Something's the matter at Stirwaters!"

He frowned sleepily. "It's the middle of the night. You were dreaming. Go back to sleep."

"No — I felt . . ." I trailed off. What had I felt? Fear, and pain — and a cry for help. "I must go." I clambered out of bed, shrugged myself into my dressing gown, and fled for the dining room. I shoved apart the drapes and pressed my face to the glass, straining through the darkness toward the millpond.

Which was orange.

Like a glowing ember in the night, the water shone back a flickering nightmare — bright with flames, the mill buildings behind shrouded in a mist of smoke.

"Dear God — what's that?" Randall stumbled into the room.

"Stirwaters is burning! I must get down there!" Heedlessly, I ran for the front doors, and flung them open onto Rosie, clattering up the brick walk on Nathan Smith's ancient pony. They skidded to a halt just feet from the steps.

"The woolshed's afire!"

I ran out to meet her, Randall following on my heels. "What of the mill?"

"Nay, it's not caught. Randall — can you help? We need all the hands we can get."

"Of course," Randall said, pulling his boots on even as he ran.

I stared at the both of them helplessly. "I'm coming with you!"

"You are not!" Rosie said. "Phinny can only carry two." She reached down and squeezed my shoulder, and I smelled the smoke from her nightgown sleeve. "Truly, Charlotte — you'll be no help."

"Don't argue," Randall said, kissing my forehead. "For once sit tight, won't you?"

I nodded in despair, but of course I didn't mean to obey. It might take all night to carry me down the hill, but I was not going to sit safe and sound half a mile away. I delayed only long enough to don shoes and pull a frock and cloak over my nightdress before following Rosie and Randall into darkness.

I made myself take care, on the rocky road in the depths of midnight, but the same sharp cry that had wakened me urged me onward. I heard it like a voice in a dream — through the bones of my breast it resonated, silent and insistent, a distant, desperate plea. Say what you will: I say it was Stirwaters.

Calling its keeper.

As I descended the hill, the night sky before me lit up like sunset and storm together. I heard the roar of thunder before I understood it was the voice of the fire — a terrifying whoosh and howl that drowned out everything else. The baby woke and kicked me hard, just as the mill's voice cried, *Go, go!*

The scene at Stirwaters was chaos. Lit up like midday, the hands scurrying about the yard like bees at their hive, bustling everywhere with a strange, single-minded confusion as the flames leaped like windblown banners from the roof and windows. Somehow I kept myself from scrambling across the fence to join the battle. I might not have, if the baby hadn't stirred within me like a flutter of panic. I stood just outside the yard fence and hugged myself tight, and the fire burned on and on.

I saw Rosie and Randall in the bucket brigade, passing dyevats down the ranks to the pond and back. I searched for Harte but did not see him. Dear God — where was he? What of Pilot? I stared at the flames pouring out his window and knew nothing could have survived inside.

A crash brought the roof down in a shower of sparks, and everyone scattered.

The woolshed was a loss. I heard a voice barking orders, but could not make out the words. The men shifted their concentration to protecting Stirwaters and the Millhouse, but watching, I knew — I *knew* that Stirwaters would not burn. Something outside any of us kept it safe. Would it not have crumbled to dust long ago else?

The building stood in silhouette against the burning sky, a blackened face with eyes afire. A blast of heat knocked me back a few steps, and I gasped. It was like the furnace at Pinchfields — black and hungry, the impossible pink sunrise of fire swathed in clouds of smoke and sparks. It seemed to swell toward me, looming, warning.

The next thing I knew, I was sitting on the earth, in a rivulet of hot water streaming down the shale. Dazed, I could not think how I had gotten there, but strong arms were round my shoulders, easing me upward.

"Easy there, Mistress," said a wonderful, familiar voice in my ear. I whirled in his arms.

"Harte!" I was on my feet, my arms flung around his neck. "Oh, thank God. Thank God." Frantically I searched his face and shoulders with my hands — for burns, for sparks, for proof of life. He laughed and let me.

"Ah, it's all right then, Miss Charlotte. Here, easy now. You shouldn't be out here, but I'm sure it's no good tellin' you that."

"How did you get out?"

He shook his head. "I weren't *in*. Pilot woke me, sure she had some urgent mission off by the river. It were a fine night, so I took to follow her for once. She disappeared into the wood, and I couldn't find her. By the time I gave her up and turned back, the smoke was halfway up the southwest corner."

"How did it start?" I held tight to Harte's arms, unwilling to admit my legs were still trembling.

Harte frowned. In the flickering light his face was in and out of shadow, shiny and red and smudged with soot. "We might know more in the morning."

"If there's anything left by then," I said.

"Ah, the lads are trusty," he said. "If there's a way to save this old place, they'll do it for you. Look, I ought to lend a hand. Since I know you won't leave, will you at least sit down?"

I shook my head — or I nodded. With one last squeeze to my shoulders, Harte left me, to go back into the living, livid fire.

They were all helping. Someone had propped a ladder against the Millhouse, and sturdy fellows hauled water up to douse the roof. It was slate, but underneath was timber — and being slate hadn't saved the woolshed. A trench had been dug in the shale surrounding the house, and beaters staffed the mill, ready to stamp out any sparks that hit close by. In glimpses among the ruddy light I recognized millhands and villagers alike, all working frantically to protect the mill.

Except me.

And the cry in my heart was as loud as ever.

"Oh, mercy help us," I breathed into the night air, unable to do more.

I saw a sudden, bright flash — quicker and sharper than the flames — followed promptly by a clap of thunder so loud it knocked my heart into my throat. And like that, the glooming, lowering clouds broke open at last. Fat, beautiful droplets spattered the shale, and a cheer went up from the crowd.

Afterward folk told that it was like no rain Shearing had ever seen. At first it merely struck the fire and splattered into steam, but eventually the heavens gained the upper hand. Rain poured down, heavy and heavier, like a curtain of water being drawn across the Valley. In seconds I was soaked through to my skin, shivering with gooseflesh. I kept wiping my sodden hair from my forehead with the back of my hand, but it only fell back again, wetter than ever. I wanted to laugh. I wanted to scream. The voice within me crowed with triumph; I mourned for everything we had nearly lost.

From somewhere in the wet distance I heard Rosie calling. She emerged from the night, breathless and shouting. "They've got the fire out at the shed, but the roof's gone, and it looks like the loft might have collapsed as well. The stock —" She shook her head. Wool won't burn, but it will scald, stink, shrink, warp, and run. Half a season's work lay beneath tons of rubble and water, moldering as we spoke. "Do you think we'll save anything?"

"You saved the mill," I said. To my relief, Rosie grinned.

"Aye, that we did," she said, and threw her arms around me. I feared she might cry, but she pulled away again. "You should get inside and change," she said sternly, "before you catch your death. Why don't you let Randall take you home? We'll finish up here."

I looked around the sodden, ashen millyard, at my drenched and sooty sister. With every flash of lightning, I could see clean through her wet nightdress. I pulled off my wet cloak and bundled her in it.

"I am home," I said.

The rain lasted only as long as it was needed, and stopped once it had done its good deed. Work resumed near dawn — the stamping out of stubborn embers, the knocking down of walls before they could tumble on their own, the raking away of rubble. I allowed someone to find me dry clothes that more or less fit and permitted myself to be tucked under the Millhouse eaves, a mug of coffee steaming in my grip. I don't think I took a single sip. Pilot showed up at last, none the worse than the rest of us, and settled beside me.

In the cold clear light of morning, the ghostly voice retreated, and reason returned. The ruined carcass of the woolshed was devastating, but not sinister; a blackened skeleton in a grave of stones, which didn't so much as whisper to me. I understood — I had done its bidding, its wish was granted: Stirwaters was saved. The woolshed was a casualty, but it was not the mill.

The fire had one more cruel surprise. About midmorning, I heard a shout from within the ruins, where Harte and Randall and some of the other men worked to smother the last smoldering remnants of the blaze. I ran to see, stumbling over kicked-up debris and slipping on the wet shale, but Eben Fuller grabbed me bodily and held me back.

"Nay, Mistress — you won't want to see that."

"What — what is it?"

Eben hesitated. "They've found a body."

"A body? But who — who could have been in there?" All of mine were accounted for — Rosie, Randall, Harte and Pilot — I'd even seen Uncle Wheeler poke a disdainful head out a Millhouse window at one point. The millhands — weren't they all here? I looked around, frantic to see who might be missing.

"It's Bill Penny, Mistress."

I stared at him, horror seeping through me as the rain had done.

"It looks like he set the fire — there's a can of turpentine and a pile of rags over by the mill building. It's a miracle that the mill never caught. Poor old sod must've crept into the shed to watch the fire, and passed out. He had his bottle with him."

I pushed past him and clambered over the fallen stones. Harte and Randall were gathered round a shape on the floor, which someone had covered with a length of ruined cloth. Harte made to stop me, but Randall shook his head and drew me to him. His nightshirt was wet through to the skin with sweat and rain, his tanned face streaked with black. I pulled away from him before he could wrap an arm around me.

"I sacked him," I whispered. "He's the one who damaged the stock — but I never thought —" My words were lost in a violent shudder.

"Hush, it's not your fault."

I could not draw my gaze away from the pitiful form in its woollen shroud. One outflung arm was not quite covered, and I thought I could see . . . I knelt beside the heap and flipped back enough of the cloth to reveal Bill Penny's clothing. It was ruined now, of course, the color distorted by smoke and water. I glanced at Harte and Randall, to see if they recognized it, but they had not spent months staring at it across the breakfast table. For me, there could be no doubt: Bill Penny had been wearing a coat of robin's egg blue.

The master gave me a present if I did it.

I lingered among the ruins all afternoon, stepping gingerly through the wreckage, trying to salvage anything from the fire. The men had cleared away most of the debris and removed poor Bill Penny to the undertaker's. Stirwaters would pay for his funeral, such as it would be; he may have committed arson, but we shared some blame for his death.

"That's one," said a grating voice behind me. I spun, gripping tight to a length of plaid flannel that smelt of a campfire.

Jack Spinner climbed toward me over the heaped-up rubble. His ragged topcoat fluttered in a breeze that was not there, showing his scrawny frame. He looked, more than ever, like a scarecrow.

"One what?" I said crossly. I was in no mood to cross paths with him today.

"Victim, one death, one poor soul who relied on Charlotte Miller and met a bad end because of it. How many more do you suppose there will be?"

"What do you want?"

He bent and retrieved a blackened object from the ground. He brushed the dust away, and I could see it was the cover to the pattern book we'd been assembling for Porter & Byrd. "The question is, Mistress Miller, what do you want?"

"I want you to go away," I said.

"Happily," he said. "Snap my fingers, whistle a tune, and all of this disappears. You won't hear from me again, and the Millers go on their merry way."

I snatched the book cover from his hands. "No, thank you. Your skills are not necessary this time. We were insured." Randall had gone home to get cleaned up, but he was heading for Harrowgate tonight, to file our claim with the firm.

"Insurance? But, Charlotte Miller, you ought to know you can't get better insurance than with me. Why, my work is guaranteed." He chuckled, a dry, throaty sound like the rustling of leaves. I suppressed a shiver, as if brushed by Spinner's phantom breeze.

"Your offer is appreciated, sir, but Stirwaters will not be needing your services again. I thank you to remove yourself from my property at once, or I shall send for the authorities."

Spinner grinned and jammed his hands into his pockets. "Aye? And who do you imagine has authority over me, Mistress?"

Now I knew I felt the shiver, and I wrapped my arms around my breast. "Go away," I repeated, but my voice was not so strong this time.

Behind me, I heard the crunch of shale, and I turned. Mr. Mordant was hobbling up the yard. "You all right there, missie? That little feller ain't bothering you, is he?"

"No, Mr. Mordant, our friend was just leaving." I turned to shoo Mr. Spinner on his way again.

He had disappeared.

*　　*　　*

Something bothered me about this whole affair, and it was more than just the loss of the woolshed or poor Bill's death. Standing in the lee of the mill, watching the last lingering steam rise from the ruin of the woolshed, I almost understood everything. The fire, Bill's blue coat, his urgent explanations about "the master." I thought I knew who that was, at least.

A few days later I carried my suspicions across the yard, to the Millhouse.

I found my uncle having a drink in the parlor, in a curious state of undress: embroidered waistcoat and shirtsleeves, covered over with a satin half-cape, as if he were getting ready to powder his wig. The idea of him wandering about my home with such an informal air was oddly disconcerting to me. I hesitated in the doorway, and had to force myself into the room.

"My dear Charlotte, what a pleasure to see you!" He turned to me and downed the remainder of his wine. "Come, sit down."

I held my ground. "I'd rather not, thank you. Uncle, might I have a word with you?"

He drew me closer with his hand, a line of concern creasing his powdered face. "Of course, my dear. Is there something bothering you? I daresay you do look a little peaked. Perhaps this weather isn't the ideal thing for a girl in your condition. Why don't you have that husband of yours take you into the city, where you can rest and have your child in civilized conditions? You know I'd be more than happy to look after your interests here."

"Yes, well, Uncle, that's rather what I wanted to discuss."

Uncle Wheeler's face brightened under raised eyebrows. "Indeed? Do go on."

Trying to summon up the certainty I had felt in the shadow of the mill, I said, "I want to know what happened to the woolshed."

He shook his head. "I know — so troubling. What a distressing thing to happen, for everyone."

"I mean, I want to know what *you* know about it, sir." Behind my back, I twined my fingers together so tightly I could feel my nails biting into my flesh.

Uncle Wheeler gave a cough. "Really, I —"

"Bill Penny was wearing your coat. Your blue velvet morning coat."

He settled into the chair, a look of sympathy on his face. Shaking his head, he said, "Now, Charlotte, you know I lost that jacket over a hand of cards. If it wound up in a rag-and-bone shop, where that unfortunate fellow picked it up, I'm sure there's nothing I can do about it."

"Shearing doesn't have a rag-and-bone shop. He must have gotten it from you."

My uncle was watching me, carefully, out of those green eyes. "My dear, are you trying to accuse me of something? Because if you are, you're going to need more than girlish hysteria to do it with."

"I saw you. With the man from Pinchfields."

"Who?"

"Their wool buyer. I saw you meeting with him. At the pub, in Harrowgate. After — when we went to the city." Coming out of my mouth, it didn't sound like such damning evidence after all.

He stared at me a moment, eyes narrowed, and then laughed, a louder, heartier sound than his usual delicate twitter. "Oh, my word, Charlotte — how your imagination has run away with you! That good fellow and I are members of the same club. As is your husband, if I do remember aright. Are you going to accuse *him* of something next?"

I felt my resolve wavering, and took a deep breath to fortify myself. "Are you also not in debt to Arthur Darling?"

"Oh, dear. You've gotten all turned around. No wonder you're so upset. Surely you understand that society circles are not that large? A man like Darling and I were bound to cross paths, and when we both enjoy a game of chance . . . well. And the debt?" He waved his hand, as if brushing away a speck of lint. "A pittance. Don't trouble yourself over it."

He had an explanation for everything. Just like he always did. But I was bone weary of secrets and mysteries, and the line that marked what I would believe was wavering. I met his concerned gaze and willed him to tell me something true — something that went deeper than the powdered mask.

"Now, my dear, if you haven't any other random accusations to plague me with, why don't you run along? I'm sure you must have some little task to occupy you, and as you can see, I myself have pressing matters to attend to." He rose, arranging the fall of his cape as he turned away from me. I stared at him, infuriated. How dare he simply dismiss me, from my own home!

"We're not finished here, Uncle. The fire —"

Uncle Wheeler clucked his tongue. "Oh, Charlotte, I wouldn't look too closely at that fire, if I were you. Especially not with Randall involved."

I flinched as if he'd slapped me. "What about him?"

"But it's just such an odd coincidence, isn't it? Taking out that sizable insurance policy on his wife's property, shortly before that same property was burned to the ground by one of her employees? I wonder, what is the penalty for insurance fraud these days?"

"What are you saying? You know Randall had nothing to do with the fire."

"Do I? My dear, truly. It's *so hard* to know who to trust these days. But wouldn't it be a pity if anything were to happen to disrupt your pretty marriage? No, let's not tamper with an arrangement that has been working beautifully for months. You run home to that dear little husband of yours, and I will try very hard to forget we ever had this conversation."

I was trembling. He was right. I had nothing. No evidence, no proof, no credibility. And too much to lose. I could say nothing, make no move. I was trapped.

Chapter Twenty-One

Randall returned from Harrowgate with the news
that the insurance settlement would more than cover
the amount still owed to Uplands Mercantile. Stirwaters put
a claim in for both the value of the cloth and the damage to the
woolshed, but we saw very little of the money by the time our
debts were paid off. The success of finally ridding ourselves
of Father's mortgage was somehow not the joyous relief I had
once anticipated.

Porter & Byrd were not well pleased to learn their entire
order had perished by fire, of course, but I was able to pacify
them by offering positively scandalous rates on replacement
stock, and by some miracle they put their faith in me again.
We resumed work on the new order immediately, the bales
of cloth stored now in the great hollow rooms at the Grange.
Rosie had suggested the Millhouse, but I pled space concerns,
unable to tell the real reason I could not have the cloth under
that roof.

I told no one of my conversation with Uncle Wheeler. I
didn't dare. The days drew closer to the birth of our child,
and when I should have been sewing lace to Christening
bonnets and pressing sprigs of lavender between the tiny

nightgowns sent by Randall's sisters, all I could do was fret and worry.

Randall couldn't understand me. "Won't you tell me what's bothering you?" he asked one night as we got ready for bed. He crept behind me and circled my shoulder with his arm. I bit back tears and pulled away.

"It's nothing," I said. "The — the baby's wakeful." I choked on the words.

"Darling, please. I can help you, whatever it is."

The words were gentle, but I felt them with a sense of panic. How could he help? With effort, I summoned up that serene smile from so many months ago. "Truly, there's nothing."

Nothing but a curse that kills children. Nothing but a baby brother, dead at a week, and his mother with him. Nothing but an uncle I had harbored for a year and yet did not know at all. Nothing but a marriage built on secrets. Nothing but a haunted mill that had threatened my husband with ter-rifying visions.

Nothing but a wife going mad with the strain of it all.

Randall sighed, rose, squeezed my shoulder. "Have you seen Mrs. Tom?

I started. "What?"

"For some tea, or a tonic. To calm your nerves. Charlotte, anyone would be under a strain at a time like this — and you've had some extra worries on top of everything."

Hadn't I just. Still, I lifted my hand to his and stroked his wrist. "That's a good idea," I said. "Maybe I will."

But I didn't.

*　　*　　*

Impatient, perhaps, for the child to be born, over the next weeks I was more "broodsome" than ever, as Randall put it — some word he'd picked up in the village. But in truth, I seemed to feel something else looming — some further crisis preparing to rear its head, and I wished to be ready for it.

It was a steamy day in August when the pending storm broke at last. I was in a sulky mood, feeling ponderous and ungainly under the increasingly awkward weight of the baby. I had quarrelled with Randall the day before, over something trivial, and he had departed for Harrowgate in an untalkative mood. I could not decide whether or not to miss him. Under an ever-widening prohibition of labor at the mill — we'd been plagued with low water, and production had come to a stop until some rain replenished the millpond — I had heard the word *curse* mumbled more than once that week, and I could not bring myself to silence those murmurs.

Deep in contemplation, I heard Harte or Rosie's hammer in the distance. Rosie poked her head in the office. "What's that pounding?"

"Well, if it's not you, it must be Harte."

"No, Ma'am," Harte said, sliding in beside Rosie. I could not help noting, yet again, how well matched they were. "Perhaps it's your ghost."

"You're not funny," I said wearily, prying myself free from the chair. "But if it is, I'll wring its wispy neck if it doesn't stop that. Well, I'm up. I may as well go home." We made our way down the stairs and outside. When Harte pulled the great doors closed, we saw the source of the hammering.

A notice had been tacked up on one door. Rosie yanked it down and read it aloud.

By orders of the Firm of Harrier & Price, debt brokers by Royal Appointment: This property, STIRWATERS WOOLLEN MILL, located approximately three-quarter miles inside the eastern borders of the village of Shearing-upon-Stowe, in the Gold Valley, and consisting of one large mill building, one residence, and two smaller outbuildings, is hereby Seized pending auction of its land, premises, buildings, and assets, to pay the debts incurred by one Charlotte Constance Woodstone, née Miller, of the same.

"What?" My voice was shrill. "Auction?"

"Is this some sort of prank?" Harte asked, steadying Rosie's wrist to study the notice. But, no — we could clearly see the royal seal and a coat of arms for the brokerage; if a prank, it was an elaborate one.

"I don't understand," Rosie said. "What debts are they talking about? And what do they mean, 'seized'?"

"Just what it says there, miss," said a new voice. We turned as a group to see the man with the hammer, crossing back over the yard. He tipped his hat to us. "This Woodstone woman has defaulted on her debts, and her creditors are calling them in. Our firm's been agented to recover said debts, and we're authorized by his Majesty's law to seize any and all assets necessary in the recovery thereof." He thrust his hand forward. "Stephen Harrier, at your service."

No one moved. He was an oddly dressed fellow, with dark, oiled hair and an overbright green frock coat. He looked — seedy, like somebody you'd meet in a dark alley in Harrowgate. Or a gambling den. "And you are?" he prompted, his face breaking into a wide smile.

"I am that Woodstone woman," I said, just to see that smile fade. "What is the meaning of this? I demand to know who brought these charges against me!"

"Ah." He withdrew a sheaf of papers from his coat and flipped through them. "Well, to begin with — one Burke's and Taylor, haberdashers, of Harrowgate. Philip Prentiss, Perukier, Harrowgate. Stark —"

I peered over his hands, searching the names. "But I've never heard of any of these people! How can I be in debt to them?"

"Well, it seems *you* aren't. A Mr. Ellison Wheeler is, but apparently your name was given as surety on all the loans."

"What?" This from Rosie. "So what! Seize Uncle Wheeler's assets, auction him off!"

"I don't understand," I said. "What —?" I gave up, helpless.

Harte's easy voice broke in. "What's the sum, then, of all these charges?"

We examined the lists together. The charges were enormous — a hundred pounds here, fifty there — one staggering sum of *fifteen hundred pounds* to none other than Arthur Darling — all adding up to an insurmountable debt of more than twenty-three hundred pounds. Easily the value of Stirwaters, and then some. "I can't pay these!"

Mr. Harrier gave his oily smile. "Well, then, you have *two* options: Submit to the auction, or be thrown in gaol."

Rosie gasped. "Debtors' prison?"

"Oh, surely not!" Harte said. "In her condition?"

Mr. Harrier looked me up and down in a way that made me feel stripped bare — down to my "assets."

"Well, it would not be ideal," he said. "But it's been done before. Still, we can turn to her husband —"

"My husband!"

Mr. Harrier reached across me to turn a page. "Though the bulk of these debts were incurred prior to your marriage of — December fifteenth last — by virtue of said marriage, a Mr. Randall Woodstone, of Eamside and Harrowgate, became legally and financially responsible for you, Mrs. Woodstone. Now, if he'd be willing to cover the debts — say, in cash, plus our twenty percent handling fee . . ." He gave me a pointed look. "If not, there's a bench in Wardensgate sittin' cold and drafty, just waiting for an occupant."

My head spun. Everything we had been through to save Stirwaters since my father's death — the lost workers, the battle with Pinchfields, the crazy bargains with Jack Spinner — all the sneaking around and making up wild excuses . . . And our own Uncle Wheeler had been pulling us under, all along.

And now not only was Stirwaters in danger, but Randall's good name would be blackened as well. It was unthinkable. "What can I do?" I said.

Mr. Harrier gave me that oily smile again. "The auction's scheduled for tomorrow night. You come up with the money by then, well, you may forget you ever met me. If not . . ." He plucked the auction notice from Rosie's hand and tacked it back up on Stirwaters's doors. He tipped his hat, bowed to us all once again, and sauntered off into the village.

"The nerve of that man!" Rosie cried. "He can't — he can't just *do* that, can he?"

"There must be something you can do," Harte said. "In the meantime, we'll have to send for Randall, Ma'am."

I turned on him. "Certainly not. We'll do no such thing. Do you think selling Stirwaters will satisfy them? If he comes near Shearing, they'll haul him off to prison!"

"But if he has the money —"

"No, no, no. This is *not* Randall's debt, and I'll not involve him."

"But —" Harte scowled, and it was as close to angry as I'd ever seen him. "You're not planning on submitting to this, then?"

I could almost smile. "Not on your life."

Anger fueling me like a fire, I yanked the notice down once more and marched into the Millhouse, where my uncle sat, calmly busy at some correspondence at the desk. It was stuffy in the parlor, despite the open windows; no breeze shifted the curtains in the heavy air. Uncle Wheeler worked steadily, painstakingly, occasionally lifting the paper to the light, as if to check that he had given each *f* the proper graceful swoop of tail; every *W* just the right flourish. I stepped a little farther into the room, and it was only when the bulk of my body cast a shadow over him that he looked up.

"Charlotte! What — what a pleasant surprise." Uncle Wheeler swept his papers into a hasty pile, knocking his sleeve against the inkwell. He scrambled to right it. "What — that is, what brings you here, my dear?"

"What is the meaning of this?" I demanded, thrusting the auction notice toward him.

For a moment, I could not read the expression on his face. "I did warn you, my dear, that managing a business was no job for a girl." He was tapping his quill against the inkwell, and a great droplet of ink flicked into the air, coming to land on the white lace of his cravat.

"These aren't my debts!" I stepped in closer, and he leaned in over his work — but not quickly enough to hide the letter he was writing. I thought I recognized a familiar combination of letters, in an all-too-familiar script. Ignoring propriety, I pulled it out from the others, a hot, sick feeling seeping into my throat.

"Charlotte, don't —"

Dear Sir,
Please advance Mr. Ellison Wheeler the sum of fifty pounds, with my compliments. The money is secured by deposit at Uplands Mercantile Bank, Harrowgate.
Yours sincerely,
his niece,
Mrs. Randall Woodstone
Woolhampton Grange, Shearing-on-the-Stowe

And another:

Milord,
Having become aware of some misunderstanding between you and my uncle, Mr. Ellison Wheeler of Shearing & Harrowgate, I am confident this should put to rest any fears regarding his solvency. Please do not hesitate to complete your business —

I stared at the papers in my hand — my *handwriting*. "What is this? What are you doing?"

"Now, Charlotte, just let me have that back." He reached for the letter, but I pulled it out of his grasp. "Let's not get carried away, here. This is just a —"

"I don't have this kind of money! And you've *forged* my signature! How could you?"

His expression hardened. "How could I? A man has to live on something, my dear, and it's not as if you girls were the very font of ready cash, after all. What else was I supposed to do?"

I stared at him, utterly dumbfounded. My head swam from the heat of the room, and the back of my bodice was damp with sweat. "You've ruined us," I said, appalled at how reasonable I sounded. "We've lost everything now."

He hesitated. "Yes, well. I didn't expect Darling to go that far. But, look, it's only —"

"Darling?" The sick feeling spread to my belly, and then to my hands, until they trembled. I'd been such a fool — how could I ever have believed a word he said to me? "You *planned* this, with Pinchfields, all along. The meeting in Harrowgate, and the fire, and now this auction —"

"No! Of course not. Charlotte, look. Try and calm yourself. You're in no state to be getting so upset." He rose from the desk and put a hand on my arm. I wrenched away from him. "Now, my dear, just listen a moment. I'm sure it's all a misunderstanding."

"I've *misunderstood* your forgery? I've misunderstood this auction notice? I hardly think so, Uncle. It all seems perfectly clear to me." I swallowed hard, a bitter taste in my mouth. "What did he offer you?"

For a moment he looked confused. "Who?"

"Darling! Arthur Darling. What did Pinchfields offer you to steal my mill from me?"

Uncle Wheeler gave a sharp, mirthless laugh. "Offer? My dear, understand me: A man like Arthur Darling doesn't make offers. He makes threats, and as you have seen for yourself, he is not afraid to carry them out."

"I don't —" But suddenly I did understand. Fifteen hundred pounds was a lot of incentive. "So that was it, then? Find a way to deliver Stirwaters, or go back to debtors' prison?"

His lip curled. "That's close enough. I'd say he's finally run out of patience with us both."

I pressed a hand to my forehead, trying to quiet my raging thoughts. This was it, then. Pinchfields had won, and the game had been stacked against us all along. I balled up the forged letters, crushing them in my damp fist. Slowly, a terrible thought surfaced, and I beheld the crumpled letters in my hand, the strokes of my own penmanship creased and twisted into something unfamiliar. I smoothed a finger down the letters of my name.

"The letter from my father. You wrote that."

Uncle Wheeler gave me a long, steady look, and shrugged almost imperceptibly.

"He never wanted you to come here," I said, my voice verging on shrill. "He never asked you to be our guardian!"

He gave a wan smile, as if to say, "What can you do?"

"I want you out of this house." I reached inside the desk and grabbed at the contents, stacking everything into an untidy heap, which I pushed toward him. "Take your lies and your debts and your — your purple ink, and get out of my home."

My uncle folded his arms across his chest. "Well, now, I'm sure I'd like that very much — but, ah, this won't be your house for very much longer, will it?"

My arms trembling, I dumped the papers on the desk. I met his gaze, until he flicked his eyes away. "I see," I said quietly. "And what do you suppose will become of *you* now, Uncle?"

Chapter Twenty-Two

I *fled* the Millhouse then, as close to tears as I'd been since Father died. I didn't want to believe it. Father's letter — it had been in his hand, his blotchy, inky script; his grief-stricken voice rising up from so many years ago. *Motherless babes now. I can't believe she's gone — and the boy.* How could that be false?

How could I have been taken in?

Rosie and Harte were still huddled in the millyard, and they watched me anxiously as I lurched toward Stirwaters.

"Charlotte —" My sister reached for my arm, but I shook her off. "Where are you going?"

"Where do you think?"

Up in the office, I searched like a mad thing. Where was it? I flipped through the atlas and could not find the page. The gears in the spinning room rattled and shook as if some phantom wind tore through them. At last I remembered — that page had come loose after our first encounter, and I'd tucked it away. But it was not in the drawer where I was sure I had left it, so I pulled the contents of the desk out willy-nilly, strewing papers and pen nibs everywhere. Finally, one of the drawers stuck, so I knelt and reached back inside. There! I found it jammed behind the drawer.

I twisted it free, and yanked my hand back with a hiss when I caught my skin on a sharp corner. I stuck my bleeding knuckle into my mouth and gently withdrew the paper with my other hand. Smoothing out the creases, I read aloud the words of Father's spell to summon aid.

Nothing happened. I read it again.

"Bluh —" It came out as a croak. I swallowed, my mouth dry, and started over. "Blood and bone, I summon thee. Hearth and home, I summon thee. Earth and sky, I summon thee." Something rustled in the corner of the office. I glanced up, but there was nothing. "From far and nigh, come now to me. Blood to bone, I summon thee . . ."

Over and over I read the spell, with the same result each time. I found a lump of chalk in the desk and scrawled a hasty circle round myself on the floor. I cast aside the glass from a lamp, to serve as a candle. I emptied a packet of mandrake root from the dyeshed into the circle. *Blood to bone, I summon thee. . . .*

I spent all night in Stirwaters — pacing, waiting. I sat in the office for as long as I could be still. I climbed the stairs to the attic twenty times or more. I came outside and circled the building. I went *anywhere* I thought he might be. I stood by the wall with the hex sign for an hour, then knelt there, then sat, then lay down on my side with my head on my elbow, and at last fell asleep. I awoke sometime before dawn, horribly stiff. And alone.

Someone had been there — some time in the night someone had covered me with a length of plaid blanket cloth, tucked some folds beneath my head. Was it Harte or Rosie? I knew not, but it was a measure of our desperation that whoever it was had not awakened me, but left me to my vigil.

By half past seven in the morning, the guards had arrived: Two burly men with the look of tavern-brawlers set themselves up at Stirwaters's yardside doors. Another walked the yard, and one much gentler gaoler arrived to confine Rosie and me to the Millhouse. Rachel and Harte were not permitted to enter; they waved sadly from the very edge of the Baker property. We saw no sign of Uncle Wheeler. The millhands crowded round the fence and millrace, their anxious murmurs turning to shouts both angry and supportive. One of the guards produced a musket, and Rosie grabbed my arm and gasped, but the crowd dispersed at last.

And he did not come.

Around noon, Harte finally talked his way through, with Jack Townley at his side. Townley doffed his hat — which I had not once in all the years of our acquaintance seen him do — and gave me a kind nod.

"We've — some of the lads and me, and some of the women as well, too — we've put together what we could." He held out a feed sack, hanging heavy from his meaty fist. "My Ruthie had some extra tucked away, and old Fuller sold that knife what Drover's been after him to sell, and . . . Anyways, Stirwaters is our home, too, Mistress." He thrust the bag at me, pouring its contents at my feet. "We've got together near a hundred pound there, believe it or not."

I felt lost somewhere between laughter and tears, and he was very red in the face. Rosie came to our rescue.

"Townley, you're a bloody fool. This won't buy back the machines, let alone the whole mill." She put her hands on his shoulders and kissed him on the cheek. "But you're a good man. And I'll lay out any man who says otherwise." Still furiously red, Townley took his leave, waving to us as he crossed the yard.

Rosie and Harte knelt to collect the coins. "We'll find a way to get this back to everyone," Harte said. "After — whenever."

Afternoon descended, and he did not come.

Had I truly managed to cast him off, with the burning of the woolshed? Had he taken me at my word, and I could not now count on him swooping to our rescue? Oh, blasted Miller pride! I had played my very last card, and I had lost.

As the evening wore down, I fell back to the Millhouse steps and watched in a sort of numb trance. The brokers — Harrier and Price — had thrown open the mill doors, and I heard the crunch of wagonwheels on the roadway as a gaily painted chaise rolled into the yard. The door sprang open, and Arthur Darling climbed out, huffing and grunting. The Pinchfields overseer plopped to the ground like a blot of black ink, and strutted round the yard as though his inheritance had just come due, the wool buyer close at his heels. I tucked myself tighter behind the tangle of ivy so they would not see me, as Darling's covetous gaze crawled up the Millhouse walls.

I watched and waited, expecting other carriages to come, other bidders — but when Darling reached the mill, Mr. Harrier shook his hand firmly, and said in a voice that carried across the yard, "Good. If you gentlemen are ready, let's get this started."

I stared into the fading light, sick with understanding. There were to be no other bidders; this was a private auction, arranged for the benefit of one buyer only. I fished the rumpled atlas page from my pocket, my heart like a stone in my breast.

I mouthed the lines, heard their haunting rhythm echo in my mind. Why hadn't it worked?

"You realize, of course, that particular spell requires *actual* blood from the one you're conjuring."

He was just there — as always, standing a mere arm's reach away from me. Spinner tipped that horrible old hat to me and consulted his pocket watch. My watch.

"You came, didn't you?"

With a flick of his hand, the page flew from my grip and fluttered to the shale.

"I am here because you have need of my unique services, Mistress Miller, not for a scrap of doggerel by some overblown scholar who fancied himself a cunning man!"

I twined my stinging fingers together. "What do you want?"

A twisted smile crossed his lined face. "You summoned me, remember?"

"As payment! To save my mill — again." I had to force the words over my lips.

The smile grew in earnest. "Ah. You won't want to pay what I'm asking this time."

"Try me."

He stepped closer, close enough I should feel the heat from his breath on my flesh, but there was nothing. "What would you pay me?"

I held my place, much as I wanted to fall back a step. "Anything."

"Are you sure about that?"

I could see the lines in his face — the thin red veins in his eyes, the pores from which his whiskers sprang. He smelt of — of earth, of rotting leaves and mushrooms. "Anything. Anything you want."

He eased off a little, but the dead-earth smell still lingered. "I suggest you give that some thought, there, Mistress Miller."

"Thought!" I cried. "They're ready to auction Stirwaters off at this moment. How much time do you think I have?"

"Ah, I just meant — before you go pledging your heart's treasures to someone like me, you decide if it's what you really want."

"I have no choice." My voice was smaller than I liked.

Spinner eyed me gravely. "There's always a choice."

My gaze travelled across the darkening millyard, to where the men gathered in Stirwaters. Among the auctioneers and the men from Pinchfields I caught a glimpse of shadowed lilac and felt something hot creep into my throat.

"Let my uncle win? Is that the choice?"

"That's one choice, aye."

I swallowed hard. "Never."

Something crossed Spinner's craggy face — a smile, perhaps. "You Millers and your pride. It will ever be your downfall."

"I do not pay you to counsel me."

"Ha. Perhaps you should. You could learn well from what I know. You're fixing to spend an unimaginable sum —"

I waved him to silence. I did not think I could sustain this conversation much longer. "Just go and do — whatever you do. The terms are these: You will use whatever means necessary to prevent the sale of Stirwaters to Arth — to *anyone* in that room, and I will pay you a fee to be determined at your discretion later."

Spinner regarded me a moment longer, from eyes whose depths I could not fathom. "All right, missie, I'll be bringin' you the bill of sale, then."

Whistling, he turned on his heel and shambled across the yard. As he stepped he swung his left hand in a curious arc — and I watched as a pearl-handled cane appeared in his fist, a feathered hat formed itself on his head. By the time he reached the yard doors to Stirwaters, he was the very picture of a gentleman.

I sank to my knees in a sea of crumpled flannel and pressed my hands into the sharp shale of the yard, as if bites from the stones could remind me who I was.

Rosie joined me then, coming down the Millhouse steps to ease me to my feet. She stooped for the atlas page, still lying in the shale, and there was understanding in her eyes. "I can't stand this," she said. "I'll go mad if I stay here one minute longer."

"Where will you go?"

She shrugged. "Drover's. Harte's there — and most of the hands, too, I should think. Will you come with us?"

"How can I?"

She laid a hand on my arm, and one of us was trembling. "We couldn't watch him before," she reminded me. "What if it won't work if you're there?"

I agreed to go as far as the Millhouse stoop, where I sank hard against the stone steps. I sat there for what couldn't have been more than a quarter hour, straining to hear anything beyond the low, ordinary creaks and rustles, the splash of water over the wheel. Pilot wandered over after a few minutes, settling herself at my feet with a bedraggled sigh. I trailed my fingers in her ruff, counted the bats wheeling overhead, counted the beats of my heart banging in my throat. Once she whimpered; I had twisted her fur so tightly it had hurt her.

At last Spinner emerged, calmly shaking the hands of everyone present. He stood like a bright, hazy spot in the circle of the other men, who drifted about like sheep who've lost their shepherd. I watched Mr. Harrier hand over my keys, but slowly, as if he were not quite certain what had just happened. A flash of lavender betrayed my uncle, slinking out the opposite doors. I expected to see him livid, red with fury as he'd been when I announced my engagement — but his expression was something entirely different, something altogether new. Uncle Wheeler's face was absolutely as white as his hair, his green eyes wide with — shock? Recognition?

My uncle *knew* Jack Spinner. And he feared him.

I had no time to digest that — for in a moment Spinner was upon me, the ring of keys in his outstretched hand, a document in the other.

I reached out, thanks forming reluctantly on my lips, but he would not release them.

"You'll pay?" he said, and the tone in his voice was odd, uncertain.

"I said I would." I was still watching Uncle Wheeler, who seemed frozen in place scant yards from us.

"Whatever I ask?"

"I said I would. A Miller doesn't go back on her bargains."

I thought for a moment I saw him hesitate — but before I could be certain, Arthur Darling and his henchman bustled up to me, competing degrees of nastiness in their expressions.

"What is the meaning of this? What do you think you're playing, missie?" Mr. Darling grunted, as if it required that much effort to force the words past his too-tight cravat.

"Why, Mr. Darling, I don't know what you mean," I said, and though I sounded very blithe, it was all a sham. My legs were ready to buckle, and I felt terribly like a dead horse that's been left too long in the sun. "But I would venture to guess that you've been outbid."

"You think you're awfully clever, don't you?" The wool buyer's thin lip twisted. "But you haven't heard the last from —"

"No," I said, and he froze, his sharp jaw hanging open. "I think we have heard the last from Pinchfields, don't you, Mr. Spinner? You see, gentlemen, it seems I no longer own this mill. And unless Mr. Spinner is entertaining offers — are you entertaining offers, Mr. Spinner?"

"No, no, I don't believe I am," he said. "In fact, I have some ideas of my own I'd like to see through."

"What are you talking about?" said Mr. Darling, beginning to turn red. "I thought your name was Smart!"

"Frankly, sir, I don't care what he calls himself, so long as it's not Pinchfields. Now, do you plan to leave Stirwaters peacefully, or will Mr. Smart have to throw you out?"

The wool buyer leaned in toward me, jabbing his finger at my chest. "Now see here, you little —"

"Oh, I wouldn't do that, sir," Spinner said, and it was the same old rusty-metal voice I knew so well. The men from

Pinchfields drew back from Spinner, frowning. I took advantage of the moment.

"Accept it, gentlemen, you've lost."

Darling flushed, a bloom of Saxon red all across his fat face. "I — I —" He turned on Spinner, who eyed him back levelly.

"Good night," Spinner said, and it was as if he had let loose all the foul air from a tomb. Darling and the wool buyer sprang back, startled. Mopping his damp face with an oversized handkerchief, Darling hurried away across the shale, muttering what sounded like "Blasted Millers!"

Oh, why wasn't Rosie here to witness this? I wanted to laugh, watching our rivals waddle ignominiously into the dusk, but a stab of pain deep in my belly made it come out as a gasp. I turned to Spinner, who was watching me with a strange intensity. He untwisted his fingers from the brass ring, and I snatched the keys and the bill of sale from his grasp. I stared at his signature on the title, scribed in a lovely, swooping hand I could not make out. As I watched, the letters straightened, compressed. . . . Like the lines in my father's atlas, changing by themselves, the signature now read *Charlotte Miller Woodstone.*

"What — what did you do for the other Millers here?"

He cocked his head and smiled vaguely, the grand hat tipped precariously on his unruly red hair. "Who said I did anything *for* them?"

"But you — you said they knew your work." I gripped the keys so hard I thought my fingers should snap, as another twinge struck me. "You said —"

"Aye," he said, and his gravelly voice was tinged with satisfaction. "So I did. Well, Mistress, as I was sayin' — ye've got your keys now, the mill is yourn for good and all. I have your word, then?"

"Of course —" I said, still trembling. "But —"

"I best go," Spinner said. Something about him was shifting, blurring — I thought to see him returning to the form I knew — the tradesman's dress, the shabby clothes. But instead his fine hat, his topcoat, the cane all became more distinct. The ruddy side-whiskers receded; the unruly hair grew long and neat. "I'll come for my payment, Mistress Miller. I know you're good for it. But right now — right now I've another debt to collect on!"

He turned from me, and something about him was still hazy. Feeling light-headed, I reached for Stirwaters's doorframe, but felt myself sinking, terribly slowly, toward the ground.

The great ring of keys slipped from my fingers.

Chapter Twenty-Three

William Miller Woodstone arrived in this world on a hot afternoon in August, with considerable screaming and indignation, and then, as if satisfied that he had made his point, settled into life as a very amiable baby. Right from the first he was plump and jolly, with a soft pale fluff of hair and eyes of indeterminate color, like his father's. Do other mothers behold their newborn sons as I did? Do they all find themselves stopped, breathless, in what they were doing to merely *stare*, in wonder, at the tiny life before them? Do they hold fast to their hungry babes and think fierce thoughts about their futures? Do they draw out a wide circle and say, *"Nothing will intrude upon this sacred space?"* I do not know; I think they must — but I must also admit I felt as though I had brought forth the only child in the universe, that I had performed the greatest miracle in the history of creation, and that nothing since time began was blessed with quite the brilliance and perfection of my son William.

I gave birth in the Millhouse — in my own old bedroom — the shock and disorientation I had felt upon Jack Spinner's departure being nothing more than the first stages of my labor. Perhaps it was required — perhaps Miller children were destined to be born at Stirwaters. Randall was sent for straightaway; but in the meantime, William and I had Rosie. Never in the history of children has a boy had such a proprietary auntie. During the first weary hours of my motherhood, Rosie held him, changed him, cooed to him, laid him in my arms, and gingerly lifted him out again. She sat by his basket as I slept, and admitted no one into my bedchamber but herself, Rachel, and Biddy Tom.

Eventually, we all insisted that she sleep, and she went reluctantly. I carefully shifted my position in the bed, and Mrs. Tom swept in to brusquely tuck and adjust my bedclothes.

"I'm so tired," I said, straining to see past her to where William lay, more than an arm's reach away.

"It will pass," she said. "*If* you have the good sense to stay abed and listen to those as know better. I've birthed more babies than you can count, Mrs. Woodstone, and they all do better if their mams take care of themselves first."

"Can't you move him closer? I want to see him."

"I cannot. He is close enough, and you will see enough of him once you're up and about." She gave a little chuckle, but I didn't find anything amusing.

"But I need —" My voice was raw.

Mrs. Tom looked at me sharply, and I felt the power of that penetrating gaze. "Now don't you worrit," she said sternly. "Your mam were plumb wore out from a forty-hour labor, and that little boy was born small and sickly. Yours is not. He's a big strapping lad like his da', and you will only make yourself sick frettin' for him!" She did, however, slightly turn the basket so I could peek inside it without stretching too far.

I fell back into an uneasy sleep, plagued by dreams I could not remember when I woke. Mrs. Tom appeared one last time, with a cup of foul-smelling tea she pressed on me, and after that I slept soundly. I awoke at last to morning sunlight pouring through the windows. Feeling the satisfied weariness of staying abed longer than I was accustomed to, I gingerly stretched my sore body and took a deep breath — and nearly choked on it.

I smelled lilacs.

My eyes flew open, and I struggled to sitting, darting my gaze round the room. There was no one there, of course, but the sickly sweet fragrance of lilacs gone past their prime was heavy in the air. Confused, I swung my bare feet to the floor and, a little wobbly, managed to stand. I was reaching for William's basket, sure something was wrong, when Rachel burst into the room.

"What's this, then? Charlotte Miller, get yourself back in that bed this instant." She swept William up in a froth of lacy blankets, as if I meant to do him some harm. He regarded me solemnly out of round eyes, his plump face drooped into a frown.

"Please —" I held out a beseeching hand. "Let me have him."

"Back to bed," Rachel repeated. She had me firmly by one shoulder, and I had not the strength to push past her. "Calm down, love. Your baby's right here, and he is just fine. Now if you'll *sit down*, I'll let you hold him."

I frowned. "Was — was my uncle here?"

Rachel watched me carefully. "Your uncle? No. No one's seen him since the auction."

"But I thought —" What had I thought? I couldn't seem to remember, now.

With some effort, Rachel got me settled once more. She put William in my arms, and I held him with a grip like iron, until she had to untwine my fingers from his tiny body. "I have to go," I whispered. Something was wrong here, but I could not wrench my thoughts from their muddled fog to tell me what it was. Everything had run together into one great confusion. "This place, it —" I faltered, uncertain. William nuzzled his face against me, and for a moment I forgot everything. When I looked up and met Rachel's wide, concerned eyes, my mind was clear again.

"Rachel, can you wake Rosie and send for someone with a carriage? I want to take William home as soon as possible."

"But, Charlotte —" she clearly had half a dozen protests to this demand, but the only one that made it out was "This is your home."

"Rosie can come with me," I continued. "And if there's trouble, Biddy Tom is right next door." I simply could not keep William in Stirwaters Millhouse any longer. Whatever danger sought my son . . . it was close to the mill.

I was happier once I had William at the Grange. I had Rosie and Colly to help, and a huge frothy nursery prepared for him, all yellow and green and full of sunlight. The windows looked onto the lush, sheep-dotted hillsides — not down on the village and the mill. There was a bed in the nursery, meant for the nurse; I installed myself there, awaiting Randall's return.

For the first time ever, the Grange felt like home.

Randall descended on the village like a triumphant general, beaming wider than ever and practically bursting with pride. I was quite recovered by the time he arrived, so when he swept me up in his arms and squeezed all the breath out of me, I only laughed and kissed him back. At William's cradle, he hesitated, reaching out a tentative hand but not touching him.

"A son!" he whispered. "Can you credit it? My son — our son!"

I looked from my dozing child to my husband, a cold spot growing in my belly. I wanted to shush him, wave him to silence, hold myself tight and pretend I had not heard all the joy and wonder and hope in his voice. "Yes, well, you can hold him, you know," I said, forcing the briskness into my voice. I scooped William from the crib and held him out to his father.

"I — no, no —" Randall stuttered, recoiling. I burst out laughing, William gurgled sleepily, and the chill passed. Randall's face lit up like a sunrise, and he eagerly took hold of his son, cooing over him in an absolutely besotted fashion that would have had the bank fellows in tears behind their laughter.

"We'll have to get a nurse," Randall said some hours later, when we had managed to convince ourselves to leave the boy alone for exactly long enough to eat dinner.

I hesitated. Rosie and I had grown up in the mill; Mam would have died from shame having a stranger raise her babies! I remembered rocking Rosie in the office as my mother pored over the books; the spools and shuttles were our playthings and our teething-toys. I had always assumed that I would tote my child to the mill and back, but now the thought of it filled me with a strange, cold fear. Yet the idea of a nurse, of leaving William alone where I could not see him every minute . . . We may have defeated Pinchfields and thwarted my uncle's plans, but I still could not feel completely safe.

"Can't we wait a bit? He's only tiny. I don't think I could leave him with anybody else."

Randall polished off a dish of custard and reached for my hand. "I know what you mean," he said. "I couldn't bear it when I heard I'd missed it all!"

I smiled, but it waned too quickly. "That's not all you missed," I said under my breath, but he heard me.

"What?" He looked up sharply. "Did something happen while I was gone?"

It took all the strength I could summon to maintain my placid expression. "No, of course not. Just — I quarrelled with Uncle Wheeler. That's all."

Randall eyed me carefully, until I squirmed under his gaze and looked away. What could I tell him? That I had narrowly missed condemning him to debtors' prison? That I had harbored a forger and an imposter in my home all these months, and that my poor judgement had nearly cost not only my mill, but my husband, as well? He didn't deserve that. He did not, in fact, deserve to be tangled up in any of the misfortunes that clung to me and the Millers. I had done a very unfair thing, marrying Randall Woodstone, and I would keep him from as much as I could, for as long as I could. But I felt I owed him . . . *something.*

"He had these letters!" It just tumbled out, as if it were the last item stuffed into an overpacked trunk. "These letters — with my name on them. Asking for money. He made them look as if I'd written them."

"Wheeler? That blasted rogue! I knew he was a rake — but I never expected him to go that far." Randall sighed. "I offered him some money. A few months ago. To let us have Rosie, to leave Shearing, to forget he ever met you girls. . . . He just laughed in my face. Said he was satisfied with the 'current arrangements,' and until I could offer him something better, he was staying."

"You what? Oh, Randall." Like a light breaking into a dark room, I felt something give way inside me. I remembered what I had felt when Randall asked me to marry him — as if he could protect me from anything. He would know what to do — about Uncle Wheeler, about Spinner, about the curse — about everything. If I just opened my mouth and let the words out, we would be safe again.

But as I looked at him, the set of his jaw, the tight hold he still had on my hand — I knew it was all an illusion. Less tangible even than the vision of him drowning in the flooded mill pit. There wasn't anything he could do. There wasn't anything anybody could do.

So I just sat, staring at my hands folded in my lap, my fingers turning pink from the tightness of my grip.

"Charlotte." Randall's hand was on my shoulder.

I shook my head miserably. There was so much more I wanted to say, so much I *needed* him to know, to understand, but I didn't dare.

William's cry, startling me to standing, was a welcome relief.

"I'll come with you," Randall said.

"No," I said. "I've got him. Truly."

He caught my hand and watched me with some deep concern. I wanted to meet his eyes, answer all the questions I found there — but I couldn't. I couldn't take the risk. I turned my face toward the stairs and pulled — just slightly — on his hand. A moment more, and he let me go.

*   *   *

I slept poorly that night, separated from Randall in the nursery. Very late my restlessness turned to wakefulness, and I pulled myself up in bed, listening for William, but he slept silently in his cradle. Sounds from the study below, where Randall kept his office, shook me fully awake, and I scrambled out of bed and into my dressing gown. I crept down the stairs to the subtle, frantic sounds of drawers being pulled open, little locks broken, papers rifled.

I rounded the doorway to the study and found, in a pool of low lamplight, Uncle Wheeler scrabbling through the bric-a-brac on the bookcase.

"What are you doing?" I demanded. "Get out of here at once!"

He whirled on me, his sharp features sinister in the lamplight. "Happily, my dear. I do believe there was an offer on the table," he said. "If I recall correctly, five hundred pounds? I'll be availing myself of that money now, if you don't mind."

I stumbled backward and grabbed the edge of the library table for support. Five hundred pounds! Randall must be mad. "I — I don't know what you're talking about."

"Oh, no, no, no." He shook one pointed finger right in my face. "I am getting out of this town while I still have a chance, and thanks to your little stunt the other day, I'm finding myself just a bit inconvenienced at the moment."

"What do you mean?" I said. His eyes were wild, and I thought perhaps he'd been drinking.

"My God!" he roared. "Is your head stuffed with wool? You really have no idea who you're dealing with, do you? Take some friendly advice, my dear niece, for once: You'll get out, too, while there's time! When he comes back — and believe me, he *will* be back — all bets are off."

I snaked my arm behind me, feeling for a candlestick. What I should do with it, I had no real idea, but I liked its heavy presence in my hand. "I don't understand."

He threw open the desk and swept through the papers, spilling most out onto the floor. "He's not here all the time. I don't — I don't quite understand it, but there's always a moment — a few days, weeks, sometimes, when it's possible to elude him. Maybe he — never mind, it doesn't matter. All I know is, I'm making a run for it while I can, and if you were smart, you'd do the same."

And like that, faster than I'd imagined he could move, my uncle had wheeled on me and grabbed me by the wrists, pinning my arms behind me. The candlestick clattered to the floor, and I was too surprised to struggle. "Now where," he said, in a hideous parody of his velvet voice, "is that bloody money?"

I whipped my hands out of his grip. "Never. You're not touching my husband's money! Not a farthing of it."

That threw him. He drew back as if he'd been struck, and regarded me with an entirely unreadable expression. "Now, be a good girl," he said in a wheedling voice. "All I need is a few guineas — just to see me on the road."

My lip bloodied by the pressure of my teeth, I shook my head.

He stepped away, began pacing the room like a mad thing. "Come on, Charlotte — just a little. You can spare it, I know you can. For family's sake?"

"How dare you?" I cried. "Break into my home in the middle of the night, after what you did? If you walk out that door right now, and never look back, I will not tell the magistrates everything you've done."

He hung back, his arms seeming too loose for his body, his velvet jacket too large. "Is that how it is, then?"

"Yes, sir," I said, sincerely hoping that was the last time I should ever have to utter those words to my uncle's face. I strode to the study door on legs no longer trembling, and pointed an arm toward the front door. "Get out."

He stepped closer toward me, leaned his smooth face toward mine, pleadingly.

"Out." I no longer even felt like screaming.

Uncle Wheeler regarded me a moment longer, and then gave a little shrug. He tugged on the hem of his coat, patted down his wig, and sniffed. He gave me a low bow, tipped his hat. "Very well, then. I have enjoyed my little sojourn in your village, my dear. May we do it again very soon."

And like that, in a whirl of black velvet, he was gone into the darkness once more. I turned and ran upstairs, pulled my sleeping infant from his cradle, squeezed him to my breast, and wept as if my world had ended, all over again.

Chapter Twenty-Four

It seemed impossible that Uncle Wheeler was finally gone. He had arrived in our lives with such pomp and fanfare; for him just to slip out again, in the middle of the night . . . it was hard to credit. The Millhouse felt strangely empty without his lilac-scented presence, although he'd left his largest trunk and most of his fine clothing behind, and I found myself lingering in the parlor, or by the breakfast table, trying to convince myself that he had truly left us.

"Good riddance," Rosie said, slamming the door to his room, as if that alone could blot out the memories of the last year. "We ought to have a holiday for it. Let's build a bonfire and burn an effigy. I think there might still be a wig here."

The idea struck too close to a chill place in my heart, so I made no response to the suggestion.

Rosie joined us up at the Grange, at least part time. She was still too young to live completely unchaperoned, although I doubted that even Shearing gossip would condemn such action overmuch. She happily took up my place in William's nursery, allowing me to return to my marriage bed. When Randall left for Harrowgate, she and I were bedfellows once again, and very often William slept between us.

One of those nights, my sister's voice whispered against my neck. "Do you think he'll come back?"

I didn't answer at first, stroking the unbearably soft skin of William's tiny hand and staring into the darkness. "I don't know," I finally said.

"What do you think he'll ask for?" she said, and then I understood.

"Jack Spinner? Don't let's speak of him."

"We should be prepared. And you haven't any more jewelry."

William was very warm against my heart, his breath a damp sweetness on my skin. "No, that's true. Do you think Uncle Wheeler left any of his cravat pins?"

For a moment, at least, Rosie and I giggled into our pillows until we nearly woke the baby.

We tried to settle back into our lives as if the auction had never happened. Stirwaters rejoiced in the news of its salvation, and as for Stirwaters's heir? I could not help but feel some trepidation carrying him across the old threshold the first time, but when William jerked his downy head to view the gears passing by above, and his face melted into an expression of contentment, I had to smile.

"Yes, my sweet," I whispered into the lace of his bonnet. "I feel quite the same."

I fought the urge to peek into corners for something that might be lurking there, something that wished my son ill. I told myself it was ridiculous. My mother had never had the chance to bring Thomas here; if danger threatened my son, it could reach him anywhere.

And, truly, in that company that bright September morning, it was hard to believe in ghosts and curses. The Stirwaters family threw open its arms to William as if he belonged to all of them. As William was passed hand to hand for the better part of an hour, I watched grizzled old millworkers turn to putty in his baby fists. Jack Townley, who was about to become a father for at least the sixth time, looked fit to burst with pride as he lifted William aloft in one huge hand, allowing the new prince to survey his kingdom.

I held onto those moments, pressed them close to my breast. This is what it had all been for — all the last year's struggles had been worth it. The wind whistling through the cracks in the walls was only wind; the splash of water hid no sinister whispers. William — *my son* — would be safe.

There came a morning late in the month, when I woke in my own bed at the Grange, and felt sure that everything would be all right. Randall was home, having gotten a full month off to spend with us.

Sunlight pricking at my eyelids, I rolled over lazily, and saw that Randall had gotten up already. I rose and slipped into a crewelwork dressing gown and padded easily down the hallway to the nursery. He was there, his long frame crammed into a rocking chair intended for someone of my size, our son tucked in his elbow. Colly grinned at me over a heap of William's laundry as she slipped past. I hesitated in the doorway; it was such a pretty scene, the morning sun slanting over them both, broken into jewelled fragments by a ball of colored glass hung in the window.

"What's this?" I said, walking over and lifting it before my face. The Woodstone clan had been inundating us with gifts, an almost daily shower of embroidered nappies, beribboned gowns, spoons, blocks, and a blue porcelain dog who watched William's cradle with a vigilance that would do Pilot proud. The orb in the window was stuffed with swirls of ribbon, the blown glass twined through with streaks of blue and yellow. It was too strange a bauble to be an ordinary nursery toy.

My eye went to the arch of the window frame, which was decked with bunches of herbs and flowers. They had been there for weeks; I had thought them decoration, or to make the air smell sweet. But as I looked closer I recognized the plants — henbane, nightshade, keyflower. Those weren't ordinary herbs; they were the sort that grew in Biddy Tom's garden, away from the cooking greens.

I cast my gaze around the room. How had I not noticed this before? Above William's bed there now hung a jumbled collection of oddments — iron nails, a burnt-down candle, a pair of shears splayed wide.

"What is all this?" I strode to the bed and had to cross a circle of soot scribed on the green-and-yellow checked floor. "Iron above the bed, herbs by the window? What's next, dark incantations by moonlight?"

"It's just some old country charms," Randall said, rising. "I didn't think you'd mind." The easy way he shifted tiny William to his broad shoulder belied his scant weeks' experience with babies. I wanted to hold that image forever, like a picture — of Randall with his son in his arms. I didn't want to live in a world where babies had to have circles drawn round them to keep bad air from their sleep, wear silver to keep from drowning, fear for curses that threatened their lives.

I yanked down the candles, pulled the nails free, used the scissors to snip down all the ribbons and flowers. "I do not see how hanging sharp objects above my sleeping child makes him *safer*," I said. "I love my sister, and I know she means well — but there are days I could just shake her."

"Rosie? But —" Randall said, frowning slightly. After a moment, he nodded. "I'll — I'll talk to her."

I went to take William from his arms. Randall watched me, an odd look in his eyes. "Charlotte?"

"What?" I busied myself dressing William in the most complicated concoction of ribbons and lace I could find in his wardrobe. My fingers shook on one of the tiny knots.

Randall strode over and put his arms round us both. "What's wrong? Why does this scare you?"

"It doesn't," I said stoutly. "It's just foolishness, and I don't see why we must expose William to superstition in the cradle. He'll see enough —"

"You don't have to lie to me."

I paused. "I don't know what you mean." But my heart quickened in my breast, and the hand that Randall caught was damp.

"Charlotte, I love you," he said. "And I *know* something's bothering you. You don't have to tell me. But I wish you would."

His great eyes were on me, soft and probing, and I should probably have crumbled completely if I stood there long enough. Instead I whisked William up from his bed and patted him on the back.

"Oh, nothing — it's just that Mrs. Tom said the Townley baby came down with a grippe, and I hope that William doesn't get it." It was true — it was certainly true, but it was hardly the whole truth, and I'm sure Randall knew it. Still, what good could come of telling Randall what did worry me? He would only want to help somehow, which would bring him closer to Stirwaters. . . . It was not to be thought of.

He reached for us, tried to reel us into his embrace, but I stepped into the hallway. I was halfway down the corridor when I heard him say, very softly, "Is it me?"

I turned back, to see him silhouetted in the doorframe, his head cocked to the side, as if that were a perfectly natural question.

"How can you think that?"

He shrugged. "What else can I think? You won't talk to me, you pull away when I touch you. You don't include me in anything. I had hoped, once the baby was born . . . Charlotte, do you know that everyone in this village treats me as though I belong here, except you?"

"I'm sorry," I said. "I — I didn't mean to. I'll do better —" I had no idea what I meant by that, and I was still standing there, gripping William as if he were the only thing holding me together, when Randall bundled us up in his arms again.

"Oh, Charlotte," he breathed into my hair, "why did you marry me?"

My damp face pressed against his shirt, I told the truth. "You made me feel safe."

He pulled back slightly, his face set. "Well," he said. "That's more than I hoped."

Something shifted between Randall and me that morning, and I'm not sure either of us knew what. Perhaps it was inevitable — like a split in floorboards, growing wider with each passing season. I did not know how to reach past the gap between us, and Randall did not seem to know if he wanted to. His weeks in Harrowgate grew longer and longer, and I was seldom certain whether I would find him at home when I returned every evening — as return I did. Stirwaters at night now had too many shadows I did not wish to fall on William. Often as not I brought Rosie with me, and we would look through Stirwaters's records or rapture over the baby together.

I had been through all the records I had found at the mill, and still the picture they created was incomplete. The dead sons, the Wheeler millwheel, the drowning no one could remember. What did it all mean? I could not ignore it; I could not pretend I did not feel some sort of spectral hand tightening around us. *What dark dealings in Miller past?* Whatever they were, they were well hidden, and why in the world didn't I have sense enough to let them stay that way?

One evening I had the memorandum books and journals spread before me on the dining table at the Grange. William was in my lap, and I was bent awkwardly over him to study papers I had already memorized. Randall strolled in, looking roadworn and a bit dusty, and kissed me briefly on the top of my head. I looked up, waiting for him to say something, straining to reach past the gap between us, and not knowing how. He sat beside me, and lifted William into his own lap.

"What's this, then?" Randall turned one of the old ledgers face-to — but I snapped it shut before he could read anything.

"You and your secrets," he said. He was smiling, but there was an element of seriousness in his voice.

"What's that supposed to mean?" I said crossly. It was patently unfair — I *was* secretive, and why shouldn't Randall notice that? So I relented a little and passed him Father's atlas instead.

"Now, this is interesting," he said, turning past the map of Shearing to the schematic of Stirwaters. "Your father drew these? See — that's what I'm talking about. We've been married almost a year now and there's still so much about you I don't know." He reached for my hand, but I pulled it back.

"Gods, Charlotte! Why do you do that? You never talk to me like you used to — I thought . . ." He shook his head and lapsed into silence. William made a fussy little cry, and Randall bounced him gently on his knees, saying nothing.

"Look." Randall sighed and traced his finger along the binding of an old journal. "I've tried to be what I thought you wanted — I don't interfere at Stirwaters, I'm not home too much, I tried not to pry into that madhouse where you kept your uncle." He put out a long hand to stroke William's cheek. "But in return, I guess I'd like just a hint of what goes on behind those grey eyes of yours. I can't read your mind, Charlotte."

I sat in stony silence — a crack in my foundations growing wider and wider by the moment. What would I tell him? There was nothing to me but Stirwaters and its secrets, and keeping safe everything I cared about.

Randall reached for his hair — the long shock of bronze he had cut away months ago — and, finding nothing, made a frustrated gesture in the air with his hand. "Aren't you going to say anything? No, never mind — I don't know why I expected you to." He tapped his finger thoughtfully on Father's book. "You're like the mill building, you know — this wall here. There's no reason for it, but you've built it up anyway." Shaking his head, he rose with William. "It's late," he said.

"I'm tired, and William should be in bed." He left, heading upstairs.

I let him go; I was no longer listening. I was staring at my father's schematic of Stirwaters. Randall had seen it — why hadn't I? Had my father realized what he'd recorded? Had he never thought it strange? There was a foot's difference in the depth of the second floor — the floor with the hex sign on its back wall.

Father's atlas clamped in my arm, I practically threw myself outside and down the hill to Stirwaters. Pounding up the stairs, I paused only to grab a hammer from the shop table and the lamp from my office. I hit the spinning room at a dead run and dropped the atlas with a bang on the floor. My heart crashed against my ribcage, but I don't think it was all from running.

The hex sign, in all its blue and yellow fire, was clearly illuminated by the full moon streaming in the windows. I cast a black shadow over it as I stared hard, studying the wall. This wall was plaster — but it was the back of the mill and ought to have been stone. The same wall, on the floor above and below, had never even been painted. Suddenly I was sure my suspicions were correct. The hex sign wasn't protecting us from anything — it was *hiding* something.

Pressing my forehead and palms to the wall, I whispered, "Oh, please forgive me," and then, before I could talk myself out of it, struck the head of the hammer deep into the plaster. It hit something soft, resistant — not the stone wall behind it. Bracing my heel against the wall, I pulled out the hammer and struck again, forcing open a hole big enough for my hand. Frantically, I pulled apart plaster and lathing, crumbling into dust with age and air. The gap, like every other wall in

Stirwaters, was stuffed with paper. I took a deep breath that almost didn't make it past my throat and reached inside.

What came out first was mostly tattered ruins, shreds of worthless packing. I let it spill to the floor without a second glance, scrabbling deep in the hole I'd made. At last my fingers found whole papers — a stack here, a scrap there. I pulled the first one out and knelt into the lamplight to read it.

Hours later, moonlight had turned to morning, and I was still crouched beside the ruined wall, surrounded by a sea of papers. There in the dim light, I had pieced together a grim impression of Stirwaters's early days. Out of all the tattered remnants of our past, a picture emerged: of Harlan Miller, ambitious, ruthless, driven and driving. His stamp was all over the mill, in the blueprint and footprint, the engineering of the dam, raceways, pond, and powertrain. His wife, five daughters, and son Josiah seemed an afterthought.

An old map of the Valley, before there was a Shearing village, showed the undammed Stowe tumbling free through a golden landscape. Notations in red — Harlan Miller's hand; I knew it well by then — had scratched out the spot where he would build his mill: a circle, a sketch, initials. One word did the map bear: SIMPLE, in block capitals spaced wide across the Miller land. I shook my head sadly; nothing would be simple about Stirwaters.

Another stack of papers, once bound together with a ribbon that fell to bits when I went to untie it, revealed itself to be an age-old journal in an unknown hand. Most was illegible — the pages stuck together and crumbled when I separated them; age and mildew had obscured the writing, none-too-readable to begin with. Here and there I found a phrase I could make out: *building continues slowly; money owed, Miller impatient for* something-something *Wheel*. I spent hours carefully peeling those pages apart and trying to understand them; here was the account of the building of Stirwaters, from some anonymous workman perhaps? One of my ancestors? But the more I read, the less clear the journal became. Words leapt out: *fighting, delay, boy, rain, hanging, Wheeler*, and, close to the end and most ominous: *drown'd in Pit*.

I felt as if I'd plunged into the icy millpond myself. *Who* was drowned? But nothing else on that page was legible, the writer made no more mention of any such incident, and the journal ended a few pages later. One page looked promising, but in my haste I pulled too forcefully, and it scattered to the floor, hopelessly lost. The back of the old book was blank; the author had abandoned his account — but stuck inside the mildewed binding was a fragile scrap of broadside, bearing a brief newspaper account on one side, a recipe for slug repellant on the other. I'd have tossed it aside with the other miscellany, but for five bold words marching across the page: **WITCHCRAFT IN THE GOLD VALLEY**, blazed the headline.

A late instance in this neighborhood has shewn that the primitive and wicked practise of witchcraft still lingers in the rural places, near for instance to the town of Haymarket, where Friday last was arrested a man for the same. The unhappy incident arose when one Mr. M — , of Shearing, made claim against a townsfellow, that the latter had endeavored to act against him in a manner not befitting a godly man, namely that he had schemed against his health and prosperity and likewise those of his family, by means of foul Poison, graven Images, and curses —

Curses! I read and reread the account, trying to make sense of it. Mr. *M* — Harlan Miller? Involved in a witch hunt? Such an act seemed almost too far-fetched to credit, coming from my kinsman, and yet wasn't the evidence of his superstition all around me? A burst of night wind howled around the mill and hit the windows with a shudder I felt in my very bones. "I know," I whispered back. "You're trying to tell me something. But what?"

Knowing I still did not have the full story, I reached again into the wall. Deep in a stack of receipts and correspondence regarding the construction, I found part of a letter, torn at the fold:

. . . did not take you for a squeamish man. I know you feel pity for that sorry fellow, but forget that dirty business at the crossroads and put your mind back to work. I am not a patient man, and I expect to see a profit from my investment by year's end. If the mill is not up and running by then, do not doubt I will have my money from this enterprise, one way or another.

I pray God delivers your son from this terrible illness.

I remain your partner in this affair,

Malton Wheeler

I traced my fingers along the name of *Wheeler*, scribed there among the records of the building of Stirwaters. I should have felt surprised, but I did not. It seemed the Wheelers had contributed more than just the millwheel; our very foundations were built upon Wheeler money as well as Miller will. Perhaps it was inevitable, then, that Uncle Wheeler had come here, and it had taken a reunion of the two Stirwaters founding families to stir up all the old ghosts of this mill.

But something in that letter did chill me. What was the "dirty business" Malton alluded to? What had Harlan Miller and Malton Wheeler done — what was the secret so dark it had to be boarded up into a wall, guarded by a hex symbol? I laid the broadside and the letter side by side in the lamplight, trying to trace the threads that wove them together.

I tapped my fingers along the torn edge of the broadside. I could not imagine accusations of witchcraft were often resolved happily. *Dark dealings in Miller past,* Biddy Tom had said: *Anger, pain . . .*

Violent death.

"Oh, mercy," I breathed aloud. *"What did you two do?"*

I fell back on my heels, as the threads twisted tighter and tighter together, binding us all in a web of violence and revenge. Was there blood — innocent blood — on Miller hands? If we were cursed, then surely we deserved it. And perhaps doubly so — for were Rosie and William and I not just Millers, but Wheelers as well?

Something still troubled me. I found myself peering back into the wall, as if it would yield up more dark secrets, but I had fair emptied it. If there was a death on Harlan Miller's conscience — something that had happened far from here, in Haymarket — who, then, had drowned in the wheelpit? Why show me a vision of Randall drowning? And why had our curse taken the form it did: that no Miller would ever raise a son to inherit after him?

I pray God delivers your son. . . .

Suddenly, the distance between me and William was too much. I left the crumbled plaster, the hammer, and the scraps there on the spinning-room floor, gathered up my evidence, and fled back to the Grange. Randall was standing at the top of the stairs when I got home. The look he gave me was almost as terrible as anything I'd read that night. I swallowed hard, watched my husband, and — as always, waited for him to speak first. His eyes were shadowed, his hair a straggled mess where his hand must have passed through it over and over.

"I spent the night packing — I'm supposed to be in Harrowgate later this week, but I need know if you want me to come back again."

I stared at him. What was he saying?

"Are — are you leaving?" It was somehow the only thing I could get out.

He nodded wearily. I had never seen him so exhausted. "Where did you go, Charlotte? What were you doing, running about in the middle of the night? What's that all over your clothes, or are you even going to tell me?" There was no expression in his voice — he knew already that this was another secret I would not divulge. I wanted to run to him, throw my arms around him, weep on his shoulder and beg for his help. But what would that do but bind him tighter to a cursed family and their inevitable doom? I could not take the chance. Randall was a good man. He did not deserve to be tainted forever by the hand of Miller luck.

Randall left us later that morning, and I don't think we exchanged another word. I watched him drag his valise down the hill to the village, felt myself crumble away, stone by stone, and knew that Stirwaters was taking away another man I loved.

Randall's departure raised a few eyebrows in the village, and I did not even try to explain it. Occasionally Rosie would mumble something about the busy season for banking, but the sympathetic clucks William and I received told me that Shearing gossip, as usual, had gotten the better of the Millers. Randall wrote, at first — painful, hesitant letters asking after William, Rosie, me . . . but my answers grew less frequent, lest I give away something that should have him bolting back to Shearing — until at last his stopped, as well. Thus autumn waned toward winter, with none of last year's hope and promise.

One of those dreary mornings I sat in my office, my back to the ruined wall, listening to the roar of water below my feet. I had done the right thing. *I had done the right thing.* I turned the words over and over in my mind, but the water drowned them out, every time.

Rosie was with us, bent over William, cooing and tickling him. Even my son's laughter, the latest in a list of infant miracles his father would never witness, could not cheer me.

The door swung open, and the very world stopped turning.

Jack Spinner was back.

Chapter Twenty-Five

Rosie and I both fell utterly silent. I stood and straightened my skirts, put out a hand to steady William's basket. An autumn wind I'd not noticed before howled outside.

"Good day, Mr. Spinner," I said, trying to keep the tremor from my voice.

He tipped his battered hat to me, bowed low to Rosie. I could feel the tension off her, like a frightened horse.

"You girls didn't forget I was coming, now, did you?"

"No, of course not," I said, coming round the desk. "Would you —" I had to swallow; my mouth had gone very dry. "Would you care for some tea?"

Spinner looked round the office. The wind shrieked through the cracks in the floor and straight up my skirts. "No, no," he said slowly. "I think I'll just take what I came for, thank you."

"And what is that, then? Have you decided?"

Spinner took a step closer to me. I seemed to have trouble fixing him in my vision — I had had him for a much taller man, once.

"What was the offer, again?"

"Anything," I said, the word a faint croak. I tried again. "Whatever you want."

"Your wedding ring?" He said it so quickly I barely heard him. My heart jumped, but I slipped the ring from my finger and laid it on the desk. I thought I heard Rosie whimper. Spinner reached for it, barely brushing it with his fingers.

"What about your father's drawings?"

The cold wind had wrapped round my chest. "Yes." I pushed the atlas toward him, telling myself I did not feel the pang.

Spinner turned his eyes on William. "His christening blanket?"

Rosie cried out. "What could you possibly want —"

I laid a hand on her arm. I nodded. He could list them all, every treasure of my heart, and it would be worth it. My son's blanket, to keep my husband out of prison? My father's album, to save twenty jobs? I bit my lip and stood firm. "Take it all. Whatever you want. That was the bargain."

"Good." Spinner did not look at me — his eyes were still on William. Slowly, as slowly as snow melting, his hand reached toward the basket, the blanket, the baby. "I'll take your son."

"What?" Rosie shrieked — but I was numb with silence. I could not move or speak; the chill wind had cut off my voice from my heart. All I could think was, *I cut the scissors down from his bed, I swept up the circle of ash. . . .*

In the silence, the mill's voice was very loud — the thumping belts, the hissing machinery, the throbbing of the stocks. From somewhere very distant came a low, urgent rush. The water crashed off the millwheel, tumbling endlessly into the pit. I thought I heard screaming — and I knew it for generations of Millers who had faced this very moment.

"Charlotte, for the love of God, do something!" Rosie and Spinner were locked in a preposterous struggle over William's basket, like something from a puppet show.

"Put him down."

"What?" They echoed one another.

"Put him down. You cannot have him; that was not our bargain."

Spinner hesitated, and Rosie yanked the basket from his grip.

"No — it was. Anything I ask — you said so. You wouldn't break your word as a Miller now, would you?"

"Of course not, but you can't expect —"

"Can't I? I can give up my time, my energies, my *money* . . . all for the service of the Millers and Stirwaters, but I can't expect fair payment in return? Use him up, he won't care — he's no *Miller*, after all! What does it matter how *I* am abused, as long as the Millers have prospered?"

Rosie gave a strangled cry, and I felt my grip on the situation slip away. He was mad — terrible, powerful, and beyond reason. "You can't take him — he's so new; I barely know him yet." I was aware how I sounded, but I could not help myself. "Please — choose something else. Anything."

"Charlotte . . ." Rosie's voice had warning all through it, but I was past caring.

"Please. Anything else."

Spinner regarded me with — what? Pity? Loathing? I could not see him clearly enough to make out his expression. Something was wrong with my hearing, too — I could only hear the shrill, mournful wailing of the wind.

"You have only two things I want," Spinner said. "I didn't think it fair to take them both."

"Fair?" Rosie burst out.

I shook my head, confused, as he blurred before my eyes. "What other thing?"

"The mill."

There — like a kick to the stomach, I felt that. The mill gasped in all its breath at once, the air rushing in through every crack and broken windowpane. I wanted to grab my son and scream, "Take it, take it, *take it!*" But the words would not shape themselves, would not venture past my lips. I had a vision — like the glimpse I'd once caught of Randall falling into the pit — of what Stirwaters would suffer if Jack Spinner got his hands on it.

I saw the stones crumble, one by one, into the river, the rotting wood give way and spill the floors and all the machines into the icy water. I saw slates shuck off the roof, plaster dissolve, the millwheel splinter . . . all the ruin of the ages, in a breath, if Spinner touched it.

Something was squeezing me tightly — like a too-firm hug, or stays grown too small. I stared at Spinner, and as if the millwheel had finally completed its last great turning, I understood. All this time — all these years — *all the Millers have known my work*. The accidents, the mysterious mishaps, the bad luck. The lost sons.

"You did this to us," I whispered, scarcely aware I was speaking. There was no hope now; the Stirwaters Curse had come to claim one final victim. And I had called it down upon myself. Upon William.

William! Like a bowstring releasing, I could breathe again, and I stared, bewildered, at my child. I wanted to give it all up for him, cast the mill behind me, flee to Harrowgate or Eamside — or Atlantis! — but I couldn't. Stirwaters still held me too tightly.

"Your mill or your baby, Mistress. Make up your mind."

"I — I need time — to —" I faltered. To do what, exactly? I held out my hand. "Please, consider what you're asking me."

"Nay! You consider it. All your fine talk of Miller honor, of keeping your bargains. Well, this is your reckoning. Pay up."

I shook my head, as Rosie whimpered. "I will! I mean to, only the price —" I held myself together by sheer force of will alone. "It's more than I was expecting. You must give me time to decide."

Spinner hesitated, looking from me to William. I saw him lift a tentative hand in the baby's direction, as Rosie held fast to the basket and glared at him. At last he nodded. "I understand. You've treated me fairly. I'll do the same for you. I'll give you three days. At midnight Sunday, I'll be here, awaiting your decision. Miss Rosie, Miss Miller — good day." And like that — as if he had never been there — he was gone.

I slumped to the floor.

"Charlotte!" Rosie flung herself to my side. "Charlotte!"

I reached for her hand; she squeezed me tightly, her eyes wide with terror.

"What are we going to do?" she whispered.

Father's atlas teetered off the edge of the desk, and fell to the floor with a sound that shook us both. Rosie grabbed my arms, and for one hysterical moment I thought she might start laughing.

Instead, we pulled each other upright, and I lifted William from his basket and laid him gently against my shoulder. Impossibly, he had fallen asleep. I patted his little backside and felt the warmth of his breath against my neck. I longed to do nothing more than clutch him to my breast and breathe in the sweet baby smell of him . . . but that would not save us. I must use the days I had bought us wisely.

"Oh, it's bent," Rosie said mournfully, showing me Father's atlas. It had landed on its edge, crushing one corner and popping the binding loose. As she tried to mend it, it fell open to the drawing of the spinning jack. Wincing, I looked away, but a draft from the doorway swept in and fluttered the pages. They came to rest at the map of the Gold Valley. Rosie and I stared at each other, and then at the map.

Suddenly, like the walls of the mill reinforcing themselves brick by brick, everything began to fall into place. I slammed the album shut and shoved it at my sister.

"Here, take this." I swept to the shelves and wrangled out the pressboard box containing Stirwaters's journals and the papers I'd torn from the wall. I pushed it into Rosie's arms, gathered up William's basket, and threw my shawl round my shoulders.

"Where are we going?" Rosie asked.

"We're paying a visit to Biddy Tom."

By some miracle, Mrs. Tom was in, and answered my first set of demanding knocks. She eyed us with some surprise, but swung the friendship door open to admit us.

"I have three days to break the curse on Stirwaters," I said, and Rosie held out the carton of documents. "Here's everything I know."

Mrs. Tom fixed us tea with honey and listened attentively to our tale — all our dealings with Jack Spinner, stretching back to last summer's first meeting. She came as close to ruffled as I'd ever seen her, holding William very tightly and rocking faster and faster in the old ladderback rocker. I sat at her feet and spread the journals and letters all round me on the floor. At Stirwaters, for a moment, I thought I could glimpse the answer, but in Mrs. Tom's cosy parlor at dusk, I could not seem to catch hold of it again.

"What must we do?" I kept repeating. "Spinner must be the man — or the *spirit* of the man; oh, mercy — who cursed Stirwaters."

"Aye, lass, there seems little doubt of that now." Mrs. Tom lifted the broadside account and read it over William's tiny shoulder, and I remembered sitting here with her, months earlier, talking of these matters over a casual cup of tea. "You've wandered into dark territory indeed, then, if there's witchcraft involved."

"But how can we stop him?" Rosie's voice was desperate.

Mrs. Tom pursed her lips. "You must know what brought about the curse — and how it were laid down. Who cast it, and why."

"But we know who cast it," Rosie said.

"Do we? Truly? What do we *really* know of him — of what happened to him?" I shook my head, sweeping through the papers. "There's nothing here." But there was. If I could only understand it — if only I could marshal my thoughts and lay the pieces all in order, clear and plain, before me.

Idly, I flipped the pages of Father's book to the old map and traced my fingers over the odd names and inky figures. My finger came to a stop on SIMPLECROSS, and I paused for a moment and peered in closer. Farther up the river was a bridge labelled HARD CROSSING; I had always assumed they were companions, comparisons: *Ford the Stowe here, where it is easier.* But the cold, still feeling in my heart intensified as I stared at Simple Cross and saw that it was nowhere near the river. It was the convergence of four roads — one marked by parallel lines, the other by dashes.

"Oh, mercy," I said. "The crossroads."

Rosie peered in closer, and Mrs. Tom rocked thoughtfully. "Aye," the old woman finally said. "Powerful magic at work in a cross-ways. Folk've been known to make dark bargains there — and worse."

"Dark bargains?" Rosie echoed, but I merely nodded, recalling Malton Wheeler's letter.

"I think that's what Harlan Miller did," I said. *And worse.* "And whatever he did there — I have to undo it."

"Well," Mrs. Tom said gently, still holding the broadside, "from the looks of this, I'd wager your Mr. Spinner met a bad end there."

Rosie gasped. "You don't mean —"

Mrs. Tom continued. "There's no good to come of pairing a cross-ways and a witch, and only one thing that would bring God-fearing men into the mix, as well."

"I must go there," I said. My voice was very soft, little more than a thread through the lamplight, but I felt the rightness, the certainty of it like a warm weight settling into my bones.

Biddy Tom nodded. "Tomorrow." The clock chimed the quarter hour, and as I glanced its way, I saw that Mrs. Tom's parlor was decked for autumn, in boughs of golden foliage, grape wreath, apples. They were fading now — somehow we had reached the end of October without me realizing it.

"All Souls' Night. When the dead walk."

"Oh, truly!" Rosie said. "You're both mad, you are! There are —" she grabbed the map and counted. "One, two — five crossroads outside Haymarket. What makes you think *this* is the right one? It could take days to cover all of them — and then where will we be?"

It is always a bad sign when Rosie is the voice of reason.

"Look —" I spread the map Harlan Miller had drawn before her on the atlas, pointing to the facing page. The letters spread wide across the land Stirwaters was built on: SIMPLE. "This is the one it wants me to see. There's something about *this* crossroads I'm meant to understand."

"How can you tell? They're all on the same page!"

What could I tell her? There was no rhyme or reason to it — I just *knew*. The way I heard the voice of the mill, the way the atlas had fallen open to that page, the way the pit had given me back Mam's ring. I had closed my ears and eyes to Stirwaters's messages too long; when would I believe *before* it was too late?

We stayed at Mrs. Tom's a few more hours, during which she told us dark things about restless spirits and the hold that great anger could have. Things I had glimpsed for myself already.

"When the old year draws to a close — and I'm not talkin' about the calendar year, mind, but of *seasons* and nature, and things the elements of the land understand — when the earth turns, it brings us round closer to the Other World. The wall between their world and ours is thinner, then, and all sort of things may pass between. The Fair Folk come down from their hills, and the ones who have gone before us sometimes come back."

"But Spinner's *been* back," Rosie said. "Why should tomorrow be different?"

Mrs. Tom stirred her tea with slow hypnotic strokes. I thought if I looked long enough, she might conjure a vision in the murky liquid. "Tomorrow he'll be drawn to the place where he died — he won't be able to help it. All things return to their beginnings."

I listened to her, my thoughts turning hazy and indistinct in the shadows swirling round us. "My father —" I could not keep the wistfulness, or the grief, out of my voice.

Mrs. Tom set her teaspoon down with a snap. "Your father died a peaceful death, Charlotte Miller. He'll have no reason to come back, and don't you go meddlin' with them that's resting comfortable."

I rose from the table and lifted William from his basket. He murmured sleepily as I stroked his tiny plump hand. I whispered meaningless commentary into his wispy hair, and Rosie took a shaky sip of her tea.

"Very well," I said at last. "What must I do?"

It was decided that Harte would accompany me, for Biddy Tom pronounced the journey too dangerous to make alone.

"Understand — this is not just a night when the spirits wander. They're also at their most powerful, their most unforgiving. Take that strapping lad what's so keen on Rosie; he's got a head on his shoulders."

Rosie would stay behind in Shearing, watching William at the Grange, Biddy Tom nearby.

But things never go smoothly in this world, not for the Millers of Shearing, not for those they love. Saturday morning, Harte and I both came first to Stirwaters, of course, to tidy up last-minute loose ends and, I suppose, have a sort of heroic farewell. I don't know how heroic Harte felt; I was only sick and desperate and angry.

I watched it happen, watched and did not move, merely held fast to William and shook my head as the ladder Harte was standing on — his own perfectly sturdy ladder, hardly high enough to fall from, and from which he was certainly not overreaching himself — simply *pulled* itself out from beneath him. I don't believe it, but that's what I saw — Harte standing strong and easy no higher than the third or fourth rung, fixing a pulley into place, and then, for one sickening moment, hanging there in the air with nothing at all beneath his feet.

He was lucky not to break his neck. I saw him land, saw the look of surprise on his face as the leg buckled and bent. I saw Rosie screaming from the other side of the room. I saw her throw down her tools and run to him, as I had done, once, long ago when my father fell at that spot. My breath stilled in my chest and I could not move.

But then, there I was — at his side, barking orders. "Ian Lamb!" I bellowed, and the boy, running toward us, froze in his tracks. "Fetch Biddy Tom. Now!" Was I even thinking it was *medicinal* aid we needed?

Harte lay stunned, a distorted heap of a body, one leg bent up under his back, his face twisted with pain. Rosie had hold of one hand, up close to her lips, and her fingers brushed at his forehead as if she were a little afraid to touch him. But her eyes, wide and blue as the Stowe, were on me. If Rosie never looks at me that way again, I may one day forget what it was like; as if the sum of every strange and awful thing of the last two years was in that look — the accidents and deaths, the magic we *had* to believe, and above all, the Stirwaters Curse.

Mrs. Lamb took Rosie round the shoulders and moved her gently aside as two strong men came and lifted Harte from the floor. He screamed then, a raw, awful sound that could not have come from our Harte. They got him half to his feet, the broken leg dangling sickeningly at his side.

"Take him to the house," Rosie said, and her voice was clear and steady. With a slowness that was excruciating for everyone, they carried their burden down two narrow flights of stairs, across the rough shale yard, and into the Millhouse. It took them twenty minutes, for every few steps they had to stop and let Harte rest. I thought Rosie was going to faint, each time they paused, or jostled him, or bumped his leg against the stairway wall.

Outside in the yard, someone said at my elbow, "Here's the laddie, Mistress." I glanced back to see Tory Weaver holding a jolly, gurgling William.

"Merciful Lord," I said. "I'd forgotten. How —"

"You handed him straight to me, Mistress," Tory said. "No harm done. He's the picture of a prince, this a'one."

William grinned his drooling smile at good old Tory, gripping his collar in a tiny wet fist. And Tory beamed right back at him, proud as any grandfather. Fighting back hysteria,

I took William from his arms as calmly as I could. It was all I could do to hold him normally, not grip him as tightly as I wanted — tight enough to make him part of me again.

God help me, it was done so easily. One moment's distraction, and William was parted from me. How little would it take to make that parting permanent?

In the Millhouse, Harte was laid out awkwardly on the parlor sofa, blankets heaped up beneath his leg. Pilot and Rosie stood guard over him, keeping the crowd well back and offering gentle comfort where they could.

He looked like a man shot and dying, pale and sweating, his face a rictus of agony with every shallow breath. Rosie, at least, had recovered: She produced a knife and split Harte's boot and trouser leg apart as smoothly as I'd seen her gut trout from the millstream.

"Hold his hand — hard," she said to me, and I grabbed Harte's fingers in a grip like iron. "I'm taking the boot off; it's going to hurt like the devil."

"Keep breathing," I whispered — though to whom I am not certain. All the strength I wanted to pour into my grip on William was transferred to that poor man's hand. Harte's eyes rolled my way, but if he saw me, I have no idea.

Rosie made another cut in the boot leather, and then with no sympathy whatever, pulled it away from the foot. Harte gasped and squeezed me hard, nearly pulling me down beside him. It seemed I could hear his heart beating, even from where I stood, and new beads of sweat rose up on his forehead.

"All right," Rosie said. "Now your stocking."

Harte mumbled something that might have been a curse, but his free hand fumbled out and touched Rosie's hair, then her cheek. She paused a little and smiled at him.

The boot and stocking free, it was plain how bad the break was. The very skin of the leg had turned purple; the knee pointed out in a direction contrary to nature, other bumps and protrusions taking its place. It made me sick to look at it, for while it could have gone so much worse, that morning a broken leg was bad enough.

Biddy Tom arrived at last, her simples bag and another, much larger carpetbag in tow. She set to work briskly, dosing Harte first with some sleeping powder so she could set the limb with as little pain as possible.

"He may not sleep," she warned, "but this will help him bear it. Mr. Harte, if you could release Charlotte's hand; I believe your mistress would like to sit down." His grip softened and his hand fell away, but I could not feel my own fingers. I sank down, right atop the little tea table, and jostled William on my knee as we watched Biddy Tom set to work on Harte's leg.

The setting and plaster complete, she shooed the crowd away. Harte did sleep, which was a relief to all of us — his face relaxed at last, and he stopped shivering.

"Good work, Rosie," Biddy Tom said, and Rosie only nodded. She was looking us over with a strained and wary expression.

"What do we do now?" she said. "This wasn't a coincidence. Harte falling off a ladder, today of all days? Harte's never fallen off a ladder in his life!"

"No," said Mrs. Tom, "no coincidence. The danger you are in is very real —"

"It's not him," I said. "The mill didn't want him to go."

"You mean the mill doesn't want *you* to go," Rosie said.

I shook my head, the understanding so clear it was almost painful. "No, I must go. Otherwise *I'd* have fallen off the ladder — or come down with fever. But Harte doesn't have to come with me. He isn't a Miller; this curse has nothing to do with him." It seemed a foolish thing to say, with him lying broken on our sofa, but I knew I was right.

Rosie was shaking her head as she took my meaning in. "I won't leave him," she said, and I leaned over and touched her hand.

"No," I said. "You must still stay here and watch Harte, and watch William. Just as we planned." And before I could feel the pang in my breast, I handed William over to his favorite aunt, my fingers lingering on his gown longer, perhaps, than necessary. "Mrs. Tom, will you stay with them?" She nodded.

"You can't mean to go alone!" Rosie said.

"I must," I said, certain down to my very bones. "I won't risk what's happened to Harte happening to anyone else. It's put to *me* to break this curse, and I'll not see anyone else endangered by it."

Chapter Twenty-Six

*R*osie wasn't happy, releasing me to the unknown dark, alone, unaided. But in the end she agreed it was unavoidable. She insisted that I take Pilot, at least, and I confess I am surprised that dog left her master's side for me that night. In the distance, a bonfire burned at the churchyard, the guidelight for the dead, casting its baleful glow into the rising night. I bit my lip and tried not to think what might be watching for those flames.

I set off in Randall's father's carriage, the horses sprightly and glad to see me. There was no moon, just a glowering stormy overhang of clouds, and as we left the last of the village behind, I was grateful for the coachlights. The groom at Drover's had filled and lit them, and as they swung in graceful rhythm to the horses' steps, they cast a welcome arc of light around me.

I pulled my collar up against the breeze. Those clouds did not look welcoming, and I could only hope my errand would not detain me in bad weather. It was a drive of four hours, and Harte's accident had already delayed me. I had an overnight valise packed, in case I must stay at an inn, but I hoped not to use it. Pilot's warm presence, tucked against my ankles on the footboards, was more welcome than I would admit.

As I drove, I went over Biddy Tom's instructions for the journey in my mind. I was not sure what I expected to find — some evidence, perhaps, of what had passed among Harlan Miller, Malton Wheeler, and Jack Spinner in the crossroads, so many years ago. I could only hope I had not misinterpreted the information — the mill's intent — and that I was being drawn toward the *breaking* of the curse, and not my own fate at its fell hand. To that end, Mrs. Tom had given me clear instructions. I was to find something that witnessed the setting of the curse, and, if possible, the identity of the man who set it. She had likewise pressed me to accept a charm of protection — a blue string, tied round my wrist — but I had declined, fearing that any such might form a barrier between me and — whatever I was driving toward.

No one else was on the road. We trotted along the pressed earth for miles, seeing no more than a light in a cottage window, so I was surprised when Bonny gave a neigh and shied slightly at a figure walking along the verge toward Shearing. I slowed to pass the pedestrian more carefully, and then gave the reins such a hard yank I nearly spun the carriage round in the road.

I hadn't recognized him, at first. Dressed all in black, he blended into the shadows, and might have been a highwayman. But he was so disheveled! His jacket was half off one shoulder, his waistcoat unbuttoned, shoes and stockings scuffed with dust. Beneath his hat, pulled low over his brow, his white wig stood out brightly in the night, a ragged halo round his drawn face.

"My God," I breathed, my hand trembling on the reins.

For a moment, my uncle seemed not to know me. "Charlotte?" he said, at last, gazing upward. A faint smile broke on his lips. "My angel of salvation. Why does it not surprise me to see you here?"

This was impossible — and alarming. I shook my head, not sure what to make of it all. "Where are you going?"

Uncle Wheeler hesitated, a hand on Bonny's bridle. The black horse leaned into his touch, and he stroked her nose as if it were second nature to him. "As a matter of fact, I found myself rather compelled to go back to Shearing. Much as I adore the place." The words were all in place, but his voice sounded odd, uncertain.

"You're mad."

His fingers paused on the horse's soft nose. "I wonder," was all he said. I could read no answers in his face. He was gazing into the distance and frowning vaguely, as if he could not quite recall how he had come to be there. A furrow appeared on his forehead, and a fog of confusion seemed to waft from him.

"How did you get here?"

He never looked up, his gaze still locked westward, into the last, fading light. "There was a gentl — an obliging gentleman, with a wain . . . ." As he trailed off, he shook his head, but more as if to clear it. He brushed futilely at the dust on his jacket. "Now if you don't mind, I really must be on my way."

"What can you possibly have to gain by going back to Shearing?" I said.

He paused. "Ah, well, you know how it is. Just a little . . . ah, unfinished business to attend to. . . ."

I shook off the chill I felt. I could tell he was only half attending to what he said. Something was amiss, out of place, in the smooth mask of his face. He truly did not know where he was going — or why.

"You heard it, didn't you?" I said softly. I could scarcely believe I was saying such things, but it seemed so obvious now. "Stirwaters — calling you back?" The mill was drawing us all together, and onward, along some unknown path for some purpose yet to be made plain.

"Don't be absurd." But he said it absently, from mere force of habit. Pilot had risen, tense, and stared hard at Uncle Wheeler, her ears pricked forward with attention. I frowned into the dusky moonlight, then sighed. I was running out of time. The last thing in the world I wanted was to bring Uncle Wheeler along on my journey tonight. But the idea that some other carriage might come along and actually take him back to Shearing disturbed me even more.

"Get in."

The shadowed coachlight made his face paler than ever, and I thought he looked thin. "Agreed. I don't suppose there's any chance you'd allow me to drive?"

The look I gave him was all the answer he needed.

We rode in silence for some time. I had nothing whatever to say to the man, but I did wonder where he'd been these two months. Had he found more rich friends to cadge off? Had Spinner caught him up?

Perhaps I did not wish to know after all.

Once inside the carriage, my uncle seemed free of the strange spell. He sprawled lazily on the seat beside me, one leg propped upon the dash rail, his hat drawn low over his brow. Finally, he said, "And where are you headed, by dark of night, all, all alone?"

I started. His voice, smooth and languid as always, did not make those words any less chilling. He had not shown himself to be a violent man — but, then, did I truly know him?

He could easily be concealing a knife in that black jacket, and we were as good as nowhere, out here on the long stretch of dark road.

But, oddly, that thought no longer frightened me. I had faced this man down before, and he was no comparison to the threat that awaited me back home. "Haymarket," I said.

He eyed me from beneath his hat brim. "Haymarket's a big city — well, compared to what you're used to. Where, *precisely*?"

I let the reins droop, trusting Blithe and Bonny to keep up their steady forward progression. From beneath my cloak I withdrew the rolled-up form of my father's map, which I had, with no little pain, cut from his atlas. If it survived the journey, I would frame it above my fireplace. I showed the map to my uncle, and pointed a gloved finger at Simple Cross. There was just enough light to read by. Uncle Wheeler grabbed my hand.

"That's not Haymarket — that is the middle of nowhere. What sort of business could you possibly have there?"

I didn't answer, but my face must have given something away. Uncle Wheeler grabbed the reins and gave them a brutal jerk. The horses scrambled to slow down, rocking the trap madly, and I grabbed for the dash rail as Pilot rolled against my feet and barked.

"Are you out of your mind? Do you have any idea what night it is?"

"Are you superstitious, Uncle?"

"Hardly. But I'm no fool, either. You must be mad; no good can come of this."

"I'm not looking for good," I said softly. "I'm trying to save my son."

He eyed me warily, but a slow smile spread across his face. "Oh, I see," he said. "This wouldn't have anything to do with our mutual acquaintance, now, would it? You wouldn't perhaps have gotten yourself involved in any . . . unfortunate bargains?"

I drew back, stung. "Please, just give me the reins."

Uncle Wheeler made no response. He was staring past me into the shadowed trees. Pilot whined softly from beneath my feet, and the horses neighed, restless. A low wind had risen in the wood; branches rustled and creaked in the distance. I turned; among the shifting leaves ahead I saw the flash of lamplight — there and then gone again. I blinked, uncertain I had really seen anything. And then it was back, bobbing along steadily. I shook my head — someone walking home by the margin, carrying a lantern. Several yards farther along, another light — larger, yellower. A cottage. I reached across for the reins.

"No, wait —"

I glanced his way. "Uncle, let me say again: I really am pressed for time. I am happy for you to ride with me, but if you intend to distract me from my errand, I will leave you here." Voice of the mill or no.

He turned toward me. "Leave me? You'd like that, I'm sure."

When I made no reply to this, Uncle Wheeler looked sharply at me — and gave a strangled laugh. "Good God, girl, do you know *nothing*? Look —" I followed his finger into the darkness. The lights winked out, quick as that. "Keep looking." Another light, deeper into the forest, now coming our way again, now gone. I watched in confusion for several minutes. Even Pilot climbed up to see what the delay was.

"That isn't lamplight. They're corpse-lights — will-o'-the-wisps. There's likely to be a bog back there, or a ravine."

I shook my head, lost.

"*You'd* call it superstition, no doubt. But the local peasantry will tell you those lights are the spirits of lost souls, leading unwary travellers to their doom."

All Souls' Night.

"So unless you mean to see me stumble off a cliff and break my neck — which, I have no doubt, should please you no end — I'll thank you to keep driving."

The odd lights followed us all evening, first on one side of the road, then the other, then ahead. I told myself my uncle was having a jest at my expense — it *was* a cottager, out searching for a lost dog, or perhaps some drunken farmhand, stumbling home from a long weekend. Nothing more eldritch than that. But if that were all, my drunken cottager made as good time on foot as my horses. I reached down for Pilot's feathered head, glad for her solid presence.

Eventually we came in sight of Haymarket, or the first scattering of houses and farmsteads leading into town. The map was still open across Uncle Wheeler's lap, and I peered at it again. I thought I could make out the shape of our path — and the tree-coated hill before us looked like the one marked out on the map. We were close; we had to be.

Turning onto an outlying road, eerily bereft of habitation, I drove along flat pasture, toward the river. Drawing as close to the trees as I dared, I leaned forward and tried to make out a gap, a strange shadow — anything in the darkness that might once have been a path. I drove a quarter mile in both directions and saw nothing but more will-o'-the-wisp. Finally I stopped the carriage and sighed.

"I'm sure you have no intention of divulging the true nature of this errand to me," Uncle Wheeler said peevishly, "but you might offer some sort of hint. No doubt —"

"Uncle, if you wish to contribute something to this journey, then you may at least look for that turning."

"You presume it's still there, of course."

"What do you mean?"

His expression clearly indicated that I was the most ignorant person he could imagine. "Although it obviously has never occurred to you that time could cause something to progress, instead of decay, woods do grow up. Trees fall over paths. Underbrush closes in. A road falls out of use, and the wood reclaims it. Likely no decent person's stepped foot on that path in fifty years."

I stared at him, and then back to the map. Oh, he was right, and we were on a fool's errand. We'd never find the cross-ways, not in the middle of the night — not in a week of trying.

I didn't have a week.

"No," I said, and started the horses forward again. "If it was there once, it's there now — and we'll find it. We must."

Suddenly, Pilot barked. "What is it, lass?" She nudged my hand absently, her eyes keen on the woods. The bobbing lights had swept toward us, and back out again, and they were coming near once more. First one dim glow on my left, pushing eastward . . . then another far off to the right, flickering on and out again. I watched in odd fascination for several moments.

"No," I said to Pilot. "You're imagining things."

But was she? After a few minutes, I didn't think so. The lights, like signal flares, bobbed and flashed in a way that could not have been random. I drove a few yards to the right, eastward, and stopped. The floating yellow orb followed, paused, and began a frantic flashing in much the same pattern as before. East. Was I being led east? And that second light, the stationary one — what did that mark?

I decided to find out. I clucked the horses into action and drove straight for the still, eastward beacon. My lefthand companion winked out and only appeared again if I seemed to pause. As I approached the light, it seemed to sink deeper into the woods.

"Stop!" I hadn't meant to, but I cried out aloud. Uncle Wheeler sprang forward in the seat and grabbed my arm.

"What are you doing?" he said. "What did I just tell you? Were you not listening?"

"I heard you," I said grimly. "But look — they want us to follow."

"Of *course* they want us to follow. That's what they *do*. Bogs and ravines, remember?"

But he was wrong. As I neared the spot where the light had hung, waiting, the trees broke open and a shadowy path appeared beneath the tangled branches.

"Look," Uncle Wheeler whispered — or I'd not have seen it, myself. An ancient stone marker, probably once a gatepost, sat by the wayside, signaling the now-obscured path.

The corpse-lights winked and sparked among the branches, far into the depths of the wood. I pulled up close to the post and alit from the trap, preceded by a cautious-tailed Pilot. Some of the old fence boards were still attached, and I tied the horses to them.

"Are you out of your mind?" Uncle Wheeler said, still sitting stubbornly in the trap. "You'll be killed — and for what?"

"I don't think so, Uncle. Look — you don't have to come with us. Someone should probably stay with the horses anyway."

"Don't be ridiculous. Stay right there; I'm coming down. If you fall and break your neck in there, someone is bound to assume I've done you in."

The woods were very dark, even stripped bare for winter. And Uncle Wheeler's assessment proved accurate: No one could possibly have walked this tangled path in the last century. We stumbled across roots and fallen branches, ducked low-hanging limbs, pushed saplings out of our way. Pilot scrabbled through the dead leaves at our feet, her steps sure and light. We had only the corpse-lights and Pilot's white breech to light our way.

It's a wonder we *didn't* break our necks, and after a quarter hour of fighting that wood I began to regret disregarding Uncle Wheeler's warnings. Clearly we were being led to our doom. And then, when I was almost ready to give up and turn back, we stumbled out into a clearing, where the path spread out wide before us, and at a long, oblique angle into the distance.

"The cross-ways," I murmured, and I saw Uncle Wheeler's hat nod once.

"And now?" he said, in that old arch voice.

I sank gratefully onto the remnants of a low stone post. "Now we wait."

The will-o'-the-wisps had stopped travelling and were clustered across the clearing. Where there had been two, there were now five — then eight, then I lost count as they sprang into being. I stiffened and heard Uncle Wheeler draw a sharp breath. Pilot made a sound that was half growl, half moan, and pressed herself tight to my legs.

I saw something else, then — the lights had gathered round an ancient beech tree, white with age and stooped under the weight of its massive branches. A raw scar on the trunk, high above the path, showed where a limb had fallen. The branch itself lay in the middle of the road, big as a tree in its own right. I found myself rising from my perch and scrabbling my way across the fallen limb toward the old beech.

"Charlotte!" Uncle Wheeler's whisper rang out loud and hoarse. I waved him to silence and crept on.

"*Charlotte!*" Some urgency in his call made me turn back, and I nearly fell back across the branch at what I saw.

A mist had risen — one tiny patch of floating, ragged fog hung above the center of the crossroads. It wafted upward like a puff of smoke, but with its own preternatural light. The blue-white glow, if nothing else, would have told me this was no ordinary mist. Hastily I clambered over the limb and underbrush and ducked back behind the beech tree.

The mist congealed, taking on the form of — of a man, unbending himself from a stooped and gnarled posture. As the form solidified, I began to shake. I dug my hands into my skirts and felt my knuckles go white. A minute more, and the semi-solid, somewhat glowing man-shape stepped — stepped! — out into the roadway. I wanted to turn away, hide my face in my skirts — but I couldn't.

It was Jack Spinner. Something was different — but he was unmistakable. His carriage, the way he moved — I sat and trembled as Spinner took a few steps *that did not touch the ground*, paused to give himself a doglike shake, and looked around the clearing, as if confused. I thought he looked like someone awakening after a deep sleep and not, for a moment, recognizing the place he has found himself.

He lifted his hands to his face, turned them back to front, flexed the fingers. He touched his face, his head, his ears and neck — his neck. He pulled at the collar of his ghostly shirt and felt below it with frantic fingers. For a moment he faded.

Suddenly, he brightened, solidified — flashed like a burst of flame, and cried out like an enraged animal. Only there was no sound, and he clapped his hands to his silent mouth. I watched him bend to take a deep breath — he seemed to struggle to remember how — and cry out again. This time the roar rattled the dry dead leaves on the roadway and seemed to roll toward me like a slow, hot wind which shook me to my very bones.

Spinner fell to his knees and caught up handsful of the earth and leaves, letting them spill through his fingers. For a moment he stayed there, head bent low, and when he lifted his face, it seemed to me that he wept.

Horrified, fascinated, I could not draw my eyes away from the spectacle — the spectre. I leaned in closer, nearly lost my balance, and grabbed the trunk of the beech for support.

Suddenly — the clearing disappeared, or *cleared*. The fallen limb vanished from the decaying underbrush; the underbrush itself was absolutely gone — the very clearing became wider, more open, more like the crossroads of old. Gone were the tangled, overgrown weeds, and *back* were the stone-posted fences, the wide, clean, dusty roads. I looked up, and instead of the raw gash in the beech's trunk, a stately limb arched gracefully overhead, fully leafed. I pulled back from the tree with a gasp, but nothing changed. Or rather, everything remained changed, the roads, the cross-ways, the fences and hale summertime trees.

A bright, full moon shone overhead in a clear starlit sky. The corpse-lights had vanished. Where they had been was now a mob.

Perhaps twenty men emerged from the woods, from the road, from the darkness. They were armed — some with muskets, some with pitchforks, some with sticks. One man carried a rope. As they materialized, I heard shouting — laughter. They did not walk, exactly, but seemed to float onward, inexorable, as if it was not necessary, now, to remember footsteps.

Jack Spinner stood rooted to his spot at the heart of the crossroads, and shook.

They overtook him, like a fog rolling across the land. Caught by the arms and struggling like a mad thing, Spinner screamed and wept and made not a single sound.

"Kill the witch!" I did not note who said it first, but it thereafter spilled from the lips of every man assembled there.

"Kill him!"

"Devil!"

"String him up!"

"Stop! Don't — help me, please!"

My eyes flew open. For a wild moment I thought he was speaking to me, but no one took any notice of me, though surely I was in plain enough view. My heart rattling like a loose shutter, I held fast to the tree and trembled.

"Shouldn't we wait for the magistrates?"

"And risk them letting him go? Not a chance. You know what he is."

"Aye, confessed, he did."

A man stepped forward out of the mob. I knew immediately who he must be. The arrogant height, the stern features . . . they did not belong to anyone I knew. But something — a stirring in my blood, perhaps, like iron to a magnet — connected me to him across the years: Harlan Miller. He drew a rolled-up paper from his coat and unfurled it.

"I have the confession here, if there is any doubt. This man is a dangerous criminal, and I think it best we take care of him once and for all."

"No — it's me! Joseph, Peter, you know me, it's John — John Simple." The words were a whimper, but they pierced my soul. *Simple.* It was a name.

Harlan Miller laughed, an ugly, ugly sound. "Your very name condemns you! For what is a *simple*, but a spell?"

"Aye," someone agreed. "Wheeler makes wheels, and Miller runs the mill — what does *your* name mean, then?"

Simple only sobbed harder. They brought the rope. I closed my eyes; I could not watch further. I buried my face in my arms and realized I was weeping. It didn't matter that this scene was ages old, over and past. We were all trapped now — those men had condemned us all.

"John Simple, you are charged with the crime of witchcraft and bedevilment. You have confessed to bewitching the sheep of Farmer Sherman and preventing Mrs. Woolsey's butter from taking."

"That were a lease I signed, for you to build yon mill on my land — and you know as much." I was surprised at the venom in Simple's voice — now, when it was too late.

Miller laughed again. "Was it? Well, here — why don't you have a closer look and read me what you signed?"

Against my will, I found myself peering out at them again. Miller held the paper right up to Simple's face. He closed his eyes and turned away. "You know I don't read."

"Well, then — you ought to be more careful what you put your hand to. Have at it, lads!"

I braced myself for the creaking of the rope against the branch — but what I heard was Simple, speaking out low and softly over the mob.

"Harlan Miller, you will have no good of what you took from me, and you and yourn will suffer the loss I felt, until the Miller line may die out. Malton Wheeler, I see you here, too — and I'll see you and yours in Hell!"

"Charlotte!"

I jumped, a scream caught in my throat. Uncle Wheeler had crept up behind me and grabbed me by the shoulder. Somewhere, Pilot was barking. Frantic, dazzled, I stared wildly round me. I was crouched in a pile of dead leaves and vines, a long white limb stretched out on the ground before me. The mob was gone — Simple, Miller, all the others, disappeared into the dark night. I choked back a sob.

"Where did they go?"

"They?" Uncle Wheeler blinked at me. "If you mean our friends the ghost lights, they've winked out — and left us stranded here in the middle of nowhere, no doubt."

I stared at him. Had he not seen it? But, no — surely . . . I *knew* he had seen Spinner materialize from the earth in a puff of fog. But the rest of it? I was never to know for certain what, if anything, my uncle witnessed in that crossroads on All Souls' Night.

All manners, he helped me to my feet and only lightly

brushed his hands after touching me. Unruffled, he headed back toward the trees.

"Wait —"

He turned back, glaring at me. "What *now?*"

Biddy Tom had said to bring something back, and I had a little jar tucked into my cloak; but for the beech tree, nothing stood to remember or commemorate the dreadful scene I'd witnessed. Unless someone happened upon this spot on All Soul's Night, who would know? Or was I privy to that performance solely by virtue of my name and legacy?

I glanced around hurriedly. What was there? The beech limb was obviously too heavy; perhaps I could prize free a stone from one of the fence posts. I made my way across the fallen branch. Souvenir-hunting at the haunted crossroads: Such a lovely way to spend an evening. Exhausted, hysterical, I wanted to laugh.

As I scraped my fingers trying to pull a stone from one of the posts, a glint of white in the moldering leaves below caught my eye. I brushed aside the debris to reveal the tiny fragile bones of a mouse. Thoughtful, I glanced back over the deserted crossroads. I couldn't bring John Simple's bones back, but I could bring the next best thing. I pulled the fallen limb aside and scrabbled through the dirt at what I hoped was the spot I'd seen the mist appear. The earth was dry and soft, and I had no trouble filling the jar with it.

As I gathered the earth into the glass, I nearly shrieked as my hands brushed something hard and cold. But it was only metal — a silver coin, its denomination obscured with age. Something else was in the ground, as well: a glint of garnet enamel in the moonlight, a glow from a mother-of-pearl watch face, showing the time: ten past twelve. I rubbed the dirt from the case with trembling fingers. My watch . . . what else might I find, if I dug deep enough? Would I find something, perhaps, of my father's?

That thought made a ribbon of fear slip through me, and I hastened to my feet, the jar of earth in one hand, the coin and my watch in the other. It seemed a bit sacrilegious to steal earth from a man's grave — no matter how unhallowed it may be — so I mumbled a benediction, best I could remember one.

"Please forgive us," I whispered, and fled back into the trees.

Chapter Twenty-Seven

I climbed back into the carriage feeling cold and sick and close to tears. I could barely look at my uncle; his face was drawn and nearly as pale as the spectre of Jack Spinner. Perhaps, I thought, so was I.

We were both of us silent as the carriage pulled away from the cross-ways, a clap of thunder rolling overhead. I turned toward Haymarket; I had no strength left in me for another journey tonight, and would seek out some lodging.

A cold, miserable drizzle began to fall as we drove into Haymarket, glossing the black trap and the black horses with wet lamplight. Well past midnight, the town was dark, the roadway empty. I was focused on guiding the horses through the darkness, and Uncle Wheeler was presumably lost in thoughts of his own. Pilot bore the rain with equanimity, gazing out over my shoulder into the night.

I wanted someone to explain what I had seen, to take my hand and say that it was just a trick of the moonlight, the workings of an overwrought imagination. But Uncle Wheeler was not that man — and what I had seen was important. I could not pretend, as generations of Millers before me must have done, that we were blameless in our misfortunes. I had been privileged to view what I did in the crossroads, no matter how miserable I felt about it.

A shaft of lightning shattered the darkness, lighting up the road like midday. I jumped, my heart in my throat. One of the horses skittered sideways in the reins, and the skies broke open in an icy torrent.

"We must find a stable and an inn," I said, my voice pitched to carry above the storm.

"Up the road about two miles," Uncle Wheeler cried back. He held fast to the carriage with one hand, fast to his hat with the other. "The Red Drake."

"Two miles? We'll never make it!"

"They'll be sure to be open."

"On a night like this? They won't expect anyone to be out." I shook my head, but drove ahead through the downpour. What choice was there?

Then, abruptly, there was a choice. Just ahead, down a twining side road, I glimpsed a light burning in a window, and under the crack of thunder from the heavens, the storm flashed a sign into brightness: HOSTELRY.

"There!" I said, pointing with the reins. "Straight across. It doesn't look like much, but it's right here." I snapped the reins and the horses found more speed, carrying us up the little alley.

Suddenly, Uncle Wheeler reached across and wrenched the reins from my hands. He gave them a firm tug and eased the horses to a halt. "I thank you for the lift, my dear girl — but if that is where you intend to go, then I shall indeed be leaving you now."

"Are you crazy? It's pouring rain — you'll freeze to death!" I wondered why I cared. "What's the matter — what's up there?"

He gave a hint of his old thin smile. "If you're so keen to know, go have a look for yourself. I think you'll enjoy the irony." With the ghost of a bow, he strode off into the rain, his black coat glossy wet.

I watched him leave, weary and perplexed, but eventually weariness won out. All I wanted was a hot bath and a warm bed, and a good thousand cups of tea. I pulled into the inn yard and descended from the carriage. My foot slipped on the rain-slick running board, landing me in a puddle that splashed icy muck up to my waist. Close to, I saw the hostelry as a rather shabby affair; unpainted for years, the yard littered with bits of moldering harness, rotting straw, and the droppings of horses. Still, I stepped gratefully under the overhanging roof and rang the bell. As I was wringing water from my skirts, the door swung open, warmth and light pouring out across the threshold.

"Gracious me!" said the woman who answered. "Oh, dear — come in out of that, then, won't you? I'll send Hank to see to your horses and your wee damp doggie, poor things."

But I was staring at her, just a tavern maid in a patched and dingy frock, and in a flash like storm light, I understood it all. I saw it in the arch of her eyebrows, the dainty pink mouth, the sharp chin — everything that had distinguished Uncle Wheeler's appearance from my mother's. Behind her, an older man with the same features leaned against the bar, his sharp eyes keenly green, even from where I stood. A rank smell of unwashed floors and unwashed bodies wafted into the rain, like steam. I whipped round to look at my uncle again, but he had all but disappeared, only a moving black shape in the endless black night. I don't know how long I stood there, gaping like some open-mouthed half-wit.

"No —" I said finally, senselessly. "No, I'm sorry to bother you, Miss —"

"Lowman," she said with a smile, pointing at the sign. "Ellie Lowman." And there in the lamplight were the words, in weathered, peeling paint, that spelled out a name, a life, a world that my Uncle Wheeler could never have been able to accept: LOWMAN, it read. LOWMAN & SONS, LODGING FOR MEN & BEASTS.

"Well, don't stand staring," she said with a laugh. "Get inside before you're drowned!"

"No —" I said. "No, I don't want lodgings. I'm sorry, I — I've made a mistake."

I found him, soaked to the skin, a quarter mile away. I pulled alongside him, but he did not look up. "Get in," I said, but he only kept walking. "Don't be an idiot — get back in the trap!"

He turned his face to me then, and what I saw there was nothing like the man I knew. Just a flash, mind you, and well I knew that by the time I truly looked at him again, the old sneer would have returned, the haughty lift of his chin. But what I saw then was bitterness and rage, and it twisted any beauty out of his face. It made him look, in fact, like an angry little boy.

"Are you truly my mother's brother, then?"

He gave a laugh, sharp and mirthless. "In the flesh, my dear Charlotte. Born side by side in the muck, we two, both of us Wheeler bastards. Does that surprise you? Does that offend your merchant-class sensibilities?"

I said nothing, but in truth, I wasn't surprised. It seemed to make sense of so many things. But Uncle Wheeler took my silence for disgrace.

"Oh, now I've hurt your feelings, have I? Can't stand the ugly truth? How will your society banker like knowing he's married the daughter of a baseborn factory girl? I don't suppose she ever told your sainted father, either."

My father wouldn't have held such a thing against her — he wouldn't have known how. "Why would it matter?"

He was incredulous. "Why would it matter? Why, it's the *only* thing that matters, you foolish chit!" The rain streaming down his face made him look waxen, fiendish, as though a mask were melting away.

"Get in," I said again, my voice low and weary. "We must get out of this weather."

Finally, finally, he consented, climbing into the trap with something still of his fastidious grace. The drive to the new inn was very long, and as the wheels of the carriage spun over the pocked road, I heard an echo of Biddy Tom's words: *All things return to their beginnings.* The great millwheel turns, bringing us all back round again. Inevitably.

By the time we pulled into the yard at the Red Drake, the embittered young man from the gutters of Haymarket had faded away, becoming once again the refined Ellison Wheeler, Esquire, gentleman from Harrowgate. The transformation left a cold pit in my belly, well out of proportion to the chill night.

It must have been nearly two in the morning by the time Uncle Wheeler and I were settled in the cosy private parlor, swathed in borrowed dressing gowns, our cloaks and clothes hung to dry by the kitchen fire. We ought to have gone straight to bed, but we had to wait for bricks to be heated and beds turned down, and our own nightclothes were near as wet as our travelling dress. Besides, I'm sure neither of us was relaxed enough for sleep just then.

They had wakened an upstairs maid to help undress me, her sleepy fingers fumbling with the wet buttons and soaked stay-laces. Peeled out of my sodden clothes, I was still freezing, despite pot upon pot of steaming tea and the roaring fire in the parlor grate. The maid heaped a very fine eider quilt atop me, but it helped little. I think the shivering went bone deep — deeper, even; the night in its wild entirety had left me cold to the very soul.

Uncle Wheeler paced the room like a clock that won't wind down. He had doffed even his wig, and though his damask dressing gown was as fine as they come, the difference in his appearance shocked me. His hair, cropped close, was an untidy smear of red; without powder, his face was blotched and freckled. He did look more like my mother, then; but still more like the folk I had seen at Lowman's.

"The woman I saw," I said, tucking my numb toes beneath my legs. "Who was she?"

Uncle Wheeler made a little sound, full of derision.

"A sister? A cousin? Who can tell? They all look alike," he said, and the venom in his voice was enough to sting me from across the room. "They breed like rabbits and live like roaches, and by God, I wasn't going to spend my life among them, kissing the gentry's pompous behinds and scraping dung from their boots! I was Harrison Wheeler's son — I had every bit as much Wheeler blood in my veins as any rich brat up at

Highton Park, and nobody was going to keep me from what was mine by birthright."

He turned to me then, one hand still on the fireplace mantel. "You'll be thinking it didn't look so bad, I'm sure. But trust me, my sweet niece, you have no idea what it *really* means to be poor — so poor you know you'll never be able to clean the grime from your fingernails or wash the stench from your clothes. You play at genteel poverty, but you wouldn't last a day if you had a taste of the real thing."

"What about your mother?" I said, very quietly.

"She? Oh, she had the decency to die in childbirth, rather than live out life as a fallen woman. Left me at the mercy of her big brother, she did — didn't even leave word as to what I should be called. So I became —" he nearly spat out the words, "*Enoch Lowman*. Enoch! Named for my generous patron, who thought enough hard, dirty work would wash the stain of illegitimacy right off me."

"And my mother?" I said, and his face softened — but briefly.

"Who knows? I think her mother — oh, yes, Charlotte, different mothers. Are you scandalized more than ever now? I think she must have been a servant at the big house; that sort of thing is common enough, after all."

My mother had weathered it well, it seemed; her half-brother, caught between worlds, had nurtured a keen resentment that burned still to this day. He had emerged from behind the mask he wore, and it was like pulling a scab off a wound. The man underneath was raw and festering, and far more frightening than the face on the surface.

"How did Spinner — our mutual acquaintance — come into it?" I said.

"My father died when I was fifteen," he said. "By that time, I understood who he was — what I was. Picture me then, Charlotte — not only a bastard, but an orphan. I knew better than to expect a legacy, or a nod, or the least little crumb off the dead man's table. A man like Harrison Wheeler can give his name to a dozen little girls and no one so much as drops a handkerchief over it."

"But not a boy," I said, understanding. Mercy, who knew better than I what it meant to have a son to inherit? "Not an illegitimate son."

Uncle Wheeler was lost somewhere in the past. "He found me at Highton Park, banging on the postern gate in the middle of the night, sick and drunk and looking like I'd crawled straight out of the slime I'd been born in. I don't know what he was doing there — it didn't occur to me to wonder at it. I was just a boy, and when a gentleman pulls up beside you in a four-in-hand and invites you in for a brandy and cakes before you catch your death of cold . . ."

"You climb right in," I whispered, recalling the glint of gold thread by fading sunlight. How easily had Rosie and I given in? Surely it took less to lure a desperate, angry boy into his influence. Oh, *surely* it had taken far less!

"You climb right in. He whisked me off in just such a coach as I'd been polishing since I was big enough to reach above the axle. He introduced himself as Mr. Smart, and he had calling cards to prove it. Rob Smart —" he gave me that same bitter little smile, "Esquire." Uncle Wheeler laughed, startling me. "They don't carry cards that say 'Others.'"

"No," I said. "No, indeed they do not."

The carriage had carried him all through the night, he said — but only that one night. He'd have sworn to it. By the time morning broke, they had arrived in Harrowgate, and young Enoch's filthy working clothes had become the clean, soft dress of a young gentleman: brushed wool frock coat, white stockings, tapestry waistcoat, and silver-buckled shoes.

"Dressed me up just like the rag-girl in the fairy story," Uncle Wheeler said. "And, would you believe it? He dropped me right off at the ball."

Not a ball so much as a gentlemen's club of the sort Enoch Lowman could never have gained entry. But that Enoch Lowman was gone, and a new young dandy stood in his place. He could hardly believe his luck.

"What did he want from you?" I asked. "For payment?"

Uncle Wheeler laughed again, and it was a sound that had not the slightest mirth in it at all. "Oh, that *is* the best part, isn't it? What did he want? In exchange for a new life, a new identity, a new wardrobe, and a purse full of silver?" He shook his head, as if he could not quite believe it, all these years later. "I had half a crown from my father — the only thing he'd ever given me. Like a tip. I was happy to be rid of it, just then."

The boy Jack Spinner had dropped at the club in Harrowgate was already well on his way to becoming the Ellison Wheeler that had descended upon us in Shearing so many months ago. But the pouch of silver would not last forever, and young Enoch — now calling himself by an array of fancy names as varied as his wardrobe — found himself in a constant scrabble for income.

"But I was young, and handsome enough, and hungry. I found a series of diverting occupations, and more than enough willing . . . affiliates to assist me. The right clothes, the right manners, the right names . . . that was enough to get invited to their dining rooms, their game rooms, their bedrooms. And if things occasionally got too close, *he* was there. A debt I couldn't cover, a husband whose ego couldn't be soothed. Get in a scrape, and who should be round the next corner but my old pal Rob Smart?

"I knew what he was, by then, of course — or close enough. I was playing the game too well to have any illusions about the 'help' he was giving me. A whole new identity all over again, and all for just my mother's tattered handkerchief, a lock of my sister's hair? He steals from you, bit by bit, and you pay up freely. But what care had I for the scraps and trinkets of a life better forgotten? As I said, I was more than happy to be rid of them.

"But then, oh, then! I had my grand idea. I had had enough of skulking about the fringe of Harrowgate's great society. I was tired of being Jack Harrison of the Wakefield Harrisons, William Pendleton, Edward Holmes-Whitley. I wanted my own name — my father's name."

He paced before the fire, spark animating his recollections. I felt cold and sick as I watched him. "What did you do?"

"I marched my way into Old Wheeler's — let's see, that would be your great-uncle, I believe, good old Harrison's big brother — Old Wheeler's study, and told him, flat out, what I wanted. Papers drawn up declaring me, by legal right, a Wheeler by birth and name. Once I suggested it was better worth his while than to have me start spreading the word that his precious new axle-bearings were really the work of a machinist at Spinney and Sons, he was more than happy to oblige me."

"Was that true?"

He shrugged. "Did it matter?"

I huddled deeper in my quilt to suppress a shudder. "So just your name? That was all?"

"Oh, well — there was a little matter of a thousand pounds, just to be certain I would keep the whole thing as . . . discreet as possible. Can't have word leaking out, now, can we?"

"And what about your Rob Smart?"

He paused, stroking his dressing-gown collar. "As it happened, things weren't quite so smooth as Ellison Wheeler as I may have anticipated. A few years ago I ran a bit afoul of some creditors. Crossed the wrong fellow at cards, perhaps, romanced the wrong lad's little sister. Who can remember? And thus I found myself — temporarily inconvenienced. At His Majesty's pleasure."

"Debtors' prison."

At those two words, Uncle Wheeler faltered. "Yes. Well. And there we met again. I believe you know the rest of that tale."

He turned to watch the fire, and as my eyes followed his gaze into the flames, I was sure that nonchalance was an act. *Sparrow. Virginia Byrd. The wrong lad's sister.* He did remember how he'd come to be thrown in prison — what had he paid Spinner to get out again?

Just then, however, my uncle's narrative was interrupted by that long-awaited knock at our door, announcing maids laden with bedclothes and — oh, sweet! — our warm, dry nightclothes. Instantly the familiar Uncle Wheeler was back, genteel but brusque and disapproving of the lateness of the hour and the state of our reclaimed garments. I tried to thank the girls graciously, but I was well past my limits of strength and courtesy by then. I think they must have noticed, for they tucked me into the bedroom with smiles, a wink, and a "don't worry, mistress. Sleep well."

Despite their gentle ministrations, I lay awake a long time, turning dark visions over and over in my head.

Chapter Twenty-Eight

I thought surely I would get no sleep that night — my thoughts raced among worry for Rosie and William back home and Randall wherever he might be, haunting visions of murder by moonlight, and the sorry account of my uncle's past. But the drive and the rain and the worry did me in at last, and I slept far sounder than I ought.

I awoke to a watery sunlight filtered between the drapes of my unfamiliar bedchamber. I peeled myself out of bed and bent all over to work the stiffness out of my joints, then padded to the window. My room overlooked the street below, and I watched dogs and children dart among the legs of waiting horses. Goodness, what time must it be? I rang the bell while I dressed, and asked the maid to wake my uncle and have a groom ready the trap.

She looked back at me, a little frown between her eyebrows.

"Is something wrong?" I said.

"Mistress came in with the bewigged gentleman, yes?" she said. "A new black trap and two black horses?"

"Yes, yes. What's the matter?"

"But, mistress —" She shook her head. "He left hours ago, said you weren't to be disturbed —"

"What?"

"Your uncle's gone, ma'am."

My legs went out from under me, and I sank into the little chintz armchair. "With the carriage? And the horses?"

The girl nodded. "Are you all right, ma'am? I could send for someone —"

I must pull myself together. The trap was gone, Uncle Wheeler was gone, Jack Spinner would be back at midnight, and I was twenty miles from my home and my child. I held tight to the arms of the chair so not to think too keenly of that. Where had Uncle Wheeler gone? Perhaps his confession had been merely the last act in his long performance, and, seizing opportunity and carriage both, Ellison Wheeler had fled to a new life, a new incarnation. I might never see him again. That thought gave neither sorrow nor relief. I had to get home. I forced myself to my feet.

"Yes, of course I'm all right," I lied. "Are they still serving breakfast?" Whatever else needed doing, I wasn't doing any of it on an empty stomach. I felt thin and hollow, like a strong breeze might blow me right over. And there was no having that, not today.

After a fortifying breakfast and an entire pot of hideous black coffee, I marched myself to the innkeeper and made inquiry about finding my way back home.

I was in luck — believe it — the stage comes through the Gold Valley once a week, and by some odd convergence of the stars in my favor, it was due that afternoon. There was no question of hiring a private cab; last night's rain had left the road a river of muck stretching in both directions, and no sensible driver would attempt it. And though everything told me to point toward Shearing and *go* — run, fly, just get home however I could — a foot journey of near twenty miles is not undertaken lightly, and stranding myself even five miles down the road would not get me passage on the stage. I had to wait a good four or five hours I could not afford to spare, but the cost was minimal, and it would have me home by evening. Just in time — should we not break an axle or be beset by highwaymen — to make my meeting with Jack Spinner.

Since the landlord clearly did not want me loitering about his common room while I waited all day for the stage to arrive, I collected Pilot from the stables and set off walking into town. For a Sunday morning, it was surprisingly lively. Much larger than Shearing, Haymarket made her living from the farmers in the widening valley to the south and supported a booming mercantile economy. It gave me a pang to walk through those paved streets and know that if one of the shops I saw — the cartwright's, the brewery, the tannery — failed, the whole town would not crumble behind it.

It seemed as though the Wheelers had all but built this town. In addition to the splendid brick storefront of Wheeler & Sons, Ltd, Wheelwrights & Carriage-Maker, Haymarket boasted a Wheeler Square, Wheeler Street, some business proclaiming itself Wheeler & Roper, and a public house called Wheeler's. Even the imposing city market hall bore the Wheeler name. Signs were evident, too, of the Lowman family — in the shabby little hostelry, in a sign for a dressmaker in a dingy upstairs window, in an abandoned butcher shop. No wonder young Enoch had longed for grander things.

In a noisy little square surrounding a dry fountain, I stopped and bought lunch from a cart. As I was counting out coins for the pasty, I saw that the awning was bedecked with strings of small figures twisted from straw. I looked down at Pilot, who bore a wise expression that seemed to answer all my questions. I brushed my fingers against her ears.

"How much for the corn dollies?" I asked, peering into my reticule.

"For you, miss? I'll throw one in for a penny."

I went to choose one, but the old woman stopped my hand as I reached for a little figure.

"That's not for you," she said. "Here." She pulled down a dolly from the back of the cart and pressed it into my hand. It was a small figure and somewhat misshapen, almost impish, with a little hat crudely shaped from the straw. I frowned at it.

"Are you sure?"

The old woman nodded, tucking her hands inside her cloak. "I think that's the one you want."

Pilot let out one short sharp bark and gave the old woman her most engaging smile. She may just have been impatient for her share of the pasty, but it's hard to say.

The old woman nodded comfortably. "You mind her, missie," she said. "*She* knows."

By the time the stage was due, I was convinced that it had become enmired or overturned, but it finally lumbered into the coachyard. The only passengers disembarked at the Red Drake, and the coachman generously allowed me to bring Pilot aboard.

"How long will it take to get to Shearing?" I asked as the coachman helped me aboard.

"In this muck?" He shook his head. "It's hard to say. But I haven't lost a wheel yet, and Heavy and Pull are two of the best horses for this kind of weather. Don't you fret — I'll have you home for your supper." And then, with a jolt and a groan and an alarming mechanical creaking, we were off at last.

Well past my promised supper-hour arrival and deep under cover of starlight, the coach heaved and slid its way into Shearing. Although the journey itself had been relatively uneventful — we only got stuck once, and the coachman and the horses had us unstuck in minutes — I had been frantic the last few miles. I was half out of my seat and ready to dive out the narrow coach door the moment we crossed the Stowe bridge and passed the smithy.

The stage normally stops at the Drover's Arms, but the coachman kindly let me off at Stirwaters. Pilot leaped out the moment he opened the door, disappearing after some skittering shadow, and I was scarcely far behind. I had a moment of indecision when I alit from the coach — home or mill? *Home or mill?* William and Rosie were at home, but Spinner would surely be at the mill by now. Oh, mercy, what was the hour? I fumbled through my cloak for my earth-encrusted watch, but my numb fingers could not seem to find it.

I was saved the choosing, for the Millhouse door flew open with a clatter and Rosie burst out, sliding as her feet hit the wet shale. She righted herself and threw herself at me headlong.

"He has William!" she gasped, and I saw with horror that my sister had been crying. I grabbed her roughly by the shoulders.

"What? Who has William?" Oh, Lord — was I too late?

Rosie couldn't catch her breath. "Uncle Wheeler!" she finally managed, and I was so relieved I didn't understand her.

"He came back here? Where are the horses?"

Rosie stared at me. "Mr. Carter took them," she said. "Charlotte — I didn't know — it just happened before I could do anything. When he came back here, in your carriage — by God, Charlotte, I thought he'd killed you!"

"Rosie, slow down. What happened?"

She took a ragged breath, holding fast to my arms. "Uncle Wheeler came back this afternoon — we didn't know when to expect you, and I had just put William down. He burst into the house like a madman, and when he ran upstairs — I didn't know what he was doing! I was helping Harte, so I couldn't follow straightaway. I swear, Charlotte — I was expecting you to come at any moment! And then you *didn't* — so I went to check on William — and they were both gone."

"Where was Rachel? Biddy Tom?"

"Josie Lawson's baby came due, and her mam couldn't manage by herself, and I sent Rachel to the Grange to fetch more nappies for William. She never came back."

I looked across the yard to the grey shadow that was Stirwaters. A faint flickering light burned in the spinning room — not lamplight or the horrible red blaze of fire, but a cold, shadowy glow like moonlight.

"They're in the mill," I said quietly. It seemed so obvious now, I could barely believe I hadn't known it as soon as I heard Uncle Wheeler had abandoned me. Now that Spinner had caught him up at last, Uncle Wheeler thought to make a better bargain with him.

"I know they're in the mill!" Rosie cried. "But I can't get in! Don't you think I've tried? I've *been* trying, all bloody day!"

She was sobbing now, a wild, robust sob of red runny nose and shrill hysterical breathing.

"What do you mean, you can't get in?"

She shook her head. "I just can't, that's all. The doors aren't locked, but they won't budge, nor the windows. I even tried breaking a couple, but rocks just bounce off. I can't explain it —"

"No," I said, my thoughts far away from my voice. I was watching the shifting moonlight pouring from the spinning room windows. "I'll get in. I'm the Miller he wants."

Altogether too calmly, I took my sister by the elbow and steered her back into the Millhouse, relating all — well, most — of what I had learned on my journey.

A voice carried in from the parlor. "Rosie, is that you?" Rosie popped her head around the door.

"George Harte, you put yourself back into that chair this bloody instant! And I mean it this time! Charlotte's back."

"Thank God." With a scrape and shuffle, Harte's curly head appeared in the doorway. He was leaning heavily on a crutch, his face red with effort. "Charlotte — we were worried. What happened to you?"

"I lost my way a little," I said, "but I've made it now. Let's go get William back. You — sit back down. You're not fit to be moving about yet."

Harte gave a grunt that may well have been pain. "Forget it," he said. "I'm coming with you."

"The devil you are," Rosie said.

"Harte," I said, "William's half lost already, and Randall . . . I cannot risk you, too. I want at least one of the men I care about safe at home. Do you hear me?" And there, at last: I was shaking.

Harte reached out to put his hand on my shoulder. "Don't," I said. "I won't make it if you do that." I turned away from Harte before I could see the look in his eyes.

What I beheld instead was almost as disturbing — and as fortifying. Our home looked like Biddy Tom's cottage, bedecked for some harvest festival that only we would observe. Apples and broom arched over the doorways, colored glass balls hung in every window. Great symbols were sketched on the glass and the chimneys, marks drawn out in chalk or soot on the floor before any threshold leading outdoors. An odd, herby effusion burned over the kitchen fire, casting the room in a heady smoke.

Rosie was watching me. "I'm not taking any chances," she said.

I stared at the salt sprinkled on the windowsills, for once not thinking how dear it was. I'd pour out a dozen salt cellars if we made it through this night.

And there was the crux of it all. I probably would make it through the night, alive and intact, and Rosie, too — but what of William? What of Stirwaters? Could I save either of them? Could I save them both? And if I couldn't —? My breath struggled up through my breast. It didn't bear thinking of. I must save them. I *must*.

Suddenly, we heard the front door fling open with a bang. Rosie jumped, and I thought she might come clear out of her skin.

"Charlotte! Rosie! What are you girls playing at?"

I whirled at the sound of the voice, to see Randall framed in the doorway, moonlight silvering his hair and shoulders. All the strength went out of my knees, and I sank against the kitchen table. He strode into the house and threw his hat onto an armchair, slamming the door behind him. "What is this? Charlotte, you look a mess. Where's William?"

"One question at a time, please, brother," Rosie said.

"No," Randall said. His face was hard and lined, the same look he'd worn when I saw him last. "I want all the answers at once. What is this you're doing — you've got wards on every door in the house — I couldn't even get *near* the kitchen! Straw dollies and salt and — is that henbane? Gods, Charlotte, what have you two been messing with?"

And then, before I could answer, he had taken three long strides from the doorway and caught me up in his arms, squeezing me so tightly I couldn't breathe. "What's going on?" he said into my neck. "The Grange is ice cold, and it looks like you haven't been there in days. How's William?" He pulled back and looked likely to bend down to kiss me.

"William's been taken." I blurted it out, just like that. I don't think I could have managed it any other way. In the space of a heartbeat his face went ashen, and he sank to the floor, somehow finding a chair on his way down.

"Taken? You mean *kidnapped*? How — when?" He could barely shape the words, and his hand reached out, not finding me. I grabbed it and held it close to my beating heart, as if I had any right to do so.

"Looks like the girls' uncle took the lad," Harte broke in gently. "We're not sure why, but there may be some bad debts involved."

Randall stared from one of us to the other. I put his hand to my lips and shook my head at Harte.

"No," I said. "That's not the truth." The time for secrets was long past. I took a deep breath. "Randall, I've made some very poor decisions, and I've put our son's life in danger." He went stiff under my touch, but I forged on. "And I will tell you *everything*, just as soon as I can. But for now, I have to go."

I forced myself to meet his eyes, as I said those words to him, yet again. His gaze was hard and cold and colored of steel. Very well, I could take my strength from that. I squeezed Randall's fingers far too tightly and then dropped his hand. I withdrew the glass jar from my rain-spattered cloak and shook it in the lamplight.

Randall rose and caught my hand, stilling the jar in mid-air. "What is that?"

"It's earth," I replied as calmly as I could. "I must take it to Stirwaters immediately if I'm to ransom William."

"Earth? What kind of earth — Charlotte, are you working *magic?*"

I was unprepared for the vehemence in his voice — the surprise, yes, but not the other thing . . . what was it? His grip on my wrist was like a vise. "Let me go," I said, twisting in his grasp. His hand loosened but did not free me.

"No. You tell me what this is."

"Please," I said. "You must trust me."

His shoulders slumped, and I thought he might fall. I pulled him closer to me. "Charlotte, of *course* I trust you. Always. But trust *me*. Is this about that curse?"

I nearly dropped the jar, but Randall saved it. "Charlotte. Did you really think I could live for any time in this village without hearing the rumors? Especially since William was born. You can't take such talk seriously. Whatever danger William is in, I'm sure there's nothing unnatural about it."

I shook my head. "No," I said. "It's very real." And then I spent precious time accounting for the dark deeds of Millers past. It seemed fitting, truly, for if I failed tonight, I should be no better than any of them: The Miller who sold her child to save the mill.

"Ah," he said finally. "Sad business. So many years — that's a long time for a curse to stand. He must have been quite powerful. Or very angry. If you mean to try and break it, you'll need something that witnessed the laying down of the curse — this earth, I suppose? And an image of the man himself wouldn't go amiss." He reached a hand toward me and brushed his fingertips against the dolly still pinned to my collar.

We were all staring at him. Incongruously, Randall laughed, but the laughter died on his lips. "Well, I wasn't born under a brick, was I? My grandmother taught me a useful thing or two. I'm no cunning man, but I can cast a circle of protection as well as the next fellow. The one I laid down at our wedding has held up pretty well."

I backed away. "You cast a spell on me?"

He followed, drawing me back in. "Shh. No. I put my arms around you, *like this*, and promised to protect you. I swore no harm would come to you. I've seen you do it, too — to everyone you love. You have amazing strength, you know, when you put your mind to it."

"No," I said. "No, no, no. . . ." But as I whispered that one word, I knew he spoke the truth. I had felt it, all these months. That sense of peace, that overwhelming security — the strong wall that pushed all my troubles back a few paces. It was real. And it was at work on me, now. I held his arms tightly and let myself draw in just a bit of that Randall calm.

"I did William, too — we both did," he was saying. "But sometimes when you have forces working against you even before you're born . . ." He shook his head. "You seemed so worried about it all; that's why I hung the charms in his room. But when you reacted the way you did . . . I know I should have told you earlier, but I didn't think you'd want to hear it. I've been trying to tell you, Charlotte — I'm pretty handy to have around."

It was too much. "You are my *husband*, and a banker from Harrowgate. You can't be a — a —" Not thinking of the word I wanted, I gave up.

Randall held me tighter. "I am the man you married," he said. "I'm William's father. I'm not anything else. But I can help, if you let me."

I still had hold of his arms, and was afraid I might fall if I let go. I closed my eyes, and felt Randall lay his chin atop my head. The warmth from the hollow of his neck was almost enough to chase away the chill of the night and the day and the night before. All the chills, forever.

"I'd move quick if I were you, Miss Charlotte," Harte said. "It's after eleven."

I drew in a shaky breath. "We must go," I said, pulling away from Randall at last. The four of us stepped out into the yard together.

Straight into a crowd. Well, not so much a crowd, exactly, but a smallish gathering of Shearing folk and millfolk, standing shoulder-to-shoulder in an arc around the millhouse. They looked like a makeshift chorus.

"Mrs. Lamb? *Rachel?* What is this?"

Biddy Tom stepped out from where she'd stood among them. "We heard there was a bit o' trouble up at the mill, lass."

I shook my head. "How?"

A sharp bark answered me. "That dog o' yourn," came Mr. Mordant's voice from out of the group. "Right strange creature, that-a-one."

"Ah, she's a good pup," said Nathan Smith, his hand on Pilot's head.

Janet Lamb came up to me and put her arm round my shoulders. "Woke up the last lot of us, she did," she said. "My Dan'll have words to say about it on the morning, that's sure. But for now, I think we're needed here."

"Aye, what are the Friendlies for, then?"

"I don't understand," I said, and then I saw that pinned to every collar and cloak was a small badge, monogrammed in blue: the letters *FS*, twining together. The Friendly Society. Of course.

"It's about time someone took on to break that old curse," said Jon Graves, the undertaker.

"Ah, and we knew you'd be just the one to do it, too," Mrs. Lamb added.

"But it concerns us all, too, then, don't it?" And that, believe it, was Lonnie Clayborn.

"An' we just thought you could use what help you could get."

I shook my head. "I must do this alone. I can't ask you to involve yourselves. This is a Miller matter — Miller and Stirwaters."

"Aye, and ain't we Stirwaters, then? That's what we've been trying to tell you, Ma'am."

"Charlotte." That was Randall, come up behind me. His strong hand was on my shoulder.

"Good, ye made it, lad. Stand between me and Dag, there," said Mrs. Tom, maneuvering my husband into the

367

circle beside the dyer. Pilot skirted the group, eyeing them with satisfaction.

I stared at them a long moment, all the circle of my acquaintance — my friends and neighbors and workers — my husband! — come forth to protect and defend me and mine. I wanted to say something, thank them for standing by me all the while, but the words wouldn't come. As I looked helplessly at them all, Biddy Tom gave me one curt nod.

"Off ye go, then, Charlotte Miller. Put that curse to rest with the past."

And I went.

Chapter Twenty-Nine

Clutching my jar, I stood outside the yard doors to Stirwaters. I put key to lock before noticing that the latch was undone already. Uncle Wheeler must have broken in.

The door wouldn't open. Rosie was right — unlocked and shut tight. I gave it an almighty tug, but it was stuck fast.

"Help her!" I think that was Randall's voice. The crowd pressed closer.

I turned to them. "No," I said. "Please, you all must stand back. I think — *ahem*, I think it's a little frightened." When I turned back to the door, I slipped the jar into my bag and put both hands on the door latch.

"This is Charlotte Miller Woodstone," I said. "Let me enter."

Nothing happened. I gave a little cough, self-conscious, and tried again. I had to repeat my name three times; finally, the whole mill shook with a gasp and a shudder like a hard wind blowing through, and the door creaked open.

"Wait here," I told my Friendly Society. "Do — whatever you were going to do." I sought the crowd, for Rosie, for Harte and Randall, and seeing strength reflected in all those blue eyes, I stepped over my threshold.

A second hard shudder nearly knocked me to the floor. I had to grab a corner post to keep from falling, and a handful of items crashed off tables. An awl rolled past my feet.

"Charlotte *Miller*," I said again, pulling myself back to standing as a third jolt shook through.

I crept across the finishing room, past the machine shop and the stacked-up dyevats, toward the stair at the back. As I passed the fulling stocks I heard the squeal of a tight lever being shoved into place. I jumped just as the great fulling hammers banged down into the dry stocks, the collision like thunder through my bones. My heart still hammering in echo, I edged past, wishing I'd thought to bring a light.

The strange wavering glow we had seen from the windows did not reach the lower floors, and I picked my way through the mill in almost total darkness. My hands out to guide me, I still managed to trip over something and crash hiplong into the hard corner of a table. Bruised and cursing, I found the opening to the stairwell at last.

Just as the never-used door to the stairs slammed shut in my face. I jumped back in time to spare my fingers. I forced myself to breathe easily and laid my hand very gently on the knob.

"Charlotte Miller," I said reasonably, and felt the knob turn under my hand.

The stairs are always dim, so the lack of light was no impediment there, and the spinning room's windows gave depth and texture to the shadows. I could see the great hulking bodies of the machines, could make out the spindles and frames and the long tracks they rode along. I looked away. How could we say "jackspinner" casually in Stirwaters after this?

As if driven by some mad brutal wind, all the bobbins came flying off the near jack, hailing down on me. One struck the side of my head and I cried out.

"Charlotte Miller," I whimpered, crouching in the lee of the jack, my arms up over my face. The bobbins clattered to the floor and rolled around crazily, trailing thread everywhere. I rose again and kicked them out of my path. The last stairs seemed impossibly far away.

But I reached the attic soon enough. My stomach gave a cold lurch as I stepped up into the grey glow of the room, and I couldn't move any farther.

William lay not ten feet from where I stood. In his basket, on a heap of snow-white carded wool, he cooed and twitched and kicked his bare feet against the wicker. His eyes — those enormous changing-color eyes he gets from Randall — were wide with delight, and his chubby hands waved in the air above his face, reaching for — I took a deep breath. Reaching for a gleaming spindle, dangled above his face. Jack Spinner knelt beside him, his clever hands bouncing and bobbing the spindle by a length of red thread.

I stood in the doorway, icy cold all through and shaking. I did not know what to make of the expression on Spinner's face. I had expected bitterness, or triumph, but this — this *gentleness* stopped me dead in my tracks, and seemed the most horrifying thing of all. Suddenly, realization hit me so hard I had to grab the doorframe for support. I understood at last why our curse had taken the form it did. Why generations of Millers had lost their sons to Stirwaters. *The young one, the angry one . . . drown'd in Pit.* The evidence was all around me. Something dark and terrible had happened here, all those years ago: Jack Spinner had lost his son.

I took a shaky breath. One hundred years ago, perhaps, this same scene had played out many times. Somewhere on this property — a sunlit room in a tidy farmhouse, or a dew-swept meadow beside the river — John Simple had played with his infant son. I had known Jack Spinner but a little — had seen his cleverness and cunning and his *power*, but this was a different man: younger, tender, as if the cold unnatural light had burned away the years to show the father who had lost so much.

A flicker in the light showed up the older Simple, then, and I thought my heart might split apart with a sudden desperate longing. I could almost see — and, oh! How I wanted to — my own father in his place, there with his grandchild. What would I have paid to have that, even for the merest breath of a moment? I could have wept for all of us.

And then I saw where the light was coming from.

In the far corner, back under the cobwebbed rafters, the old loom my father had tinkered with still stood. And there, as if held to the bench by unseen straps, was my uncle. His slim hands worked the loom — but madly, threads twining round his fingers, his feet beating at the treadles with a wild unnatural rhythm. Slumped like a broken marionette left to dangle in the wind, he wove frantically as the threads in his glittering topcoat unwound themselves and reworked into the crazy tapestry before him. He was bound up in a web of gold and silver, his bare head bobbing and jerking like something — like someone hanged. The flickering light surrounded him, shone through him. A will-o'-the-wisp.

"Let him go." I barely recognized my own low voice.

Spinner looked up and calmly twisted the red thread onto the spindle. William watched with wide solemn eyes.

"Ah, Miss Miller. Have you made your choice, then? You see your son is unharmed. I will take those keys you carry now, if you don't mind."

"Let him go," I repeated, gesturing toward Uncle Wheeler. "He has no part in this."

Spinner rose. "No part? No part? Nay, Mistress — he has the *finer* part in this!" With a wave of his hand, the greying light burst into brilliance and, as if with a sudden rush of water over the millwheel, Uncle Wheeler's weaving took on a frenzied pace. The shuttle banged back and forth across the shed as his arms stretched and scrabbled over the workings.

"He didn't pay you," I whispered, understanding. "For getting him out of prison."

Spinner smiled, all tenderness gone. "Surprised? You shouldn't be. Enoch Lowman has spent his life skirting his debts, as I'm sure you know well enough. But you see, he finally did come through, with a deposit of sorts."

I closed my eyes before I could see him point to my son.

"What was the fee?" I barely heard myself speak the words, but perhaps he could read even my thoughts.

"The fee? Oh, the *littlest* thing; he never would have missed it." Spinner laughed, and tonight it was the sound of a cold wind through dead trees. "Just his name."

Impossible bargains. Unimaginable costs. No wonder Uncle Wheeler had run away, before Spinner could strip him of the very identity he'd worked so hard to possess. I'd seen it last night; he never would have — never *could* have — gone back to life as Enoch Lowman, stable boy.

"What have you done to him?"

"Done? Why, nothing! Merely supposed it was time our dear Ellison Wheeler, Esquire, learned a trade of his own. This seemed fitting, don't you agree, as he has such a fondness for clothes. They make the man, or so I've heard."

Oh, indeed, all the tenderness was gone. Turned to madness and — who knows how else such pain may twist itself, so many years beyond the grave? Before I could utter a single word, Jack Spinner swept down with a too-quick motion and scooped William up in his arms.

William crowed with delight. I positively stopped breathing altogether.

"Don't hurt him," I prayed, and it seems I said those words aloud.

Spinner's smile twisted in his lined face. "I'm not the one who harms defenseless children. *Millers* do that," he said, clutching William to his chest. Wildly, I thought of poor baby Thomas, dead at seven days. Oh, mercy. What had we done to this man? We were all bound together, by loss and grief and vengeance. It was time to end this. But if Spinner had no tenderness, I must find some of my own to spare.

"What happened to your son?" Very quietly, almost a breath.

"My boy," Spinner — *Simple* — murmured to William. "My Robin."

I took a tiny step closer. "What happened to Robin?"

He gave a sigh and stroked William's downy temple with a cracked and grimy finger. A working man's hand; I had thought it before, but his memory of his own hands was stronger now. As he was.

"It were a dirty spring, we called it then," he began. I watched William carefully. We say that, too. "One freeze after another, melting into mud and muck under the sun. 'Twouldn't rain, and won't dry out neither. But Old Man Harlan, he would have his mill. Dug that pit too deep and too close to the river. Oh, he were warned, weren't he? But that one paid no mind to anyone. My Robin were just a lad then — no bigger'n your rosy sister. Fourteen . . ." The word slipped out in a sigh. Spinner jostled William to bring up that jolly toothless grin, and began again. "He would work the mill site. Said 'twere our land and our duty to see it used proper. Wanted so to be a man, my Robin. I were proud of him, and proud he were, too, to be workin' a man's job day and day over.

"He thought to do a mason's work, a real builder. Trained alongside men who worked but for money — never for love. Followed Old Miller's say-so to the letter, and my Robin didn't know no better. When they bricked in the pit it were too cold, too wet. It never set up right. A hard rain at last, and those men kep' right on working."

"The wall collapsed." I hadn't meant to say anything, but I could see it all so clearly as he spoke. The pit *was* too close to the river; it had plagued Stirwaters forever with cracks and seepage. Poor workmanship and unlucky weather — it had surely been a disaster in the asking.

Spinner nodded. "The wall collapsed, with my Robin at the bottom. Buried under a half ton of mud and sludge and brick, he were. Not even a proper burial, and no one to mourn him but me. My boy, my only child . . ."

"I'm so sorry," I said. It was a mistake.

"Save your apologies!" he cried. "Keep your sympathy! We don't need them. I have what I need!" He spasmed with laughter as William reached a wavering hand toward his twisted face. "You'll pay, too," Spinner said. "As all Millers have paid."

"Please," I whispered.

"Please?" He echoed. "Did your Harlan yield when I begged him *please*? Please return my son's body to me? Please clear off my land and let us be? Please let me see the magistrate? Please don't string me up to yonder *tree*?"

His words rang out like claps of thunder — sparked through with lightning as my uncle thrashed against his bonds. The loom banged and shuddered like a mad thing, deafening. Suddenly, another great gasp heaved through the mill, spilling me to the floor. Spinner stumbled and William nearly fell from his arms.

"*Charlotte Miller!*" I screamed it to the rafters. "Stop it!" I smacked my hands hard against the floorboards. As I struggled to my feet, my skirts bunched up round my ankles, I saw the floor at Spinner's feet peel apart like a raw wound. The boards cracked and splintered, a nail prized free. *Oh, please, Lord — don't drop him.*

Righted now, Spinner clutched William still tighter. "Make your choice!" he shrilled.

"Let my uncle go!" I yelled back.

"No! He is not part of our bargain!"

"You made him part! And he did, himself, by bringing William here. A third party. The terms have changed. I'll not leave without him." I gripped my poor abused apron with trembling hands and stood firm.

Spinner stared at me, his shadowed eyes wild. "What care you?" he cried. "He's betrayed you every step of the way. He cares nothing for you!"

I nodded and dared a step closer. "He has," I agreed. "But he is my uncle, and . . . and family is precious. Life is precious. I think you know that better than anyone."

He stepped back from me, his tattered sleeve curved round William's white nightie. He looked so small, then — not William, who is a positively *huge* baby — Spinner. I have said before, he was little above my own height; now, whether from remembered years or grief or defeat, he diminished before me. The colors in his motley clothing faded, the texture of that tweedy topcoat blurred. The flickering light and mad clatter from the loom overwhelmed him; I lost him for a moment in the shadows.

"Sir —" I stepped toward him, uncertain. He reappeared, the crack in the floor a hair's-breadth from his feet. He had changed in that brief instant. The scarecrow's clothing had vanished, replaced by simpler garb — brownish trousers, tucked into stockings, a linen shirt and bracers. Bareheaded now, his ruddy hair damp with sweat and streaked with grey, he seemed a different man.

He held William gently, like his own child. "What are you proposing?" The reedy grate of his voice had changed — deepened into weariness and age, I think. My heart stoppering up my throat, I stepped right up to the near side of the gap in the floor and fished the jar of earth from my bag.

"I have seen the cross-way," I said, holding up the jar. "I know your name. I can arrange for your . . . remains to receive a Christian burial, in a churchyard in this village.

With a proper headstone — for you and your son. Everyone will know the wrong that was done to you. In return, you will free my uncle, return my son to me, and vow never to trouble Stirwaters or my family again."

Spinner faltered. The arm holding William trembled, and he reached out for the jar with his other hand. I held it just out of his grasp.

"Let me have it." His voice was a scarce whisper. I might have imagined it under the din from the clattering loom. I steeled myself not to look at Uncle Wheeler.

"Make your choice," I said.

All at once, his eyes narrowed and the grey glow flared up. "Take the mill and your uncle. I keep the boy."

"What? No!" I could feel the floor giving way beneath me. "Don't —"

"I like him," he said. I couldn't look at them. "He's a fine boy, like his da'. You go, lass — make some other bairns with that pretty city gentleman of yourn."

I had failed. After everything. I felt ill, a wave of something washed over me, and for a moment I forgot myself. The thumping of the belts, the rattle of the window glass, the endless racket of the loom . . . I felt it all, deep in my bones as if I were part of the mill itself. But beyond the din of the millrooms, I heard a steady, calm cadence of soft voices coming out of the night. I could not make out what they said, but my mind formed their chanting into words: *Great courage breaks ill luck.*

They had not come, all those Shearing folk, to stand in the cold November air and see me fail. This was no moment for my resolve to crumble.

With fumbling fingers I unpinned the corn dolly from my collar and pulled the cork from the neck of my jar. Spinner's head turned toward me, his eyes narrowing. I stepped over the crack in the floor.

"John Simple!" I said, loud over the voice of the mill. "You will leave this place. Give me my son."

"Never!" He squeezed William to his chest and William began to whimper. "See what you've done?" Spinner cried, bouncing my baby with a nervousness I had not seen before. "Shh, little one," he crooned. "Your da's here." William's whimper became a wail.

"Give me my son." I dropped the corn dolly on the floor and poured a little of the earth atop it. Spinner started, grabbing for the bottle. William screamed.

"Stop! Stop it!" Spinner patted William on the back, clutching him against his shoulder. *He won't hurt him*, I told myself, willing myself to believe it.

"Give him to me," I said, very gently, holding out my arms.

"No! He needs me!"

I shook my head. "He needs his mother." I spilled a few more grains of dirt. Spinner moaned.

"What will happen if I pour all this out?" I said. "Will you vanish? What would become of William then? He cannot go where you must go."

"He needs me." Two great tears rolled down his lined cheeks.

"Robin needs you. You can go to him."

A shudder rumbled the mill beneath our feet — the gentlest of sighs, barely more than a breath through the old stone and wood. I stared down at the cracked boards beneath my feet with a sudden, belated understanding. My heart pounded. "Robin needs you," I repeated. "He's been alone all these years."

"Robin?"

The mill sighed, creaking in the corners, whispering through the gears.

Spinner listened, hope lighting his face. "My Robin?"

"Go to him," I said. I poured out a thin stream of earth, straight into the gap in the floor.

Suddenly, Spinner thrust William into my arms, nearly knocking me over, twisting the jar from my hand. He fell to his knees and turned over the jar.

"Wait!" I lunged for him, grabbed him by the wrist, staying the flow of earth into the gap. His arm was so thin — like a child's. "You will never return. We are free of your curse. Those are the terms."

Spinner met my frantic gaze with eyes as clear and sane as anyone's. He nodded. "Those are the terms."

"And my uncle?"

"He'd not do the same for you."

I shook my head. "You do not know that."

Spinner shook his own head, but waved a hand toward the loom. All at once the light disappeared, and I heard a sickening thump as Uncle Wheeler slumped forward against the loom.

I reached out my hand, open, to take his own. After a moment, Spinner grabbed it, shaking firmly. But he was fading, and I could barely feel the rough, cold flesh in my grip.

"John Simple," I said, "I will hold you to your word."

"Charlotte Woodstone," he replied, "you have my bond." He reached out one last time and brushed William's fair head with his clever, clever hand. "He's a fine boy," he said.

And dashed the jar to the floor, scattering the earth from his unhallowed grave all across Stirwaters's floor. I jumped back, shielding William with my arms, but it was not necessary. Spinner — evaporated. Like a mist in the sunlight, like sand through a glass, he spun into air and slipped like a shadow down through the floorboards, and was gone.

The mill gave one last great sigh, and the crack in the floor sealed itself tight once more. I sank to the floor, cradling William in my lap, sobbing. William reached up toward my face, and I let him grab as big a handful of my hair as he wanted.

Chapter Thirty

W^e sat there a long moment — not nearly as long as I'd have liked. It took all my strength and a considerable quantity of my will to pry myself to standing and lay William in his basket. The red spindle was on the floor beside him, and after only a moment's hesitation, I passed it into his baby grip.

Uncle Wheeler was silent, sagged against the loom. I could make out only his shape among the varied shadows in the corner.

"Mercy, but it's dark in here," I said — and the moon came out. I almost smiled, but I didn't have it in me then. I went to the windows and looked down. I could make out every single face in the little company below — Rosie and a strained Randall looking anxiously up at the mill; Rachel and Harte; Biddy Tom, grey head bent in concentration, hands busy with something I could not see. I had little time — they would not wait much longer for me.

"Open the window, please," I said, and the long-stuck frame fell out of the casement on top of me. I caught it and eased it to the floor. There was a soft creak, a small embarrassed rustle that was more than the November wind rushing through.

"It's all right," I said softly. "No harm done." I stuck my head out into the chill air. "Randall, I need you! Come here, please." He gave me a quick nod and disappeared into the mill.

"You need anyone else up there, Miss Charlotte?" Lonnie Clayborn waved cheerily.

"No, just Randall for now, but there's a bit of a mess here we'll need to take care of tomorrow," I said. "Rosie, take Harte home. He looks ready to fall over." She'd probably be furious — but I didn't want her up here. Not yet. "Rachel, go to the house and build a fire in the master bedroom. Mrs. Lamb, Mr. Smith, can you see to it that everyone gets home? Mrs. Tom, could you join Rosie and Harte at home, please? The rest of you —" I paused and *forced* myself to smile. I felt my jaw would crack because of it. "Thank you all for your help. I shall never forget it."

The Friendlies separated, satisfied that they'd done their part. I never should be able to thank them all properly, but saving Stirwaters would go a long way in the right direction.

I had put it off long enough. I went to my uncle. He was breathing — merely unconscious — but an angry red bruise had flared up on his temple, where he must have struck the loom. He looked naked now, small and vulnerable without his wig; the tapestry jacket and waistcoat were nothing more than ravelling fringe held together by a band of cloth at his shoulders. The fine linen underneath was streaked with sweat. I put out a hand toward his cheek — pulled it back again. Had he always been so small?

All at once, I whipped off my own cloak and wrapped it round his frail shoulders. He was tangled in the glittering threads, and I fumbled for the scissors I *knew* had to be somewhere at hand, and cut them away. I took him in my arms as gently as I could, and could have wept when his head rolled back against my chest. His feet would not obey me, and he was heavier than he'd appeared — and I had reached the limits of my own endurance for one night.

Finally, I got him laid out on the millroom floor near to William. I knelt between them. Uncle Wheeler's pale face looked waxen in the moonlight, and I was surprised — no, I was *shocked* by how young he was. It seemed impossible that this was the man I'd known. I wanted to hold his hand, and couldn't bring myself to.

With a truly incredible thumping of feet and banging of doors, Randall sprang into the room. Ah — a lantern. Have I mentioned he is clever and practical?

Before I could make a sound, Randall was on the floor beside me, bundling me up in those strong arms, and holding me in a grip so tight it crushed every bone in my body. I've never felt anything quite so wonderful. Then we were both speaking, frantically, wildly, at once — and one of us was weeping; I don't know who.

"It's all right — it's over now."

"He's gone — William's safe."

"Shh — don't worry. I'm here now."

I pulled back and looked into his tear-streaked face. His eyes were grey now, like the ragged sky outside. "I love you," I said, not meaning for it to sound quite so desperate.

He smiled and brushed the damp hair from my forehead. "I know."

For all that, it was a brief reunion. William had settled down to the serious business of sucking on his fists, and after a moment of admiring the perfection of his tiny wet fingers, we turned to my uncle.

"Is he —" Randall leaned over his body, his cheek close to Uncle Wheeler's mouth. "No — just out cold."

"He's freezing — we must get him back to the house. Can he wear your coat?"

At once Randall was stripping down to his jacket. "But I haven't brought a hat. Do you think anyone will recognize him?"

His compassion still surprises me. He saw clearly that some things are too private — too painful — to be borne in public. I shook my head. "Not — not like this. Can you carry him? He's heavier than he looks."

Randall nodded. "Looks like the first strong wind will blow him right away. What's happened to him? No — there'll be plenty of time to tell me, soon enough."

I did, too, hours later. Randall got Uncle Wheeler propped upright against him, and we half carried, half dragged him back to the Millhouse. Our scene of welcome was — well, a bit awkward, really. Rosie'd have liked to have left Uncle Wheeler out on the street ("for the crows to find," I believe was her precise wording), and I was too weary to fight with her. Harte took a convenient moment to crack his plaster painfully against a doorjamb, and distracted her. Since he couldn't manage the stairs, Rosie stayed down in the parlor with him. I can never repay that George Harte for all I owe him. It bears repeating.

Rachel determined that the lot of us must be starving, and took it upon herself to whip together a hearty early breakfast. I was far too tired to eat, but William wasn't, so we withdrew to my uncle's room for a quiet vigil. Randall came with us, and we sat there in silence a long, long moment.

"Biddy Tom says there isn't anything wrong that rest won't mend," Randall said at last. I nodded, not so sure. My uncle had suffered injuries in the last twenty-four hours that would surely take more than rest to heal. He slept fitfully now, twisting the bedcovers in his torn fingers.

"He really does look so much like you," Randall said. I had seen it, too — up in the mill in the shadow of the moon.

I told Randall everything, then. I wished to spare Uncle Wheeler something, so I sketched out his sad dark tale as briefly as I could, but left out nothing important. This family had been burdened by secrets for far too long.

Randall made no comment, passed no judgement; just sat and listened, nodding and holding my hand. He asked intelligent questions, some of which I had no answers for, others whose answers I shared in full, however reluctantly. I shouldn't have been surprised if, now he knew everything, he turned right around and walked away again. But he is Randall, and of course he didn't. Great courage, indeed. It had to do with more than breaking curses. It meant taking risks and giving your heart into the care of a stranger. Why must I nearly lose everything to learn that?

Rosie wouldn't stay with us, but she couldn't stay away, either. Through the long telling and the long hours of that endless night, she was in and out of Uncle Wheeler's room. Once she came to fetch William off to bed, once to bring us a tray of coffee and hash, once on an errand never fully explained. She never stayed long, never got closer to our uncle than a glance from the doorway. I could see she was troubled and bursting at the seams to know what had happened in the mill, but she could not bring herself to ask.

Randall finally slipped into a doze, his hand still on mine, and I sent him off to sleep in my old bedroom, with William. He wanted me to join them, but I wouldn't leave Uncle Wheeler. Rosie finally came in near dawn. Uncle Wheeler had not awakened. She sat on the edge of the bed and stared at him, silently.

"What happens now?" she said, at long last.

"I don't know," I said. I was so tired the room seemed darker, instead of lighter, and I leaned my head back against the wall. Rosie took a blanket from the heap on the bed and moved to drape it over me. I shook my head.

"I don't understand you!" she cried, flinging the blanket back down on our uncle. "After everything he did, you're treating him like a wounded war hero!"

I sighed. "Show some compassion, Rosie."

"Why? He never did."

I pulled her closer. Her hands were cold; she must be as weary as I. "I've seen what comes of an unwillingness to forgive, and I'll not pass that legacy on to William. And nor will you."

She glared at me, her face set hard, and then sank to the floor and laid her head in my lap. She sighed, and I twined my fingers into hers. I brushed her golden hair with my hand as she closed her eyes.

Uncle Wheeler finally awoke, sometime late the next day. No one was with him — Randall and Rosie had finally persuaded me to sleep in a real bed, and I fear I overdid it a bit. When I rose late in the afternoon, I looked into the bedroom to find my uncle up and dressed, or partially so. He had donned a fresh shirt and the very plainest trousers I'd ever seen him wear; the shirt was open down the front and he wore no cravat, no wig. It was hard to see this man as *our* Uncle Wheeler. But I could see, at last, my Mam's brother.

I let myself in but did not sit down. He did not speak to me. There was a tray of tea and rolls beside the bed, so someone else had been first to talk to him. I wondered who.

He was packing, and I watched him fold his beautiful things and lay them slowly in his trunks. There was the spring-green damask frock coat, the silver waistcoat, the purple shoes. Was it possible I could miss them?

"I'll clear out straightaway," he said — and it was like his old voice, and unlike it. "I'll get a room at Drover's until the stage comes through at the end of the week."

"You don't have to do that," I said, and he almost smiled.

"We both know that's not true."

"Where will you go?"

The thin shoulders shrugged — the briefest gesture. I could not tell if that meant he would not tell me, or if he did not know himself. I stepped in closer and — I do not know if I meant to put out my hand toward him or not, but I did not get the chance.

"Please, just go," he said, and turned away from me.

I hesitated in the doorway. "He's gone. It's truly over now."

I could not see the expression on his face. "It's never over," he said, so softly I almost could not hear him. As I said, some things should not be borne in public. I shut the door behind me.

True to his word, he left us that afternoon. Randall drove him over in the trap, and painful as it was to watch, our growing household all turned out for their departure.

"Good riddance," Rosie said as they pulled away. I think she might have spit on the ground behind him, if Harte hadn't been there. I shook my head.

"Rosie, we're family."

"He's not our family. Not the way he treated us."

The trap rolled down the road. No one turned back. I took Rosie by the hand.

"We're *his* family."

We took another day to repair the damage to Stirwaters, but save for a scattering of bobbins in the spinning room and a crack in the fulling stock headframe, the mill was in remarkably good shape. The broken floorboards had mended themselves, seamlessly, overnight; we could no longer feel each breath of wind through the walls. I held William to my shoulder and watched as Rosie and Randall hefted the attic window back into place; it fitted snugly in its frame and gave Rosie no trouble — no screws popped loose, no panes of glass cracked inexplicably.

Was it the breaking of the curse that did it? Was John Simple's ill will no longer fighting with the protective spirit of Robin, who had given his life to the building of the mill, and stayed many long years hence, watching over us all, speaking to us in the mill's voice of creaking floors and crashing water? Which happenings were Simple's doing, I wondered, and which Robin's? And which were truly no more than bad luck? I should never know for certain.

Except once.

Stirwaters had one last surprise for us. In the commotion, my father's desk had slid a foot or more off its accustomed spot, and as Randall went to push it back into place, he found a thick envelope stuck between the floorboards. It was addressed to Barr & Courtland, Solicitors, Harrowgate. I knew the untidy script immediately, and my hand shook as I opened it.

Inside were pages cut from Father's atlas — schemata, diagrams, and a patent application for a new sort of loom, powered — oh, mercy! — by steam. *They have a loom here that runs by itself — they say it's a wonder!*

"Father made something that worked?" Rosie said, prying the pages from my hand. "But what —"

"He was suing them," I said, reading the letter that accompanied it all. It was dated the day before he died. "Pinchfields — for stealing his invention. That must have been what he needed the money for — your money, Randall, from the bank. These diagrams are dated — it says here that they can prove he had the idea a year before Pinchfields built their looms — no, before they built the *factory*. Mercy — do you know what this means? That whole factory is built up around Father's machines."

Randall was studying the papers over my shoulder. "I should say it means a great deal more than that," he said. "If it's true — and it looks to be; this looks like pretty clear proof of their theft — you Millers would be entitled to share in Pinchfields' profits for all this time, and they'd have to pay you for the use of those looms. And that, I daresay, could be quite a tidy sum indeed."

"Now what," Rosie said, a grin overtaking her face, "would we ever do with that kind of money?"

"I can think of one thing." I thought I heard the mill's voice sigh, ever so slightly, followed by the churning of the waterwheel. A bigger wheel, a deeper pit . . . we could make Stirwaters competitive again. And perhaps, just perhaps, right one more wrong in the process, return something that had been taken, so long ago.

There was one last thing to be done. Everyone else wanted to wait 'til spring, but I insisted, and before the week was out we had assembled in the cross-ways — Randall, me and Rosie, Harte on his crutches (he'd let us down the first time, he said; he'd not miss again), Biddy Tom, and William; as well as Shearing's vicar and two strong Haymarket lads. We did not make it more public than that, although Randall had to put it before the magistrates in Haymarket. They were quick enough to agree once he showed them the broadside. A haunted cross-roads is all very entertaining — until you find an actual body buried there.

It took hours, and to their credit, they had only my word to go on. Eventually the spades in the cold earth struck something unyielding — and then again, and again. As the vicar read Scripture over the diggers, and Biddy Tom traced a great chalk circle round us all, the men gingerly lifted the bones from the earth and laid them in their new coffin. Some shreds of clothing were found, too — remains of a shirt, what may once have been leather bracers. I clutched William tight and fought back tears.

We laid John Simple to rest in the Shearing churchyard, a few plots down from my father, under a cold November drizzle. A dark cloud hung overhead, and I held fast to my sister with one arm, my husband and son with the other, as a flash of sunlight fought to break free. A warm wind rolled off the river, like a soft voice bidding us farewell, and I knew that the end had come at last.

The End

Author's Note

This is a work of fantasy, and Charlotte's village is not based on any real place. Her world, however, *is* strongly influenced by the real woolen industries of Britain and America during the early years of the Industrial Revolution (for our purposes, the late 1700s). While serving my own need for a completely imaginary setting, I have tried to be true to the history and society in as many ways as possible, and hope that a real woolworker of the era would not find it too unfamiliar.

That said, I have departed from history where it was necessary for the story I wished to tell — most notably in my use of a machine called the "spinning jack." This is a real machine, and the men who operated them really were called jackspinners. But they were not in common use until the 1820s, and I have no proof that any were ever water-powered. There certainly *were* water-powered spinning machines during Charlotte's day, but no other had a name so delightfully apt. I was fortunate enough to get a firsthand glimpse of the processes of wool production — including the spinning jacks — at Watkins Woolen Mill State Park in Lawson, Missouri, a later-period, steam-run operation that has been beautifully preserved and is open to the public.

Another major departure was making Stirwaters's weavers female. In truth, weaving was one of the most important careers available to men of the era, and many period weavers made quite a good living at it. However, this fact of reality broke faith with a longtime association of women with textile work that stretches back to the Fates of Greek mythology and gives the story of "Rumpelstiltskin" its backbone. Women would return to dominate the profession with the advent of cheap cotton production in the 1800s, when operating a power loom became unskilled labor.

The folklore and folk magic illustrated here are also based in tradition. Corn dollies, hex signs, and other charms all existed, though they were not necessarily used quite as I have presented them. I am deeply indebted to Katherine Briggs, Christina Hole, and Jacqueline Simpson and Stephen Roud for their work in English folk tradition, and urge anyone interested in pursuing the subject to look them up. I have only scratched the surface here, and the depths are astoundingly rich.

The story of Rumpelstiltskin is what folklorists call a "Name of the Helper" tale, in which a character must defeat a mysterious helper by discovering his True Name (or Secret Name or Hidden Name). Germany's "Rumpelstiltskin" is certainly the most familiar of these, having been collected by the Grimm brothers in the nineteenth century, but the motif occurs in at least fifteen versions worldwide, including the English "Tom-Tit-Tot" and the Scottish "Whuppity Stoorie," in which, like Rumpelstiltskin, the title characters assist the heroines with their spinning. My work with the fairy tale elements of this novel has been greatly informed by the discussion and scholarship at Heidi Anne Heiner's marvelous Web site, the SurLaLune Fairy Tale Pages (www.surlalunefairytales.com), which should be a frequent stop for any fairy tale enthusiast.

I have always found "Rumpelstiltskin" to be a troubling tale, probably because it violates my sense of justice. The greedy father and merciless king go unpunished, and the miller's daughter betrays the only character who tried to help her. The anti-Semitic overtones of the Grimm version are also deeply disturbing to me — and should be to any modern audience — and I have tried to steer well clear of them.

Other readers disagree with a sympathetic view of Rumpelstiltskin. Folklorist Veronica Schanoes writes, "Some deals can't and shouldn't be enforced, and those deals include ones made under duress and those that involve taking a mother's child away from her." In other words, Rumpelstiltskin gets what he deserves.

I've also found it fascinating that in "Rumpelstiltskin," the heroine is known only as "the miller's daughter" or "the queen," while Rumpelstiltskin's name becomes a magical talisman — an object of power in and of itself. In a story about the potency of names, the heroine is anonymous.

Charlotte Miller's story began there.

This book was edited by Cheryl Klein and designed by Alison Klapthor.

The text was set in Adobe Jenson Pro, a typeface designed by Robert Slimbach in the 1990s for Adobe, which was adapted from the original book typefaces designed by Nicolas Jenson in the 1470s. The display type was set in P22Michelangelo, designed by Denis Kegler and Richard Kegler at P22 type foundry in association with the Philadelphia Museum of Art.

The book was printed and bound at RR Donnelley in Crawfordsville, Indiana.

The production was supervised by Susan Jeffers Casel, and the manufacturing was supervised by Jaime Capifali.